Praise for Jennifer L. Wright

"A fiercely woven tale from the birth of the atomic age, Jennifer Wright's unflinching look at fractured friendship, war-tested families, and hard-won faith grabs the reader from its start and won't let go. It's a powerfully rendered testament of how the implements of war, in the end, must come down somewhere, even when our hearts struggle to hold the fallout that only God can redeem."

PATRICIA RAYBON
award-winning author of *All That Is Secret* and *My First White Friend*

"Jennifer L. Wright is a storyteller with the distinct gift of bringing history to life in full color. I knew from the very first page of *Come Down Somewhere* that I was going to experience a powerhouse novel with deeply complex characters, an engaging and heartfelt story, and master level writing. Wright's sophomore effort exceeded my expectations. Jo and Olive have taken up residence in my heart where I believe they will stay for a long time. This novel is a triumph."

SUSIE FINKBEINER
author of *The Nature of Small Birds* and *Stories That Bind Us*

"An emotive novel, Jennifer L. Wright's *Come Down Somewhere* takes readers to the deserts of New Mexico in 1945 where an unthinkable, top secret event took place. Wright's command of historical facts allows her to craft a fascinating tale that introduces us to Jo and Olive, two young women coming of age in dark and frightening times, revealing what life was like in the shadow of the Trinity nuclear bomb test. Their story serves as a powerful reminder that friendship is a precious gift worth fighting for, even when all seems lost."

MICHELLE SHOCKLEE
author of *Under the Tulip Tree* and *Count the Nights by Stars*

"When it comes to writing haunting prose, Jennifer L. Wright positively shines, and her second novel is no exception. . . . Unique, suspenseful, and meticulously researched, *Come Down Somewhere* is a raw and masterful exploration of estrangement in its many forms and one of the finest works of Christian fiction I've ever read."

NAOMI STEPHENS
Carol Award–winning author of *Shadow among Sheaves*

"*Come Down Somewhere* is a heart-wrenching story of friendship, war on the home front, and all that threatens the deepest parts of our souls. The story touches on a lesser known part of WWII, of an atomic nature, and allows the reader to take a journey with Olive and Jo through an explosive friendship that will be tested by the fires of loyalty. A must-read of 2022—the fallout of this novel will stay with you long after you've finished it."

JAIME JO WRIGHT
Christy Award–winning author of *The Souls of Lost Lake* and *The House on Foster Hill*

"Jenn L. Wright brings a devastating event in our nation's history to light with a poignant story of friendship and faith. In a landscape fraught with heartbreak, *Come Down Somewhere* speaks a life-giving message of forgiveness—for our friends, our enemies, and ourselves. For readers who crave a story with the grit of real life and the grace redemption, *Come Down Somewhere* will satisfy and enlighten."

STEPHANIE LANDSEM
author *In a Far-Off Land*

"The Jornada del Muerto and the Trinity test create a powerful and unique backdrop for this thoughtful coming-of-age story. I love the sincerity of Jenn's writing and the earnestness with which she portrays complicated relationships. This is the perfect choice for readers who love historical fiction as well as women's fiction."

KATIE POWNER
author of *A Flicker of Light* and *Where the Blue Sky Begins*

"[A] lovely debut. . . . Wright's adept depiction of the times capture the grit of the Dust Bowl. Fans of Tracie Peterson should check this out."

PUBLISHERS WEEKLY on *If It Rains*

"The treatment of historical events is gritty and unflinching, similar to other Dust Bowl fiction, like Susie Finkbeiner's *Cup of Dust* and Kristin Hannah's *Four Winds*. Character growth is the highlight of this novel."

LIBRARY JOURNAL on *If It Rains*

"A moving story about the struggles of those who endured the Dust Bowl period in Oklahoma's history. . . . The reader will find themselves completely engrossed in its unfolding."

FRESH FICTION on *If It Rains*

"Reminiscent of the striking narrative of Delia Owens and with the poetic grace of Julie Cantrell, Wright exhibits an inimitable voice and pitch-perfect historical acumen. Wholly immersive and gorgeously spun. . . . One of the freshest debuts I have read in an age by a uniquely talented author to watch!"

RACHEL MCMILLAN
author of *The London Restoration* and *The Mozart Code,* on *If It Rains*

"Set against the suffocating cloud of the Oklahoma Dust Bowl, *If It Rains* is an unforgettable debut. Wright's evocative descriptions of grief and grace will echo with readers long after the last page has been turned."

NAOMI STEPHENS
Carol Award–winning author of *Shadow among Sheaves*

"*If It Rains* transports you so fully, you catch yourself gasping for breath and praying for rain alongside the characters. And the characters! . . . Sisters Kathryn and Melissa are loyal but complicated, sincere but imperfect—and fiercely lovable. As they cling to courage and fight for faith, you find yourself doing the same. Their story stays with you long after you reach 'The End.'"

ELIZABETH LAING THOMPSON
author of *All the Feels* and the When God Says series

COME DOWN SOMEWHERE

COME

A NOVEL # DOWN

SOMEWHERE

JENNIFER L.

WRIGHT

Tyndale House Publishers
Carol Stream, Illinois

Visit Tyndale online at tyndale.com.

Visit Jennifer L. Wright's website at jennwrightwrites.com.

Tyndale and Tyndale's quill logo are registered trademarks of Tyndale House Ministries.

Come Down Somewhere

Designed by Jennifer Phelps

Edited by Sarah Mason Rische

Published in association with the literary agency of Martin Literary & Media Management, 914 164th Street SE, Suite B12, #307, Mill Creek, WA 98012.

Scripture quotations are taken from the Holy Bible, *New International Version*,® *NIV*.® Copyright © 1973, 1978, 1984, 2011 by Biblica, Inc.® Used by permission. All rights reserved worldwide.

Come Down Somewhere is a work of fiction. Where real people, events, establishments, organizations, or locales appear, they are used fictitiously. All other elements of the novel are drawn from the author's imagination.

For information about special discounts for bulk purchases, please contact Tyndale House Publishers at csresponse@tyndale.com, or call 1-855-277-9400.

Library of Congress Cataloging-in-Publication Data

A catalog record for this book is available from the Library of Congress.

ISBN 978-1-4964-7167-3 (HC)

ISBN 978-1-4964-4934-4 (SC)

Printed in the United States of America

28	27	26	25	24	23	22
7	6	5	4	3	2	1

To Jonathan, Matthew, and Meredith
This was truly a team effort.

PROVERBS 17:17

CHAPTER ONE

OLIVE

OCTOBER 1944

The Army moved in on a Sunday.

Moved in. That's what Uncle Hershel called it. Like they'd been a happy family out house hunting and found the perfect little bungalow. Like they hadn't just walked in and taken what was ours, claiming the government needed it for the war effort. Uncle Hershel could call it anything he pleased. I called it stealing.

I was in the hayloft when they arrived. Pushing things to the side, sweeping away years of dust and bird droppings, making space for boxes of things we were no longer allowed to keep in our house. Because our house, and over 75 percent of our land, was no longer ours. It was now property of the US government.

"Olive!" Ma's voice came from outside, just below the window.

I didn't answer. Instead, I jumped over a hole in the loft floor—one more thing we didn't have the time or money to fix—and tossed a bag of old grain to the corner with a bang. Dust floated up from the impact, shimmering in the afternoon sun.

"Olive, come on down. Your brother can finish up there. I need you to help me move the last of this stuff into the casita."

I stuck my head out of the narrow opening. "Make Avery do it. I'm already up here."

Ma shielded her eyes as she looked up at me. "Avery is stronger than you. It'll be easier for him to carry the boxes up the ladder. Besides—"

Her sentence was interrupted by a distant rumble. She and I turned at the same moment, searching for the source of the commotion. From my vantage point in the loft, the land spread out beneath me, shades of brown and green. Dirt and shrubs, rock and hills, miles of withered land fading in a pale sky. Ugly. Barren. *Home.* But now, in the distance, on the last hill before our house—the one with the Arizona sycamore, my initials carved in the trunk, bark worn smooth from climbing and that one branch perfect for reading . . . beside that hill, *my* hill, a large truck rolled to a stop, the words *US Army* stamped on the sides.

"They're here," Ma said unnecessarily. "Avery! Hershel! They're here."

I pulled back from the loft window as another truck reached the barn. Tires on gravel, engines cut, and in their absence, a stifling silence. I pressed myself against the wall. Unable to breathe. Unwilling to move. A slamming door, muffled voices. A man. And then my mother. Laughing.

I dug my fingernails into my arm and stared at my boots, inhaling the smell of manure and hay and memories of a place that was fading before my eyes.

And my mother was laughing.

From below came the squeak of the barn door being shoved aside and the rush of sunlight across gray, weathered beams. "Olive?"

Uncle Hershel. I pushed myself further against the wall.

"I know you're up there," he hissed. "Get down here. Now." The last word cut through my resolve the way only Uncle Hershel could.

The ladder creaked as I swung my feet over the side, shuddering beneath my hands as if it too felt my apprehension. As I jumped off the last rung, a small cloud of dust billowed out from under my boots. I straightened my back and jutted my chin against Uncle Hershel's glare.

The buttons of his flannel shirt strained over his chest as he wiped sweat from his thinning black hair. Sneering, he placed a battered cowboy hat back atop his head. "Get out here and say hello like is proper. Ain't gonna have these men thinking we've raised a bunch of savages."

"So today we care what the Army thinks, huh? Seems just a few weeks ago we hated Roosevelt and the war. Then your CPUSA buddies tell you that they've changed their mind, so now we *do* support the war. I can't keep—"

"Shut your mouth, Olive."

Hershel raised his hand, prepared to strike, but I ducked out of his way. He would always be bigger than me but now, at fifteen, I was faster.

He scowled. "When are you going to grow up and think about someone other than yourself? This country has made you soft and stupid, girl. When I was your age—"

But I withdrew from the barn before he could finish. I did not care what Hershel was like when he was my age. My bet was brooding and Russian—just like he was now.

The October sun was harsh and bright, summer refusing to give in to fall, as was often the case in this part of New Mexico. I walked with my head hung low. Staring at the ground, I tried to avoid the reality of what I knew I'd have to see eventually.

"Olive? Olive, this is Sergeant Hawthorne." My mother's tone was light, fake, grating.

"Olive, so nice to meet you."

Sergeant Hawthorne had dark hair, slick with pomade, and eyes as green as the Rio Grande valley in spring. He was tall—over six feet, if I had to guess—and muscular, evident even under the drab brown of his uniform. He stared at me with a smile that dimpled his cheeks. On a normal person, I would have found all of these traits appealing. Downright handsome.

Too bad I'd already decided to hate him.

He extended his hand. I didn't take it.

Beside me, my mother tittered and tugged at her dress. "Olive."

But still I did not shake his hand. After a moment, Sergeant Hawthorne pulled his arm back to his side but kept that stupidly handsome grin on his face. "It's alright, Mrs. Alexander. I've got a daughter around her same age. I know all about teenage girls."

The two of them laughed at his joke like it was funny, my mother's giggles morphing into one of her coughing fits.

"I'm sorry," she croaked. "This dust. You never really get used to it." Finally catching her breath, she cleared her throat and gestured as my brother strode forward. "And this is my son, Avery."

Tall and wiry, with a mop of jet-black hair that would never lay flat, my brother looked younger than his nineteen years, though lately he more than made up for it with his ridiculous manly posturing. He thrust his shoulders back and shook Sergeant Hawthorne's hand with enough force for the both of us.

Sergeant Hawthorne's eyes widened as his arm jerked forward under the intensity of Avery's grip. He stiffened, regaining his bearing, and let out an amused laugh. "Quite a handshake there, son."

Avery pressed his lips into an absurd, overly serious non-smile. "We could use a man like you in the ranks!"

"I actually leave in two days, sir."

Sergeant Hawthorne dipped his head and grinned, completely oblivious to the effect Avery's words had on my mother. The slight shift in her stance. The imperceptible intake of breath.

His initial application the year before had been rejected for medical reasons, though I knew nothing more about the story than Avery's return from the enlistment office with fire in his eyes and whiskey on his breath, along with a string of curse words that made even Uncle Hershel's mouth seem tame. Avery had never exactly been light, but his darkness had grown heavier since then. He spent less time in the house and more time in the casita, his bad temper exacerbated by our uncle's own and fueled with a steady diet of Hershel's never-ending rhetoric on this country and its problems.

Still, despite it all, I thought that was the end of it. The world would war, but we would continue on, untouched. And we did . . . for a while. Then the Army sent a letter. Next thing I knew, Hershel's friends from California had shown up, and their loud meetings in the casita—which now included Avery—grew louder and then markedly quieter. All manner of strange men came and went from the ranch for days before the whole lot of them just up and disappeared. That was when Avery announced the Army had changed its mind and he was leaving soon too.

Since then, my brother had started smiling more, my mother less and less. I had kept my head down, doing my chores and trying to pretend none of it was happening.

But here we were.

Uncle Hershel brushed past me, knocking my arm a little harder than necessary. "Sergeant Hawthorne, Hershel Alexander."

"Hershel, yes. Nice to meet you. I can't thank you enough for this."

I glowered at the ground. As if we had a choice.

"It's temporary, of course," Sergeant Hawthorne was saying. "Just a billet for the men while construction is ongoing. Your house will be yours again before you know it. But the land could take longer. It's all a matter of . . ." He swallowed whatever he was about to say. Awkwardness seeped into the air around us.

Because he couldn't tell us when. He couldn't tell us why. But he knew. He knew what all of this was for, what secrets the government was hiding beneath its "war effort" label. And that knowledge was a power over us no amount of smiles or small talk could ever erase.

"Let me show you around," Uncle Hershel barked, breaking the tension. "We're just about finished in the main house—a few odds and ends here and there—but let me go ahead and give you the lay of the land. Now, over here . . ." He put a hand at Sergeant Hawthorne's elbow, leading him away.

My mother's shoulders collapsed as she watched their retreat. The smile, the joy, the facade faded as quickly as it had begun; she pulled a cigarette from her dress pocket and lit it with shaking hands. "Come on, Olive," she said wearily after taking a drag. "We still have work to do."

Inside the main house, Avery returned to stacking boxes in the hallway, Ma to loading dishes in the kitchen. I joined them, biting the inside of my cheek to stem tears as I folded blankets in the living room.

Pa had died seven years ago in a farming accident with a wayward bull. His brother, Hershel, had returned from California and moved into the casita not long after, sulking but dutiful; his temper and bad mood were a cloud the ranch had never quite been able to shake since. I couldn't help thinking that if Pa were still alive, none of this would be happening. It wasn't true, obviously—my father's presence couldn't stop the war any more than his absence—but I clung to the fantasy anyway.

"Olive, grab that pile there and take it to the casita. Avery, that stuff goes in the barn."

Avery grunted as he lifted two boxes at once. "You sure they're okay with us storing this stuff in the barn?"

My mother lit another cigarette, inhaling deeply before answering. "The barn is still ours. At least according to the papers they gave us. 'Eminent domain' or not, we still have to make a living, and we need that barn to do it. Though heaven knows how we're going to—"

"It'll be fine, Ma."

A look passed between my mother and brother, fleeting but pointed, before Avery broke off and disappeared out the door.

The smoke from Ma's cigarette curled around her gaze as she watched him walk away. It was several moments before she finally blinked and turned to me with a tepid smile.

I did not return it. Instead, I punched at a pile of blankets, trying to force them into a ball small enough to carry in one trip, and stalked from the house. I didn't want to look at her. Or Avery. And I sure as anything didn't want to hear the words *eminent domain* again. The government kept using them over and over. As if naming a thing made it right.

Uncle Hershel and Sergeant Hawthorne stood next to the Army truck, laughing and talking like old friends. I stuck my nose in the air as I passed them, not caring when the blankets began to slip, dragging in the dry New Mexico dirt. Let Ma sleep in filthy blankets tonight. At least she'd still be here at our ranch. Yes, the Army would be here. The land would be smaller, the big house no longer our own. But even in the casita, she'd still fall asleep to the coyotes howling, to the smell of sagebrush floating on the breeze. Tomorrow morning, she'd still wake up and watch the sun wash over the Jornada, the gray of night giving way to reds and browns and yellows, before stepping outside with Hershel, doing their work, living their lives, just as they'd always done.

And Avery? In a few days Avery would be shipping out, his duty finally realized, his restless anxiety now fused with purpose and a plan. With meaning.

But tomorrow morning I'd be in Alamogordo, opening my eyes to the pale-blue wallpaper at my grandmother's house on Delaware Avenue. The one with the cracked chimney that made the whole house smell like smoke and the fenced-in front yard that wasn't even big enough to grow a row of corn. The one where the mountain view was obstructed by rows of other houses just like hers and where, instead of painted desert sunsets coloring the walls, there were portraits of Jesus in every room.

Sixty miles away but it might as well have been a million.

I should have been grateful. According to the posters, we all had a role to play in the war effort. We'd get our land back eventually, the Army had promised, when the war was over and the government was done. I should be proud to sacrifice in such a way.

And I was. I truly was. I wasn't necessarily happy about being forced to surrender our land and our livelihood, but we *were* at war. Deep down, I knew it wasn't really the Army's fault. But it was easier to rage against a stranger than stomach the truth. Less painful. No, it wasn't the Army I was mad at.

It was everybody else.

I didn't understand why *my* sacrifice meant relocating while Ma and Hershel got to stay. Why Avery moved closer to war and I had to move further away. Why I was being pushed out, treated like an in-the-way toddler rather than a useful part of the family. All around me, there was a great need for help . . . but apparently not the kind I could offer.

I threw the blankets on the floor of the casita, not bothering to take them all the way to the bedroom, and returned to the main house. My grief and anger rose with each step. The living room was empty, voices coming from the back part of the house.

No, not just the back part of the house. *My* part of the house. *No. No, no, no.*

I ran toward the sound, skidding to a halt in the doorway. Avery was pulling books off my shelf, tucking them into a box labeled *Alamogordo*.

My mother, perched on the corner of my bed, was the first to see me. "Now, Olive, it's the last room. We've waited as long as we could—"

I didn't bother to listen to the rest of her words. I flung myself across the room at Avery as something between a scream and a wail erupted from my throat. The book in his hands—*Treasure Island*, one of Pa's favorites—landed with a thud on the floor as he raised his arms, shielding himself from my blows.

"Get out of my room!" I screamed. My nails stabbed into his flesh. "Get out! Get out!"

"Olive! Olive, stop that!" My mother's voice sounded far away, muted inside my anger.

Blood sprouted across Avery's arm. I kept swinging anyway. It was immature, childish, as if we were kids again and he'd broken my favorite toy. But I didn't care. Surprise shone in his eyes as he wriggled and dodged, trying both to block me and escape. I moved to connect with his cheek and felt my arm jerked back painfully.

"Knock it off!" The stink of sweat and tobacco pressed into me. Uncle Hershel pinned my wrist to my spine with one hand. His other dug into my bicep. "What in sam hill has gotten into you?"

My mother stood to one side, hands in front of her mouth. Sergeant Hawthorne hovered in the doorway. That stupid smile was finally gone from his face, and his shiny black shoes were covered in dust. At the sight of him—this stranger, this intruder, standing in my bedroom as if he owned it, because he did—the blood drained from my limbs. My body deflated.

Avery puffed out his chest and snatched the book from the ground. The cover ripped as he shoved it unceremoniously into the box. He smirked, daring me to say something or come at him again.

But instead of inciting me, that rip—that small rip in the cover of a book I hadn't read since childhood—broke me. I wrenched from Uncle Hershel's grasp, barely registering the tears on my mother's face through my own, and fled from the room. Momentarily blinded by the sun, I kept running, past the casita and the barn, past the corral, out into the open desert.

Ragged sobs choked me as the ground began to slope upward, stealing my breath but not my misery. I dodged the yuccas and juniper trees easily despite my blurry vision. The Chupadera Mesa was as familiar to me as my own hands. Every hill and valley, every sprig of creosote and blade of tobosa. I knew it all.

But now I was leaving. How long would it be before I forgot?

I didn't stop running until I came to the top of that particular slope, to the corner where the big boulder split, a cleft in its side shaped like lightning, opening into a secret space no one but us ever bothered to notice.

The burrow. My brother had called it that because we'd had to pretend to be small animals just to fit inside. Through the crack, a hidden ledge jutted like a makeshift balcony in front of a shallow cave that was really nothing more than a crawl space. We'd outfitted it with a door made of rotted wood and stuffed the inside with old moth-eaten blankets and pillows, comic books and dime-store novels.

It had been our spot, Avery's and mine. Back before Pa died and Hershel moved in. When we were still friends and life was still fun. But now it was *my* spot, my safe spot, a place to escape from Mama's grief, Avery's sullenness, and Uncle Hershel's temper. A remnant of childhood I refused to let go. Because up here, among the rocks and the shrubs, I could still pretend life made sense.

From this spot, I was perfectly hidden, yet I could see our ranch hundreds of feet below, shimmering in the heat. In the distance rose the ragged top of Oscura Peak; across the gentle slopes of the mesa came the dark stain of the ancient lava field to the east and the faint glint of the gypsum dunes to the south. I slid to my knees as a fresh wave of sorrow washed over me.

The ranch had been in our family for over half a century, before New Mexico was even New Mexico. Since my grandparents had emigrated from the motherland with their two small boys in tow. Back then, no one wanted a piece of the Jornada del Muerto. And why would they? The "Route of the Dead Man" was nothing but a wasteland, a ninety-mile stretch of desert between Socorro and El Paso with no water, little vegetation, and summer temperatures hot enough to boil your blood.

But the land "called" to my grandparents, or so the story went. Grandpa built the adobe walls of our home with his bare hands. The pitched roof, the chicken coop, the barn, the horse corral . . . everything here bore his mark. As a teenager, Hershel had fled, claiming he was going back to Russia to fight in the revolution. (Pa swore he never made it out of California, though, joking his mouth was bigger than his courage—a rumor I quickly learned not to bring up in my uncle's presence, lest I wanted to be on the wrong end of his violent rebuttal.) But my father had stayed in his adopted homeland, his Soviet blood thawing in the New Mexico sun. My grandfather added the casita, attached to the house by a courtyard wall, a year after my parents' wedding. He and my grandmother planned to finish out their days there while my parents started a family of their own in the main house.

And they did. Grandpa died in the casita's back bedroom and

was buried in the far corner lot. My grandmother followed soon after.

Pa took over after that, making the ranch his own by adding a third bedroom onto the main house for his daughter. Me. Every memory I had—of him, of my family, of my life—centered around this ranch.

New Mexico. Our home. *My* home. Only it wasn't mine anymore.

I wept for what seemed like hours, until my eyes burned and my cheeks cracked beneath dry tears. Until the sun lay only a finger width above the mountains and the shadows began to stretch, dappling the landscape with previews of the coming night. That's when I heard the sound of crunching rocks; Avery's eyes appeared through the crack in the boulder.

I swatted at my face, wiping away the grit of evaporated sorrow.

"You look awful," he said, crawling through and dropping down beside me. He stretched his long legs in front of him, draping them over the edge of the cliff.

I scooted away, scowling. "At least my clothes match."

He glanced down at his outfit. "Mine don't?"

A pair of jeans and a dingy-white shirt matched well enough, but Avery had been color-blind since birth; making fun of him for it was stupid but routine. A pathetic grasp at normal when the world was anything but.

"I'm sorry about your book."

I glanced at the welts on his arms and the subtle swelling of his cheek. It looked painful enough to cause a smidge of regret. "I'm sorry for blowing a fuse and kicking your rear."

"Psssh. You didn't."

"Sure about that?"

He tapped his fingers lightly against the beginnings of a bruise. "I was just trying to be a good big brother. Letting you win."

"Oh, shut up, Avery."

But I couldn't stop a smile from creeping over my lips. He grinned and gave me a playful jab in the shoulder.

We turned our attention to the sunset, watching the sky melt from yellow to orange to red. After a moment, I heard him sigh. "You know, you can't hide up here forever, Olive."

"I wasn't hiding. I just wanted to be *alone*," I added pointedly.

But my attempt at humor fell flat. Instead, Avery's face remained serious. "Ma's worried about you."

"Good."

"Now, stop it. That ain't no way to be."

"Ain't no way to be? You don't have any right to tell me which way to be. You're *leaving*."

"Just because I'm leaving don't mean I don't care about what happens here."

I stared at my boots. The laces were frayed, the toes scratched. Memories of a place that no longer existed. I pulled my elbows into my sides. "Why are they making me go?" I had thought my tears were spent but here they were, springing up once again. "It's not fair. Especially with you gone. I'm practically an adult. I can help! They can't do this all on their own."

"Olive . . ."

"Why don't they want me here?"

Avery shifted, his discomfort obvious. "Olive, there are some things in this world that are bigger than us. Bigger than our family, bigger than our home. I know you don't understand that yet—"

"Oh, just dry up, will you?" That was another thing Avery had started doing. He was only four years older than me, but he acted like it was ten. Like he was so wise and worldly, when the farthest he'd ever been was Albuquerque. "I know there's a war going on, same as you."

"I ain't talking about the war."

I turned to look at him, but his face remained forward, staring at the spot where the sun had just dipped below the horizon. He pushed a strand of dark hair off his forehead.

"I mean, I am talking about the war. But there's more to it than that. There are some things . . ." He stopped and sighed deeply. "What I'm trying to say is there are some things even bigger than the war, Olive. I . . . I can't explain. But I hope one day you'll understand."

I tilted my head to one side. "What do you mean, Avery?"

"Nothing. It's nothing." He gave me a small smile. "Just . . . just know that I do care, okay? No matter what you think, no matter what you see or hear. I do care. About you, about Ma, about this." He took my hand, pressing one finger into the dirt. Up to a point, then down again. An upside-down *V*. It was the same symbol carved into the rock behind us. The one we'd sign in the air when Hershel got ugly, write on papers slid under each other's door when we'd been sent to our rooms, or leave written in the dirt when Mama's incapacitating grief made the chore load overwhelming.

The three points representing the only stable things in a world of instability: me, Avery, the mesa. Home.

We hadn't used the symbol in over two years. But the weight of it now beneath our entwined fingers made the lapse evaporate.

I leaned against him, wanting to cling to this feeling but knowing it was pointless.

He must have known it too. Rather than hug me back, he pulled away. "That's why I'm going, Olive. And that's why you have to go too. We all have our parts to play."

And then he was gone. His words hung in the air. Although I knew he was only going back to the ranch, it felt as if he were already a thousand miles away. Because he was; he had been for months. And no amount of childish reminiscing was going to change that.

Below me, clouds of dust rose from the desert floor as three more Army trucks made their way up our long drive. As I watched them, I knew I should have felt something like pride. Comradery. Duty. The honor of sacrifice, of being a part of something bigger.

And I tried. Because he was right—all of that stuff was meaningful and important. All of that stuff mattered.

The only thing that didn't matter was me.

CHAPTER TWO

JO

MARCH 1952

Everything about Alamogordo was different now. And somehow completely the same. From behind dark glasses, Jo Hawthorne stared out the bus window as it rumbled up Highway 54 and merged with 70, dropping all numbers and becoming Pennsylvania Avenue as it passed a sign declaring the town limits of "Rocket City."

Rocket City. That's what they were calling it now. Because "Fat Cottonwood" didn't sound nearly as cool. And because this town—this Podunk town in the middle of New Mexico, where dust hung in the air like confetti and the wind was dry enough to suck the moisture straight from your skin—was the epicenter of the future, thanks to Holloman Air Force Base and the New

17

Mexico Joint Guided Missile Test Range. Her seatmate, an over-eager new airman with baby fat still hugging his cheeks, couldn't shut up about it. Cutting-edge missiles and bombs and weapons that could vaporize a city in a fraction of a second.

As if that was what the world needed more of.

Jo hunched lower in her seat, pulling her hat down over her face as the bus vibrated to a stop at a red light. The airman, Michael (he'd told her again and again before she'd conceded enough brain space to remember), craned his neck to look past her out the window, practically drooling with anticipation. She should switch him seats. But she didn't. Instead, she stared forward and fingered the letter in the pocket of her black trousers. She'd read it so many times over the course of the trip, the ink was starting to smudge. With her other hand, she rubbed her temple, fighting the urge to read it again. She had a headache. She'd had one since she stepped onto this hot, smelly bus.

But she didn't want to read it again. And she didn't want to look out the window again. The memory of Alamogordo had been better in her mind, where the earth had swallowed the whole town as she had driven away all those years ago, tears streaming down her face, darkness swallowing her heart. She knew it hadn't, of course, but it was easier to live with the fantasy. She had thought she was strong enough to face it, but now, as the bus groaned beneath her, pulling her through the congested main drag, she realized she had been wrong.

It wasn't fair. This place had marked the end of her life as she knew it, had signaled the ruination of all things innocent and right. Like a seed of poison sown into her very core. It had nearly killed her—and yet still, it survived. And not just survived. It *thrived*. All around her rose new buildings, fresh landscaping, neon signs, signals of growth where there should have been none. The place flourished like a parasite, feeding off her pain. It was enough to roll her stomach. Or perhaps that was just the stench of a three-day bus ride.

"Tenth and Pennsylvania!" the driver called, ringing a bell that could barely be heard over the exhausted engine. "Next stop downtown! Tenth and Pennsylvania!"

Jo stood, removing her sunglasses and gulping down nausea. "Get it over with," she whispered to herself. "Just get it over with."

"What did you say?"

Michael stood too, reaching for an olive-green duffel bag. He had freckles and red hair, cut short enough Jo could see a puffy white scar above his ear. He'd gotten on in Tucson, and by now, the smell of his cheap cologne could barely mask his lingering body odor.

"Nothing." She swayed as the bus turned.

"Oh. Thought you were talking to me." He stretched and yawned, releasing a wave of sour breath.

"Tenth and Pennsylvania!"

Jo closed her eyes, trying to calm herself. But at that moment, the bus jerked to a complete stop, causing her to tumble back into her seat. Her head snapped forward violently, smashing into Michael's thigh.

"Easy!" he said, gripping her arm. "Easy there. You okay?"

Jo wrenched from his grasp and stood again, trying to ignore her throbbing nose and watery eyes. "Fine," she huffed as she straightened her hat. "I'm fine."

Michael gave her a lopsided smile. "Alright. Well . . . ladies first." He made an awkward, exaggerated bow.

She didn't say thank you. Instead, she pushed toward the door, forgoing the usual bus exit etiquette of allowing those in front to disembark first. She ignored the annoyed stares of the other passengers as her handbag bumped their seats on the way out. She didn't care. She didn't want to set foot in Alamogordo; she wanted to stay on this bus even less.

The sun blinded her as she stepped onto the sidewalk. That relentless New Mexico *sun*. It was like stepping into an oven. She pulled her hat lower, already feeling her skin starting to burn through the thin fabric of her white button-down blouse. Alamogordo was different, but that sun was still the same. And she realized, wrinkling her nose, so was the smell. Like dirt and gasoline and cow poop.

She moved into the shade of the nearest building to rummage through her bag. Inside was a paper with the bus schedule. The afternoon bus left at five; it was the only afternoon bus back to San Diego all week. Otherwise she'd have to snag a morning bus that wound through Phoenix. The long way. Not that it mattered. She *would* be on the afternoon bus. Do what she needed to do and get out of this wretched desert.

Blood pounded behind her eyes. Her sunglasses . . . she'd just had them. They were right . . .

The bus roared to life in front of her once more, sputtering as it struggled to pick up speed heading north, out of Alamogordo.

. . . on her seat.

Fantastic.

The other passengers milled around on the sidewalk, all smiles and hugs, apparently unaffected by the sun or the heat or the dust. No one was squinting. No one was frowning. Some of them were even laughing. They *wanted* to be here.

It made Jo even more irritable. And being irritable made her headache worse. She snapped her bag closed and headed east, keeping her head low and refusing to look at the buildings around her. Woolworth's. The Texaco station. Nu-Way Beauty Center and White Auto Store. They pushed in on all sides, calling to her, begging her to remember. Even half-shut, her eyes burned. People bumped into her as if she wasn't there, mumbling muted apologies. They were all in a hurry to be someplace, to go on with their lives, unaware that, on the inside, she was struggling to keep her heart beating.

She hesitated under the shadow of a familiar copper turret, greened with age, antiquity clashing with the modern neon Coca-Cola sign hanging at its base. *Don't do it, Jo,* her mind screamed. *Don't go inside.* And yet she did, pulling open those wooden doors as if she were sixteen again.

Because she was. Inside Corner Drugs, it was still 1945. The tiled ceiling, the wooden counter, the stools, and the soda machine. The smell of cigarettes and syrup. The shelves lined with trinkets and candy and elixirs. And there, in the corner, where the counter curved around to meet the wall, that perfect spot where the breeze from the fan was just so, sat a girl, short dark hair pulled away from her face, dungarees and dirty boots, red-and-white straw poking up out of a root beer float.

Jo sucked in her breath. Hope and anger and indignation swirled inside her, nailing her to the floor.

The girl took one final slurp and stood, wiping the last of the brown liquid from her lips. It wasn't her. Of course it wasn't her. Relief and disappointment washed over her in a conflicting wave. *Don't be stupid, Jo.*

She strode forward with a confidence she didn't feel. Grabbing the first pair of sunglasses she saw off the revolving rack, she hurried to the counter.

"Hot one out there, ain't it?" The cashier was old, stooped, and missing his front two teeth. He turned the sunglasses over in his hands, smudging the lenses. "Definitely need a pair of these today. Good choice. Is there anything else I can get you?"

"No, that's it. I'm—" She stopped. "Actually, yes. Aspirin."

"Headache?"

"Obviously."

The man grabbed a bottle of white pills from the shelf behind him. "Anything else?"

She shook her head, rooting through her bag for her wallet.

He stared at her with raised eyebrows as he punched numbers into the register at an impossibly slow pace. "You're not from round here, are you?"

"What gave it away?" she asked wearily.

"Your hair, actually. I ain't never seen hair like that before." He nodded toward her shoulder.

She lifted a hand to her head. Some of her hair had indeed come free from under her floppy hat. Frustrated, she shoved the silvery strands back into place. "It's just hair."

"Unique, though, ain't it? That color. Blonder than blonde."

"Sure." She pulled a wrinkled five from her wallet and thrust it onto the counter. "Is this enough?"

He leaned toward the register. "Let me get you your change."

"Keep it." She grabbed her items and pushed through the door. Yanking the tag from the sunglasses, she placed them on her nose, took them off again to wipe the smudges from the lenses, then returned them to her face. They barely muted the glare, but it was better than nothing. She popped the cap from the bottle and downed three aspirin without water. Now she was ready, she told herself. Now she could do what she needed to do.

She rounded the corner to Tenth Street, once again keeping her head low. She made it past Michigan Avenue without looking. One hurdle down. A million to go.

"There you are!"

She quickened her pace.

"Hey, wait! Wait up!"

No. She would not stop. In and out, she told herself, before anyone could recognize her. The place was bad enough. If she had to face the people . . .

"Hey!"

She tensed as a hand landed on her arm. "I was looking for you when we got off, but you disappeared."

Michael. It was just Michael. Jo rolled her arm, pulling it free from his touch.

He didn't take the hint. "Listen, I was thinking—"

"Michael, where is it you're going?"

His mouth snapped closed, making a wet-sounding pop. "Um, well, I'm heading to the USO right now. My mama said she'd have a package waiting for me. Then I'll go over to the base—"

"The USO is that way," Jo said, jerking her thumb to the left. "You need to backtrack. It's at the corner of New York and Eleventh."

He blinked. "How do you know that?"

"Lucky guess."

Michael rubbed the back of his neck with one hand. "Listen, I was hoping maybe we could, um, grab a cup of coffee? I'm gonna be stationed at the range for a while, so I thought maybe . . ."

"I don't date Army guys."

"Good thing I'm in the Air Force then."

His smile was hopeful. Painfully pathetic. The old Jo would have taken pity. Heck, the new Jo might even have too if she wasn't here, in this place. This place where she was surrounded by ghosts, too sickened by the ground beneath her feet to consider becoming someone else's remedy.

So instead, she spun on her heel, scraping the sidewalk with her shoes as she resumed her pace. She held her breath, waiting to see if Michael's footsteps would follow. They didn't.

"If you change your mind," he called, "I'll be at the Coronado Café tonight. I'll buy you a drink. Whatever you want. Think about it?"

She didn't turn around. There was nothing to think about. She'd be gone before nightfall.

If it hadn't been for Michael, she could have kept her bearings. She could have turned when she was supposed to and taken the longer—but less painful—route to her destination. But now, here she was, tugged by some invisible force toward a familiar brick facade. She tried not to look. She didn't need to. The image of the high school was burned into her mind. The doors. The classrooms. The ringing of the bell, the shouts in the hallways, the dark-haired girl under the tree in the corner of the lawn, brown paper bag in her hand. It was silent, a Saturday, and yet she saw and heard it all nonetheless, whether she acknowledged it or not, as if the very bricks themselves were calling her.

She hurried her stride, but it was no use. Because just beyond the high school lay another building. "Pastor R. J. Hamilton" was still emblazoned on the sign out front. "Sunday's Sermon: The Beatitudes and You, Sunday School at 8:30, Worship at 9:30." Memories trickled from the stained-glass windows.

Or maybe just from one of them.

She was surprised to see how new the glass looked even all these years later. Still out of place next to the others. Jesus, vines encircling His outstretched hands. The words around Him, hard to read from the outside but, Jo knew, there just the same: *Abide In Me.*

An instruction. A command. A promise.

Broken.

She pushed her eyes to the ground. Coldness seeped into her limbs from somewhere inside, untouchable by the sun's warmth. She passed the building quickly, but distance brought no relief. The past seeped from every stone and tree, bearing down on the place inside her heart she had vowed to keep sealed.

CHAPTER THREE

OLIVE

NOVEMBER 1944

School was the worst part about living in Alamogordo.

I'd been homeschooled my entire life. Ma had taught me to read at age four. Math was learned by measuring feed and yield. History was alive in the land around me. My lessons were the shared work of the ranch. Those kids just sitting at desks all day, regurgitating facts spewed at them by teachers—they were only getting half an education and were brainwashed at that. At least according to Uncle Hershel. Life, he said, echoing my father in sentiment if not in tone, was the best teacher.

I tried to reiterate this to both my mother and grandmother. When that didn't work, I tried to reason that, at age fifteen, I pretty much knew everything I needed to know already. My mother had pinched the bridge of her nose and said I was giving her a head-ache. My grandmother said if I was done with school, I was more than welcome to spend my time with the Ladies Auxiliary at the church instead.

So that's how I found myself in early November, seated in front of the principal's desk. Mr. Williams's beady eyes peered at me from beneath bushy gray eyebrows as he pulled a paper from a pile on his overcrowded desk. Under a thin mustache, his lips stretched into what was supposed to be a smile . . . at least I thought it was.

"I believe we have everything in order here." His voice was one of too many cigarettes and not enough sleep. "I've got your class schedule here—" he thrust a piece of paper toward me—"and your book list here. You do know how to read?"

I laughed but stopped when I realized he wasn't. "Yes?"

He sat back in his chair, the wood popping under his weight. "Keep in mind, Miss Alexander, that this schedule is entirely sub-jective. Without any sort of benchmark, there's no way for us to know for sure the level to which you've progressed in relation to your age. We'll strive to keep you among your peers, but we have to make certain allowances for your skill level."

I blinked, my comprehension arriving before my emotions. *He thinks I'm stupid. He's too professional to say it, but he thinks I'm stupid.*

His eyebrows merged into one long gray caterpillar across his forehead.

Say something! I screamed at myself. But my mouth remained closed, every comeback, every intelligent thought I'd ever had left back on the ranch, where my "skill level" had never been ques-tioned.

After several moments, Mr. Williams sighed, and I was well aware I had somehow simultaneously met and failed his expectations. A sensation like a deflating balloon moved through my stomach. "Well, let's get you to class, shall we?"

First period science was taught by an ancient, wobbly-chinned woman named Mrs. Wheeler. Within five minutes of being introduced and shoved into a desk in the back corner, I was being asked to explain the difference between igneous and sedimentary rocks.

On the ranch, a rock was a rock. They were objects to be cleared, lest the tractor kick one up and kill you. Or break a window. But in high school, apparently there were different kinds. With different names, all of which sounded made up.

"I . . . I don't know." Heat rose in my cheeks as snickers erupted from somewhere up front.

"Oh. Dear." Not even a shred of pity in her voice. Instead, she shook her head and moved on to the next student, a pretty redhead who answered the question without hesitation.

I slumped down in my seat.

And that was just the beginning.

In history class I got in trouble for getting up to go to the bathroom without asking. Because evidently my *peers* needed permission to answer nature's call. In math, Mr. Dusky said they were studying something called "algebra," which sounded like a kind of fish disease but turned out to be nothing more complicated than figuring out the dimensions for a replacement piece on the windmill blade that broke during that big thunderstorm two springs ago. Unfortunately, algebra muddled it up with numbers and letters making it way more confusing than it needed to be.

And in PE, the girls were learning to play tennis. That was the actual lesson. Tennis.

I didn't agree with Uncle Hershel on most things. But when it came to traditional school, I was starting to think he might be right.

If the classes were bad, the hallways were worse. I looked like my peers—same calf-length skirt; same plain, fuzzy sweater; same bobby socks and loafers. I could have easily swapped places with any number of girls wandering the corridors. And yet something about me was different. People stared without staring. Whispered without moving their mouths. I was both completely ignored and put on display at the same time.

When the bell finally rang for lunch, I gathered my books and followed the other students out the door, focusing my attention on the class list in hand. Health this afternoon, followed by home economics, art, and—

I didn't see the black mass appear in front of me until too late. I crashed into it with a thud, my books and pencils flying into the air in slow motion.

"Oh, wow! I'm so sorry!"

The voice belonged to a boy. More than a boy. A man, really. Tall and broad-shouldered. Dark hair, blue eyes. And full, pink, beautiful lips that were twisted into a smile.

"Um, I . . . um . . ."

"Here, let me help you."

He crouched down and began to gather my belongings into a pile. I stared at him stupidly. Finally I knelt down next to him, so close I could smell the scent of Barbasol on his skin.

"*The Scarlet Letter*, huh?" he said, handing me a book.

"For class," I mumbled. My lips and brain were refusing to cooperate with one another. "Read. In class."

I wanted to die.

But the boy only laughed. "Yeah, I remember that class. Mrs. Parker's, right?" I nodded as he handed me my pencil. "I'm Tim, by the way. Bucknam."

"Olive." At least I thought I said Olive.

"You new, Olive?"

I felt my cheeks redden. "That obvious?"

"No, I didn't mean . . ." He shoved one hand in his pocket. "I've just never seen you around here before, that's all."

I tried to smile, although it probably came out more like a grimace.

"Well . . . it was nice to meet you. Welcome to Alamo High." He tapped the cover of my book with one finger. "Enjoy your book, Olive." Then he winked before walking away, turning down a side hallway and disappearing out of sight.

Boys had never held much interest for me. The summer farm-hands who frequented the ranch were sweaty and immature. Their teenage mouths spewed what I suspected was more confidence than they actually felt. I'd tested this theory last summer when, having had enough of their whistles and hollers, I approached one—Ben, I thought his name was—and placed a hand upon his arm. Trying to maintain an air of serious sensuality, I asked if he'd like to accompany me behind the barn. He'd fallen straight off the fence post.

That shut the rest of them up for a while.

But Tim . . .

"Olive? Olive Alexander?"

A soft voice broke me from my thoughts. I spun around, coming face-to-face with a ghost. I blinked. Not a ghost. A girl. A girl with hair so blonde it was white and skin so fair I could see snakes of blue veins underneath. Her black sweater, layered over a gray skirt, only made her look more colorless. The lone item of any substance was a small golden cross around her neck, which shimmered under the hallway lights.

"Olive Alexander?" she repeated.

"Yes?"

The girl broke into a smile that reached deep into her pale-blue eyes. "I thought so. I mean, I hoped so. I've been looking for you all morning."

"Why?"

She crossed her arms over her chest. "That came out wrong. I mean, yes, I was looking for you, but not *looking* looking like some kind of loony. I—"

"Who are you?"

The girl let out a nervous titter. "How rude of me. I'm Jo." She stuck out one bony hand.

I shook it tentatively, trying not to flinch at its coldness. Even at arm's length, I could smell her soap—like flowers and fresh air. Immaculately, impossibly *clean*.

"It's only my second week here. It's been . . . hard." The last word came out slowly, as if she wasn't sure it was the correct one. "Anyway, Mr. Williams mentioned that you were starting today— another new student—and suggested I find you. And here you are."

I pressed my lips together. I wasn't looking for a friend. I wasn't *not* looking for one either. Aside from Tim, Jo was the first benevolent presence I'd encountered all day. I forced a smile.

Her body visibly relaxed at the sight. "So . . . how's your first day going?"

I shrugged. "It's not bad. But it's not good, either."

"I understand. Everything here is so different from my old school. Everyone seems to know each other already."

"That's because they do. I take it you're not from a small town?"

She shook her head.

"These kids have probably known each other since kindergarten. Heck, maybe even longer. They probably potty-trained together."

She laughed. "Do you want to sit with me at lunch? There's nothing worse than eating alone."

I grinned—a real grin, the first one all day. "Sure."

The lunchroom at Alamogordo High School was louder and more crowded than an Albuquerque rodeo. About the same level of refinement too. Boys whooped and hollered, showing off for the girls by tossing food in the air—or at each other. Groups of girls responded either by giggling, which was annoying, or ignoring, which only made the boys try harder. A frazzled monitor scurried from one table to the next in a futile attempt to maintain order.

Jo and I took one look at the scene and made our way outside. It was still crowded, groups of students lounging beneath trees that were just starting to change their shade, but at least it was quieter out here, even with the whistle of a nearby train.

We found a spot on the corner of the lawn, away from the other students. There was a slight nip in the air, but the noon sun warmed our backs as Jo removed a peanut butter sandwich from her lunch pail, crusts removed and the halves cut into neat triangles. A box of raisins followed, along with a small container of carrot sticks.

I pulled my lunch from its rumpled paper sack. Spam on smooshed bread. I should have expected nothing less from my grandma, whose fascination with the "wonder meat" was a lesson I'd learned after only a few days living in her house. It had been in our potato casserole at dinner last night. It had been in my eggs this morning. It would probably be in my dinner tonight. At the bottom, I found a crumpled bag of Smith's Potato Crisps, its contents mashed into a greasy mess.

Perhaps I'd insist on packing my own lunch tomorrow.

I glanced up to find Jo looking at me, eyebrows raised. I shoved the chips back into the sack. "It's been a while since my grandma has had to pack a lunch. Guess she's a little out of practice."

Jo gave a slight nod as she raised two fingers to her mouth. I realized she was holding back a laugh.

I should have been offended. But instead I laughed too. Because it *was* funny. And because I needed to laugh. There hadn't been anything to laugh about in such a long time, and no one to laugh with.

"Do you want some of my carrots?" Jo asked between sniggers. "I have plenty."

"Thanks," I said. The carrots were crisp and sweet on my tongue, distinct against the blandness of my Spam.

"So you live with your grandma?" Jo smoothed her skirt as she stretched her legs out in front of her. "I used to live with my grandma too. Back in California. My mom died when I was a baby, so my grandma practically raised me."

Her voice was so steady, so matter-of-fact. Her mother was dead. Just like the sky was blue.

"My dad died too," I blurted out. "Seven years ago. He fell off his horse chasing a runaway bull and broke his back."

If she thought it was a weird reply, she didn't show it. Instead, she nodded. "But you knew him."

"Yes, I knew him."

"So it was harder, I'm sure. I didn't know my mom. So I don't feel sad about it, even though I know I'm supposed to. It was much harder to lose my grandma. She died a couple months ago."

I started. Again that tone. So matter-of-fact. "I'm . . . I'm sorry."

"Thanks. I miss her. Every day I miss her. But she'd been sick for a long time. Not in her body, but in her mind, if that makes sense? I'd been pretty much taking care of myself for a year, as well as her. And there toward the end, she didn't even know who I was anymore." She cleared away the first trace of emotion with a slight cough. "So it's sad, but it's better now. She's better now. I know she's in heaven."

I could almost hear Uncle Hershel's raging in my ears. *"Heaven. God. Garbage. Delusions for the weak."* I should have realized from the cross around Jo's neck that she was one of *those* kinds of people. I rolled my eyes before I could stop myself.

Unfortunately, Jo was watching. "What?"

"Nothing," I said quickly, shaking my uncle from my brain. Christian or not, I wasn't ready to burn the bridge to the only friendship I'd made that day. "So she passed . . ."

"She passed and now I'm here. I didn't want to leave California, but it wasn't really up to me. I'm still a minor, at least according to the government, and legally I had to be placed with a guardian."

"A guardian?"

"My dad. Although I hadn't seen him in over a year before he came to get me. The war and all, you know? He's in the Army."

A chill washed over me like a cold breeze. Only there was no breeze. "The Army?"

"Yeah." She tucked a strand of loose hair behind her ear. "He's working on that project north of here. The one by your ranch."

And suddenly I was falling. Not literally, no. On the outside, I was still just sitting next to Jo, listening with a look of interest on my face. I gave no outward sign of the darkness spreading throughout my body. "What . . . what did you say your last name was?"

Jo frowned. "I . . . I don't think I said. I thought . . . well, I thought you already knew. I recognized your name right away. And my dad said he mentioned me to you." She gave a tight smile. "Hawthorne. Jo Hawthorne."

I knew before she said it. Of course I knew. The sheer amount of desperation it had taken to blind me to the truth. I'd been so lonely, lonelier than I'd admit even to myself. And this girl—this strange, pale, friendly girl—appeared at the hour of my greatest need. A new girl, just like me. How *stupid* I'd been. How wretchedly, willfully naive.

"Olive, are you okay?"

I scrambled to my feet. Carrot sticks dropped to the ground with dull thuds.

"Olive, what—?"

"Stay away from me," I hissed. "Don't you ever come near me again, do you hear?"

Jo recoiled. "What did I—?"

"Your father may think he can come prancing onto my family's land, taking whatever he wants just because he has some piece of paper saying it's legal. But just 'cause it's legal doesn't make it right. And it certainly doesn't mean we're friends."

Jo's eyes flitted around the yard nervously. "I'm sorry; I just thought . . ." Her voice trembled. "I thought, we're here, you know? Together. God has a reason, even if we don't understand it. And—I don't know—we might as well find a way to make the most of it?"

Splotches of red flashed at the corners of my eyes, blurring out everything but her. This girl with the stupid, hopeful smile on her face. This girl who thought this was all part of some imaginary God's *plan*. Pity wrestled with anger. Her naiveté was worse than my own.

Because at least I could see that there was no *divine force* bringing us together. There were only human hands pushing us aside.

I'd never know what Mrs. Arnold taught in home economics that day. I wouldn't hear the crude jokes from the football players who sat in the back of study hall. I wouldn't even get to see Bobby Reskey shoved into the girls' locker room at the end of the day. Because I spent the rest of the afternoon under a blanket in the bedroom on Delaware Avenue, vowing never to return to Alamogordo High.

CHAPTER FOUR

JO

MARCH 1952

The law offices of Purcell and Pamona were located on Delaware Avenue, next to an optometrist and across the street from a bank. Jo couldn't remember if these buildings had always been here or not. They looked old and new at the same time, the white stucco gleaming around dusty, opaque windows, their painted letters cracked from the relentless sun.

Jo stopped out front. The heat shimmering above the concrete waved her on down the street. She knew what she'd find if she kept walking. Two blocks down, the shops gave way to little gray houses, dead grass, and sagging fences. All of them with different inhabitants but the same stories.

Except for one.

One pulled at her, beckoning with a piece of her own story. But, she vowed, ripping her eyes from the past and pushing open the heavy door of the office, that didn't mean she had to read it.

A small brass bell tinkled as she stepped inside and removed her hat. The interior of the building was dim and blissfully cool. Three large fans oscillated around her, circulating the smell of old cigarettes. Her hair blew onto her forehead, where it stuck, glued in place by sweat.

She pushed her sunglasses up. "Hello?"

The front desk sat empty. Behind it were three more desks, also empty, each covered with stacks of paper and ashtrays filled to the brim. A green lamp illuminated one, its light making the dust motes beneath it sparkle. Rows of file cabinets lined the back wall, next to a shelf of thick volumes with faded-gold lettering.

"Hello?" Jo called again.

"Hello!" The red, round face of a man appeared from around the corner, a narrow hallway Jo hadn't even realized was there.

She jumped before she could stop herself, then stuck out her chin, pretending she hadn't. "I'm here to see Mr. Purcell."

"Then you're in luck because that's exactly who I am!" He stepped forward with a grand gesture, holding stubby arms out from his rounded sides. Puddles of sweat stained the white fabric under his arms. Over his shoulders, navy-blue suspenders held up khaki pants that sagged at the sides. He beamed at Jo beneath hooded, sleepy eyes.

She did not smile back. "I have an appointment."

"Of course, of course. Yes, yes. Come in, come in."

She wondered if he was going to say everything twice. She certainly didn't have time for that. She brushed past him, heading for the lit desk, assuming it was his and hoping he could read her impatience.

He couldn't. Or if he could, he didn't care. He waddled slowly behind her, stopping to grab a taffy from the front desk. He unwrapped it with maddening precision, one side of the paper and then the next, before popping it into his mouth. "Want one?"

"No," Jo said pointedly.

He pocketed two more before finally joining her at his desk, which was a hurricane of loose papers, stacked books, and candy wrappers. The chair squeaked as he sat. The papers threatened to take flight as another pass of the fan swept over them, but he put a hand on them without looking, eyes focused on the open calendar upon his desk. "Let's see, let's see. Ah, yes. The power of attorney." He looked up at her, smiling. "You must be Miss Hawthorne. Thank you for coming all the way out here."

"Did I have a choice?"

Mr. Purcell grimaced. "No, I'm sorry. I suppose not. We were worried the state was going to have to step in. You were, um, rather difficult to contact."

"I was . . ." *Running. Hiding. Somewhere—anywhere—but here.* ". . . in and out of the country."

"Yes. Well, water under the bridge. You're here now, right? Let's get started, shall we?"

"Please."

"As I stated in my letter, the reason I've asked you to come here, rather than doing this by mail, is because of the urgency of the matter at hand. Your father has reached a state of incapacitation in the, um, physical sense."

"He's dying." She kept her voice flat. Emotionless.

Mr. Purcell started, coughing in an attempt to cover his surprise. "Yes. Yes, he's dying." His eyes flickered between Jo and the paper on his desk. "If there's anything good in all of this, it's that his condition was not unexpected, and Sergeant Hawthorne made arrangements. In the event that he is no longer able to support himself by his own person, he has authorized you to be his power of attorney, making all legal and financial decisions for him and his estate. Do you understand what that means?"

Jo nodded.

"Your father has been in the hospital for the past month, hence the frequency of my letters and telegraphs." He fiddled with the cap of his pen. "During that time, his condition has deteriorated rapidly, and according to hospital staff, he has been in and out of consciousness over the past week."

Jo pulled at the fabric of her pants. She should feel something at this news, laid out more plainly in front of her than the black and white of the oft-read letter. But the only thing she felt was a strange sense of detachment, as if she were hearing the news about a stranger, rather than her own flesh and blood.

Mr. Purcell shifted in his seat. "By all intents and purposes, he is no longer able to make decisions for himself, and unfortunately, there *are* decisions that must be made."

"Like what?"

"Well, for starters, the house on Michigan Avenue—"

Memories swirled. None of them good and certainly none in which she wanted to linger.

"Sell it."

Mr. Purcell gave her a sidelong glance. "That's not possible, I'm afraid. The house is not yours to sell."

"But I'm the power of attorney. I'm here to make his decisions, right?"

"Well, yes, but—"

"Then I've decided to sell."

"Yes, but the power of attorney does not negate legal matters already settled. Like his will. And in such, the matter of the house has already been decided."

A chill crept down Jo's spine that had nothing to do with another pass of the fan. "Who did he leave it to?"

"I beg your pardon?"

"His will . . . Who did he leave the house to?"

"I'm afraid that's a sealed document and I'm not at liberty to discuss it. Until his . . ."

"Until he dies."

"Yes."

Jo blinked several times. Mr. Purcell's scarlet face grew hazy as she focused on sealing the cracks she could not let break. She pulled her coldness from deep within, wrapping it around her like armor until all she felt was a stifling, overwhelming nothingness.

Mr. Purcell's chair squeaked again as he shifted. "Um, anyways, I really just need you to sign some papers and then your authorization to pay some bills."

Jo rubbed her temples. The aspirin had done little for her headache; it was returning now in full force. "Pay whatever needs to be paid. Hospital bills, utility bills, whatever. I assume he has the money?"

"He has money."

"Then just do it. Whatever needs to be done."

He scribbled something down on a pad of paper. "Very well. I need you to sign here." She did. "And here. And here."

Jo signed away, not bothering to read or listen to Mr. Purcell's explanation of each document. By the end, her signature had become nothing more than a smudge. "Is there anything else?"

Mr. Purcell shuffled the papers, licking his thumb before flipping through the stack. "Have you seen your father yet, Miss Hawthorne?"

She detected a note of condescension in his voice. It made her bristle. "It's on my to-do list."

"I see. Well, your father and I, we became . . . close . . . over these last few years. More than client and attorney. And I can tell you that Mr. Hawthorne had many demons he was fighting long before this illness became the bigger battle. I hope—"

"You know his side of the story," Jo interrupted. Heat rose in her cheeks. "Don't presume it's the only one."

Mr. Purcell opened and closed his mouth twice before clearing his throat. "Naturally. Yes. But I . . . I do hope you see him sooner rather than later. I know he . . . well, he really wants to see you."

The muscles in her throat seized but she allowed no outward display. This town was already doing it, already making her dig up things that should remain buried. Like any sort of pity or compassion she felt for the man who had shown none for her. She clung to her anger like an anchor.

"If we're quite finished here?"

Mr. Purcell broke his gaze and sighed. "For now."

Jo rose swiftly, nearly knocking over her chair in the process. Placing her sunglasses upon her nose, she nodded once in his direction. "Mr. Purcell." Then she marched from the office without giving him a chance to respond.

The heat rushed to meet her as she stepped outside. She tucked her hair under her hat and stalked down the sidewalk. Focusing on the click of her low heels, she tried to steady her breathing. Mr. Purcell's words replayed inside her head. As if he knew anything about her. About the things that happened that summer.

As if any of it could ever be forgotten. Or fixed. She pushed forward, shaking her head, willing the thoughts to fall from her mind like snowflakes. Trying to ignore the heat, the anger, the relentless *guilt*.

Gosh, she hated this town.

There was just one more thing to do. One more stop and she could leave. Be done with this place forever. And yet, in her self-absorption, she had not walked toward her destination. Instead, she was standing in front of a familiar house. Weeds climbed up the chain-link fence now encircling the dirt yard. It was a coincidence. She hadn't come this way on purpose. And the idea that she'd been led here by something—something that had been tugging at her heart since she stepped off that bus, something that had never really left her alone, even after all these years away—was absurd.

The house looked nicer than she remembered. Fresh paint on the siding, a new door on the small porch. Only the yard remained the same: brown and rocky, cracked in the sun. Nothing but a miracle could make grass grow in New Mexico.

She swallowed hard, her throat raw from the dry air.

"Can I help you?" A woman emerged from the house, dark hair falling over her sunburnt shoulders.

Jo drew a sharp breath and took a step back. The sun was bright, obscuring the woman's face. But she didn't need to see her to know.

Olive. Olive was walking toward her. Barefoot on the earth, somehow not flinching as rocks and goat heads pressed into her skin.

"Can I help you?" Olive repeated.

She doesn't recognize me, Jo thought, wounded. And then, even harsher: *She has forgotten.*

But then she was there, right on the other side of the fence. Hand over her brow, shielding her eyes from the glare. Not Olive at all. Not even close.

The woman was older than she'd first appeared, forties perhaps, with streaks of gray in her hair that Jo had somehow missed. Freckles peppered every inch of exposed skin.

"No, I, uh," Jo stammered, embarrassed at her childishness. "I'm sorry. I'm, um, I'm lost and—"

"Military?"

Jo shook her head.

The woman's mouth pressed into a line. "Oh. I just assumed. Nurse or USO volunteer or something. Those are the only ones we get wandering around out here, lost and looking for directions. I swear, you get 'em off base, and they can't find their rear from a hole in the ground. How they ever find enemy troops is beyond me." She snorted.

"Well, I'm not a nurse, but I'm headed for the hospital."

"Ah. Wrong direction. It's thataway." She jerked one cigarette-stained thumb back toward Tenth Street.

"Right," Jo said, pretending to be grateful. "Of course. Thank you. Have a nice day." She found her legs again and took a step back in the direction she'd come. She needed to get out of here. She was going crazy. The last bus left at five o'clock and she would be on it. It was the only truth she knew for sure.

And yet she found herself turning on her heel. "Excuse me?"

The woman was halfway across her yard but stopped at the sound of Jo's voice.

"I'm sorry," Jo said. "I . . . I used to know someone who lived here. Last name was Burke? Or perhaps Alexander?"

The woman cocked her head, closing one eye. "Well, there ain't no Alexanders or Burkes here now."

"Right. Okay. Thank you anyway."

The woman lit a cigarette, her eyes boring into Jo's back until Jo had crossed Ninth Street and ducked under an awning, finally out of sight.

Leaning against the cool stone of the shaded storefront, Jo pulled off her sunglasses and wiped the sweat from her nose before replacing them. What had she been thinking, going over there like that? She hadn't been thinking, she reminded herself. That was the problem. It had been her emotions—her weak, unchecked emotions. Like the Jo Hawthorne who'd left here all those years ago.

But she was not that girl anymore. She was no longer a victim of her own naiveté and youth. She did not care what had happened to Olive. The bond between them—if there ever had been one—was severed long ago, the wound cauterized and scarred. It was over. Done. And Alamogordo would not slice it open again. She was too strong now, her heart sealed against whatever this town would throw at her. The meeting with Mr. Purcell had created a fissure, but she would not let that happen again.

She took a deep breath and turned down Tenth Street, head held erect, more clear-minded than she'd been in days. It was time to finish her business and leave this place. Once and for all.

CHAPTER FIVE

OLIVE

NOVEMBER 1944

Grandma had other ideas about me not going back to school.

She was out shopping when I snuck back to her house. I heard her return not twenty minutes after I'd hidden myself under the scratchy green comforter she'd promised I'd get used to.

I stopped sniffling, wiping my face on my sleeve, and listened as she moved around the kitchen. She hummed as she put groceries away in the small pantry. The walls were so thin I could even hear the rustle of her stockings as her legs rubbed together. No wonder Grandma still insisted on garters.

After a few minutes, the shuffling stopped, and I knew she'd retreated to the living room, more than likely with the newspaper in tow. She'd probably be asleep within the hour. More than enough time for me to sneak out and pretend to be coming home from school. I exhaled deeply, closing my eyes, and snuggled further into my blanket to wait.

"There's Spam and crackers on the table."

My eyes fluttered back open.

"You can let it get sticky if you want, but I'd recommend eating it now rather than later because I sure ain't letting it go to waste."

I held my breath. She couldn't possibly be talking to me. There was no way.

"Suit yourself. But I'd planned on washing those sheets today, so if you're going to keep up this charade, at least do it under the bed so I can finish my work."

I sighed and flipped the blanket down to my waist. Grandma stood in the doorway, one hand on her thick hip, the other drumming on the doorframe. Her simple button-down dress was purple and faded, traces of flowers barely visible after so many washings. Graying curls caught the afternoon sun, creating a halo around the crown of her head. Her face, however, looked anything but angelic.

"How did you know I was here?"

"I may be old but I ain't blind, child. And I don't ever leave my house with a bedspread as rumpled as that one." She waggled her eyebrows. "So tell me: when did they start letting school out before 1:42?"

I turned my eyes to the comforter.

"Uh-huh. I thought so." She motioned toward the bed, and I pulled up my knees, allowing her a place to sit. "So what happened?"

Everything. "Nothing."

"*Nothing* don't hide under a blanket in the middle of the day."
She puckered her lips, a gesture so much like my mother's it forced
a slight gasp from my throat. It was easy to forget she was my
mother's mother when we saw so little of her out on the ranch.
Even as a small child, I'd been very aware she and my father didn't
get along; the tension was even worse with Uncle Hershel. Our
relationship was measured in sporadic visits, birthday cards, and—
once in a blue moon—trips to Alamogordo to prove we were still
alive and kicking. Out on the ranch, it wasn't difficult to pretend
Mama had just always been there, that she had never had another
life—with other people—someplace else.

But now I was here, and Grandma was real—more real than
she'd ever been. Her skin was soft and worn, like a favorite pair of
mittens. She smelled of the butterscotch candies she was forever
sucking on. And while her mouth was usually set in a frown—a
result of a stroke a few years back and years of impatience for
stupidity—her smile, when she managed one, was warm. She
managed one now.

I barely knew the woman. But her face made me want to tell
her everything—the whole stupid mess of it. "Why am I here,
Grandma?"

"That's what I'm trying to figure out."

"No, I don't mean here. I mean *here*. Why did I have to move
to town . . . and why did she get to stay?" I began to blubber.
"Why did they take our land in the first place? Why—?"

"Goodness, child. Slow down. One question at a time." Her
doughy hand enveloped my own. "Now, I'll pretend not to be
offended by how awful you think it is to have to come and stay
with your own grandmother."

My chest went tight. "Grandma, I—"

But she spoke over me. "That aside, I could try to answer if you want, but I have a feeling you wouldn't like what I have to say. Plus, truth be told, you already know the answers." She crossed and then uncrossed her arms, waiting for me to respond.

I didn't.

"Suit yourself. You had to move to town because you're a child, and it's better for you here. Safer, while all this Army stuff is going on." She held up a hand to my objection. "Yes, better, even if you don't see it that way yet. And your mother stayed because she had work to do there. Her and Hershel."

"But I could have stayed—"

"And done what?"

"Helped!"

"By doing what?"

"Avery's work!" I swallowed hard, frustrated at the wobbliness in my voice. "He's gone, and there's way too much for just two people."

"Both you and I know the ranch ain't nearly as big as it used to be." She raised her hand again as I started to disagree. "I know you don't like hearing it, but it's true. Even before the government came in and took half of it for . . . well, whatever it is. Hershel's been selling it bit by bit since your father died just to keep you all afloat. All them government men keep saying the Depression is over, but ain't no one told New Mexico yet. Having you here takes a bit of the financial burden—"

"Oh, so I'm a burden?"

"You stop that right now, Olive Marie. You know that's not what I meant."

I frowned into my pillow. I was being juvenile and petty, sure, but just once I wished my grandmother would let me. I knew things had been bad for a long time—since Pa died, really—but I didn't want to hear about it. Not right now. I was too busy feeling sorry for myself to worry about a little thing called the truth.

She sighed. "You may not like it. You may not agree with it. But your mother made a choice, and you have to believe she did so with your best interests in mind. That's what mothers do. Everyone has their part to play, Evelyn. Even you."

I wrenched my mind out of its misery. "What?"

"I said everyone has their part to play. Even you."

"You called me Evelyn."

My grandmother stared at me blankly, scratching at her temple with two fingers. "No, no, I . . ."

Evelyn was my mother's name, and aside from the dark hair, I looked nothing like her. She was tall, slim, beautiful, with high cheekbones and eyes as blue as the sky. I, on the other hand, took after my father—short, stocky (or "sturdy," as he used to say) with eyes so dark, my pupils seemed to disappear inside them.

No one had ever mistaken me for Evelyn before.

The silver chain at my grandmother's neck jingled with each jerk of her head. "You misheard me, Olive. That's all." She rolled her shoulders, shaking off the moment. "But anyways, like I said, we all have to do our part. Anything that helps us win this awful war and bring our boys home."

I nodded, thinking of Avery with a twinge of guilt. Consumed by my own misery, I'd barely thought about him. I wondered where he was now, what he was doing. If he was safe.

"Your mother's part is out there. But your part . . . your part is here, with me. In this house. And in that school." Her eyes narrowed pointedly.

I hung my head. I'd almost thought she was going to let it slide. How stupidly optimistic.

She rose and smoothed out the bedspread beneath her. "Now you come and have your Spam and crackers. I won't have you wasting away to nothing while you're in my care." She moved to the doorway but paused in the opening. "Today you get a snack. But tomorrow, Olive? Tomorrow if I catch you out of school, you won't be hiding in this room. You'll be scrubbing every inch of it with a toothbrush."

———◆❖◆———

I know I said school was the worst part of Alamogordo. And it was.

But church? Church was right behind it, nipping at its heels.

My family didn't go to church. Not only for practical reasons—the nearest church was over thirty miles away in Carrizozo—but because my father never saw the point. While Uncle Hershel, who moved in after my father's death, was a flat-out atheist, railing against the dangers of organized religion and the absurdity of some "wizard in the clouds," my father was more agnostic. If there was a God who created the world, he reckoned, what good would it do to sit in a building made by a man, reading a book written by a man, and singing songs composed by a man? Wouldn't it be better to spend our time outside in the very creation God was supposed to have formed?

I didn't care either way. Whether it was Papa's apathy or, later, Hershel's rage, whatever kept my body out of an itchy dress and my behind off of a hard pew on a Sunday morning was okay by me. Instead, I was free to spend the day reading in the burrow or napping in the hayloft. I didn't waste my time thinking about God because, if He *was* real, I was pretty sure He didn't spend His time thinking about me.

But Grandma . . . Grandma didn't just spend her time thinking about God. She spent her time *working* for God, or so she said. There was Ladies Auxiliary and Tuesday morning prayer circle, food pantry service, and care package preparation for the troops. There was Sunday school class followed by Sunday service, as well as Monday afternoon Bible study and Wednesday night worship.

And guess who was now expected to accompany her?

It never set well with my grandma that her only child had so readily given up her faith after her marriage to my father or that she was content to defer to her husband's viewpoints when it came to raising children outside the church. Though the time to repair the former had passed, she was intent on fixing the latter, she told me as she drove me to church on Wednesday evening, now that the Lord had dropped the opportunity into her lap.

I sulked in the passenger seat but said nothing. I'd gotten a pass from church activities during my first week in Alamogordo because Grandma wanted to give me time to settle in. But the honeymoon was over (if it had ever really happened in the first place), and at exactly 6:15, Grandma had grabbed her purse and her Bible and instructed me to get in the car. I'd almost put up a fight, but considering the earlier stay of execution from my truancy, I decided now was not the time to push it.

And even though she'd traded her faded old housedress for a nicer, belted navy-blue one, at least she'd let me stay in my school clothes.

She bumped the curb as she parked. I winced at the scrape of the old Ford on concrete.

She patted her hair and inspected her teeth in the rearview mirror before turning to me. "What?" she asked, seeing my face.

"There was a curb there."

"A what?"

"A curb. You hit the curb."

She gathered her things from the seat beside me. "Oh, Olive. We don't have time for such nonsense. We're late." And she scooted out the door without a backward glance.

The church was loud and crowded. The congregation was already deep into their hymnals by the time we pushed through the heavy oak doors. The smell of old lady perfume was thick, all fake floral and musk. Any hopes I had about slipping into a back pew unnoticed were dashed when Grandma seized my elbow and dragged me straight up the center aisle to the front, where two seats were still open despite the push of bodies around them.

Grandma shoved a hymnal in my hands, flipping expertly to the correct page and pointing to the text before turning her attention forward. The words of the song fell from her lips without the need of a silly thing like a book.

But I didn't sing. Instead I watched.

I'd never given more than a passing thought to religion, but now that I was here, forced to confront it, I studied the congregation with a critical eye. It was like being in a zoo—an outsider gawking at a foreign species in its native habitat. Just who were all these people singing to? And why? What did God—if there was one—want with their weak, pitiful song? It was silly at best, an insult at worst.

I was more inclined to believe, however, that He didn't exist at all.

Because a good God wouldn't let wars happen. Wouldn't kill fathers in farming accidents. Wouldn't let the government steal land and break apart families. No, Grandma's God couldn't be real. Because if He was, then it meant He sure didn't care too much about us.

About me.

The incessant voices droned on. I focused on inspecting the building instead. Both the carpet and the cushions on the wooden pews were maroon, faded from years and use. Stained-glass windows lined either side of the sanctuary, each of them displaying what I guessed was a scene from the Bible. The one nearest me showed Jesus, vines encircling His outstretched hands, shards of red glass spelling the words *Abide In Me* near His head.

Hogwash. How could you abide in a person?

But it wasn't even the words that bothered me most. It was His eyes. Inanimate and lifeless, yet they bored into me, the shards of cool-blue glass somehow burning my skin. It was stupid—they were just pieces of glass arranged to look like eyes. But still they reflected a presence—a pain—I found unbearable to witness.

I tore my own away, only to have them land on something even more unsettling. A head of bright-blonde hair in the pew across the aisle. Too bright. And too blonde to be anyone else.

Jo. Jo Hawthorne was here. And she was staring right at me.

Quickly I buried my nose in the hymnal. I could hear her now. Her soft voice rose above the chorus around me. She was singing without looking, the words drifting forth from her very soul, more an outpouring of her heart than a mandated exercise in faithfulness.

In my state of already-heightened irritation, this annoyed me most of all.

At long last the singing stopped, replaced by the creak of dozens of pews as everyone took their seats. The preacher ("Pastor Hamilton," my grandmother whispered in a wave of butterscotch) was younger than I expected. Only a few traces of gray seasoned his temples. He wore a black suit, sweat glistening on his forehead from the heat of the overhead lights. His smile extended into his deep-set eyes as he opened his palms to the ceiling.

"Brothers and sisters, I am so happy you could join us this evening to worship our Lord, the risen Christ."

A loud "hallelujah" from the back caused me to jump. Grandma smiled and patted my arm.

"As it says in the book of Matthew, 'For where two or three gather in my name, there am I with them.' May the Lord's presence be in this place today as we raise our voices and glorify Him not just for what He has done, but for who He is."

Another "hallelujah," but this time I was ready for it.

"Let us pause in our worship to remember our brothers and sisters at war, whether in Europe, in Asia, or at the Army base right down the road. Let us take this moment to lift them up to God and ask for His blessing over the lives of those who are willing to die for ours." He bowed his head. The congregation followed. "Lord, protect our soldiers and bring them home safely. May their hearts and ours be molded and shaped into ones of sacrifice and service, seeking Your will above all else, even now, in times of great hardship."

A sharp jab in my side. I flinched. Grandma had poked me. Her eyes narrowed as she gestured toward the preacher, her meaning obvious. *Bow your head.* I scowled as I did it. But I did not close my eyes. That would have been too much. Instead I stared at my fingers, twisting and untwisting them as I waited for the preacher to finish.

All these people around me, praying for husbands and sons and brothers. I'd never prayed for Avery. Grandma probably had. These strangers—these people who didn't even know my brother—probably had too. In a world where everything was so out of control, these people came together as one, thinking they could do something about it. And it didn't necessarily make them seem bigger or better.

But it did, somehow, make me feel smaller.

After more singing and more praying and then even more singing, it was finally time to go home. Or at least I thought it was. I nudged Grandma from the pew, hoping to usher her ahead of the crowd and especially ahead of Jo. But I hadn't anticipated the sheer amount of hugs and small talk I would have to endure just to get us out the door.

"So this is the granddaughter!" a gray-haired woman shrieked, embracing me as if I were *her* granddaughter. "Edna has told me so much about you! I'm so happy you're here!"

"The famous Olive!" another man said. His starched brown jacket barely moved as he embraced me. "Finally!"

And more like that. Over and over and over again. People acting like they knew me, people hugging Grandma like she was their own, people talking about potlucks and sewing circles and letters from the front. No one else was in a hurry to leave. These people *wanted* to be here. Instead of dispersing, the crowd swelled toward one another.

It felt suffocating. And not just physically.

It was as if they were a family, bound by shared delusion but genuine in affection. My peers at school had found me wanting, but somehow, this was worse. Through their hugs and handshakes, these people welcomed me, extending an invitation I would never—could never—accept. I wasn't one of them, no matter how much they pretended otherwise.

Their religion was not mine. Their God was not mine. But more importantly, Alamogordo was not mine. It would never truly be home.

And yet . . . neither was the ranch.

I was an outcast. Everywhere. In this place where these people seemed so at home, I had never felt more home*less*.

I was finally able to break free during a particularly lively discussion about a care package collection system. Ducking in between bodies, I pressed my back against the wall and took a deep breath. Unfortunately, the place in which I'd found refuge was directly under the window with the stained-glass vines and the eyes I wasn't sure were actually made from glass. I tried to ignore the sensation of being watched as I lowered my head, hoping to avoid any more attempts at conversation, and waited for Grandma.

"Hi, Olive. Surprised to see you here, but in a good way."

I knew it was her without looking up. So I didn't.

"The people here are so welcoming, don't you think? I can feel the Holy Spirit when I walk in the door. It's so refreshing."

There was a snag in the carpet. I picked at it with the toe of my shoe. My silence might have seemed impolite, but it was better than what I wanted to say to her.

"The war makes me feel hopeless sometimes, you know? Like it's never going to end, and there's nothing I can do about it. Coming here gives me hope. God is still in control."

I gritted my teeth. I wished she would stop talking. I needed her to stop talking. Right *now*.

She moved closer. I could feel her, even though I still refused to look. "I prayed for your brother," she said softly.

I jerked my head up. "How did you—?"

"His name is on the prayer list," she said quickly. "The one with boys at the front. He's the only Alexander and I . . . well, I put two and two together. I just want you to know—" she lowered her voice—"that I understand. I know how hard it is. The worry and uncertainty."

Her words severed the last nerve binding my anger in its place. "Oh, you know, do you? How do you know, Jo?"

She took a step back, the surprise in her eyes delighting me.

"It must be so hard for you, Jo. All that worry and uncertainty. Do you worry about your father, sitting all cozy in my living room? The uncertainty of whether he'll get a goat head in his shoe as he tramples all over my land?"

"Olive, I didn't mean—"

"You have no idea, Jo. No idea what any of this is like. So stop pretending like you do. We are not in this together." I'd never felt anything as powerful as this hatred, this sheer contempt for the girl standing in front of me. Deep down somewhere, I knew she hadn't done anything wrong; she was only a fool, after all. There was nothing malicious in her words or actions. And yet here, in this moment, her kindness served only to shine a spotlight on my own deficiency. Everything I was feeling—all the hurt, rejection, and my own crippling isolation—everything that was unfair in this world was personified in Jo Hawthorne.

"How dare you pray for him!" My voice rose but I was powerless to stop it. "He doesn't need prayers and he especially doesn't need them from you! What he needs is our house, our *lives* from before your father showed up and took it out from beneath us."

Tears welled in the corners of her eyes. "It wasn't him," she stammered. "It's for the war. He was just following orders. He was—"

"He needs his home!" I shouted. The words were just as much for my brother as they were for me. The events of the past few days, weeks, years pulled at my heart, threatening to drown me in grief if I released the buoy of my anger. "A place where he belongs! A place—"

"Olive, what is the meaning of this?"

Suddenly Grandma was there, hand on my arm, her eyes wide. Her nails dug into my skin, causing my vision to clear. The whole congregation encircled us, staring with open mouths, many with hands on their chests. But Grandma . . . Grandma's face was the worst of all. Shock and disappointment.

Disappointment over *me*.

Shame flooded into my body. I'd embarrassed her. I'd embarrassed the person who took me in when no one else wanted me. Who was feeding and sheltering me. Who cared.

I was awful.

I hung my head and allowed her to lead me away from the crowd. I would be better, I vowed. I'd try harder next time. For her. I would. And the vow would have stuck if I hadn't heard Jo as we passed her.

"I'll pray for you, Olive."

It wasn't a conscious decision. At least that's what I told the pastor afterward. But maybe it was. I knew what I was doing when I lunged at her, when I grabbed her hair and my fist connected with her cheek. But still I felt out of control. It was as if my rage were a thing separate from my brain, controlling my muscles without the benefit of reason or temperance. I seemed to be floating outside my body, watching myself attack Jo from above. Because surely that couldn't have been me. I was just as horrified as the crowd, which swelled and pushed, rushing to separate us, only to retreat as Jo finally gathered herself enough to hit back. Her fist landed on my nose with an intensity I saw rather than felt. And it certainly couldn't have been me who lunged at her again, knocking her into the candelabra. Because I know I shrieked just as loudly as everyone else when it toppled backward and smashed into the stained-glass window, shattering Jesus' watching eyes into a million shards that cascaded onto the floor like snow.

CHAPTER SIX

JO

MARCH 1952

By the time she arrived at the adobe building on Cuba Avenue, Jo was panting. She had run without running from the house on Delaware Avenue. Her low heels were not meant for speed; now her feet were aching. And as she stepped into the lobby, sweat dripped down her temple. Her makeup was most likely completely gone. But, she thought, she had made it. She had successfully dodged one ghost. Now it was time to deal with the other and leave this place for good.

The receptionist at the front desk smiled as she approached. She had dark hair pulled back in a tight bun and black cat-eye glasses on her nose. Her makeup was flawless, red lipstick and golden eye shadow, not the tiniest hint of sweat anywhere.

"Can I help you?"

Trying not to feel self-conscious about her own disheveled appearance, Jo pulled a crumpled paper from her bag and held it out. "I'm here to see Richard Hawthorne."

The woman did not take the paper. Instead she raised her eyebrows above the rims of her glasses and stared at Jo with a look of barely contained disapproval. Or was it just Jo's imagination? Because there was no way Miss Betty Thomas—for that was her name; her blue name tag said as much—could possibly know anything about her. Still, her lips oozed unspoken criticism as she pressed them together. "Sign in here, please."

Jo scribbled her name on the sheet, aggravation squeezing her chest, before following Miss Betty Know-It-All Thomas through a set of large double doors. The smell of antiseptic gagged her. They walked quickly, footsteps echoing on the linoleum, and stopped at another set of doors. "Last bed on the right."

Jo hesitated. It was only the impatient, judgmental look from Betty that compelled her forward. Taking a deep breath, she pushed open the door with shaky hands.

It smelled different in here, but not better. Sweaty sheets and sterile gloves and infections. Hopelessness. Death.

The corridor stretched for miles. At least it felt that way. Each drawn curtain and rumpled bed held a story. Held a *life*. All unique and different . . . yet ending in the same place. The harshness of it all. The inevitability.

She paused before the last curtain, unsure she had the strength to take the final step. She'd wrestled for weeks with the decision to come, buying a ticket and hopping on that bus after yet another sleepless night, delirious enough to make a choice she regretted less than fifty miles into the trip. But still, she was here. And he was there. And she couldn't bring herself to take another step.

A small cough to her right caused her to jump. She'd forgotten she was standing outside another patient's "room." Inside the curtain, a woman with pale hair and dull skin lay sleeping in a stiff-looking bed. To her right, on a plastic chair, sat a man in a navy-blue suit. His legs were crossed. A yellow pad of paper lay in his lap. He cleared his throat again, smiling in Jo's direction.

Despite the warmth in his face, goose bumps formed along her spine. She looked away and took a quick step forward, out of his gaze . . . and into her father's.

At least, it used to be her father. Gone were the muscles broadening his shoulders. His thick dark hair—always so perfectly coifed—was now gray and thinning, patches of transparent skin visible beneath. The dimples on his cheeks—the only physical trait he'd passed on to Jo—were gone, sunken into his jawline with the rest of his skin. The sole bits of him still holding any color were his eyes. But even they were tinged with a cloudiness that lessened their green hue.

They widened at the sight of her.

A small, unexpected cry escaped her throat. She'd known he was bad. Dying, even. But to see it firsthand . . .

The doctor at his bedside turned. She hadn't noticed he was there. He had a large stomach and a bulbous nose upon which sat round glasses. His white coat swished as he approached her, wrapping his stethoscope around his neck. "You have a visitor, Richard! How wonderful!"

His name tag read Dr. Pope. It bounced as he shook her hand. "It's so lovely to meet you, Miss . . ."

"Jo. Just Jo."

"Well, 'just Jo,' I'm glad you're here." He laughed at his own joke. "I was just finishing my rounds. Usually Richard here gives me some grief. Grabs my hand and wants me to stay." He winked at his patient, but the patient wasn't looking at him. "But now you're here, maybe I can get out of here on time for once!" Another laugh.

Jo struggled to respond, unable to tear her eyes from her father's.

The doctor scribbled a few notes on his clipboard. The click of his pen was way too loud in the stillness. "Well, I'll give you two some privacy. Richard, enjoy your visit. It was nice to meet you, 'just Jo.'" He gave her a large smile before disappearing behind the curtain.

"Wait!" Jo said, finding her voice again. "Please, Dr. Pope, wait."

He stuck his head back through the white sheet.

She gave her father a backward glance as she lowered her voice. "How . . . how is he?" A stupid question; she knew the answer. Anyone looking at her father would know the answer. Yet she needed to hear it from the doctor's lips.

"I'm sorry, but I'm not at liberty to discuss prognosis."

"But I'm his daughter." She pressed a hand to her lips. It was the truth, but it had been years since she'd thought of herself that way. The words felt deceitful coming out of her mouth.

The doctor's face softened. He motioned for her to step outside. "Let's not sour your visit with specifics. Please, just go and enjoy some time with him."

"But . . . what is it? Do you know?"

"Cancer. Advanced and aggressive. In his throat. Very rare, especially for his age. It's eaten away at his voice box—"

Jo's stomach dropped to her knees. "You mean he can't talk?"

"You didn't know?"

"I knew he was sick. I didn't know he couldn't talk."

Dr. Pope rubbed at the metal on his stethoscope. "Oh, dear. Well, I'm sorry to be the bearer of bad news. He's been like this for several weeks now, over a month, and I assumed . . . well, I guess I shouldn't have assumed, but still I . . ." He blinked. Cleared this throat. "Just go spend time with him. Talk to him. He can still understand, even if he can't answer." He gave her elbow a gentle squeeze before walking away, vanishing through the double doors that led to the hallway, the lobby, the freedom beyond.

Jo stood staring at the empty corridor. It would be so easy to follow. The easiest thing in the world, really. She'd come here for answers, answers she now would never receive. There was no point in staying. She owed that man, the one in the bed just behind her, nothing.

"Miss? Are you okay?"

Jo jumped as a person materialized in front of her.

"Do you . . . do you need something?"

It was the man from the next room over. The one in the suit. His yellow pad was on the chair now, the woman in the bed still asleep. He was good-looking, Jo realized. Dark hair, blue eyes, strong jaw peppered with the slightest hint of stubble. He moved his arm to touch hers.

"Miss?"

Jo pulled back, suddenly embarrassed. "I'm fine."

"He yours?" The man nodded toward her father's bed.

"No."

He waved a hand toward the bed behind them. "She's not mine either. She—"

"Excuse me." Jo brushed past him, leaving his mouth open in midsentence. She barely even registered her own rudeness. There was no space for anyone else. Not here. Not now. She stepped around the side of her father's curtain, pulling it closed for emphasis.

Now it was just him and her. Alone. For the first time in seven years.

She looked down at her fingers, picking at a hangnail until it bled, trying not to see the pleading in her father's eyes. In the heavy silence, the noises of the hospital were magnified. Murmurs. Rustling sheets. Coughs. Private grief in a public space. But that stare—somehow that stare was the loudest of all.

"I came," she said finally. There was nothing else to say. *Hello* wasn't right. It wasn't good to see him. He didn't look well. None of the niceties seemed appropriate. So instead, she stated the obvious.

The shell of her father blinked.

"I got a letter from Mr. Purcell. Telling me you were here. And then another one. And another one. I didn't . . . I wasn't going to come. But I did."

He extended one clawlike hand in her direction. She took a step back.

"Funny how after all these years of silence, it was your lawyer who reached out first. Not you. Your lawyer."

Her father's arm dropped. He clutched it to his chest, hollow eyes watering.

"You know, if he could find me, you could have too. If you had wanted. If you had tried." She gave a bitter laugh, tasting the heavy antiseptic smell in the back of her throat. "Not that I should have expected you to ever do that. You made it pretty clear what you thought of me, what you wanted of me. To never come back, right? Wasn't that what you said? And yet here I am. Disappointing you. Again."

His mouth opened. He let out a deep, croaking rasp.

She kicked at a black scuff mark on the sickly green tile. For once, she was thankful for his silence. It was an evil thought, she knew. But his muteness gave her speech all the more power. "I've been overseas. South America first, building houses and passing out Bibles in Ecuador. Did that for a few months and then came home." She laughed again, though nothing was funny. "Not that I had a home anymore, really. So I jumped at the next opportunity. A hospital in Costa Rica needed volunteers. So I went."

She didn't know why she was telling him all of this. He didn't care. And yet she continued. "After that it was Mexico for a while. Small villages outside Guadalajara, Mexico City."

The years rolled through her mind like a silent movie. The dirty people. The unsanitary houses. The despair covering each village like a blanket. How readily nearly all of them had accepted Jesus, how eager and desperate they were for any kind of hope. Any kind of faith. The sheer brokenness of the world had shocked her, shattering what was left of her innocence.

"And then, once the dust had settled from the war, I went to Japan."

She glanced at her father, wondering if he recognized the heaviness of that word. But though his fingers twitched at his sides, his face was vacant. Only his eyes betrayed any hint of remorse.

Or was that just what she wanted to see?

"It wasn't easy to be there. I walked around a small town outside Tokyo, looking at faces, trying to reconcile these people with the enemies we'd been told about. Wondering how many of them had killed our boys or had their own killed in return. Wondering how we could be so different and yet so very much the same."

She could feel her father's eyes boring into her. She refused to meet them.

"I saw it, you know. Hiroshima. I'd seen pictures, of course. After it happened. I knew. But I didn't really *know* until I saw it. Until I stood there. All these years later, and it still smelled like burned flesh. I swear. It used to smell like cherry blossoms, they said. But maybe it never will again. And the people. *The people.*" She closed her eyes as the memories swam before her. The blackened landscape. The tired, empty masses. "And you did it."

On his bed, her father made a move as if to get up and reach for her.

She shrank back further against the curtain. "I walked around that big old city knowing you—my father—had a hand in this. Halfway across the world, you helped make this happen. And I didn't know what I was supposed to feel. Proud? The cutting edge of technology. The bomb that ended the war. Saved thousands of American lives. All those slogans they threw at us after it happened. Or was I supposed to be disgusted? Seeing the truth of it all. The devastation, the ruin—not like Germany. Not like a bomb that knocks down walls that they can pick up and rebuild again. No, this turned the walls—and the people—to dust. You can't rebuild dust."

Jo glanced at her father just long enough to see a lone tear roll down his cheek.

"I spent two whole days wandering that city, trying to figure out how I should feel. I wondered if maybe that was why you did it—if what you did to me, what you said, was because of Hiroshima, because of what you knew was going to happen. Or perhaps because you didn't know."

There was a slight gurgle, the strain of a plea against the cancer. He was trying to speak. To defend himself. But Jo would not give him the chance.

"But now I know that seeing Hiroshima didn't change a thing. Between us, at least. Because when it comes down to it, selfish or not, the way I feel about you has nothing to do with Hiroshima. Nothing to do with that bomb. I don't hate you for what you were a part of, as wretched and morally complicated as it was." For the first time, Jo met that tearful gaze and held it. "I hate you for what you chose *not* to be a part of."

The words came without preface, without planning, though now it occurred to her they were the real reason she'd come. It had never really been about answers; it had been about proving to him that he hadn't destroyed her, no matter how hard he'd tried. About giving him back the poison he'd injected into her all those years ago.

Because maybe then she would finally be free.

The man in the bed released a pitiful, silent whimper. His tongue rolled about as if choking on the words he could no longer speak, eyes disappearing behind a wall of tears.

Jo bit the inside of her cheek until she tasted blood. "It doesn't matter that you can't talk. Because I wouldn't listen anyway. I just needed you to hear me. For the first time. And the last." Chin high, she brushed past his bed and headed for the exit. She stopped short, however, when an icy hand made contact with her fingers.

Tangles of blue veins popped through the papery surface of her father's skin. His grip was weak, the muscles barely strong enough to maintain contact, and yet the shock of his touch was enough to moor Jo to the bed as if by some invisible chain.

His chest heaved. Sweat beaded across his forehead. His entire face twisted in agony as his lips twitched with a single, soundless word. *"Jo."*

Inaudible, and yet she heard it all the same.

He exhaled, breathing her name again, all of his excuses and apologies rolled into a single whisper. His fingers trembled against her own. In that moment, they were father and daughter once more. After all this time. After all this *hurt*.

She would not cry; she hadn't cried since that day and she would not start now—not for him. Instead, summoning all her strength, she snatched back her hand. Her skin felt cold and tingly where he had touched her. Refusing to look at him, she rushed from the room. It did not escape her mind that she had forgotten the only word she'd meant to say, the one word her father had denied her all those years ago: *"Goodbye."*

Ignoring Miss Betty Thomas, she burst from the hospital and out into dry, desert air. The stench of dirt and manure was an oddly welcome reprieve from the sterile smell just inside. She collapsed on a nearby bench, elbows on her knees, and tried to catch her breath. In front of her, cars whizzed by; pedestrians strolled; a gentle breeze whispered through the cottonwoods. The world went on. And yet she remained frozen, paralyzed by the finality of the moment, waiting for the relief to wash over her now that it was done, over, finished.

But it never came.

For years, those words had bubbled inside her. It felt like she'd waited a lifetime for a chance to say them, to pay her father back. And now she had. But rather than liberated, she felt empty.

She'd come here to fix herself. Somehow, instead, she'd only become more broken.

"Are you okay?"

Jo started. How long had she been sitting here? The sun was waning in the western sky. And there was a man in front of her, handsome face bathed in gentle evening light.

"Are you okay?" he repeated.

It was the man from the room next door. Again. Jo stood quickly and put her hands on her hips. "Are you following me?"

"No, I . . . Well, yes. Kind of." His eyes flickered to the ground. "I saw you rush out of there. And you looked like you were upset. So I just wanted to . . ."

"What do you care?" Anger filled that empty place inside, its presence comforting and familiar. Anger was strong. Anger was easier.

The man held up two hands. "I'm sorry. I didn't mean to intrude."

"Well, you did."

"Okay. Sorry. I'll go." He took two steps backward, hands still held in the air.

Feeling suddenly weak, Jo sank onto the bench, rubbing her fingers across her forehead. Her headache was back.

"Was he there?"

The man remained. Farther away now but still within earshot. Hands in his pockets, he rolled himself up on the balls of his feet, though he was careful not to move any closer.

"Your father, I mean. Trinity. Was he there?"

Inside her bag, Jo's hand closed around the aspirin bottle and paused.

"I didn't mean to overhear. It's just kind of hard not to." He took a step forward as if testing the waters. "The woman I was with—the one in the bed—she's got something similar. Can't talk. Can barely eat. She lived in Tularosa during the test, and now she's got this cancer." He shook his head. "So that's why I was wondering."

Jo grabbed two aspirin and then, on second thought, pulled out a third. She swallowed them dry.

"I'm Charlie," he said, extending his hand. "Charlie Wilson."

She did not take it. "Jo Hawthorne."

He nodded once as he stuffed his hand back into his pocket. In front of them, a truck rumbled down Tenth, carrying their gaze with it, westward toward the setting sun. They watched in silence as the sky turned from pink to orange to red.

"Were you there too?" he said finally.

She did not answer. Because even though Jo's eyes remained on the sky, on the inside, she was thousands of miles—and years—away. Her mind floated over the ocean, to Hiroshima. To her father, the last time she'd seen him—not that thing in there, that shell of a man, but her real father. The one she had loved. The one she had thought loved her.

To Olive. The girl who'd been her friend. No, more than a friend. Her family.

And to God. The One she'd known or thought she'd known. To the last time she'd felt His presence . . . before the flash changed everything.

Changed *her*.

All around them, streetlights began to flicker on, pressing the darkness closer to her. Jo's headache lingered and her eyes burned, exhaustion radiating from her core. She glanced at her watch. Her bus. She'd missed her bus. She'd have to spend the night here, something she'd sworn she wouldn't do and yet somehow knew would happen. Hours in Alamogordo passed in a state of suspended disbelief, lingering and flowing at will, ignoring the laws of physics, the outside world, and self-determined plans. She didn't even have the energy to be irritated.

"Buy me a drink."

"What?" Charlie looked up, his lips parted slightly.

She pinched the bridge of her nose wearily. "If you want to hear my story, you have to buy me a drink first."

"Sure! There's a bar right down the road. The beer's watered down, but—"

"Then I'll order something else." And she took off down the sidewalk, not caring if Charlie followed but knowing without a doubt he would.

CHAPTER SEVEN

OLIVE

Time stopped. Or at least the hitting did. Jo slithered out from underneath me as my muscles turned to gelatin. Rather than blowing in from the shattered window, air rushed out from the sanctuary, taking with it all noise except for the tinkle of broken glass. Beneath me, millions of fragments were now reduced to glittering white powder.

Where the window once was, there was now nothing but the blackness of night. Slivers of glass hung around the edges, giving it the appearance of a great gaping mouth surrounded by sharp teeth, menacing and sinister.

Or maybe that was just how it felt to me. I had destroyed an image of Jesus, after all.

"Olive."

My grandmother's voice, quiet. So quiet it was the loudest thing in the room. Still lying on my back in a puddle of broken glass, I shifted my head to look at her. She stood at the edge of the crowd. Chest drawn in, shoulders hunched, chin dipped, she looked smaller somehow. For a moment, I felt ashamed . . . but then I saw her eyes. For in her eyes, there was no sadness. No grief or mortification. Just wrath.

"Olive," she said again.

That was all it took. I scrambled to my feet, ignoring the sting as shards of glass penetrated my skin. As I brushed debris from my skirt, I tried to tell myself it wasn't pieces of Jesus Himself hanging from the dark-blue folds.

"Stand back, ladies and gentlemen. Stand back." Pastor Hamilton pushed forward, throwing out his hands to wrangle the crowd. "We don't want anyone to get injured. If you'll all just move toward the exit, we'll get this mess cleaned up in no time. Good as new, I promise." He swung his arms as if leading a herd of cattle, and surprisingly, the crowd moved in body, if not in spirit. Their collective eyes remained glued to my flesh, though I refused to meet them. It was only by the shuffle of feet and the dissipation of murmurs that I knew most of them had retreated to the parking lot to gossip.

The room felt colder without them, bigger and even more noiseless. I wished them back almost immediately, especially when Pastor Hamilton returned and stood in front of me, not speaking. Beside me, Jo sniffled quietly, hair hanging in curtains around her face.

"Never," the pastor said after what felt like an eternity, "in my ten years of ministry have I witnessed such behavior from young women."

"Pastor Hamilton, I apologize. I don't know what's come over Evelyn. It must be that boy she's always hanging around with. That Alexander boy. He's . . ."

My hand froze above a sliver of glass I'd been attempting to free from my shirt. She'd called me Evelyn. Again.

"He's no good!" she went on. "No good at all. Pulling her away from the church and filling her head with nonsense. And look where it's gotten her!" Her eyes, though still angry, had a misty quality to them, like fire you can't see for the smoke. "I don't even know what to say, Pastor. I'm so ashamed. Evelyn has just . . ."

Her voice trailed off as the pastor laid a hand on her arm. "Sweet Edna. Please. You don't need to apologize."

Grandma's mouth twitched like she wanted to continue but couldn't form the words. The fog began to drift from her eyes. I could practically see Evelyn melt before her, transforming back into me. Her granddaughter. Standing in a pile of broken glass. In her church.

"First things first," Pastor Hamilton was saying. "Are you alright?"

I pulled several small pieces of glass from my palms before placing a finger gingerly upon my nose. It was tender and hot to the touch. She'd gotten one punch in, and she'd made it count, I'd give her that. Not broken but it would most definitely bruise. "I'm fine."

"And you?"

"Yes, I'm alright." Jo wiped her face with the back of her hand. Her cheek was swollen and starting to purple, a blemish made all the more dramatic by her pale skin. There were several small cuts sprouting across her forehead.

Pastor Hamilton exhaled through his nose. "Do either of you care to tell me what this whole incident was all about?"

I kept my eyes on the ground, willing Jo to keep her mouth shut. I'd attacked her because she'd said she'd pray for me. Yes, that was how it started. But it went much deeper than that. Deeper than I could understand and definitely deeper than I could ever explain, especially to a pastor.

The glass beneath my feet crunched as I shifted my weight. Behind me, Jo sniffled again but said nothing.

Pastor Hamilton sighed. "That window was from Spain, you know. It was originally housed in a church built by missionaries just over the Texas border. The church was destroyed during the Texas Revolution, but the window was salvaged and brought here in Alamogordo's infancy, when this church was first founded. It was to be a testament of the past and the future, a reminder of the saving power of Christ to all peoples and all nations."

He stood staring at the empty hole as if he could still see the glass. "Having it broken now, in the midst of another war . . ." He rubbed the crease between his eyebrows with one finger. "I'm not sure what, but I know it means something. God is speaking. Lord, give us ears to hear."

A lone tear dropped from Grandma's eye onto her cheek. Jo, meanwhile, let out a full-blown sob.

I clenched my jaw, ignoring the tenderness in my face. All my life I'd believed this religion stuff was naiveté. One day inside a church had taught me it was so much more: it was willful, blind stupidity.

God did not break this window. I did. And I didn't do it because it was part of some divine plan. I did it because I was angry.

Pastor Hamilton turned. "We will replace it. Somehow we will replace it. And the two of you will lead the charge."

Grandma squeezed my arm just hard enough that I knew it to be an act of emphasis, not solidarity. "I agree, Pastor. Absolutely."

"Edna and I will discuss details. And, Jo, you can rest assured I will be calling your father and informing him of the matter as well. But for now . . ." He pointed toward the pulpit. "The two of you will get gloves and brooms from the back closet and clean this up. Tonight."

I did as I was told. I did not speak or even look at Jo during our work, but the sound of her crying mixing with the scrape of bristles on carpet grated in my ears until well after midnight.

———— ◆❖◆ ————

If I thought cleaning up glass shards with Jo was annoying, it was nothing compared to what Pastor Hamilton had planned for my Saturday morning. Autumn had arrived suddenly in southern New Mexico, a biting wind sweeping down the slopes of the Sacramentos and into the valley below, bringing with it the smell of dried leaves and pine needles. It was obvious the plastic covering he'd hastily erected over the broken window wouldn't be enough to keep out the chill. We'd need a sturdier substitute until enough funds could be raised to replace the window entirely.

And guess whose job it was to put up said substitute?

I knew I deserved to be out on a crisp morning doing manual labor. I had broken the window after all, and I was willing to put a little elbow grease into the solution, if only to ease my guilt about Grandma's shame. She had grounded me for an undetermined length of time ("Until I say so!" she had sputtered when I'd foolishly asked for an end date), but she hadn't looked me in the eye since it happened. The tension and loneliness that had filled the house on Delaware Street over the past few days was more than enough to subdue me into repentance.

Yes, I could have managed . . . if only Jo hadn't been assigned as my coworker.

"That's what you're wearing?"

Jo Hawthorne stood before me in a calf-length pink skirt, brown saddle shoes on her feet. Her top half was covered in a navy-blue cardigan with an embroidered pink *J* on her chest. The cuts on her forehead had faded, but the purple bruise on her cheek was still prominent, even despite Jo's attempt at cosmetic concealment.

"That's what *you're* wearing?" For the first time since I'd known her, scorn crept into her tone. Maybe she wasn't so perfect after all.

I held out my arms, glancing down at my dungarees, boots, and one of my father's old flannels.

Jo wrinkled her nose. "Just because I have to do boys' work doesn't mean I have to dress like one. *You* can wear whatever you'd like. I'm wearing this."

I dropped a toolbox on the ground with a thud. "Suit yourself."

Pastor Hamilton had left us the wood (for which, he emphasized, he'd need to be reimbursed), a ladder, and a collection of tools that looked as if they hadn't been used this side of the twentieth century before retreating inside, where I was sure his office was toasty and probably had at least one comfy couch just perfect for napping.

I adjusted the ladder against the building and climbed the first few steps to check the balance. My head swam as I looked toward the top of the frame. The hole seemed to have grown since I saw it last, stretching above my head for miles. I'd spent hours in the burrow hundreds of feet above the desert floor, but the prospect of climbing to the top of this ladder made my stomach flop. Living in the city was already making me soft. Gripping the ladder with sweaty hands, I closed my eyes momentarily. "Hand me the tape measure."

"The what?"

"The tape measure."

Jo kicked at the toolbox lightly, keeping her arms crossed over her chest. "What's a tape measure?"

I dropped my head to my chest and clenched my teeth. This was going to be a long day.

Jo burst out laughing. "I'm kidding! Do you honestly think I don't know what a tape measure is? I'm not *that* helpless."

Although I was tempted to admit I *did* think so little of her, doing so would acknowledge that her stupid little joke had fooled me. So instead I let out a short burst of air through my nostrils—a painful act of annoyance, due to the swelling from Jo's one good punch—and held out my hand, saying nothing.

Disappointed or irritated or perhaps both, she sighed and handed me the tape measure. She made no more jokes. In fact, she didn't try to talk at all as we set to work, a blissful concession on an otherwise-arduous and lousy morning.

I yanked off my flannel and tossed it to the ground as the sun rose higher. The air was still chilly, but I'd worked up a sweat cutting the wood with a saw that was more rust than steel.

Beside me, Jo grunted, working on her own piece with even less luck than me. Her normally perfect hair fell in sweaty strands across her face, and I noticed with no small amount of satisfaction a tiny rip in the bottom of her cardigan.

Wiping my brow with the back of my hand, I stretched and pulled a small canteen from my pocket. My throat was raw from the desert air, the water unpleasant before it was refreshing. I downed half of it in one swig. Before I had to wrestle with the question of whether or not to share, Jo removed a container from her handbag, taking graceful sips as she retreated to a spot in the shade under the window. Sliding to the ground, she took something from a side pocket.

"Do you want some?" She held out a small brick of chocolate in her palm.

I did. I wanted that beautiful, sweet square more than anything in the world. Not only because I'd already burned through my rushed breakfast of stale bread and Spam, but because it had been months since I'd tasted chocolate. It was both a luxury we couldn't afford and a rarity reserved for our troops overseas.

And yet here sat Jo Hawthorne, Hershey bar in hand, offering me a piece without even a trace of irony or self-conscious pride.

There was nothing in the world that would make me accept a piece of that chocolate.

Instead I swallowed my hunger, shoved the canteen back in my pocket, and picked up my saw. My back hurt and my fingers were stiff, but the quicker I got this done, the quicker I could leave.

We resumed our work in silence. Even when the weight of the board required teamwork to lift and secure, we communicated only with the most basic of words: "Higher." "Up." "Lift." Though years of ranch work had leaned and strengthened my muscles, by the time we were finished, I still found my arms tender. I was impressed Jo had been able to keep up, being as scrawny as she was. Not that I'd ever tell her.

The sun beat down on us as we packed our supplies away. Alamogordo was awake now. The aroma of bread from Dale's Piggly Wiggly mixed with the tang of freshly cut lumber from the nearby sawmill. Cars hummed through the downtown area, mingling with the chatter of crowds out for a lazy shopping trip or early lunch at Rolland's.

When the last of the scrap wood had been gathered and placed in the storage shed behind the sanctuary, I made no pretense of goodbyes. I simply picked up my flannel and moved toward the road, head down and hands tucked in my pockets.

"Olive!"

I wanted to keep walking. But something in her tone made me stop. It wasn't the usual obnoxious friendliness. This was firm. Purposeful.

I turned around. Jo still stood by the side of the building. Her expression was hidden, darkened by shadow, but her head jerked repeatedly to the side.

I shielded my eyes and glanced to where she was gesturing. My grandma was walking up the church sidewalk, brown handbag hanging from her forearm. Her flowered green dress was freshly pressed and stiff against her body.

"Grandma!" I called, jogging toward her. "Grandma, you didn't need to pick me up. I was getting ready to walk home. We're all done."

She kept walking, eyes only on the door ahead.

"Grandma." I touched her gently as I finally reached her side. She jumped, startled. "Evelyn! What are you doing here?"

"Grandma, I . . ." Words dried out on my tongue as her eyes met mine. They were cloudy again. Unfocused. Far away.

"I've been praying you'd join me for church." She squeezed my hand. "That man of yours filling your head with nonsense. I kept praying God would open your heart again, bring you home." Tears welled up in her milky eyes. "And here you are."

I opened my mouth to speak but closed it as she embraced me. Not only because I didn't know what to say but because the lump in my throat rendered all my words mute.

"Come on," she said, intertwining my arm with hers. "We don't want to be late."

I let myself be led into the empty sanctuary, ignoring what I was sure was a look of curiosity from a still-staring Jo Hawthorne. I was embarrassed and confused, exhausted and conflicted. But most of all, I was scared. Scared because my grandmother was standing right next to me . . . and yet I didn't know where she was.

She pulled me into a pew, oblivious to the quiet, to the dark, to the rows of empty seats we passed along the way. Placing her handbag next to her and smoothing her dress, she smiled at me before finally looking at the deserted room around us.

I held my breath, waiting for truth to douse her like cold water.

But she simply scrunched up her face and pressed her lips together. "Now where is the pastor? He usually walks around before service doing the meet and greet. I'm very surprised he wasn't at the door when we came in. That's not like him at all."

My stomach hardened, my heart in my throat. She wasn't snapping out of it. It wasn't just that I was Evelyn. Even though we were sitting side by side, my grandmother and I were in different times, different *realities*.

"Where *is* he?" Her voice betrayed the first sign of doubt as her head swung back and forth, looking but not seeing.

"Grandma." Hot tears burned my eyes but I refused to let them fall. I squeezed her hand, choking on my uselessness.

"Mrs. Burke?"

Grandma's head jerked at the sound of her name.

Jo stood at the end of the pew, hands clasped, a tight smile on her face. "Hi, Mrs. Burke. I'm Jo Hawthorne. Evelyn's friend. I don't believe we've met."

Grandma rose and cupped her cheek. "Oh, honey! It's so lovely to meet you. Any friend of Evelyn's is a friend of mine, especially if it's a godly one."

Jo's eyes flickered to mine for a moment before returning to Grandma. "I'm so glad I could finally convince her to come back to church. I know how much it means to you."

"God bless you, child. God bless you." Her voice was thick as she hugged Jo. I wondered if she was crying.

Over Grandma's shoulder, Jo nodded at me slightly. She patted Grandma's back. "Thank you, Mrs. Burke. You're so sweet to say." She pulled away gently, still keeping hold of her hand. "But I wanted to tell you that Pastor Hamilton is sick today. Nothing serious," she added quickly, clamping down on my grandma's response. "Just a little cold. But he needs his rest and he doesn't want to spread it around."

"Oh, that's too bad. Poor thing."

"Yes. But he's assured me he'll be as good as new tomorrow, and we'll have the service then. Does that sound okay?"

A look of uncertainty crossed Grandma's face. She bobbed her head without conviction and grasped at my wrist, missing several times before her palm connected with my skin. "But you'll still come tomorrow, won't you, Evelyn? Please say you'll still come tomorrow?"

I gave her a shaky nod, unable to speak.

"Of course she'll come, Mrs. Burke," Jo said. "Of course she will. She wouldn't miss it. I'll make sure of it." She draped her arm around my grandmother's shoulders. "In the meantime, let's get you home."

She led Grandma from the sanctuary, their footsteps muffled on the scuffed red carpet; I followed several paces behind, too overcome with the task of stifling my sobs. I held them in the entire walk home, which was slow and fraught with several turnaround attempts by my grandma that Jo masterfully averted. I even held them in as Jo convinced Grandma to take a nap, tucking her into bed like a child as I sat on a couch in the living room, hands shaking. But when Jo finally left, her simple goodbye inadequate and yet somehow still too long-winded, the screen door screaming as it clicked shut behind her . . . it was only then that I held them in no longer.

Burying my face in my hands, I curled up on the couch and wept.

CHAPTER EIGHT

JO

The bar smelled of menthol cigarettes and sweat. It didn't even have a name. The sign out front just said *Bar* in flashing neon red, a metal Budweiser sign in the window for emphasis.

The tables were sticky and empty, save for two other couples and an old man with a stubby cigar hanging from his scowl. From the jukebox, a woman crooned a country song Jo didn't recognize as the bartender glared at them, two strangers in nice clothes, most assuredly out-of-towners from the look of it, and definitely some with no business at a no-name bar on this side of town. But still, he accepted their money and poured the tequila—cheap and marred a funny shade of yellow—which burned in the most satisfying way.

Jo didn't normally drink. She'd never had the desire or the stomach. But after two drinks, the alcohol spread from her core to her limbs, tingling her toes. It was a new and different kind of numbness, one that was warm and blissful rather than cold and callous.

She understood now why some people drank the way they did, even if the effect was only temporary.

Charlie shrugged out of his coat and loosened his tie. "I can't remember the last time I had tequila. College, maybe?"

"Where did you go to school?" She didn't care. Not really. But the tequila made her think she could if she tried.

"UCLA."

"California man. I should have known."

"Is that where you're from?"

Jo shrugged. "Mostly. Originally. Before the Army stepped in."

"You're lucky then. Spent my whole life there. Same school. Same house. Same neighborhood. Same people. Me, my brother, baseball. Year after year after year. Even the weather was always the same."

"And that's a bad thing?"

"I guess not. But it *is* pretty boring."

"What I wouldn't have given for boring."

He pulled a pack of Camels from his pocket, offering her one. When she refused with a shake of her head, he lit one for himself and tucked the package back in his pocket. "So you were an Army kid, huh? That must have been quite an experience."

Jo crossed her arms over her chest.

He grimaced, casting his eyes downward. "I'm sorry. That was stupid of me. Obviously it wasn't good. I mean, I heard what you said to him back there. Not that I meant to," he added quickly. "I wasn't intentionally eavesdropping. But I heard, and then you ran out and then—" Smoke streamed from his nostrils as he let out a long breath. "I'm sorry. It's just that you're very pretty and I get nervous around pretty girls. I don't know what to say."

Most girls would have been flattered. A handsome man—because he *was* handsome, no matter how much she tried to ignore it—calling her pretty. But to Jo, the word merely rolled off her skin, like a whisper in an overcrowded room. She'd been called pretty a lot. Not a brag, just a fact. It was the hair, long and almost silver. Unusual. Unique. Boys were drawn to that kind of girl, like bugs to a porch light.

Not that she ever let them get close. She'd chatted with a few, kissed still fewer. At one time, it had been her commitment to God keeping them away. Now it was something else.

"It's fine." She gestured to the bar for another round. "No, it wasn't all fun and games. So let's not talk about me. Let's talk about you." A waitress approached, tray laden with glasses. Jo knew this wasn't the answer; it was just a brief and irresponsible Band-Aid for what was really bothering her. But she took the drink from the waitress anyway and downed it in one gulp.

This one . . . this one wasn't nearly as pleasant. She covered her mouth with the back of her hand, stifling a gag.

Charlie stared at her. "You okay?"

She nodded, trying to swallow a lingering burn in the back of her throat.

"Okay. Well, um, I'm a scientist from UCLA. Part of a yearly study about the effects of radiation from the Trinity test."

"A scientist, huh?" she managed to croak.

He gave a shy smile. "Yeah, but not a very good one. I just conduct interviews with the patients. Where they lived, where they were at the time of the blast, that kind of thing. That's why I was asking about your father. I'm trying to see if there's a connection between their illness and the test."

The tequila made Jo's head feel fuzzy. Still, despite the haze, her father's face loomed large, clear and decrepit. "How do you mean?"

He took a long drag on his cigarette, rolling the lighter in his hand. "This area has seen a dramatic rise in cancer over the past few years. In fact, it has one of the highest concentrations of multiple cancers—cancers afflicting more than one area of the body at a time—per capita in the nation. That doesn't just happen for no reason."

"And you think there's a connection between the cancers and Trinity?"

"I know there is."

Jo scratched at her arms. They suddenly felt itchy. But it wasn't just her arms. Her entire body tingled, like there was something in the air. Something heavy. Something dirty. The tequila sloshed in her stomach, although she was pretty sure her discomfort wasn't completely alcohol-induced.

Charlie clicked his tongue behind his teeth, studying her. "You really don't know anything about this? Even though they're still allowing us to do our tests, officially the government says there's no danger. But it's pretty common knowledge that *something* is going on around here, something that wasn't happening before Trinity. Talk to any local and you'll get an earful, believe me."

"I don't talk to many locals," Jo muttered under her breath. "And anyways, I was there, and I'm not sick. So how do you explain that?"

He didn't seem to notice her annoyance, instead tipping his cigarette into the ashtray and shrugging. "The effects seem to come from long-term exposure, not so much the initial blast. People who have lived here since then, breathing the air, using the land, drinking the water. That kind of thing. How long after the blast did you stick around?"

Rumbling buses. A sinking stomach. Feet on vibrating steps, hot seat sticking to her sweaty skin. Confusion. Hurt. Betrayal.

Jo swallowed the images down with an acidic burp. "I left that same day."

"Why?"

"Because it was time to go."

"But your father stayed."

"Obviously."

He took another drag on his cigarette. "Do you mind telling me what he did? On the project, I mean."

She did mind. She had come to this bar to forget, not to remember. And certainly not to talk about the bomb. She leaned back in her chair, stretching, eyes on the door. "I don't really know. Something about construction." She stood and gathered her things. "He wasn't actually stationed on-site. He lived on a ranch. Anyway, thank you for the drinks, Charlie. Really. But I've got—"

"The Alexander ranch?"

The words froze her blood. She gnarled her fingers around the back of the chair. "What?"

"Was he on the Alexander ranch?"

"How do you know that name?"

"It's my job to know all the homesteads in the area. For research purposes," he added, snuffing out his cigarette and immediately lighting another. "The Alexander ranch was split in three parts during the project, part of the land requisitioned for the test, part—the part with the house—leased by the Army to house construction crew, and the smallest part left over for the family to use. Naturally, I assumed . . ."

So matter-of-fact. Data memorized from a paper.

"So am I right? Was he there? On the ranch?"

Jo suddenly felt dizzy. The music from the jukebox became as shrill and piercing as broken glass.

Charlie's voice lowered, hoarse and barely audible. And yet it was as if he were screaming. "Did you ever visit him there? Did you know the Alexanders?"

She was spinning now. A flash of adobe walls, crackling piñon, and roasted green chile crowded out the bar around her.

Charlie was still talking, oblivious. "Do you still talk to them? Were you with them—at the ranch, I mean, when it happened? The test?"

She tried to drown these memories inside her anger, but they'd left a residue, a grit on the inside of her soul she'd been unable to shake since she'd arrived. Because it wasn't just Alamogordo. It wasn't even just her father. The heartache, the bitterness . . . Olive Alexander was a part of it too. The knife in her heart had been put there by her father, but it was Olive who had twisted it.

Suddenly the tequila didn't feel so warm or cozy. It felt like the bad idea it had been all along.

"I need to go to the restroom."

Charlie's face fell for a moment before brightening again. "Right. Okay. It's back there, I think."

Jo pushed herself from the table on wobbly legs. She barely made it to the stall before retching. Tequila simmered at the back of her throat but remained there. A cold sweat broke out on her forehead as she retched again. This time it came up.

She remained over the toilet for several minutes, waiting for the trembles to cease before stumbling to the sink. In the foggy mirror, her skin looked puffy. Remnants of smudged mascara darkened the area under her eyes. Trying to ignore the stench of sulfur, she splashed lukewarm water from the rusted tap onto her face. Patting it with the bottom of her shirt, she noticed a flash of motion in the corner. She spun around.

No one.

Of course there was no one. She was alone in the bathroom. And yet when she turned back to the mirror, there it was again. In the corner, just behind her. Movement. She spun around once more and noticed, for the first time, a small window. And just on the other side of the opaque glass, a face.

Chills raced down her body, dousing whatever tequila might have remained in her bloodstream. Not just any face. *Her.*

She rushed to the window and pushed against the glass, trying to reach the girl on the other side. After several frustrated groans, the pane broke free of its moldy glue, sending flecks of white paint onto the grimy tile beneath her feet.

The girl was gone.

Jo thrust her face through the opening and into the warm night air. It was an alleyway. Dark, aside from a lone streetlight at the far end, and reeking of garbage and cat urine. Empty.

Jo blinked. No. She was sure of it. There had been someone in the window. Not Olive—it couldn't have been Olive; she didn't want it to be Olive—but someone had been there. Tequila or not, she knew what she saw. She forced herself away from the wall and through the sticky bathroom door.

"Jo! Hey! Are you okay?"

Ignoring Charlie, the bartender, and the other patrons, she raced through the dimly lit bar and burst through the front door, nearly knocking over a gruff-looking man in a cowboy hat.

"Watch it, you!"

"Sorry," she gasped. "I'm so sorry. I'm—"

"Good grief, lady," he said, backing away, holding a grimy hand to his nose. "You drink all of Bill's tequila?" He laughed, revealing a row of gray teeth. "You best be getting on home. Ain't no good come from tequila."

Jo swallowed another wave of nausea. "Did you see a girl?"

"What?"

"A girl. Just now." She closed her eyes, trying to stem the headache oozing back into her temples. "Maybe coming from the alleyway? Dark hair?"

"No, I didn't see no girl. Just you." He raised his eyebrows, amusement passing from his face. "You sure you're alright?"

Jo staggered toward the alley, hanging on to the brick wall as she peered around the corner. The light from the open bathroom window cast a yellow square onto the dark pavement. The smell of urine was even stronger out here. But still nothing. No one.

"Jo. Jo, are you okay?"

Charlie's hand on her back caused her to tense. She turned to see him, eyebrows furrowed, lips creased into a frown.

"She yours?" The man in the cowboy hat gestured at Jo as if she couldn't hear him.

"Yes," Charlie said. "I mean, no. We're not together. But we were here together. Having a drink."

"I don't need your life story. I just need to know if I can wash my hands of this."

"I've got her."

"Good." The cowboy spun on his heel and walked away, boots scraping against the dusty concrete.

Charlie waited until his echo had faded before he spoke again. "Jo, are you okay? What's wrong? Did I do something?"

"Please take me to a hotel."

"Which hotel?"

"Any hotel. I don't care. I just need a room for the night. I need to lay down. I'm . . ." *Seeing things,* she wanted to say. "Not feeling like myself."

"Okay. Sure. Yeah. Let me just pay our tab. Do you need anything? Water?"

Jo shook her head slightly, the pain in her temples shifting like sand beneath her skin.

"I'll be right back. Just wait here."

As he disappeared inside the bar, Jo slid down the wall, barely even registering the rough brick that tore at her back. She pressed her palms against her eyes, willing the pounding to cease. She needed to sleep. Or vomit. Or both. That's all. That and the first bus out of town tomorrow morning. She'd check the schedule in her purse. If she was lucky, she wouldn't even be around to see the sun rise again.

She let herself be pulled to her feet. Charlie gripped her arm as he led her down Tenth Street, away from the bar, toward the blinking red light of the Atomic Inn. He was talking. She pretended to listen. She thanked him for his chivalry and apologized for her mess with a goodbye handshake outside the door to her room. Then she climbed into bed fully clothed and pretended to sleep.

Most of all, though, she pretended not to feel the eyes of the dark-haired girl watching her from her dreams.

CHAPTER NINE

OLIVE

NOVEMBER 1944

Thanksgiving 1944 was a quiet affair. Murmurs of a secret project in the desert north of town had begun to trickle southward, of people like the MacDonalds, who had been kicked off their land completely. We were the lucky ones in that respect; the Alexanders at least still had our house. Nevertheless, whispers of a secret base and a secret mission had reached Alamogordo. No one knew anything concrete, just that *something* was happening on the Jornada. Something big enough to get tongues wagging and gossip swirling.

Something big enough to make me feel sick. What exactly was happening at my home?

Avery was still abroad, and while we were hearing of victories along both fronts, including the sinking of Japanese ships off the

Philippines as well as the withdrawal of German troops from Greece, from my brother we heard only silence. It was so much easier to pretend not to care about Avery—which was how I'd lived the last few years anyway—when I didn't have to wonder if he was still alive.

But Avery's absence was just one of a thousand clouds hanging over the little house on Delaware Avenue. Thanksgiving also marked the first time I'd seen my mother since I left the ranch over a month earlier.

Gas rationing rendered her incapable of making the trip sooner, as well as the sheer amount of work needing to be done at the homestead with very few hands to do it. At least that's what she told me when she swept from the vehicle and wrapped me in a hug before Uncle Hershel had even put the truck in park.

I stood on the sidewalk stunned, reminding myself this woman was my mother, surprised at how foreign she felt in my arms. She was thinner. The fabric of her gray dress—my favorite, the one with the black buttons and satin ribbon around the waist—was loose around her shoulders now. Her cheeks were drawn, dark circles rimming her eyes. But her smile was still the same, that of the woman I'd known my entire life.

Even so, she was a stranger, a remnant of the life that was so close and yet somehow so far away. Had I really changed that much? Or had she?

"I've missed you, Olive," she breathed, gazing at me with a longing so strong I was forced to look away.

I knew she wanted me to say it back. And in fact, there were hundreds of words on my tongue, ready to slip out, but none of them were right or even sufficient. I was happy to see her, in a way, but there was more to it than that. Joy mingled with resentment, rendering me mute.

"Doggone it, Evelyn. Get over here and help me with this." Uncle Hershel emerged from behind the truck. His arms were loaded with dishes.

She released me, scurrying over to take the top two plates from his stack.

I followed, grabbing a casserole pan. "Uncle Hershel," I said, finding my voice again. "Nice to see you."

He grunted as he pulled two more dishes from the truck. "So you brainwashed yet? That grandmother of yours got you lifting your prayers to the sky? Got you giving money to street magicians claiming to be able to speak to the Creator of the universe?"

"I—"

"So what if I have?" Grandma appeared behind me suddenly. Her hands were on her hips, and there was a light dusting of flour on her cheeks. "Ain't nothing wrong with her getting exposed to new things."

"There is if those 'new things' are as poisonous as arsenic."

Grandma laughed. "Arsenic? Heavens to Betsy, Hershel. You're getting dramatic in your old age. Never seen a grown man so scared of a little Bible readin'."

Uncle Hershel thrust his shoulders back, his face as red as his flannel shirt. "I ain't scared! I'm—"

"Can we please not fight?" My mother's voice was weak and wavery but enough to silence Uncle Hershel's coming tirade. "It's Thanksgiving. Can we just have Thanksgiving?"

For a moment, no one spoke. My head whipped back and forth between Grandma and Uncle Hershel, who were glaring at one another like two dogs with their hackles raised. The air between them was crowded, years of mutual dislike coming dangerously close to a boil.

"Please," my mother said again.

It was my grandma who broke first. She licked her lips, forcing them into a tight smile as she placed one hand upon my mother's arm. "Of course, Evelyn. You're right. Forgive me, Hershel. It's Thanksgiving, and you're a guest in my home. It was wrong of me to quarrel with you."

Uncle Hershel rolled his eyes. "Ah, heck with it. I'm only here for the food, anyway."

Satisfied, my mother made her way toward the house. I followed, not wanting to be left in the company of warring parties without the truce maker. The initial tension curbed, Hershel relegated himself to the porch, settling into an ancient rocker with a pipe and book. Karl Marx. Again. Grandma, meanwhile, busied herself in the kitchen, shooing away any help my mother and I tried to offer, instead banishing us to the living room while she put her finishing touches on the meal.

I sat on the couch while Ma circled the room, black heels clicking on the wooden floor. She ran her fingers over frayed blankets and old books, doily-covered end tables and aged framed photographs, lingering at one of her and my father taken on their wedding day. My mother's hair had been longer then, pulled up at the sides and cascading down her back in soft waves. Beside her, my father was supposed to be looking at the camera, but his gaze was directed at his new bride, delight etched across his lips in a lopsided grin. The picture was so innocent and joyful, so tinged with love and hope, it made my heart cleave. I wondered how Ma could even bear to be in the same room with it.

She took a slow drag from her cigarette as she ran a finger over the tarnished silver frame. "This was the last time I set foot in a church."

I looked up from my nails. I'd bitten them to the quick in the few minutes we'd been alone together.

She smiled. At the photograph, not at me. "Christopher was so good that way. He wasn't a believer, hated churches, really . . . but he loved me. And he knew it meant a lot to my family. So he agreed to get married in the church."

I nodded, even though she wasn't looking at me.

"And I loved him enough to give it up afterward. I know it hurt my mother, but it was important for me to be one with my husband. We had to make our own path, raise our family our own way." She turned to me, and I was surprised to see a hint of sadness in her eyes. "I miss it sometimes, you know? The songs, the sermons. That feeling of being a part of something bigger."

Although I remained sitting, my stomach flopped as if I'd just done a cartwheel. My mother rarely talked about her childhood faith; I always assumed she'd grown out of it, just like fairy tales and movie star dreams. It never occurred to me that she'd been one of *those* people—the people I'd seen in the pews, the ones who *wanted* to be there. The people who returned week after week out of faith rather than obligation.

People like Grandma. And Jo.

They felt something there. *She* had once felt something there. And the fact that I didn't made me feel even further away from her than before.

"Everything has been so wrong since he died. The Depression, Hershel moving in, sucking Avery into his . . . ideas. I've felt so lost. Like I've been pushed into a corner and forced into decisions I never wanted to make. What a lonely way to live, isolated like that. Lately I've wondered if . . ." Her voice trailed off as she coughed, a clearing away of thoughts that morphed into a barking hack. She held up one hand as she waited for it to pass. "Goodness. Sorry about that. These allergies. Where was I?" She twisted the butt of her cigarette into a nearby ashtray. "Ah, it doesn't matter. Enough about the past. I don't want to waste another second of our time together. Tell me about you. How's school?"

I pulled my knees to my chest like a child, not looking at her. I hated to think of my mother miserable and alone, but my sympathy evaporated when I reminded myself her feelings were self-imposed. She lost Pa, yes, and even eventually Avery, but she could have had me. She had been emotionally distant for years. Now she had chosen to go a step further and physically push me away.

She had done this to herself.

To me.

So how could I even begin to tell her about my life here? About the girls at school who pretended I was invisible. Or worse, the ones who whispered and laughed every time I walked by, making me a part of their joke but never, ever privy to it. I couldn't tell her about the classes full of information I was suddenly expected to know but which all seemed so ridiculously useless in the real world. I especially couldn't tell her that the only good thing about Alamogordo High was the few moments each day when I passed a certain dark-haired, blue-eyed boy in the hallway who always said hello . . . or winked . . . or one time brushed my arm with his hand . . .

No, I certainly couldn't tell her about that.

"Fine," I said at last. "School is fine."

"Any friends?"

My mind immediately flitted to Jo, causing my posture to go rigid. We weren't friends. No matter what she had done for my grandmother. No matter how she'd hunted me down the next day at church and asked, with irritating sincerity, how Grandma was, how I was, and offered to come over to help whenever I needed it. No matter the knot of emotions her presence created within me—angry, ashamed, and so very, very vulnerable. I'd made a point of ducking into the bathroom at school every time I saw her coming.

No, we weren't friends.

"Not really" was all I could say instead.

"Really? Richard—oh, um, I mean Sergeant Hawthorne—" she giggled—"said his daughter had mentioned you a couple times."

The air, filled just moments before with the sweet smell of roasting yams, suddenly curdled. Each word of my mother's statement lingered for an eternity in my ears before allowing the next to enter.

Richard. She called Sergeant Hawthorne Richard. And she had giggled. Less like a schoolgirl and more like a nervous child having just been caught with her hand in the cookie jar.

My mother fiddled with the ribbon around her waist. "In passing, I mean. He mentioned it in passing." Her lighthearted tone was gone. "We live in such close quarters, is all. We're bound to run into each other sometimes. We have to find something to talk about to keep things civil."

I stared at her, confusion giving way to dread. Did she know about the window? Grandma had promised not to tell. She said my mother was under enough stress as it was without worrying about my shenanigans. I touched a hand to my nose, thankful the bruise from Jo's one good punch had faded. But *Richard* knew— Pastor Hamilton had said he would make sure of it—so did my mother know too?

Because apparently they were . . . friends? Or at least friend*ly*.

"Evelyn?" Grandma's voice came from the kitchen, muffled but startling in the heavy silence. "Will you help me set the table?"

"It would be my pleasure, Mother."

And just like that, the moment was broken. My relief at a reprieve from her questions—and a possible revelation of the "incident" (as Grandma now referred to it)—was quelled by the sheer insistence of my own. They swirled in the air like the beginnings of a monsoon cloud, casting shadows over a meal in which I was now even less sure what I was supposed to be thankful for.

Turkeys were hard to find nowadays. Most of them had been shipped overseas as a morale booster for the troops. But Grandma had managed a chicken. She'd gotten yams and green beans from her neighbor's garden, and my mother had brought corn bread with prickly pear jelly, as well as a few pies and a casserole made from green chiles and chickpeas. She'd even managed to gather a few eggs to hard-boil and season. The meal, though smaller, was every bit the picture of normalcy.

Except nothing about this was normal. Especially not the way my mother floated about, smile on her face, serving a scowling Hershel, fussing over Grandma (who insisted on giving a loud and, I could only assume, purposefully long-winded prayer before eating), and making forced, joyful small talk in the tense silence. The window was never brought up. Neither was Sergeant Hawthorne.

But still the meal couldn't end fast enough.

Afterward, Hershel retired to the porch to read again (or more likely, to nap in the swing) while my mother and I helped Grandma clear the dishes. In a moment of inspiration or desperation, my mother snapped on the radio. The room filled with soft trumpets and the soothing voice of Bing Crosby.

"'Or would you like to swing on a star,'" my mother sang along, swaying her hips as she gathered plates in her arms. "'Carry moonbeams home in a jar . . .'" She interrupted her own chorus. "Come on, Olive. I know you know the words."

Despite this day—despite these horrible, miserable last few weeks—suddenly I was six years old again, back on the ranch and dancing in the kitchen as my mother sang. My heart grasped at the memory, one of those flashbulb moments made all the more poignant by their scarcity. I smiled in spite of myself. How desperately I wanted to return to that time, that place. "'And be better off than you are.'" I tried to make my voice low, causing it to crack and the two of us to giggle.

"'Or would you rather be a . . .'"

"Mule!" my mother sang.

"Pig!" I said at the same time.

"Fish," sang Bing's voice from the speaker.

We laughed again. She took my hand to spin me, dishes momentarily forgotten, as Grandma emerged from the kitchen, wide smile on her face.

"Why, Evelyn, dear, who's your friend? I didn't realize you'd be bringing a guest to Thanksgiving dinner."

My mother's fingers tightened around my own. She stopped me midtwirl but my stomach continued to twist. "What?"

Grandma moved toward me, hand outstretched. "I'm Mrs. Burke, Evelyn's mother. I'm so happy you could join us. We have plenty of food, plenty of food." She paused. "I'm sorry . . . I didn't catch your name, dearie."

I turned my eyes to my mother, unsure how to answer.

"Mother, this is Olive," she said for me. "Your granddaughter."

"Granddaughter!" Grandma threw her head back and laughed. It sent chills down my arm. "You always were such a joker, Evelyn. Granddaughter." She walked away, shaking her head, still chuckling, before pausing at the window. "Who's that on the porch?"

"The porch?"

"There's a man asleep on our swing!" Gone was her previous giddiness, replaced by a subtle and terrifying panic. "Evelyn, there's a man on our swing!"

My mother placed a hand on Grandma's back. "That's just Hershel. Hershel," she repeated. "You know Hershel."

Grandma wrenched from her touch, swatting at the explanation like gnats. "Go in the kitchen. Call the police. Tell them we have an intruder."

"Mother—"

"*Now*, Evelyn." She grabbed a broom from behind the hatstand.

"Mother!"

But it was too late. Within seconds, Grandma was out the front door, the first blow landing with a thwack on Hershel's face.

"What the—?"

Grandma got in two more hits before Hershel awakened enough to right himself and scramble away. I stood there frozen, watching the whole thing as if it were an afternoon matinee of the newest Laurel and Hardy, though not in the least bit funny. My mother, on the other hand, had no such reservations. Dodging blows, she lunged at Grandma, taking a hit to the stomach before finally getting a hand on the broom and jerking it from her grip.

"What are you doing, Evelyn?" Grandma shrieked. Her arms waved wildly for the broom.

"You crazy old biddy!" Hershel shouted, still keeping a safe distance. "What is wrong with you?"

"Get off my porch!" she screamed. "The police are on their way, you hear me?"

Hershel's face turned a deep shade of crimson. The vein in his forehead throbbed with each syllable. "What . . . are . . . you . . . talking . . . about?"

"She's not well," my mother pleaded. "Hershel, she's not well. Her mind, it's . . ."

"Not well, my rear," Hershel spat. He grabbed his book from where it had landed on the ground. "That crazy old woman knows exactly what she's doing. Been doing it for years. And I'm done. I'm done!" He shouted the last word as he passed by her, stomping down the steps toward his truck. "Where's your Jesus in that, Edna? Smacking a sleeping man with a broom? Threatening to call the police on me for doing nothing more than taking an afternoon nap? You're a hypocrite! That's all you Christians are—a bunch of brainwashed, sissified hypocrites!" He opened the truck door with a yank. "You've got five minutes, Evelyn. And then I'm gone and you can find your own way home."

The slam of his door was the loudest thing on Delaware Avenue until Grandma finally spoke again. "What's gotten into Hershel?"

My mother and I turned to look at her.

"I thought we had a nice meal. I was civil. He was . . . well,

Hershel." She shrugged her shoulders. "Goodness. I'll be sure to say an extra prayer for him tonight." And she disappeared back into the house.

Ma took a step as if to follow but then hesitated, glancing over her shoulder at the idling vehicle. She bit her lip, her eyes dancing with tears. "Olive, sweetie . . ."

"You knew?" My throat tightened, barely releasing the words. "You knew she wasn't well, and you sent me here anyway?"

"I didn't have a choice, Olive." A single tear broke free from her eyes. She coughed into her handkerchief. "I was wrong not to tell you, I admit it. But I didn't know the spells had gotten so bad. I've . . . I've never seen her like that."

"I have."

My words landed like a slap. Ma blinked several times, momentarily stunned, then shook her head. "No, they're just spells. She comes out of them. She always comes out of them. Like just now . . ."

Uncle Hershel honked twice, short and irritably.

My mother looked back and forth between the house and the truck.

"Let us come back to the ranch," I said. I hated the desperation in my voice. "Both of us. She needs you, not me. I don't know how to take care of her—"

"But you have to, Olive. Right now, with all this . . . I'm sorry, but you have to. This is for both your sakes."

"What do you mean? Just bring us back to the ranch. We'll make room. Maybe being out there will make the spells less severe and—"

"Doggone it, Olive, I said no!" Her tone was sharper than I'd ever heard, piercing and angry. When she turned to me, her eyes were blazing. "You keep saying you're an adult. Why can't you act like it? I can't have you at the ranch right now!"

I recoiled, hand flying to my chest. Bing was long forgotten. The bitter slab of resentment and anger slid back over my heart.

Any doubt about where I stood with my mother was gone. She could make whatever excuse she wanted. But now I knew: not being at the ranch wasn't a question about what was best for me or even what was best for Grandma.

It was because she didn't want me there.

At the curb, Hershel laid on the horn, longer this time. Impatient.

The fire was gone from my mother's eyes as quickly as it had flared. Tears coated her cheeks. She reached for me but I pulled back. "Olive . . . Olive, I'm sorry. Nothing about this is fair to you, to her. It's not. And I . . ."

Hershel's horn again. More insistent.

"I have to go. I'm sorry. Know that I'm sorry. And please take care of her." She paused. "No, take care of each other. Please." Then she fled down the steps, disappeared into Uncle Hershel's truck, and roared away down Delaware Avenue without a backward glance.

CHAPTER TEN

JO

MARCH 1952

Jo was in a room. Four walls, no furniture. Just an empty room. Only not empty. The atmosphere was orange and cozy. Like a fire, but there was no fire. And Jo couldn't get warm. Outside the glow, a darkness pressed in on her; it soaked into her skin like freezing rain. Ice flowed through her veins, chattering her teeth and sprouting goose bumps across her arms.

A loud banging echoed all around.

Jo tried to lean forward but the chill held her back, frigid tendrils wrapping around her body. The warmth . . . the warmth was God. Somehow she knew it was God. And her father was there beside Him, the two of them beckoning. Calling. Waiting.

But she couldn't get to them.

Unable to move, she opened her mouth to call out, only to find her lips frozen together.

The banging increased, but this time it was coming from inside Jo's own head. Louder and louder, colder and colder.

The light and the warmth pulled further away, drawing God— and her father—with it.

No, Jo screamed. *No, wait!*

"Miss Hawthorne?"

Suddenly the banging stopped. Jo's muscles collapsed, free, exhausted, confused.

"Miss Hawthorne?"

The darkness fled, replacing one room with another. Pale green. Hard bed. A painting of White Sands inside a hideous gold frame. The motel. She was in a motel. In Alamogordo.

The events of the previous night came rushing back, sending waves of nausea and regret into her still-tender stomach. *It was a dream,* she told herself. Her father wasn't in this room. *And last night you were drunk. Olive wasn't at the bar. Neither one of them are here.* And she realized, glancing at her watch, she shouldn't be either. It was 7:42 a.m. She had less than twenty minutes to get to her bus.

"Shoot," she hissed, hopping from the bed. There was no afternoon bus today; this was her only shot until tomorrow. "Shoot, shoot, shoot."

She grabbed her bag from the chair, closing her eyes for a moment as the floor tilted and a massive headache swelled up behind her eyes. She would never drink again, she vowed. Never. Swallowing dizziness, she gave only a passing thought to brushing her teeth or washing her face. Not that she had a toothbrush. Or extra makeup. Or clothes. There was no time. Her breath would still be bad and her face still dirty at the next rest stop. She could take care of it then. The only thing that mattered now was getting out of Alamogordo.

She flung open the door, wincing at the burning sunlight.

"Miss Hawthorne?"

Jo jumped. In the bright light a woman materialized. She was in her late forties perhaps, with dark-blonde hair twisted on top of her head. Her maid's uniform was faded pink in color, and the brown shoes on her feet were scuffed. She kept her eyes down when she spoke. "Miss Hawthorne?"

"Yes?"

"You have a phone call. At the front desk."

Jo blinked as if she were speaking another language. "A phone call?"

"Yes." The woman gestured behind her. "Back there."

A sudden hardness dropped into her stomach. She was leaving. Now. Nothing was going to stop her.

And yet the chill from her dream lingered, fingers of ice sprouting from her chest into her limbs, pushing her toward the office in spite of herself. The dream didn't mean anything. At most, it was another sign she needed to get out of this place while she still could. This phone call couldn't change that. Wouldn't change that. No matter who was on the other end.

No matter the news she knew she was about to hear.

Inside the office, a bored-looking clerk pointed one finger at the phone. Shaking, Jo placed the unhooked receiver next to her ear. "Hello?"

Faint static. A woman's voice. Muffled.

"Hello?" she said again.

More static. And then, louder: "Miss Hawthorne, hello. Is that you?"

She hadn't even realized she'd been holding her breath until she let it go. One long, ragged exhale, the stench of sleep and alcohol lingering on the edges. "Yes, this is Jo Hawthorne."

"Miss Hawthorne, this is Mary Faulkner down at the hospital. I'm the overnight nurse in charge. I got your number from—" Another burst of static covered her sentence. She continued anyway, her voice rising over the crackle. "Would it be possible for you to come down here?"

No, Jo said inside her head.

"Your father is . . . He's not well. Agitated. Restless. Refusing his medicine."

Jo closed her eyes. Her father's shrunken form swam in her vision. "I'm sorry. I have a bus to catch."

Another burst of static. "Miss Hawthorne, I don't think you understand. I've never seen him like this. He's upsetting the other—"

A stab of pain shot through her temple. She was going to be sick. "Nurse Faulkner, was it?"

"Yes—"

"I appreciate you reaching out, but as I said before, I have a bus to catch. I saw my father yesterday and—"

"Miss Hawthorne . . ."

Jo talked over her. "I said everything I needed to say. Goodbye, Miss Faulkner."

"Miss Hawthorne, I think . . . I think this might be it."

It. She didn't have to explain.

The word wasn't unexpected but still her fingers grew numb, causing the receiver in her hand to slip. She pulled it back toward her ear with a trembling hand.

Another burst of static and then: "Miss Hawthorne, did you hear me?"

And she did. Curse it all, she *did*. What she wouldn't give to have not heard. To have not answered the phone and simply walked to the bus stop. It was there, right across the street. Staring at her. To have walked right in there and bought a ticket, one-way to San Diego. Clear head, clear conscience, shaking off Alamogordo, her father, Olive, this entire stinking desert once she passed that city limit sign.

And she could have. If only she hadn't *heard*.

"Are you still there?"

The tightness in her chest expanded to her throat, choking her. Her stomach was still churning, though she knew it was no longer just the residual tequila. "Yes," she managed to whisper.

Again her mind flickered to her dream, to the warmth just out of reach. Coldness pressed against her spirit, causing her to flinch, though it did little good. She couldn't escape from herself. She sighed. "I'll be right there."

Although the nurse had told her to hurry, she found her legs unwilling to cooperate. Invisible hands pulled her backward, causing her to strain with every stride. She didn't want to face what she knew she'd see when she got to the hospital. Didn't want to stare into those green eyes again and watch the light leave them. He had forsaken her, and she hated him. But he was the last of her blood on this earth, and soon he would be gone. She didn't know how she was supposed to feel about that. It was easier to pretend she felt nothing at all.

Easier still just to leave. So why wasn't she?

— ◆ ✦ ◆ —

Nurse Faulkner was not at all what Jo had pictured. Her husky voice and no-nonsense tone conveyed age and authority; when Jo entered the hospital, she was surprised to find the night nurse only a few years older than herself, pretty and pert, with soft brown eyes and a mop of blonde curls.

"Miss Hawthorne, thank heavens you're here. He's stabilized now, but I don't think we're out of the woods just yet." She grabbed Jo's arm and pulled her past the curtain partition. "Richard! Richard, someone is here to see you!"

Richard Hawthorne stood beside his bed. A pale-green hospital gown hung limply off his frame. He gripped the bedsheets with one veiny hand, flamed red, splotches of blood oozing from the wounds created by ripped-out IVs. With his other hand, he pounded weakly on his lumpy pillow. At the sight of Jo, however, he froze midstrike. Then suddenly his body gave way, folding in on itself as he collapsed on the cold, tile floor.

"Richard! What are you doing out of bed again? I—" Nurse Faulkner raced forward, catching his head just before it hit the ground.

His lips twitched in desperation, but his eyes never left Jo's face. Focused only on her, he seemed oblivious to his beleaguered state.

"Miss Hawthorne, please, can you help me get him back on the bed?"

Jo twisted her head to avoid looking at him as she reached for his emaciated arm. His bones protruded under paper-thin skin; it felt as if it would rip beneath the force of her grip. But his knobby fingers found hers and he stopped writhing, allowing himself to be lifted back into his bed.

"I don't know what's gotten into you." Nurse Faulkner rolled her eyes as she checked his pulse. "You're bound and determined today's the day, aren't you?"

Richard's chest heaved but his gaze remained fixed on Jo. He didn't even flinch when Nurse Faulkner not-so-gently shoved the IV back into his withered veins.

"I try not to let anyone die on my watch, but doggone it if you weren't itching for it. What were you thinking, climbing out of bed like that? You know you ain't strong enough. All that grunting and wheezing—enough to make your heart stop!"

The nurse busied herself smoothing down the sheets, not pausing her tirade as she made notes in his chart. Through it all, Richard Hawthorne maintained an icy grip on his daughter's hand, not allowing her to pull away.

"Don't you make me call the doc back in here." The nurse replaced the clipboard in the pouch at the foot of his bed. "Pull a stunt like that again, and you won't like the medications he puts you on next. Will you behave now that she's here?"

Richard's chest rose and fell slowly. He nodded.

The nurse narrowed her eyes. "You'll stay put in that bed? No more fits? No more tantrums?"

Richard nodded once again.

Nurse Faulkner turned her attention to Jo. "You'll let me know if he starts acting up again? Breathing heavy, making noises?"

"Yes. Sure."

With another glare, the nurse disappeared behind the curtain. The squeak of her shoes faded as she made her way from the ward.

As soon as she was gone, Jo wrenched her hand from his grasp. "Are you crazy? What was that all about?"

Her father's face crumpled. He reached for her again.

"I wouldn't be surprised if you did that on purpose. Making a fuss like you were dying just so I'd come back."

For the first time, he looked away.

Jo pushed herself from his bed, disgusted. "That's it, isn't it? That's what you did? Well, you got me here. Congratulations. But that doesn't mean I'm staying. Throw all the fits you want. I'm gone."

A fearful gasp erupted from Richard's mouth as he made a weak lunge for her, but Jo ignored him, brushing past the curtain . . . and walking straight into Charlie Wilson. "Oh!"

He grabbed her arms before she could slip. The smell of Old Spice and cigarettes wafted from his sharp black suit. "Hey there!"

Jo was suddenly aware of her own appearance, the smear of day-old makeup on her collar and the stench of her hangover clinging to rumpled fabric. She smoothed her hair, knowing it was absurd but unable to stop herself, and tried not to think about her tequila sweat and sour breath. "Charlie! What are you doing here?"

He winked. "Looking for you."

"Me?"

"I was here this morning checking on Mrs. Hahn—the lady from Tularosa," he added, seeing Jo's confused face. "The one in the bed next to your father? I was here and I heard him . . . well, you know."

Jo looked at the floor.

"I told them about you," he said quietly. "Your name. Where you were staying. I hope that's okay."

So that was how they'd found her.

"I ran out for a cup of coffee but I wanted to make sure . . . well, I wanted to make sure they got ahold of you. And I wanted to make sure you were alright."

"I'm fine."

Charlie rubbed the back of his neck. "And your father? Is he . . . ?"

"He's fine too. It was a . . . misunderstanding."

"Are you sure? He seemed pretty agitated."

"What is it exactly you want from me?" Her headache was screaming, and her stomach still burned from the leftover alcohol. On top of that, the bus she was supposed to be on was probably cresting the peaks of the Organ Mountains right now on its way west toward freedom. And before her stood this man—this overly nice, impossibly good-looking man—pretending to be concerned about any of it. "Why do you care so much? You don't know me, and I don't know you."

Charlie grimaced. "I'm sorry. I just . . ."

"Do your tests on someone else, okay? Stop asking me questions. I don't want to remember anything about that day, and I don't care what that stupid bomb did or didn't do to him. It's over, it's done, and I want to just move on already."

"Jo, I wasn't—"

Crash!

Charlie's defense was interrupted by a sudden sound behind them. They turned to find Richard Hawthorne on the floor once more. His legs knotted beneath him as one hand gripped the bed-sheets. The other reached toward his daughter.

"Mr. Hawthorne!" Charlie rushed forward and grabbed the man's arms. He pulled him into a standing position, wrapping one frail arm around his shoulders.

Jo remained where she stood, watching, rage simmering below the surface.

"Here you go. Back on the bed. Back on the bed, there." Charlie eased the man up, folding his hands over his stomach like a child's. "There you go."

Richard stared at Jo, lips twitching. Trying to communicate, for sure. But Jo stayed put, arms crossed over her chest. She was utterly uninterested in whatever it was he was trying to say.

"Easy does it." Charlie released the last of Richard's weight onto the mattress.

Jo's father looked up, taking in his rescuer for the first time. His eyes searched Charlie's face, lips in a pout, brow knit with concentration. Suddenly he shrank back, pressing his head into his pillow until it nearly swallowed his face.

"Whoa! Whoa, what—?"

Richard's arms and legs flailed. It was as if he were running without moving, grasping for some invisible rope to pull him away. From his lips came the same guttural sounds as before, like an animal cornered in its cage. Unable to garner enough strength to rise again, he instead swung at Charlie with one gnarled fist. Barely enough force to knock over a feather but so unexpected, it caused Charlie to stumble backward.

"Hey!"

Richard Hawthorne swung again. His lips twisted into a snarl.

"Stop that!"

But still he continued to swing. His aim was feeble but ferocious.

"Jo! Tell him to stop!" Charlie reached for Richard's arms, missed, then reached again. "He's going to hurt himself!"

Spittle flew from her father's mouth as Charlie finally succeeded in wrapping his large hands around the man's wrists. Richard leaned forward, attempting to push Charlie away, but only managed to free one hand, which he immediately swiped at Charlie's face. Sharp nails made contact with smooth flesh, and tiny speckles of blood erupted from the scratch.

It was the appearance of red that finally sprang Jo into action. She lunged toward the bed, ducking to avoid a blow and grabbing her father's wrist in midswing. His skin was clammy beneath her touch. "What are you doing?" she screeched. "Stop it! Stop it right now!"

At the sound of her voice, he quieted, blinking rapidly.

Charlie took a step back, one hand to his cheek.

"Are you okay?"

He wiped his palm against his face. "Yeah, I'm fine. It was more shock than anything."

Behind her, Jo's father was breathing heavily. Sweat beaded on his upper lip. "He was just trying to help you," she spat at him. She pulled down on her wrist, trying to break free from his grasp.

He held tighter.

Heat flushed under her collar. "You should go," she said to Charlie, mouth tight.

"You sure?" He looked to Richard, whose eyes remained fiery and narrowed in his direction. Frowning, he opened his mouth as if to say something but closed it again, nodding once at Jo instead. He gave Richard one more unreadable glance before backing from the room.

Jo listened to his footsteps fade before turning to face her father. "Let go of me."

His eyes flitted between her and the curtain, still swaying from Charlie's exit. His mouth twisted, thousands of words swimming just below the surface, but no sound came out.

She pulled her wrist again but he held tight, turning it over so her palm was facing upward. Taking his other hand, he traced a shape on her skin. He looked at her expectantly.

"I'm not in the mood to play games," she said, tugging once more at her wrist.

He held fast, tracing the shape again. Two lines, crossed at the middle.

"What are you doing?"

Again, two lines, crossed at the middle.

"Stop it."

He made to trace a third time, but Jo had had enough. With a huff, she yanked her wrist free. "I said stop it."

Tears formed in the corners of her father's eyes. His fingers gripped the bedsheets, his lips forming the same silent word over and over again, growing ever more agitated.

For a moment, Jo hesitated. The love she'd held for this man at one time—this man who had brought her into this world, who had guided her, who had molded her—roared forth like a wave, threating to overtake her. Just for a moment. One fleeting moment was all she would allow before swallowing that lump in her throat and taking a step away from the bed.

"Goodbye," she said, hoping the finality in her voice would solidify her resolve. "For good."

And she turned and walked from the room, scolding herself for wanting to look back but not daring to allow herself the weakness.

"Jo!"

Charlie was waiting outside the hospital door. Because of course he would be.

"You okay?"

"I'm fine."

"You seem upset."

"Wouldn't you be?"

Charlie crushed a cigarette under his heel. "Yes. That's why I'm asking. How is he?"

"Dying."

He started. "Right." His left hand fidgeted with his cigarettes, contemplating another smoke. "Did he . . . did he say anything to you?"

"He tried to." She thought of the mark in her hand. What in the world could he be getting at? Was it code? She racked her brain for any memory of a *t*, anything from her past he might have been trying to spell, but nothing came.

Maybe it was just the cancer. Seeping into her father's brain, creating letters and pictures that meant nothing. Maybe it was pulling up memories as if from a photo album, flashing them before his eyes with no semblance of logic between them. A cruel mocking of their history, the pain and suffering of that long-ago confrontation rising up through the disease to wound once more.

Another thought pushed into her mind from nowhere, causing air to rush from her lungs. Was it a cross? Her father was not a religious man. In fact, he'd made his feelings about God very clear that last day they'd spent together. And yet her dream . . . God and her father together, with her on the outside, unable to reach him. Unable to reach *Him*.

She shivered in spite of the heat. *It was just a dream,* she repeated to herself. *It didn't mean anything.*

And yet her palm tingled with the memory of her father's touch.

The sun was higher overhead than she'd anticipated, her bus long gone. Another day stuck in this town. A result of poor choices on her part, as well as her own foolish weakness.

Or something else.

"Charlie," she said, "can you take me somewhere I might find a fresh set of clothes? And maybe a toothbrush?"

Visible relief flooded through his body as he smiled and gestured toward a black Packard parked in the small lot to the left of the hospital. "Absolutely, Jo. Whatever you need."

CHAPTER ELEVEN

OLIVE

DECEMBER 1944

December brought nothing from my mother. No follow-ups, no apologies, not even a letter to check in. Instead, it brought the first freeze, my first-ever high school exams, and the first fundraising assignment from Pastor Hamilton.

So on a night I should have been studying, I was shivering in a too-light jacket (having left my winter coat at the ranch in a huff), selling coffee and ersatz hot chocolate to much happier folks lining Tenth Street for the annual Alamogordo Christmas parade. In addition to the drinks, a colorful donation box was set up on our table, in case people were feeling especially moved by holiday generosity.

Jo Hawthorne was, of course, a picture of Yuletide cheer. Her blonde hair flowed perfectly from a green-and-red stocking cap, and bells hung from the end of her scarf, tinkling infuriatingly with every move she made. "God bless!" she called with each dime dropped in our tin cashbox. "And merry Christmas!"

I poured drinks and said as little as possible.

The sidewalks were noisy and crowded. Laughter mixed with the sounds of music from carolers and bands as floats carrying papier-mâché snowmen and reindeer made their way down the street. The smell of popcorn and tamales wafted from vendor stands, a stark contrast to the hints of cinnamon and sugar coming from the USO volunteers passing out bags of roasted pecans. Overindulgence and cheer seemed to be the theme of the night. The only time the crowd grew silent was when the float carrying baby Jesus passed, a plastic doll in a wooden box, illuminated by a single flashlight tied with a string.

I wasn't ignorant. I knew the whole Jesus Christmas story. But in my house, Christmas had nothing to do with Jesus; instead it focused on family and togetherness and pride in the year's accomplishments. So my vexation was twofold: not only was I witnessing firsthand the absurdity of reverence over a baby (and a fake one at that), but the true meaning of Christmas—the Alexander meaning of Christmas—was, I realized, simply another thing to add to this year of loss.

"Olive! Olive, hey!"

Breaking through the depths of my gloom was a voice. But not just any voice. *The* voice. The only voice in this dark, confusing town that brought me any light.

Tim Bucknam appeared before me, grin stretched across those

beautiful lips. His dark hair was barely visible beneath a navy-blue stocking cap. The strings of multicolored lights above our heads made his eyes dance.

I did what any cool, calm, and collected fifteen-year-old woman would do. I dropped a cup of coffee, splashing not only myself but also the outstretched hand of the elderly woman waiting for it. Hot liquid stained her gray gloves and splattered the front of my coat.

"Ouch!" she squealed.

"I'm so sorry!"

The woman had jumped, causing her to stumble backward into Tim, who, never losing his smile, caught her with ease. "Whoa there. Are you okay?"

"Yes," we both said at the same time, though the woman's glare made it clear she assumed his query was only directed at her. And maybe it was. I'd seen her before, during Sunday service, though I didn't know her name. She was always dressed in outfits I knew hadn't come from any of the shops on Tenth Street. Tonight, for instance, her coat was ankle-length fur, dark and luxurious, beaver perhaps, with shiny black heels gleaming beneath. She pulled off her gloves—leather—and examined them with a look of horror. "I'm fine. But my gloves! My beautiful gloves!"

Embarrassed, I turned to pour her another drink, only to find Jo standing behind me with a steaming cup already in hand. She gave me a sympathetic smile.

I took the coffee, pursing my lips as I felt my ears redden. I'd almost forgotten she was there. And somehow her seeing my accident was worse than Tim.

"I'm sorry," I murmured, thrusting the cup forward with a grimace.

The woman, recovered physically, now had the energy to really tune in the dramatics. She sneered at the coffee in my hand. "Those gloves you just ruined with your careless ineptitude are from New York, and they are absolutely irreplaceable! Do you hear me? Irreplaceable!"

Heads began to turn in our direction. The woman's voice rose above the off-key rendition of "Jingle Bells" now flowing from the wobbly, streamer-covered float passing in front of us. I shrank into my coffee-covered coat as the steaming cup wobbled in my still-outstretched hand.

"Mrs. Lowe—" Tim placed a hand on the woman's shoulder.

She didn't shrug him away, but she didn't calm down, either. "I should have expected nothing less from you after the mess you already caused. You can be sure I'm going to speak to Pastor Hamilton about this. Not a good image for the church, people like you out and about. And you're going to figure out a way to pay for these gloves as well as that window. I'm—"

"Mrs. Lowe?" Jo's voice was as meek and mild as a Christmas carol. "Mrs. Lowe, please. It was an accident. Olive didn't mean to spill coffee. She was—"

"This doesn't concern you," Mrs. Lowe interrupted, twisting her nose into the air.

"But it—"

"It was my fault, Mrs. Lowe," Tim piped up.

I tipped my head, frowning.

"I startled her," Tim continued. "I didn't mean to. I was just saying hello. But these news reports from the front have us all on edge, I think. Iwo Jima and Kesternich, then Glenn Miller missing over the English Channel? It's just never-ending."

Mrs. Lowe's scowl slowly dissipated. "Yes. Yes, I suppose so. Poor Glenn Miller. I do hope they find his plane." She placed a hand on Tim's elbow. "How *is* your brother, by the way? Any news?"

He shook his head. "Last letter was a month ago. He's somewhere in the Pacific, though he can't say where. In high spirits though."

"He always was such a good boy. He fixed the rattle in my Edward's car when no one else could, you know? I pray for him—and all our boys—every day."

The change from hatred to piousness was sharp and jarring, but it was her words that stole my breath. With them, she had conjured ghosts of those who should be here but weren't. I shook them away. I didn't want to think about Tim's brother or any other soldier, especially not Avery. And I didn't want this woman—so full of vitriol and artificial holiness—to be lifting *her* prayers over any of them.

"Here." Jo moved past me, pulling the gloves from her own hands. "Take mine. I know they can't replace yours, but they'll at least keep your hands warm in the meantime."

"Child, no, I can't—"

"I insist. They're not from New York or anything, but they are from California. Lake Tahoe, actually. So they're pretty warm." She pressed the wool into Mrs. Lowe's palms.

"But I—"

"It's okay. I have another pair at home." She took the coffee from my hands and placed it in Mrs. Lowe's. "This one's on the house."

After a few more moments of sputtering disbelief, Mrs. Lowe

finally walked away, new gloves on her fingers and free cup of coffee pressed to her lips. Jo retreated to the table without a word, and the crowd swelled back around us, leaving Tim and me all alone in the middle of it.

He rolled himself up on the balls of his feet. "Well, it seems a little late now . . . but hi."

I laughed, my breath a cloud of vapor in the chilly air. "Hi."

"You having fun?"

I gave him a sideways glance.

It was his turn to laugh. "Okay, that was a stupid question. I guess I should ask if you're making money. That's the whole point, right?"

I shrugged. "I think so. I mean, I haven't counted it or anything. But business has been pretty steady. So no matter what, we're closer to our goal now than we were when we started."

"Well, that's good."

"Yeah."

Self-consciousness returned suddenly. Tim chewed on his lips. The crowd in front of us was too thick to see the parade, but I caught a few strains of "O Come, All Ye Faithful" weaving through the chatter. The song swelled and faded with the passing float before he finally spoke again.

"So I was . . . I was wondering if you were going to the winter formal?"

Warmth spread across my chest. And it wasn't because of the coffee still seeping through my coat. Was Tim Bucknam going to ask me to the dance? Could this really be happening?

But as quickly as it started, my elation plummeted. It didn't matter if he was asking me. I was still very, very grounded. No way

Grandma would make an exception for a dance, even one with a boy like Tim Bucknam.

I swallowed the lump in my throat, not meeting his eye. "No, I . . . I can't."

"Oh. Okay." He frowned.

"It's just . . ." I gestured limply to the table behind me, to the church.

"Right. I heard about that. I imagine you're in it pretty deep, huh?"

"Yeah."

"It's okay. I understand."

And maybe he did. But it didn't stop the awkwardness from growing bigger, pushing on the space between us. I opened my mouth, trying to find the words to tell him that I wanted to go, that I would go if I could. Because he was handsome and kind and perfect and the only boy who'd ever made my stomach feel as if I'd missed the bottom rung of a ladder. But then behind me, Jo cleared her throat. Tim blinked, and the moment was gone.

I let out a quiet, aggrieved sigh. "I have to get back to work."

"Sure." He scratched at the back of his head. "Well, hey, can I at least get a cup of hot chocolate before I go?"

I gave him a smile I hoped masked my unhappiness. "It's not very good."

"Then I won't be upset if you spill it on me."

With a wink and a tip, Tim Bucknam took his cocoa and disappeared back into the crowd. Trying to avoid Jo's eye, I busied myself unwrapping more cups. I could feel her staring at me, wanting to talk, but I refused to take the bait. She'd see the truth, no matter what words I said, no matter how much I shoved it down. And this feeling about Tim—whatever it was—was one I was not willing to share. Especially not with her.

The parade wound down around eight. Santa's sleigh pulled up the rear. Kids scrambled for candy canes tossed in the street as he passed, ho-ho-ho-ing over and over until the sound was mechanical and grating. The bulk of the crowd followed him, leaving only a few stragglers and ripped streamers in their wake. I started to pack up our things without waiting for Jo to say it was time.

"I think we made a dent in our debt," she said with tiresome brightness as she loaded a thermos into the wagon Pastor Hamilton had loaned us. "I'll count it later but I think it's a good start."

I stuffed napkins into a box and ignored her.

"I mean, obviously we still have a long way to go. I mentioned something to Pastor Hamilton about a rummage sale after New Year, but still—"

"Why did you do that?" I asked suddenly, spinning around to face her.

The stack of cups in her grip teetered as she jumped, lips frozen midsentence. "Why did I do what?"

"Why did you give Mrs. Lowe your gloves?" The moment, though only an hour before, seemed so long ago, but the memory had festered. Probably because it was the least painful thing my mind could dwell on. And because it was way better than allowing her to bring up what I knew she wanted to discuss.

"Why not?"

"She was horrible."

Jo chuckled as she put the cups in the wagon. "She's just a crotchety old lady. She's been through a lot. Lost her son in the first war, I think, and her husband not long after. And I really do have an extra pair at home." She shrugged. "Besides, she wasn't going to let it go. She'd have gone ranting and raving to Pastor Hamilton, getting you in even more trouble." She swung a garbage bag full of used cups and coffee grounds over her shoulder like a miner. "She likes to complain. But I saw no point in letting you take the brunt of it, especially when it was an accident."

"You didn't have to do that."

"I know."

She smiled, letting her words hang between us. And inexplicably, I felt as if I was going to cry. For no reason at all and for every reason. Because of the hypocrisy of Mrs. Lowe, singing praises to Jesus on Sunday and screaming over a spilled cup of coffee on Friday. Because of Tim Bucknam's smile and the way I'd made him frown and the dance I'd never cared about that was suddenly the only thing in the world I wanted. Because of Grandma's mind and the ease with which it floated away and the impotence I felt at being unable to make sure it returned—and the unfairness that it should be my responsibility at all. For Avery's absence. For my mother's indifference. For my own loneliness, bigger and more intense in this city full of people than it had ever been on my small, nearly empty ranch.

And for the girl standing in front of me, who had defended me. Simply because she saw me as someone worth defending. Someone worth seeing at all.

I shoved the cashbox at her, causing her to stumble. I didn't stay to help her pull the wagon back to the church. I didn't care how much we'd made toward our goal. I simply fled into the night, tears blurring the too-bright Christmas lights adorning the windows of town, where happier families huddled inside their homes, surrounded by love and joy and a peace I'd only heard preached from a pulpit.

— ❖ —

Winter formal came and went. Tim Bucknam attended with Melody Jones, a perky sophomore with wavy blonde hair and legs for days. I told myself I didn't care, a line I repeated over and over when I saw the two of them walking in the hallway a few days afterward. He mouthed a hello but didn't stop to chat. The pit of my heart burned with a jealousy I had no right to feel. I had blown my chance. But I didn't care. I *didn't*. If I said it enough, maybe it would be true.

The only plus side to my forced detachment from the world around me was that I aced my exams. Turns out, I was pretty good at regurgitating facts and figures when I didn't allow myself to think about anything but the material at hand. And I was only a *little* smug thinking about the faces of Mrs. Wheeler, Mr. Dusky, and all the others who'd viewed me as some sort of unteachable wild animal.

When the bell rang on that last day before break, it was a sense of pride and relief that carried me away from Jo and Tim, from the suffocating hallways and egotistical overlords. Christmas would be anything but merry and bright this year, but I had a stack of books, a quiet house, and three whole weeks where I could pretend to live in a world of my own design.

Or so I thought.

Unbeknownst to me, my mother had invited us back to the ranch for Christmas. A special privilege, she'd said, considering the sensitivity of the Army's work nearby. It would be the first time

I'd set foot on Alexander land in over two months. I should have been elated, grateful even.

Instead, every mile that passed beneath the tires of Grandma's car, leading away from Alamogordo and into the Jornada, brought me nothing but dread. It was December 24, a day of anticipation. But as we passed the lone yucca at the end of our drive, bouncing over the ruts and watching the Arizona sycamore rise above the horizon, it felt like a funeral.

When I saw my mother, her dark hair pulled away from her face, thin frame seeming to disappear beneath a thick red shawl, I wanted to feel something for her. Something other than hurt. But the pain and confusion of our last parting was a tangible companion, swelling between our embrace with such force that she released me after only a moment, hugging her own mother instead. I looked away, uncomfortable, and focused my attention on the land around me. It still smelled the same—hay and brittle earth. There were no fences running through the middle of the property. No change or physical barriers of any sort. And yet a definitive wall existed just the same. Separating the main house from the barn and casita, a heavy foreign presence, invisible but palpable, manifested itself just feet from where I stood.

The casita was stuffed full, the contents of a three-bedroom house crammed into a space meant for two. But my mother had tried. The roaring fire cast the entire room in an orange glow, accented with dozens of candles and several kerosene lanterns. From the old wooden Admiral came the soft sound of trumpets. Meager decorations—mainly paper chains and dried chile ristras—were hung throughout the room. And somehow, standing in the corner was a tree. A real spruce tree, garnished with small candles and strings of popcorn and red berries, filling the house with the scent of Christmas long ago.

We hadn't had a tree in years. Not since Hershel moved in.

Grandma spoke first. "Oh, Evelyn, how did you . . . ?"

"Sergeant Hawthorne," Ma said, dipping her chin. "He was trying to boost morale for his men, so he traveled all the way up to Capitan to cut down a tree. He cut down one for me, too. For us," she corrected herself.

But it was too late. Suddenly that beautiful glowing tree was the ugliest thing in the room.

"It's simply breathtaking," Grandma said. "Isn't it breathtaking, Olive?"

"Where's Uncle Hershel?" I asked instead. Surely he'd have something to say about this preposterous tree.

"In here." Uncle Hershel emerged from the kitchen. He was dressed in a plaid button-down and jeans, glass of wine in his hand. His red cheeks conveyed it wasn't his first. He eyed Grandma with a look of suspicion and decidedly un-Christmassy spirit.

"Hello, Hershel." Grandma's voice was sunny and willfully ignorant of the tension. "Merry Christmas."

He grunted. Impolite, sure, but considering their last encounter, a decided improvement.

"So . . . a tree," I said pointedly.

My uncle rolled his massive shoulders, showing dark sweat stains beneath his arms. "It's just a tree."

My mouth went slack as I watched him retreat to his easy chair with his wine and a book. Had the whole world lost its ever-loving mind?

"Well, sit down, sit down." My mother pulled my grandmother and me toward the sagging couch. In front of us, the fire crackled invitingly, warming feet I'd barely registered were freezing. "Can I get you something to drink?"

The fire cast dark circles under my mother's eyes. Her lips were chapped, and the usual soft curve of her chin jutted. There was still beauty there, of course. My mother couldn't be ugly if she tried. But there was an exhaustion just below the surface, a new sadness that hadn't been there only a few weeks before.

"I'll have some of Hershel's wine," Grandma piped up. "If he'll share, that is."

From behind his book, Uncle Hershel grunted again.

"Well, thank you, Hershel," Grandma replied with a wink. "So generous."

My mother disappeared into the kitchen, returning a moment later with a glass of deep-purple wine for my grandmother and mugs of hot cider for herself and me. We sipped in silence, staring at the flames dancing in the charred fireplace.

"So how are things here?" Grandma asked.

Hershel glanced at my mother over the top of his book. It was a gaze so quick and pointed, it felt as if I imagined it. From my mother came a barely perceptible clenching of her fist. "Things are fine."

There was a pause. A beat. No one else could have possibly noticed it. But she was still my mother. So I did.

"I need to check on dinner." The couch squeaked loudly—too loudly—as she rose suddenly.

"Let me help you," Grandma said. The buttons on her festive red dress strained as she rose.

Never one for light conversation, Hershel retreated into his book, so I went to the window instead, wiping away condensation with one hand. The main house on the other side of the courtyard was dark. I'd spent fifteen Christmases in that house. Even after Pa died, when things changed and the world shifted, there was still Christmas—our version of Christmas, at least—in that house.

And now we were here. In the guesthouse. On our own ranch.

"Where are the Army guys?"

"What?" my mother called from the kitchen.

"Where are the Army guys?"

"Most of them have been given leave for the holiday," Uncle Hershel answered for her, resting his book on his chest. "Just a few days, not really enough to travel all the way back home. But enough to take a break, at least. Most were going up to Santa Fe or Albuquerque. A few were heading down to Alamogordo. The USO down there was setting up a Christmas dinner, I believe."

I had asked the question, but hearing him answer the way he did suddenly made me angry. It was like he was one of them.

"Naturally, they couldn't all take leave. Security issue. Some are in the barracks over at the construction site. And Sergeant Hawthorne—"

A knock on the front door interrupted his speech. Tunnel vision clouded my eyes. The casita, the decorations, that stupid beautiful tree all evaporated. All I could see was the wooden door. I knew without opening it.

My mother swung it open with a chuckle. "Well, speak of the devil."

Sergeant Hawthorne stood on the stoop. Only he wasn't Sergeant Hawthorne today. No, today he wore khaki slacks and a green sweater vest over a button-down shirt. His dark hair was slick and perfect, unencumbered by his uniform hat. His face, however, was serious. "Mrs. Alexander, I'm sorry, but you're going to have to come with me."

My mother tilted her head. "What? I'm sorry; I—"

"We have reason to believe we've been infiltrated by spies."

My mother's lips quivered; her smile remained but it was stagnant and unsure. She looked as if she would laugh. Or cry. Or run. One hand still gripped the doorknob, her bony fingers white with the tense grip.

"Our intelligence has intercepted some communication between this house and German agents. I'm going to need both you and Hershel to follow me."

"What? I—"

"Hogwash!" Hershel's voice boomed from behind me. "Ain't no dirty Nazis here! Just a couple biddies and a crusty old Russian."

I stared bewildered between the three of them: my mother, tense and unmoving; Hershel, hands on his massive hips, face red with wine and indignation; and Sergeant Hawthorne, just outside the threshold, brows raised above an unreadable expression.

Suddenly both Hershel and Sergeant Hawthorne burst out laughing. I started, confused. At the door, my mother seemed to melt beneath the weight of broken suspense. She pulled her hand from the knob, grasping her skirt to steady a very noticeable shake.

"You shouldn't joke like that." Her voice wavered under a fractured giggle.

"Ah, Hershel knows I like to give him grief." Sergeant Hawthorne laughed. "He can drink me under the table—I have to save my pride somehow! And anyway, accusing Hershel of conspiring with Nazis is like saying Roosevelt is a Communist."

"He should be!" Hershel's tone was joking without quite being a joke.

"On that, my friend, we disagree. But still—the enemy of my enemy is my friend . . . even if he is a Soviet."

Hershel raised a glass. "I'll drink to that."

My mother's eye caught mine. She gave a weak smile and shook her head, coughing into her shawl. "Alright, boys. It's too cold for politics *or* jokes. Come in, Richard. Come in."

Sergeant Hawthorne—*Richard*, I thought bitterly—stepped through the door, kissing my mother on the cheek as he did so. "I've come bearing gifts!" He held out a bottle of wine wrapped in a bow.

My mother took it from him and cradled it like a child. "Thank you, Richard! So thoughtful. This will be perfect with dinner."

"And not just wine." He moved aside, allowing a rush of cold air to follow behind him . . . and someone else. "Evelyn, this is my daughter, Jo."

Jo. Jo Hawthorne was standing inside my living room. Jo with her white hair pulled back in a ponytail. With her pale skin and her stupid green Christmas sweater, rows of boxy trees and prancing reindeer across her front, paired with a perfectly pleated brown calf-length skirt. She huddled behind her father, looking genuinely, ridiculously happy to be there.

For a minute, we all stood there, staring while trying not to stare. Or maybe that was just me. Because the next thing I knew, my mother was taking coats, Hershel started pouring wine, and Grandma began passing out hugs like she had nothing else to give. I, on the other hand, still found myself unable to move.

My mother put a hand on my arm. "I asked the Hawthornes to join us for dinner this evening. Someone had to stay here for the holidays and Richard volunteered, being the senior officer and the only one whose family would be able to join him."

"Not to mention I'm a terrible cook." Sergeant Hawthorne chuckled. "Thankfully Evelyn is not, and her generosity is—"

"Oh, nonsense. It was only natural . . ."

She blushed. It was absurd, and we all knew it. There was nothing natural about this. Saying a thing didn't make it so.

My mother coughed into her shawl again, this time louder and more violently. She waved away Sergeant Hawthorne's look of concern. "I'm fine. Dinner's almost ready. Just finishing up the posole. Richard, Jo . . . won't you please have a seat? Olive, could you get Jo a cup of cider? And bring the wine in case anyone needs a refill."

Her words came out in one long string, all mashed together. I blinked as I tried to piece together her instructions. Cider. I was supposed to get cider. For Jo. Who was in my living room, settling onto the couch like she belonged there.

I retreated to the dining room and poured a mug of the thick honey-colored liquid, setting it on a tray with an open bottle of wine. Ma had returned to the kitchen, banging plates with more force than necessary. Grandma, however, had settled in next to the Hawthornes.

"So, Sergeant Hawthorne," she was saying, "You don't mind if I call you Sergeant, do you? I believe a man of your stature deserves a certain level of respect." Ever the conversationalist, she didn't wait for him to answer before continuing. "Tell me, how is morale among our boys? This war . . ."

Turning my back, I snatched the wine bottle and tipped it to my lips. I'd never had a drink before. The bitterness lingered on my tongue long after I'd swallowed. My stomach swirled dangerously for a moment before warmth began to flow outward, tingling my toes, a sensation not entirely unpleasant. My mother would kill me if she caught me. But she'd invited them here in the first place. What did she expect? I took one more discreet sip before gathering the tray and walking into the living room, a little bit of liquid boldness flowing through my veins.

"A toast," Grandma said when everyone's cup was in hand. "To our boys. May God keep them safe and bring them home soon."

I glanced at Uncle Hershel. Grandma had brought up the "G word." Surely he'd have a comment, a snarl, something, anything to snap the world right again.

But he merely nodded, a smile on his wine-stained lips. "Cheers."

What was *happening* here?

"Dinner is ready!"

The party moved into the makeshift dining room. It was really just a breakfast nook, no more than two or three chairs and the round table Grandpa had made out of a baling spool. But Ma was determined to make it work. Bodies pressed against the adobe walls, struggling to free their seats without scraping the wood or pinching fingers.

The wine inside me found the whole ordeal hilarious. No one else did.

"I hope you like tamales." My mother placed a heaping plate of steaming corn husks in front of us. "It's our Christmas Eve tradition. And Olive's favorite."

She winked at me. I did not wink back.

"Some are chicken and some are vegetable, since pork is in low supply." She was talking too fast, trying to fill the gap with excuses. "But I have both red and green chile. And potatoes and posole, stuffing and sopaipillas. I tried to mix some of our traditions with yours, so I'm—"

"It's perfect, Evelyn." Sergeant Hawthorne put a hand on her wrist. It was only for a moment; he pulled away quickly. But not quickly enough.

I narrowed my eyes as his gaze flitted in my direction, then back down again. Inside that touch, there was another secret. Another brick in the wall being erected between my mother and me. Suddenly I wanted nothing more than another sip of wine, sour stomach or not.

"Well, are we gonna eat or ain't we?"

I was the lone holdout against laughter. Everyone else apparently found Hershel's rudeness endearing. Plates were filled, condiments passed, a simple prayer uttered, though no one but Grandma and Jo partook. I kept my head lowered and my mouth filled with food, an island in the midst of this false Christmas. When dessert was served, I begged a full belly and excused myself to the living room. Once there, I snuck another sip of wine.

I turned to find Jo sitting on the couch, a plate of pumpkin pie held daintily in her lap. She smiled.

I scowled and wrapped myself in Hershel's easy chair.

"So have you heard from Avery lately?" Sergeant Hawthorne's voice floated in from the dining room, followed by the sound of my mother's cough and a rough smack. Uncle Hershel, no doubt, "helping" her.

"You alright there?" The next smack was lighter but still audible.

"Yes," she croaked. "I'm sorry. The wine . . . it just . . . it went down the wrong pipe." She coughed again. "But to answer your question, no. No, we haven't heard from Avery. Not lately."

"Last we knew he was somewhere in the Pacific," Uncle Hershel interjected.

The tamales curdled in my stomach. Avery, in the Pacific? How did they know? When had they heard from him? And why hadn't anyone told me?

Jo's fork was frozen in midbite. When she saw me looking, she pretended she hadn't been listening by shoving the pie in her mouth hastily.

"We're in the same boat," Sergeant Hawthorne was saying. "It's been months since I've heard from Josh. Although mail service is limited here with all the classified—" He bit down on this last sentence, swallowed, then started over. "His last letter said France, but I imagine he's made his way into Germany by now. Most of the boys have."

"Won't be long before they're storming into Berlin!" Grandma's tone was triumphant.

"Ah, my son will be the front line of that march, if he has any say in it. Always was a . . ."

But I didn't bother listening to the rest of it. I was too busy staring at Jo. She was concentrating on her pie as if she couldn't remember how to eat. Every bite required the attention and care of a tightwire act.

"You have a brother." It was supposed to be a question, but the wine muddled my tongue.

"Yes." She still did not look at me.

"In the war."

"Yes."

I took another sip of wine, no longer bothering to hide it. I shouldn't be surprised there were parts of her life she hadn't told me about. But I was. Not because there were things about her I didn't know, but because *this* was one of them. Jo Hawthorne, Miss Perfect, Miss Joyful, Miss Peace and Prayer, had a brother in the war, just like me. That, in addition to dealing with a sick grandmother and being forced from her home . . . just like me. Beneath that calm exterior, she had the same uncertainty, the same fear, the same worry.

And yet despite the brokenness and heartache that bound us, we lived in two entirely separate worlds. Mine was dark; hers was inexplicably, overwhelmingly light. And it was that realization that somehow made everything else unbearable.

I took another drink, trying to drown myself inside the bitter liquid.

"Olive, maybe you shouldn't . . ."

"Fine," I shot back at her. My tongue felt heavy. "Is fine. I mean, *it*. It's fine."

Laughter drifted in from the kitchen, my mother's mixing with Sergeant Hawthorne's in a way I hadn't heard in years. Even Uncle Hershel's guffaws sounded genuine.

Jo glanced over her shoulder. "Maybe we should go back in there and join them? Get you a glass of water?"

I licked my lips, rolling the fuzz around in my mouth. I wanted a glass of water. More than that, I wanted to join my family, to laugh, and to make-believe myself into the past. I wanted warmth and joy in spite of it all.

But those things were out of reach for me. Because I was no Jo Hawthorne. And for the first time ever, a part of me wished that I was.

Something else rose in my throat. This time it wasn't grief. I pushed past Jo and out the door, into the cold night air. My goal was the outhouse, but I didn't make it.

Chile and wine exited my body violently, coating the ground near the barn and splattering the whitewashed walls. The smell of it was enough to make me retch again. And again. And again.

"Olive?" my mother called from the doorway. "Are you okay?"

"Yes," I barked, my throat cracking. "I'm fine. Just . . . going to the bathroom."

"Well, you forgot the lantern," she called. "You're gonna trip over a rock, running like that."

I closed my eyes and swallowed a wave of nausea. "Right. Sorry. I . . . really had to go." My mouth tasted of bile. "Just leave it on the stoop. I'll come grab it."

"Are you sure? I can bring it to you."

"No, no, I'm coming. I'll get it. You just . . . you go on inside. I'll be back in a minute."

I waited until I heard the door click before stumbling to the front stoop. The glow from the lantern was muted. I'd forgotten just how dark it got out here. The massive New Mexico sky was filled with stars I hadn't seen in months behind Alamogordo's city lights. They blurred together as I staggered from the house, their beauty corrupted by the ground spinning beneath my feet.

I felt like I might be sick again. I couldn't go inside yet. Instead, I pushed my way into the barn, where I tripped over a bucket and nearly impaled myself on an overturned rake. The panic sent a surge of blood toward my head, causing my veins to throb. I slid to the ground in the corner and rubbed my temples with numb fingers, willing the floor to still. The cold was biting, but not enough to freeze the smell of gasoline and manure in the air. I felt another swell of nausea rise within me. This wouldn't do; I'd have to wait it out somewhere else.

I rose on one knee, grabbing a nearby shelf for support, only to have it collapse under my weight. A pile of gloves and overalls cascaded down onto me. Cursing under my breath, I gathered them in my hands to replace them but stopped when I felt something hard inside one of the pockets. I dug it out, ignoring my swimming head.

It was a notepad. Plain and nondescript, it had an unmarked brown cover over yellow paper. Probably Grandpa's. Farming notes, most likely.

I flipped open the cover. In handwriting much neater than any man's were numbers. Page after page of numbers and letters. Nearly a dozen, each line filled. I ran my finger though it, blinking, trying to find something familiar, something that stuck out. But the writing swirled on the page, combining into an undecipherable jumble. One of the pages was folded over, three small letters tucked into the corner: *GUS.*

Gus? What's a gus? Or is it a who?

And then, beneath it, the letters *MMRS* with the word *STRAWBERRY* in small block letters, crossed out, replaced with the word *LIME.*

I was drunker than I thought.

"Olive? Are you still out there?"

"Coming!" I shoved the notepad back inside the pocket and stuffed the overalls onto the shelf.

Ma stood on the front stoop, one hand shielding her eyes, squinting against the darkness. The glowing orange tip from her cigarette bobbed between her fingertips.

I approached slowly, begging my stomach to behave.

"There you are!" she said. "I was worried you were . . ." Her eyes flickered toward the barn. "Everything okay?"

The look was so quick I could have imagined it. But I knew didn't. Even in my woozy state, I knew I didn't. Because in that look, there was something I'd never seen before in my mother's eyes. Something unmistakably like panic.

Soberness chilled my heart, even as another round of queasiness filled my gut. For some reason, my mother did not want me inside the barn.

"Fine," I said. "I . . . tripped. Just like you said I would." The lie released easily, the wine removing the edge from my voice.

"Goodness." The word came out like a breath. Her shoulders relaxed beneath a warm smile. "Well, let's get you inside."

While the rest of the group settled in for a game of dominoes, I begged a headache and retreated to the back bedroom to lie down. The room spun and my head throbbed. I retched several more times before settling into a restless sleep.

I dreamed of a storm of letters and numbers, encircling my mother and sweeping her away. The fear in her eyes was still etched in my mind when I awoke hours later to vomit again.

CHAPTER TWELVE

JO

MARCH 1952

It was the smell that got her. Outside the doors of the church, time had moved on, *progress* was the word of day, and—no matter how much Alamogordo clung to its small-town past—the streets buzzed with the promise of a future that was already here. The cloak of memory draped over every building could do nothing to stifle the "days of the rockets" just ahead.

But inside the sanctuary of the church, the smell of spent candles and polished wood, worn carpet and cracked leather—the outside world had no chance against these scents. Within these walls, it would forever and always be 1945.

She still knew the way to Pastor Hamilton's office. Naturally. Because in here, she was Jo Hawthorne, good little church girl, again. Optimistic. Innocent. Hopelessly naive and on fire for the Lord.

Only she wasn't. And the dichotomy between her two selves had never felt so poignant.

She smoothed down her itchy gray sweater and wiped her hands on the stiff khaki of her slacks. Those two items, in addition to a wide black belt, were the only decent things she'd found in a small boutique on New York Avenue called Chappell's. For all its emphasis on the future, Alamogordo's available fashion still screamed rural chic. Taking a deep breath, she continued down the aisle, passing the window without looking. *That* window. It was late morning now, and she knew the sunlight would be hitting the glass just so, making the colors sparkle and dance. It would be beautiful. But she couldn't look. Images of Jesus surrounded her and yet it was only that window where she truly felt His eyes watching, staring at her. No, not *at* her. He was looking *through* her to the tangled darkness of her heart. To the truth.

She didn't exhale until she'd left the sanctuary, closing the door of the hallway firmly behind her.

Pastor Hamilton was, as expected, hunched over his desk, leafing through a stack of paper and scribbling notes with a pen that clicked as it moved. Books still spilled from the shelves lining the walls of his office, though the stacks of them on the floor had grown taller. Mugs sat scattered haphazardly throughout the room. Jo knew most of them were probably half-full of day-old coffee, set down in haste and then forgotten, replaced by a fresher cup, which was also soon abandoned. The thought made Jo let out a small chuckle.

Pastor Hamilton looked up from his work. His face was fuller, the lines around his eyes more pronounced, but otherwise—much like the church itself—he looked exactly the same. He blinked several times before a wide smile broke not just on his lips, but across his entire face.

"Jo! Jo Hawthorne! Is that really you?"

His chair nearly toppled in his rush to meet her. Jo stiffened momentarily under his embrace, fighting the impulse to flee. How long had it been since she'd allowed anyone to hug her? To touch her even? And yet she found herself crumbling, that rush of safety she'd always felt in this place pushing against the wall she'd erected inside when she'd left.

"It's so good to see you! Sit, sit." He gestured to her usual spot in the corner.

She sat. Same chair. Same view. Different Jo.

"What brings you back to this neck of the woods?" He settled himself behind his desk, interlocking his long fingers over a yellow legal pad. He always wrote his sermons on yellow paper. He said it was impossible to be anything but joyful staring at the color yellow.

Gosh, the things she remembered.

"How long has it been? Five years?"

"Almost seven."

"Seven years!" He sat back, causing his chair to squeak—he still hadn't fixed that squeak!—and scratched the back of his head with one hand. "Seems hard to believe. Well, how have you been? What have you been up to?"

"I've been doing mission work, actually. South America, Asia, all over, really."

"Is that so?"

She nodded. "Humanitarian stuff. Health care, medicine, that kind of thing. But also some housing, schools, churches. Whatever came up."

"Spreading the love of Jesus." He grinned. "That's amazing, Jo. Really amazing."

She shrugged, looking away. The joy and pride in his eyes was excruciating. "So what about you?"

"Same old, same old," he said with a laugh. "But the church is doing well. Growing. Slowly, but growing nonetheless. The town and the times are a-changing, as they say. We're trying to figure out how to change with them but still remain the same. Lot of new folks comin' into town with the military, and we're trying to reach 'em before work becomes the only god they know."

The hangnail on her pinkie started to bleed. She hadn't even realized she'd been picking at it.

"So," Pastor Hamilton said, "what brings you back to Alamogordo?"

"My father." It surprised her how easily the words came. She'd thought it would be hard to bring it up; somehow, after all these years—and all these changes—Pastor Hamilton's very presence still had the ability to loosen her tongue.

"Oh?"

She took a deep breath. No reason to hold back now. "He's . . . not well."

Distress flashed across his face. "I see. I'm sorry to hear that. Trinity?"

"They think so."

He pressed his lips together. "Doesn't surprise me. Ever since Trinity—and what a word for it, *Trinity*—ever since then, there's been so much . . . affliction. The government says—officially at least—there's no correlation, but I've lived here my entire life, and the rate of cancers in people, animals, you name it, has simply exploded in the past few years. And the only thing that's changed was that doggone test. I'm just a simple preacher, of course, but even I can connect the dots. I'm actually working together with some of the elders to start up a ministry specifically for those affected. I wish I could do more but . . ." He leaned back once again, letting out a deep sigh through his nose. "Progress, they call it, but at what cost?"

"But how can they get away with that?" Jo asked. "If the test is making people sick? How is that even legal?"

"No proof," he replied with a grimace. "In their rush to send up the bomb and end the war, they didn't take the time to think about what would come afterward. The damage it might leave behind." He rubbed his forehead. "From what I hear, scientists have been collecting data. It's a start, I suppose. But what about the people who are sick now? The people who are still being exposed every single day—with the water they drink, the food they eat, the homes in which they live? What are *those* people supposed to do?"

Jo crossed her arms over her chest, feeling suddenly cold. In her mind, she saw her father's emaciated face, heard the croak of his stolen voice. She tried to suppress an involuntary shudder at the memory and—if Pastor Hamilton's words were true—at the image of thousands of others just like him, scattered all across the Tularosa Basin.

It made her feel sick. It made her feel sad. It made her feel angry.

And therein was the danger: that it made her feel anything at all. Because she was not here to get involved. She was not here to care.

He pressed a hand lightly to his lips. "But all that is neither here nor there. Not when it's personal. How are you? With everything, I mean."

Jo's throat tightened. Even if she'd been able, she couldn't have answered him. She couldn't lie—not to this man, not in this place—and she couldn't tell the truth. Instead she raised her hand and gave a shake of her head, waiting for the ache to subside, hoping her gesture passed for stoicism rather than evasion.

"Fine," she said thickly. "I'm fine."

He pulled his head back slightly and gave a tentative nod.

"I was actually . . ." She paused. She needed to pull herself together before she gave too much away. "I was wondering if you'd seen him."

"Seen him?"

"At the church, I mean. After I left."

Pastor Hamilton's lips puckered as he considered. "No," he said slowly. "No, I never saw him."

"Are you sure? He might have come in and sat near the back." Her belt was too tight. It was digging into her navel, making it hard to breathe.

"I suppose, yes, he could have. But I don't recall ever having seen him here. Why do you—?"

"So you never spoke to him?" She steadied her voice, trying to check the rising dread.

"No, Jo, I'm sorry."

Her shoulders drooped. It was stupid of her to have gotten her hopes up. It wasn't like her atheist father would ever set foot in a church. The cross he'd drawn in her palm wasn't a cross; it didn't mean anything. He clearly hadn't meant for her to come here, of all places, for answers.

It was just the cancer. Not her father. And certainly not God.

Maybe she really was still that same silly, naive fool who'd boarded a bus all those years ago.

Pastor Hamilton let out a small cough. "Well, um, since you're here, let me ask *you* a question. How's Olive?"

Her hands clenched around each other. "What?"

"Olive Alexander." He let out a soft laugh. "You two certainly got into some shenanigans, didn't you? How is she?"

"I don't . . ."

The smile faded from his lips. "Oh, I'm sorry. I assumed . . . well, I assumed you'd kept in touch, seeing as how you're friends and—"

"We're not."

For the first time since she'd stepped into his office, something changed in his eyes. It was as if, for a split second, he saw the truth. Of who she was, who she had become. The lie she'd worn like armor dissolved in one knowing glance, crushing her beneath the weight of his unspoken disappointment. And then, with just a blink, it was gone, compassion and nostalgia once again emanating from his smile.

The sting of that moment, however, was not so easily repaired. Jo returned her attention to her hangnail. "I mean, we were," she mumbled. "But I haven't spoken to her since I left."

"Oh." The word was simple yet harsh. "Well, I haven't seen her for years, so I thought I'd ask. Last I knew she'd moved back to the ranch with her mother and grandmother. Edna passed away about five years ago . . ." He paused, giving Jo a moment to react.

She didn't. At least not on the outside.

"And the last time I saw Olive was at the funeral, I believe. If I remember correctly, she didn't stick around. I tried to talk to her, give her some words of comfort, but I don't know that it really got through. It was like she wasn't really there at all, like she just wanted to get the thing done and get out of there."

He leaned forward suddenly. "Now that I think about it . . . yes; yes, I have seen your father."

Jo had the sensation of tripping, though she was sitting completely still.

"Just that once. He was there. At the funeral, I mean. Sat with the family, arm around Olive, hand on Evelyn's shoulder. I only remember because I was surprised. I wasn't aware there was any sort of relationship there. Aside from Army business, I mean."

Jo kept her eyes on her bleeding nail. She couldn't let him see just how hard his words had landed. Like a punch to the gut or a stab to the heart. Edna was dead. And her father had been there. Not for her; never for her. He'd made sure of that. But he'd been there. With Olive. *For* Olive.

Not only had they all pushed her away, but then they'd come back together. Without her.

There was an acidic taste in her mouth. She tried swallowing several times, gagging on her own tongue. "So the ranch," she managed. "Last you knew she was at the ranch?"

"Yes," Pastor Hamilton said quietly. "That was the last I'd heard."

Jo stood suddenly. She closed her eyes as the blood rushed to her head. Her muscles felt weak, her very soul crumbling within.

"Thank you," she said. "It was really nice to see you, Pastor Hamilton. But I have to get going."

"Jo—"

She kept her back turned as she gathered her bag, still trying to swallow the agony. She had to get it down, way down, behind the wall where it was supposed to be, before it could consume her. Again. She made it to the threshold of his office before a hand on her shoulder caused her to pause. And that one pause—a fraction of a second, a blink of an eye—was all it took.

If she'd still been able to cry, she would have then. It was the closest she'd come in years.

Instead, the pounding of her own heart swallowed her. Pain radiated from her chest. The room was spinning, and she was falling. She was only vaguely aware of Pastor Hamilton's embrace, his whispered words of comfort as he led her to his battered couch. They were the only things keeping her from collapsing completely into the darkness.

"Jo, please tell me what's wrong. Why are you really here? What's going on?"

She tried to shake her head but only managed the slightest of movements with what little energy remained in her. She concentrated on returning her breathing to normal, on sending the ache in her chest back into its assigned place.

He sighed, sitting back against the cracked leather. "Okay. I won't force it. You don't have to talk to me. But I . . . well, I just hope you at least talk to Him." His eyes flitted toward the ceiling as Jo's went downward.

Of all the things he could have said, of all the advice he could have given . . . If only he knew. Or maybe it was because somehow he did.

Jo hadn't spoken to God in years. He hadn't spoken to her for even longer.

On all her mission trips, in every project in which she professed to be working for the Lord, she had been silent. And so had He. Her heart was as far from God's as His presence had been from her since that day.

Since Trinity. The day they all left . . . including Him.

She had tried. Oh, how she had tried. She had chased Him all over the world but come up empty. Well, not empty. Pain and betrayal, loneliness and grief filled the shell where her faith had once lived. And this journey of disbelief had brought her right back here, where it had all started, to the place where He had fled. The only thing in her life she had ever been sure of evaporated that day, along with everything else in that cursed New Mexico desert.

She stood on legs she could not feel. "Thank you again," she murmured. "I have to . . . I have to go."

Pastor Hamilton rose but did not try to stop her. Instead, he held his hands behind his back as his chin dropped slightly toward his chest. "Well, it was nice to see you again, Jo. I hope you'll stop by again before you leave. If you get a chance."

She gave a half smile she hoped would suffice rather than the answer she could not give and he would not believe. She reached out as if to touch him again but changed her mind and swept from the office. Keeping her eyes on the frayed carpet, she walked through the sanctuary, looking up only when she reached the wooden doors. It was then that she noticed a sign hanging just over the frame.

It was new. It had to have been new. She'd never noticed it in all her time here. And yet the wood was worn, the etched letters faded with time.

"You will seek me and find me when you seek me with all your heart." Jeremiah 29:13.

Another twinge, another nudge. Only a few short years ago, she would have taken it for a sign. The Word of God speaking to her, telling her exactly what she needed to hear, when she needed to hear it. But it wasn't possible anymore.

It was too late now. God was a shadow and her heart too far gone. She pushed aside the notion, pulling Pastor Hamilton's words from the depths instead. Her father and Olive, together. Without her. Fresh, comforting rage spilled forth once more, sealing the crack threatening the wall she'd spent years building.

She pushed out into the sunlight. The only thing she was seeking now was Olive Alexander . . . and the answers that would put an end to this nightmare once and for all.

◆ ❖ ◆

Back at the motel, she splashed cold water on her face and phoned the front office to confirm another night's stay. Before hanging up, she asked the clerk for the number of a taxi company, not surprised to learn there wasn't one, and settled for the location of a rental car company instead. Another quick phone call led to the irritating—but also not surprising—revelation that they only had five cars, and all were currently in use.

Aggravated, she slammed down the receiver. There had to be another way. Maybe there was a bus that passed by there? Unlikely but worth a shot. She stuffed her hair under her hat and stepped out into the sun once again. The heat had intensified while she'd been inside, which only deepened her bad mood.

"Jo! Hey—Jo!"

She jumped and spun around, shielding her eyes. Charlie was jogging across the street, waving at her. Despite the blazing heat, when he reached her, not a bead of sweat could be found on his face.

"Hey," he said again. "I thought that was you."

"Are you following me?" She hadn't meant to say it out loud. Or maybe she had. The morning had frayed what little nerves she had left.

His brow crinkled but his smile remained. "What? No. No, of course not. I was grabbing some lunch." He gestured back in the direction he'd come, toward a shabby diner with opaque windows. The words *Plaza Café* were emblazoned on the top in dull, unlit neon. "And I happened to see you."

A prickle of regret. "Oh," she replied. "Right."

"How did it go? At the church, I mean?"

When he'd dropped her off at the boutique, she'd told him she was going to visit an old friend at the church afterward. It was as much as she was willing to share, a sentiment that her disastrous chat with Pastor Hamilton certainly hadn't changed.

"It was fine."

"That's good." He pulled a cigarette from his pocket but paused before lighting. "You want to grab a bite with me?"

She shook her head even as the smell from across the street caused her stomach to rumble with sudden hunger. Her motel vending machine breakfast—a bag of Blue Bell chips and a Coca-Cola—felt years rather than hours in the past. "No, I'm in a hurry. I was actually on my way . . ." Her voice trailed off, a very bad idea suddenly materializing inside her brain.

"On your way where?"

She bit the inside of her cheek. It was wrong. He was a man very obviously pining for a date, and taking advantage of that was wrong.

But she *was* hungry. And she needed a car.

"How would you feel about getting lunch somewhere else?"

Charlie's face reddened. A line of smoke trailed from his mouth as he smiled. "Sure, Jo. Wherever you want."

CHAPTER THIRTEEN

OLIVE

JANUARY 1945

A mild December trickled into a frozen January. The weather alternated between snow and rain, the sun never daring to show its face among such cold, wet wretchedness. My Christmas hangover lasted into the New Year as a queasiness I was able to pass off as the flu when my grandmother and I returned from the ranch. Physical misery mingled with my despondency, and I spent the rest of break wrapped in a quilt, trying—and failing—to immerse myself in *Tom Sawyer*, *Robinson Crusoe*, and any other world far beyond this one.

I didn't want to think about Jo, her brother, or my own. I didn't want to think about my mother and Sergeant Hawthorne. I didn't want to think about the smiles, the giggles, that knowing touch between them. Most of all, though, I didn't want to think about the ranch. The never-ending whispers about what was happening in the desert, the fake hominess of the place that was not my home, the unfamiliarity of what used to be the most familiar place in the world, from the reorganized casita to the weird notebook of scribbles in the shed. I felt unnerved and disoriented. Nothing made sense there anymore.

I didn't make sense anymore.

In the hallways of Alamogordo High School, the mood wasn't much better. The after-holiday doldrums had the student body firmly in their grip; the constant freezing drizzle and gloomy sky didn't help. New Mexicans are used to the sun. Take it away for too long, and a sort of melancholy settles over us, as if deprived of food or water. Never had I seen the weather in such a foul mood—or been in such a state myself.

"Olive!"

Like a long-lost ray of sunshine, Tim Bucknam broke through the glumness, maneuvering through the crowd with a wave and a grin. He wore a blue button-down tucked into jeans. One lock of dark hair fell across his forehead.

I felt my face flush. "Hi."

"How was your Christmas?"

I wanted to laugh. Christmas? Where to even begin? "Alright" was all I said, though. "How was yours?"

He shrugged. "First one without my brother. Everything was the same . . . and yet nothing was." He shook his head. "I know that sounds crazy."

I reached a hand into my locker, sighing. "No. Actually, it's not crazy at all."

He gave me a half smile, showing just a glimpse of those perfect white teeth. "So listen." He readjusted the notebook under his arm. "I was wondering if . . . well, since you couldn't go to the winter dance . . . if maybe we could . . . do something else?"

Inside my locker, my fingers froze around the spine of the book.

"The new Humphrey Bogart movie is playing at the Sands Theater. *To Have and Have Not.* I thought maybe we could go see it. Only if you want to, of course." He pressed his lips together, cheeks reddening and making him impossibly more handsome.

I stood there with one arm still stuck inside my locker. Tim Bucknam was asking me out. Again. I hadn't blown it; he was giving me another chance.

Say something, Olive. Anything. Anything at all will do.

But my mouth only twitched. My fingers grew sweaty around my math book.

After several seconds, he cleared his throat, toeing the ground with his shoe. "It's okay if you don't want to. I just figured I'd ask. It's no big deal. It's—"

"What about Melody?" I blurted.

"What?"

"Melody Jones. I thought . . ."

"Oh . . . that." He tipped his head to the side. "We're just friends. I think maybe she wanted more but . . ."

"Oh."

The third period bell rang. Startled, I dropped the book from my locker onto the ground. I snatched it up as bodies swelled around us, talking, laughing, and rushing toward open classroom doors, taking all the air with them as they went.

Tim took a step backward. "It's okay if you don't want to," he repeated, glancing over his shoulder down the hall. "It was just a thought. I mean—"

"Yes."

He paused midstep. "What?"

"Yes." There it was. So help me, I'd actually said it out loud. "Yes, I'd love to."

Visible relief flooded his face. "Great! This Friday okay?"

I bit down on the grin trying to stretch across my face. I couldn't let it give away too much of my giddiness. "Yes. I mean, I have to check with my grandma first. Pretty sure I'm still grounded but I think I've paid at least part of my dues. I'm sure it will be fine."

In truth, I had no idea if it would be fine. But I would do everything in my power to make it be. Extra chores, extra church even. Everything was a mess. I needed Tim's smile. It felt like the only right thing in the world, and I was not going to say no to it again.

"I'll pick you up at seven?"

He fumbled with a pen to take down my grandmother's address. When he finally walked away, I couldn't even be sure I'd given him the right one. Because it wasn't me telling him. The real Olive Alexander was a hundred feet overhead, floating on a cloud. I was oblivious to the scolding from Mr. Dusky about being late to class. In my head, I was already leaving school behind. And not only that. I was leaving behind Christmas, Ma, the ranch, and the worries of this week. In my mind, I was already heading for Friday night.

The only thing I couldn't leave behind, unfortunately, was Jo. Although I'd managed to dodge her in school, strategically ducking into bathrooms when I saw her in the hall and practically running from the classes we shared as soon as the bell rang, I couldn't avoid her forever. Because today we had an appointment with Pastor Hamilton, sorting and tagging items for the church rummage sale. And skipping that appointment would surely dash any hope I had at securing a pass for my date Friday night. So I had no choice.

I would have to face her. For Tim.

The rummage sale had been Jo's idea. Naturally. Another fundraising plan she'd pitched to Pastor Hamilton with the earnestness of one who seemed to actually *enjoy* punishment. The church had been collecting donations for a few weeks, and the choir room was filled to the brim with people's unwanted junk. The entire room smelled like mothballs. I had a headache the moment I stepped inside.

Jo was already there, bent over a notepad with Pastor Hamilton, who was gesturing to a stack of boxes in the corner. He smiled when he saw me.

"Ah, Olive. There you are." He pressed a clipboard into my hand. "I was just explaining our system to Jo. I need you to take inventory of every item we have in here, writing it on these pages and tagging it according to color code. Red for the bigger items like furniture and appliances, blue for clothes, yellow for toys, orange for home goods, and green for things like books and records. It's a lot of work, but it will make it easier for us to keep track of what's been sold in the long run. Does that make sense?"

I nodded.

"I have to finish up some sermon notes, so I'm going to leave you girls to it. But I'll come check on you in about an hour or so."

He closed the door with a click behind him, leaving Jo and me alone for the first time since Christmas.

I grabbed the nearest box. It was filled with chipped dishes and half-used candles. If this was the type of thing we were selling, we'd have enough funds for the new window . . . in about seven hundred years. I slapped an orange tag on each of the items and made a notation on my clipboard.

One box down. Fifty-eight to go.

I tried to look busy. Too busy to chitchat, at least, in hopes Jo would get the hint and focus on her own tasks rather than me.

It didn't work.

I had just finished attaching a yellow tag to a bald teddy bear with one missing eye when she spoke up:

"How have you been?" She held up a dingy white garment that might, at one time, have been a dress.

"Fine," I answered, an edge to my voice.

Jo didn't seem to notice. "Good." She folded the dress and attached a blue tag near the collar. "I had fun," she added as an afterthought. "With your mom, I mean. At your house. Your family is nice."

I thumbed through a stack of old magazines, pausing at a copy of *Life* with Joe DiMaggio on the cover. I concentrated on it like I gave more than two hoots about baseball.

"I was sorry you got sick." She placed tags on a pile of scarves. "I know there's been a stomach bug going around."

For the first time, our eyes met. She knew the reason I'd gotten sick. She'd seen me drink the wine. But her eyes spoke of our shared secret, of her complicity and discretion. She hadn't told. Wouldn't tell. Not even now.

I looked away. That knot of emotions I always seemed to get when I was around Jo was starting to tangle again. No matter what she thought, this did not bond us. I didn't want to share this secret with her. I didn't want to share anything with her.

And yet denying it wouldn't change the fact that I did.

"So your brother . . . ," she started.

"Please . . . ," I said softly, my throat thick. "I don't want to talk about my brother."

"Okay. I understand."

Turning my back to her, I flipped open the cover of the nearest book. *Harper's Reader for Children*. I slapped a tag on the title page and jotted a notation on my paper, hoping Pastor Hamilton would be able to read writing scribbled through blurry eyes.

"My brother enlisted the day he turned eighteen," she said.

I grabbed another book from the pile. She'd changed topics like I'd requested, though this one wasn't much better. I almost snapped at her to be quiet. But something held me back. Because a part of me *did* want to hear her story, if only to reassure myself that it really was different from my own.

"I haven't heard from him in months. It's like Hitler draped Europe in this giant black curtain. No news gets in, no news gets out. Sounds like the Pacific theater is the same way."

I flipped through a couple more books, trying not to think about Avery swirling inside a massive black cloud as bullets flew at him from the shadows.

"We were close," she said. "Had to be, with my father gone all the time and Grandma . . . well, Grandma being the way she was." She glanced at me quickly before looking back down at her paper. "Not that it was her fault, of course. It's a sickness."

Thinking about Grandma was even worse than thinking about Avery. Just that morning she'd been in a tizzy, searching for her missing glasses. I'd found them in the oven. When I'd handed them to her, she'd sputtered, telling me I must have been mistaken, that her glasses had been on her nightstand the whole time.

"I could have stayed in California after she died if Josh hadn't left. Just the two of us. Finished school, gone into missionary work—that's what I want to do, you know—and been happy. But he told me he had to go and that I had to do my part, which was coming here."

Avery had said something similar, that day on the mesa before he'd left. *We all have our parts to play.* Somehow the words sounded different coming out of Jo's mouth.

"But doesn't that make you mad?" My question came out fast and sharp, as if it had been bubbling on my tongue for much longer than it actually took me to say it.

Jo stopped in midfold. Faded denim lay draped over her arm. "What?"

"He left you. Not caring about what you wanted, not caring about your plans. And your dad—just packing you up and moving you. Didn't matter what you wanted or how you felt."

"I don't really think that was it."

"Wasn't it, though? They didn't care about you, either one of them. Not really."

I stuffed down a twinge of sympathy. So help me, I actually felt sorry for Jo; I understood what she'd gone through. Boy, did I understand. And yet it was anger that roared to the surface instead. Anger was easier. These words, these feelings—they weren't really for Jo. They were for my mother. For Hershel. Maybe even a little bit for Avery.

But none of them were here. Jo was. And I needed her to share in my anger not to ease it, but to validate it.

"It was . . . it was the right thing to do. Christ calls us to—"

"Don't go bringing religion into it. Do you really think Christ means for us to be shooting and dropping bombs on each other? I don't even believe in Him, and I'm pretty sure that God has nothing to do with this war."

"You're putting words in my mouth. I never said that. I was trying to say Christ tells us to go where He calls—and while He goes with us wherever He sends us, the calling itself looks different to different people. For my brother, it was to enlist. For your brother too. We serve best when we serve in *Him*, not in ourselves."

"Serve." The word came out like a curse. And it was. I hated it. I'd heard it too much. It had been pressed on me from every angle, like a melody stuck in my head. Only this melody was one that condemned rather than pacified.

Avery was gone. Uncle Hershel was indifferent. My mother didn't want me at home. And here . . . my grandmother barely even registered my identity. Everyone everywhere telling me to *serve*, but how? There was no place where I fit; no place where I was needed, where I belonged. I had no part to play.

And no one seemed to care. Least of all this God Jo kept talking about.

"Yes," Jo said slowly. "To serve—"

"Leave the sermon for the preacher, Jo. If it makes you feel better, go ahead and pretend God had some grand plan for all of this. But if He did, I'd say His plan is a pretty doggone crummy one. Even downright mean. Doesn't sound like a god I'd want anything to do with, and I'm not sure why you would either. You can pretty it all up with whatever words you want: service or sacrifice or whatever. But when it comes down to it, they didn't care about you. Not really. They just wanted to get you out of the way. You were abandoned. Period."

Jo's lip quivered. Her wide blue eyes brimmed with tears.

I turned from her and grabbed another box, this one filled with old records. I busied myself sorting them into piles. From across the room, I heard Jo cough several times, thick and fake. Pretending as if she wasn't crying. In between sniffles, silence wove itself into a curtain separating us.

I had won. Finally. And yet somehow it felt like a loss.

I'd broken Jo Hawthorne. Her shiny, happy exterior had proven to be no match for my needle of truth. I'd thought this was what I wanted, but my triumph tasted sour. Pulling her down hadn't allowed me to float; instead it had only made her drown right alongside me. Shame flared inside me, making it impossible to concentrate on the task at hand. After a few minutes, I let out a long sigh and turned to her, hating what I had to say but knowing I'd hate even more if I didn't.

"Look . . . I . . . I'm sorry. I didn't mean to make you cry. I don't believe in this God stuff, but I shouldn't have . . ." I licked my lips, trying to wet my dry mouth. "All I'm saying is . . . I know what it feels like to be rejected. And even if you don't want to call it that, it still hurts. It's rotten, and it's unfair, and I'm sorry you had to go through it too."

Jo's silvery-blonde hair obscured my view of her face. She gave a small nod but still didn't look at me. She did, however, continue to cry. Louder now. More openly.

Because apparently I was garbage at apologies too.

When Pastor Hamilton returned a short time later, I didn't say goodbye. Instead I mumbled a promise to return next week to finish tagging and swept from the room as quickly as I could. The evening air was brisk on my skin as I walked down Delaware Avenue, trying to shake Jo—and my own guilt—from my mind. I needed a clear head. I had more important things to deal with at the moment.

Like how I was going to convince Grandma to un-ground me long enough for a date with Tim Bucknam.

"Olive? Olive? Is that you?"

"Yes." I shrugged off my jacket. The room was sweltering, just the way Grandma liked it.

She poked her head out from the kitchen. "I have a surprise for you." A butterscotch candy clicked against her teeth as she pulled something from behind her back. "We got a letter from Avery! Well, your mother did. She forwarded it here via post with a note saying you should keep it. There's a whole section written just for you."

I stared at the envelope in her outstretched hand. Avery was alive. Or at least, he had been alive a short while ago. All these months of uncertainty laid to waste with a single piece of paper. I took it from her gingerly, afraid it would disappear. Avery and I had our differences, sure, but this letter was a link to a time before. A time when things weren't perfect but normal. When the Hawthornes didn't exist and life was contained within the boundary lines of our ranch without the interference or confusion of the messy world beyond.

Grandma winked. "I'll give you some privacy. I'm just finishing up dinner."

I settled down on the couch as she disappeared back into the kitchen, the door swinging behind her with a creak. Slowly I pulled the letter from the envelope and unfolded it. A small slip of paper fell into my lap.

What a relief to hear from Avery and know he's okay. I've read it so many times I've practically committed it to memory, so please keep it with you. Read it any time you need a reminder of why we're doing what we're doing. I love you.

Love, Ma

I dropped her note to the couch and picked up Avery's letter. It was surprisingly short. The writing was small and messy, smeared in several places. Aside from our symbol, I'd never seen his handwriting before. Part of me was surprised he even knew how; he'd always balked at any lessons involving reading or writing. I held it close to my face and breathed in, wondering if I could smell him or the ocean or even the jungle, but it smelled only like paper.

I don't know if this letter will reach you. Mail service is spotty around here. But I wanted to let you know that I am well. Cold and tired, but well. We are on a boat somewhere in the Pacific, though I can't tell you exactly where. The motion of the waves made me so sick the first few days, I thought I would die. But there is a lot of work to do on the ship, and it couldn't wait until I grew my sea legs, so I had to work, vomit and all. We're all anxious to get where we're going, ready to fight. The waiting is the worst part.

I'm not sure when I'll be able to write again, but please don't worry. I'm ready for this, and I will write when I can. Probably from an island but maybe from Japan itself! Wouldn't that be something?

Take good care of the ranch, Uncle Hershel. I know you will. And look after yourself, Ma. I'll be home as soon as the war is won and peace is secure.

A gap in the writing. A few scribbled-out words and splotches of ink. Then:

O., I know a lot has been asked of you lately. But please know how proud I am of you. What you're doing is so important, even if it doesn't feel like it. Grandma needs you now more than ever. Thank you for doing what you're doing. When I get home, we'll make a special trip to the cave to celebrate, just me and you. Until then, remember I love you.

Love, Avery

I reread the letter several times slowly, letting each word sink into my body. It was kind and encouraging, a much-needed pick-me-up and distraction from the mess an afternoon with Jo Hawthorne had left in my heart.

There was just one problem. These words were not my brother's. Avery had never called me "O.," never told me he was proud of me, never said "I love you." And he'd certainly never referred to our spot on the mesa as "the cave." It was the burrow. He'd named it himself.

But what was most striking was not what the letter contained; rather, it was what it lacked. Our secret symbol, the mark we'd carved into the rocks, the one he'd written in the dirt on the last night we'd spent together. It was the thing he'd told me to always remember. That mark was the only thing we shared that still meant something between us; he would never have neglected to include it.

Yet it was nowhere to be found.

I stared at the letter, feeling bile rise in the back of my throat. I wanted to believe he'd just forgotten. He was distracted, tired, a man changed by war. But the truth pulled at me; no matter how much I wanted to believe otherwise, the proof was there in front of me, my naive hope dashed by the smudged black ink.

No, this letter was not from my brother. But who was it from? And even more disturbing, why were they pretending to be Avery?

CHAPTER FOURTEEN

JO

MARCH 1952

Jo managed to make small talk through Tularosa, past the quaint shops with their southwestern flair. But as the car maneuvered out into open desert, the dead grass and thorny plants stretching out for miles around them, she gave up any pretense of good humor. She offered no commentary and deflected Charlie's questions with short, dead-end answers. Eventually he retreated into his cigarettes and left Jo to brood behind dark glasses. There was no use pretending. Her mind and her heart were too heavy for such lightness.

Pastor Hamilton's words coiled around her like a serpent. Olive and her father, together at Edna's funeral. She pictured his comforting arm around her shoulders. An embrace he withheld from his daughter offered to a girl who had deserted her. The two of them together, while Jo suffered and grieved alone.

She'd known Olive had let her down. Betrayed her, even. But the image of the two of them together had merged the agony of her friend's broken promises with the wounds inflicted by her father's words. And yet more than injuring her afresh, the pain acted as fuel. It gave new life to her anger. She'd been able to loose some of the poison onto her father; now it was Olive's turn.

It wasn't until they passed Three Rivers, a laughably named outpost in the middle of the desert, that Charlie spoke again. "So do I, uh, just keep going straight?"

"Yes." She did not look at him.

A long exhale. The smell of fresh tobacco. "You're going to have to tell me where we're going eventually. If you mean to actually get there, that is."

"I know."

A pause. There was a slight scratching of fabric as Charlie shifted. "Okay."

More miles passed. They stopped for lunch in Carrizozo, like Jo had promised, though she was barely able to stomach the hot dog she grabbed from a local drive-in. She insisted on paying, despite his protests—this was no date, after all. She—and he—needed to be very clear on that.

"Not hungry?" Charlie asked.

"No. You can have it." She pushed her food in his direction.

"You sure?"

She nodded.

"So," he said in between alternating bites of her hot dog and his cheeseburger, "is there a reason we came all the way out here for lunch? Not saying it wasn't delicious or that the company wasn't spectacular," he added, giving her a wink. "But this was quite a haul for a burger and fries."

She chewed the straw in her Coke bottle. Regret needled at her not for the first time since they'd left Alamogordo. He was so eager to please, so obviously attracted to her. She should never have brought him along. "Charlie," she sighed.

"Jo, it's okay. I'm not stupid. I know you're just using me for my car."

"No, I—"

"It's fine. Really. Being used by a pretty girl—even for my car—isn't necessarily a bad thing."

She looked up, surprised. A dab of mustard lay trapped in the corner of his smile. She couldn't help herself; she laughed.

"What?"

"You have mustard. There." She pointed.

"Here?" He wiped at the opposite corner.

"No!" She giggled. "The other side!"

"Here?" He dabbed the top of his lip.

"No!" She grabbed a napkin and leaned toward him. From here, she could smell his aftershave, see the smattering of freckles on his nose, feel the heat from his skin. Inside her, something stirred.

She wiped the mustard away and scooted quickly back to her side of the seat. There was no time for that. No *room* for that. She straightened her posture. "I need to go see someone. An old fri—" Her voice caught. *Friend* definitely wasn't the right word to describe Olive. Especially now. "Someone I used to know."

He tilted his head slightly, still smiling. Watching her with those *eyes*.

Stop it, she scolded herself. "I didn't . . . Well, I really am sorry. I—"

"Jo, it's fine. I'm happy to help. Just tell me where to go."

There was no malice in his tone, no sense of dismay. Nothing but genuine support.

It made her feel better. And worse.

Charlie eased the car back onto the highway. She directed him to take a left, watching the desert morph abruptly into the blackened rock of a long-dried lava field. It wouldn't be long now. Her stomach twisted, and she suddenly wished she hadn't given Charlie her lunch. It roiled dangerously as they crested a hill, her mouth filling with sour saliva. Then again, maybe it was for the best that she hadn't eaten much.

As quickly as it appeared, the lava field disappeared, replaced by the rolling hills of the Chupadera Mesa. Her memory strained. There used to be a landmark. Something that showed the way to turn. But it had been years. There was no way she'd remember.

"Jo."

Charlie's voice was a million miles away. She was inside her head, digging through memories she'd tried to forget. What was it? What *was* it?

"Here!" she shouted suddenly. "Turn here!"

Her body slammed into Charlie's as he veered right. The back of the Packard fishtailed on the loose gravel. Jo's hand shot out to steady herself, landing way too far up Charlie's leg. She snatched it back as a hint of a smirk crept over his lips. She pushed back to her side and smoothed her hair, willing the heat down from her cheeks.

"Sorry," she said under her breath. She straightened her sunglasses with more force than was necessary.

"About what?" The smirk was gone. In its place was a look of forced innocence.

He was being nice again. Always with the niceness. It was irritating. And irritatingly charming.

For a minute, she wondered if she'd made a mistake. It was a road like all the others they'd passed. No markings, no pavement. Not really a road at all. The long, rambling dirt path seeming to lead to nowhere. Just miles and miles of gently sloping desert covered in scraggly trees and withered brown grass.

Yet something had told her to turn, something she couldn't explain. Called her. *Demanded* her.

It was with a feeling of both relief and dread that she saw the house finally rise from behind a hill. She'd been here only once, but the image haunted her memory. The adobe walls of the casita were just as she remembered, still baking beneath the sun. The main house stood next to it, attached to its smaller counterpart with a curving courtyard wall. The horse corral, the chicken coop, the barn . . . it was all still there. And behind it, rising into the sky, the part of the mesa Olive talked about, the one hill that was just the same—yet completely different—from its mountain sisters.

Charlie pulled the car to a stop and killed the engine. The sudden quiet was deafening.

Jo didn't move. The same determination that had pushed her all these miles was failing now, just feet from her destination.

Beside her, Charlie lit a cigarette. "Do you want me to go with you?" His voice was quiet. Gentle. Kind. Exactly what she *didn't* want at that moment.

In response, she opened the door. Behind her, she heard Charlie exit the car and follow after her. She thought about telling him to stay, but she didn't. A pause would give her nerves another chance to fail.

She took a step toward the main house, then changed her mind; something inside her told her to head for the casita instead. Memories, perhaps. The main house was foreign to her, after all. She'd never been inside. The war was long over, but it still seemed more like construction barracks than an actual home. She couldn't picture Olive in there.

Then again, she could barely picture Olive anywhere anymore. Except beside her father.

It wasn't until she was on the front landing that she noticed all wasn't as it had first appeared. The place *had* changed. There were cracks in the adobe. The tile roof was sun-bleached, its clay color faded from brownish-orange to a sickly shade of pink. One corner of the courtyard wall was crumbling, a small pile of dust and rocks collecting at the base of a gaping hole. It seemed to grin mockingly, sending an unexplained shiver down Jo's arm.

She knocked on the door before she could stop herself.

From inside, silence.

Another knock, louder this time.

Behind her, Charlie snuffed out his cigarette. "Are you sure—?"

She knocked again, interrupting his thought.

"I don't think anyone's home."

Instead of backing down, she grabbed the knob and twisted. The thick wooden door swung open with ease. Jo sucked in her breath . . . but there was no one on the other side.

Blinking against the dim light, she crossed the threshold. She winced at the smell of dust and decay, unused air and moth-eaten fabric. The stench of abandonment.

A fine layer of sand coated the furniture. The sofa sagged, its stuffing spilling onto the floor in clumps. The fireplace, insides still charred black, was a nest of cobwebs. Farther in, the kitchen cabinets were open, scratches of animal intruders carved into the peeling paint. Mouse droppings covered the floor, so old they crunched beneath Jo's feet.

"Olive's not here."

Jo turned, surprised. "I never said—"

"I know you didn't. But I've been out here enough to know where we are. This ranch has been empty for a while."

His tests. Of course he knew. He'd probably been scouring this area for years, plucking up plants and capturing wild animals. She thought she even remembered him asking about this particular ranch. Somewhere in the middle of all that tequila.

"The main house, too?"

"All of it. Completely deserted."

"Then why didn't you say anything?" She suddenly wanted to hit him.

"You wouldn't have believed me anyway. You needed to see it for yourself."

Her jaw tightened as she drew a long, steady breath. He was right. But that didn't mean she wasn't still annoyed.

"You *did* know her, didn't you?"

Jo pressed two fingers to the bridge of her nose, trying to force her emotions back down her throat. "It was stupid to come here. I'm sorry I wasted your gas and your time."

"It wasn't stupid, Jo. The government gave the ranch back a few years ago. Well, most of it." There was a pause. "And they *were* here—Olive and her family, I mean. But now . . ."

"But now what? How do you know all this?"

"I tried to find them too." He fiddled with the collar of his shirt. "For the science interviews, I mean."

The tightness in Jo's chest deflated. Adrenaline seeped from her muscles, leaving her feeling tired . . . and defeated.

"I'm sorry, Jo. I should have told you. I should have told you the moment I realized where we were going. But you seemed so resolute. I couldn't bear to say anything. And I thought maybe you knew something I didn't. Some way to find her or contact her." He hesitated. "There's obviously some kind of . . . history between you two."

History.

She took a step, leaving a footprint in the dust behind her. Charlie lit another cigarette; the soft click of his lighter echoed in the stillness. But she barely noticed. Instead, Jo ran her hand across the mantel, stepping away from Charlie, away from the neglected present and into the vibrant past. She could feel the heat of the lit candles, smell the spice of chiles, taste the sweetness of pie on her tongue.

And see Olive. Her eyes were wide. Her lips, stained purple with contraband alcohol, spoke: *"Jo."* The first glimmer of potential friendship, the cruel world around them growing bigger and smaller at the same time.

"Jo," she said again. Her voice was deeper this time. Sharper.

A rustling at her feet as she took another step.

"Jo!"

She blinked. It wasn't Christmas. And it wasn't Olive.

"Jo, look out!"

Her eyelids were heavy as she blinked again, trying to focus. The noise at her feet morphed into something more distinct.

Not a rustle. A rattle.

A large brown snake coiled on the ground below, head arched, tongue tasting the air. Its tail shook angrily. Jo froze, paralyzed with fear. The rattling increased; the snake seemed to expand with the intensified sound.

And then three things happened simultaneously. First, the ear-splitting rattling ceased. Second, the snake lunged forward, fangs bared, aiming for a spot near Jo's ankle. And third, an explosion rang out beside her, causing the ground near her feet to splinter and Jo to fall on her backside with a teeth-jarring thump.

The seconds that followed seemed to move in slow motion. Or maybe it was Jo herself. She took in her new position on the floor. The snake, now headless, was in pieces on the wall, splatters of red against the white adobe, like some abstract painting in a museum. Above her, Charlie was staring at the bloodied corpse with a silver pistol in his hand.

"Are you okay?"

Jo nodded shakily, the ringing in her ears slowly beginning to fade.

"Here." He shoved the gun into his waistband. "Let me help you." Wrapping one arm around her waist, he pulled her to her feet.

"What happened?" she stammered.

"I don't know. You were . . . lost in thought," he finished tactfully. "I was looking out the window, trying to, um, give you some privacy, when all the sudden I heard this noise. I looked back, and there was a rattler right there at your feet." He gestured to the spot now soiled with snake innards.

Wiping her hands on her pants, Jo winced as they came back

wet. Blood. There was snake blood on her khakis. Acid pooled in her mouth.

"Here," Charlie said, handing her a hankie.

She took it gratefully, swallowing disgust as she wiped at her legs. The blood smeared into ugly, rust-colored stains but at least the snake's flesh was off her. For the most part. "Well, thank you. For being more aware than I was. For . . . saving me."

Charlie's face broke into a crooked grin. "Well, I was going to let it bite you, but then I remembered you still owe me money for drinks the other night."

Jo let out a shaky laugh. The blood began slowly returning to her limbs.

"Come on, let's get out of here. Before something else decides to claim its territory. That is," he added, eyebrows raised, "if you're done here?"

Jo took one last sweeping glance around the decrepit living room, deliberately keeping her eyes off the splattered snake remains. Olive wasn't here. Hadn't been here in a very long time. These rooms contained nothing but painful memories and broken promises.

"Yes," she said, managing a small smile in Charlie's direction. "Let's go."

He offered his arm with an exaggerated bow. She took it, letting him lead her from the gloom of the casita and into the bright sunshine beyond. Their feet crunched on rocks as they made their way back to the car. He opened her door with another silly bow, exposing a glint of silver in his waistband.

Jo hung back, a sudden thought striking her. "Why do you have a gun?"

Charlie stuck out his chin, one eyebrow cocked. "What?"

"I mean, I'm thankful for what you did and all. But . . . why would a scientist need a gun in the first place?"

"I would think it would be obvious, Miss Hawthorne." He gestured in the direction of the house. "*That* is why I carry a gun. Scientist or not, this is still New Mexico. And everything in New Mexico is trying to kill you."

"Ain't that the truth," Jo muttered under her breath as she settled down in the front seat.

After a moment, Charlie joined her. He did not, however, start the engine. Instead, he turned, draping his arm over the back of the seat. "Can I take you somewhere?"

"Huh?"

He reached toward her as if to touch her, then stopped, folding his hands in his lap instead. "I want to show you something. Can I take you somewhere?"

Jo narrowed her eyes. "Where?"

"It's a surprise."

"I don't like surprises."

"Please?"

She should say no. It didn't matter that he was attractive and nice and did she mention attractive? What's more, she was leaving tomorrow. She didn't care where Olive was or what her father had been trying to tell her. There were no answers for her here, no closure. Nothing at all but tainted dirt, old memories, and fresh pain. She needed to get out of here before this place turned her to dust, too.

But she couldn't get a bus until tomorrow morning. And Charlie *had* driven her all the way out here without complaint, even knowing her journey was in vain. Better to spend her last few hours in New Mexico with a kind, good-looking man than alone in her motel with ghosts.

She gave a slight nod. "Okay. Sure."

The Packard roared to life beneath them. Jo gave the ranch one last look before turning her attention to Charlie. He winked at her playfully as he turned the car around and started back down the long dirt road to the highway.

CHAPTER FIFTEEN

OLIVE

JANUARY 1945

The fake letter from Avery consumed me for a few days. Several times I crumpled it up, ready to throw it away, only to smooth it back open and read it again. But each study of the text left me with new questions rather than a single answer. Had my mother been fooled? My grandma? Or—even worse—had they been a part of the deception?

My first thought, obviously, was that Avery was dead. Killed in action somewhere, and my family didn't want to tell me. And yet my grandmother's face when she'd handed me the letter had been joyful, so positive, so . . . sincere. Not only did lying go against everything her precious Jesus taught, but I also doubted her ability to pull off a lie so wholeheartedly. So if Avery was dead, Grandma was likely just as in the dark as I was.

But my mother? Six months ago I would have said the same about her—incapable of lying, especially to her own daughter. Now the only thing I was sure of was that I didn't know her as well as I thought I did.

Yes, it was the easiest explanation . . . except I didn't want to believe Avery was dead. I *couldn't* believe Avery was dead. Not my brother. So if he wasn't dead, what other explanation could there possibly be?

There was only one thing strong enough to pull me from the mystery: my date with Tim Bucknam.

I almost chickened out. On Friday night, just an hour before he was due to arrive, every piece of clothing I owned suddenly looked hideous. My normally straight hair had a wave in it that had never been there before, and not a pretty one like Hedy Lamarr's. No, mine looked like I had gone to bed with wet hair underneath a burlap sack. And the skin I'd never paid attention to cried out for makeup I didn't own.

Grandma, however, was ecstatic. She'd agreed to the date without hesitation, a brief reprieve in my punishment I knew wouldn't have been granted for anything else. She gushed about me "taking an interest in myself." I knew what she really meant was taking an interest in *life*. Moving on from the ranch. From my sulking and bitterness. If a date—and a little makeup—was what it was going to take, she would gladly share her meager supply.

Perhaps I should have asked to go to the winter formal after all.

"The point of makeup," she cooed, brushing my hair from my face as she prepped it for powder, "is to make it look as if you're not wearing any." She ran a brush over my nose, making it itch. "Bring out your natural beauty. Don't hide it."

I kept my eyes closed as she dusted a trace of eye shadow across the lids. More brushes swept over my cheeks and neck. It felt silly, all this fuss. But it felt glamorous too.

"Pucker." Thick wax rolled over my lips. "Now rub them together. Gently. Gently." The dab of a tissue and a sigh. "Now open your eyes."

In the mirror was me. Only not me. My cheeks were rosy; my dark eyes popped under a hint of gold and brown. And my lips—I had lips! Pink and full where once they were thin and pale. I scrunched them together, testing them out. For all my talk about being an adult, for the first time in my life I looked—and felt—not like a girl, but truly like a woman.

Grandma's moist eyes washed over my face with a sad but approving smile. "You look so much like your mother."

And just like that, my contentment vanished. My mother. All the things I was trying to forget flashed in the mirror, blurring the face that could have been beautiful.

Pa was dead and Avery was gone and my mother was only sixty miles away . . . and yet hers was the absence I felt most. As wonderful as my grandma was, *my mother* should have been the one here, putting on my makeup, calming my nerves before my date.

But not the mother I had currently. The one from before Pa died. My real mother. Shoot, at this point, I'd even take the shadow of a mother I'd had for the past seven years. At least that mother didn't hide things from me. At least that one I could trust.

My grandmother's eyebrows knit together. "I'm sure she wishes she could be here for this. You know that, right?"

I didn't answer. Instead, I fought the urge to nibble my nails, knowing it would ruin my lipstick, and waited for the tears to retreat.

With only minutes to spare, I settled on a knee-length cornflower-blue dress with white buttons down the front and navy piping across the middle. It was an old one of my mother's, more suited for May than January, but I would rather freeze than put on the same boxy cardigan Tim saw me in at school each day.

Precisely at seven, Tim knocked on the door. He wore a white button-down with a dark tie beneath a black jacket. His khaki pants looked freshly pressed and his shoes recently polished. His hair was perfect, his smile was perfect, and his manners were perfect; he presented flowers to my grandmother, pulling a single carnation from the bouquet for me. When we left, he held the car door open for me and waved at Grandma, who lingered on the front porch, watching as we drove away, a misty smile on her face.

I don't remember anything about the movie. Something about Nazis (because everything these days was about the Nazis) and a fisherman and Lauren Bacall. I'm sure it was great. Tim said it was great afterward. But I couldn't focus. I was too aware of his breathing, the sweat forming under my armpits, the way he crossed and uncrossed his legs. Most of all, though, I couldn't stop staring at just how close his hand was to mine.

"Are you hungry?" he asked as we exited. The neon lights of the marquee seemed too bright after the intense darkness of the theater.

"Not really. I ate a lot of popcorn."

He laughed. "Right. Okay. Well, do you, um . . . do you want me to take you home?"

"No," I said quickly. Too quickly.

He smiled, shoulders relaxing. "Good. Great. Well then . . . how about a drive? It's too cold for a walk."

Tim's father's Chevrolet was black, freezing, and stank of exhaust when he tried to start the heater. He banged on the dash, apologizing profusely, and offered me his jacket instead. I snuggled inside, inhaling the scent of his aftershave—Fitch's, perhaps, though I was no expert. All I knew was that it reminded me faintly of my father—earthy and masculine.

The streets of Alamogordo were empty. The wet weather had finally broken but refused to release its chill. We drove down Pennsylvania Avenue in silence, watching the neon lights dance on the hood of the car.

"Sorry about this heat." Tim ended his fiddling with a disgusted sigh. "Do you want to listen to the radio? It's the one thing in this old car that actually works."

A click, and Dinah Shore's voice filled the car.

"I'll walk alone because to tell you the truth, I'll be lonely . . ."

"'I don't mind being lonely.'" Tim tried to harmonize with her voice—poorly—causing me to giggle.

"'When my heart tells me you are lonely too,'" I chimed in.

Tim let out a snicker. "Not bad, Olive! Not bad at all!"

It was a lie; I was no singer. But I appreciated it all the same.

"'There are dreams I must gather . . .'" Tim puffed out his chest as he sang along. Passing headlights flashed on his goofy smile. "'Dreams we fashioned the night you held me tight . . .'"

"'Ooooooooh!'"

We laughed. It felt good to laugh, to be here with him on this cold night, singing. There was too much terribleness in the world. But this . . . this was good.

"Do you want to scoot over here? I'm sorry it's still so cold."

My heart pounded as I pushed myself across the cloth seat. It nearly leapt out of my chest as his arm draped over my shoulders. His fingers squeezed my shoulder through the thick fabric of his jacket. His thigh was against mine, the crook of his arm perfectly shaped to cradle my body. I'd never been this close to a boy before. I hoped he couldn't feel me tremble.

He maneuvered the car down Indian Wells Road, moving east toward the rising Sacramento Mountains. The lights of the city faded behind us. At the foot of the mountains, the pavement turned to gravel. Our wheels crunched as we made our way slowly up the narrow embankment. At the end of the road, Tim swung the car around and put it in park, killing the engine. Below us, Alamogordo spread out like a rug, the lights flickering under a half-moon.

"Pretty up here, isn't it?"

I nodded.

"I used to come up here with my brother. It's where I had my first shot of whiskey." His body shook with a soft chuckle. "But that was before the war."

The war. It was always here, pressing down on us, refusing to let us feel anything good for too long.

"I haven't heard from him since November." His voice seemed far away, like he was talking to himself more than me. "I miss him. My dad and I . . . well, we don't see eye to eye on a lot of things. Most things, really. He wants me to take over the family garage—the one over on First? It's been in our family for two generations. Fixing up machinery is all the Bucknams know. It's all that's expected of us. It was easier when Leroy was home and everything wasn't all on me. But things are different now. He's gone and we don't know if he's coming home and . . ." He let his words trail off. "I just miss him, that's all." He turned slightly, meeting my eyes. "Do you have anyone? Fighting, I mean?"

"My brother." The words tasted funny in my mouth. "Avery."

"Europe or Pacific?"

"Pacific." At least according to his fake letter.

"Mine too." He took my hand and intertwined my fingers with his own. Despite the cold, my nerves, the mystery of Avery swirling in the air, and the absolute absurdity of Tim Bucknam sitting next to me in the dark, I felt my shoulders go limp. The weight of the past several months melted like ice from the heat and compassion in Tim's small touch.

"We weren't close," I said quietly. "My brother and I, I mean. Well, we were. When we were kids. But then my dad died and my uncle Hershel moved in and Avery . . . changed."

"Grief is like that," Tim said gently. "People respond to it in different ways."

"Yeah, maybe. He was . . . he so was angry. All the time. And him and Hershel . . . it was like they had this club. They'd read and argue and rile each other up. And I . . . it was like I disappeared. My mother was in her own world. I don't think she ever really got over losing my dad. On top of that, she was constantly worrying about money, too busy trying to keep food on the table to think about anything else. To think about me." I knew I was talking too much. But I couldn't stop. The feeling of Tim's skin had opened a gate I wasn't sure I'd be able to close even if I tried. "I was invisible. Nothing I said or did mattered. It was like I wasn't even there. And then the Army came in and Avery left and they just . . . shipped me away. I don't know why I was surprised. I guess you can't see the truth until it slaps you in the face . . . or packs up your stuff and kicks you to the curb."

Silence filled the car after I finally hushed, only this one was cumbersome, seeping into the space between us and hardening like concrete. I'd laid myself too bare, and now that I was empty, shame had been given room to sprout. I shifted, prepared to scoot away, but Tim's hand tightened around my own. I turned, surprised to see a trace of melancholy, not disgust, on his face.

And then he kissed me.

Those lips, soft and beautiful, on my own. They tasted gentle and sweet. Hands in my hair, running down the curve of my jaw, and I was lost. Lost to everything except here and now and Tim.

After a moment, he pulled away. The corner of his mouth twisted upward. "I've wanted to do that from the moment I first saw you."

I looked down, feeling myself blush.

"Was that . . . was that okay?"

I nodded and grinned stupidly at my lap.

He leaned back, sighing happily, still keeping a firm grasp on my hand. I settled against him. For what seemed like the first time since leaving the ranch, I felt safe. As we watched the lights of Alamogordo flicker, I breathed in the scent of the night, of Tim, of this moment.

"Olive," he said finally.

And with that one word, our peaceful bubble was popped; the world rushed in once more. *Please don't,* I wanted to beg. *It's too perfect to last, I know, but please don't spoil it. Not yet.*

"My birthday was last week. My eighteenth."

It felt as if my body were dropping right through the bottom of that ancient Chevy. *Stop. Please just stop. Don't say it.*

"I . . . I enlisted. I leave in two weeks."

Tim's words sliced through my body like a cold wind, shredding the tranquil cocoon of the moment into irreparable tatters.

"I can't stay here and sit in a classroom, fixing up cars after school, stealing kisses from the prettiest girl in New Mexico at night—" he squeezed my fingers—"while everyone else fights. It ain't right. I have to go. I have to play my part. I can feel it inside, like something bigger is calling. Does that make sense?"

No. Yes. No.

"Olive?"

I looked at the ceiling in an attempt to force back tears.

"Olive." Pleading.

Even in the dim light, I could tell Tim's eyes were watery. His forehead was creased. He pressed a hand to my cheek, turning my face toward his.

"I'm not going to forget you. I couldn't even if I tried." His fingers tugged gently on a stray strand of hair. "I'll come back."

I let him kiss me again, the salt of my tears mingling on our lips. I let him hold me as he drove me home, his hand stroking my shoulder through the fabric of his jacket. On the steps of my grandmother's house, I even let his lips brush my cheek, feeling his want wrestling with propriety in case eyes were spying through the curtains. I nodded my agreement that he'd see me Monday, that he'd walk me to class, that maybe we could eat lunch together on the quad.

I waited until he'd driven out of sight before stepping inside. My grandmother sat in her easy chair, knitting needles in her lap, pretending to sleep. Or maybe she really was. I didn't care. I slipped past her into my bedroom, clicking the door firmly behind me before letting myself weep. For Tim, his life and his safety. For the moments that were and never would be again. For his seeing me, hearing me, feeling me . . . and still choosing to leave.

But also for me. Because the cold and dark never felt so bitter as to one who has just touched the sun.

—◆ ❖ ◆—

Tim left on a Saturday morning.

I hung back as he said goodbye to his parents, feeling out of place. He held my hand as the bus rumbled to life behind him, as the other passengers stowed their luggage and climbed up the dirty rubber steps. We didn't speak. Instead he kissed me. Right there in front of the other passengers, in front of his parents, urgent and improper. A thousand words summed up in the softness of his lips, both promises and apologies, a boy still clinging to a hope of days to come.

A hope I wasn't sure I'd ever believe in again.

The days rolled by after he left, and somehow so did I. Teachers still taught; preachers still preached. I walked the hallways, attended church services, prepared for the rummage sale. But I didn't sleep. I barely ate, except when Grandma scolded. I tried to put on a happy face for her, begging off any attempt at heartfelt discussions with a wave of my hand, an imaginary load of home-work, or a masterful redirection about *her* latest projects like a blood drive at the USO. But the truth was, I existed so far inside myself I barely registered any of the outside world. I was a ghost, walled behind my grief, so strong that not even Jo Hawthorne could break through.

Not that she really tried. Our argument at the tagging session lingered between us. Though not unfriendly (because I doubted Jo could be unfriendly even if she tried), she remained distant. Cordial but aloof. She did not engage. She did not pry.

It was better this way. Or at least that's what I told myself.

Before I knew it, it was the second Saturday in March, and all the items we had categorized and tagged over the past few months lay spread out on tables in the church parking lot. Large, hand-painted signs reading *Help Us Replace Our Window!* were hung at the entrance. The morning air was still brisk but the sun was warm, and I found myself sweating beneath my brown sweater as I positioned myself in a chair next to the cashbox. Jo, as always, was flawless. Her long hair was pulled back in a tight ponytail, and upon her cheeks was a smile as wide as my scowl.

"Good morning, ladies," Pastor Hamilton said, striding toward us with a clipboard in hand. "Are you ready to get to work?"

"Absolutely!" Jo's enthusiasm was more than enough for the both of us.

"I'll leave you two in charge of the cashbox. At least one of you needs to be here at all times, but if necessary, the other can mean-der about, offering help and answering questions. I'll be around if you need me."

As he walked away to meet the first wave of bargain hunters already perusing the lot, Jo stripped off her pink cardigan to reveal a modest white blouse with puffy sleeves. She threw the sweater on the chair beside mine and sighed. "It's hot already. Are you hot?"

"No." I stared ahead, keeping my eyes on an elderly lady who was digging through a stack of crumbling books.

I heard gum click in Jo's mouth. "How . . . are you?"

"I'm fine."

Quite possibly the biggest lie I'd ever told.

"Of course," she said, shuffling a stack of papers on the table in front of us. "Of course you are. I just mean . . . Well, I heard about Tim. That he left, you know? And that you two were sort of . . . I don't know. It's silly gossip. I shouldn't even be asking. It's too personal. Doesn't matter what you guys are. Or were. Or . . ." She grimaced. "Anyway, I, um, tried to talk to you at school several times. And at church. Well, I almost tried. But I didn't know what to say, so I . . . well, I wanted to make sure you were okay."

I dug my nails into my thighs.

"I'm sorry, Olive," she said softly. "Please know I'm here for you. I understand. I know you don't want to hear that, but I do. It's hard when someone you care about is in harm's way. You don't have to be 'in this' with me . . . but I'll be in it with you. If ever you want."

As she was speaking, Jo's hand was hovering above my shoulder. Her fingers fluttered, the desire to land and the fear of getting burned playing out in equal parts upon her face. Finally, with a look of resolve that would have made me laugh had my heart not been broken, she brought her palm down and patted me with an almost-imperceptible tap.

And beneath that small, faint touch, my heart swelled and then shattered. For the first time, it no longer mattered to me that it was Jo Hawthorne standing beside me, the daughter of the man who had stolen my home. I didn't care that she was a happy-go-lucky Christian who smiled and talked too much. What mattered was that someone understood. Someone cared. Genuinely, truly, she cared about me.

But even more than that, she was here. When no one else

could be bothered, Jo showed up. Relentlessly. Even when I didn't deserve it. Despite everything. Despite *me*.

I grabbed her hand, causing her to jump. I couldn't bring myself to look at her; my tears were for me and me alone. And yet she didn't pull away. Instead, she stood there beside me, silently holding my hand, allowing me to fight my tears and catch my breath. She only let go when the first round of customers strolled up to the cashbox.

As much as I despised the rummage sale, I was thankful for the distraction. Smacking the tears from my cheeks, I lost myself to a group of children who were examining wooden pull toys with frayed strings while their mother tried on a pair of scuffed black heels. The bargain-hunting hagglers kept me way too preoccupied to give a front-row seat to the ache of Tim's absence or—worse—the embarrassment I was starting to feel about the unexpected vulnerability I'd just shown Jo.

By the time the sun was high overhead, the tables and blankets had been picked nearly clean, save for the rattiest and most broken items, and Pastor Hamilton finally gave us the go-ahead to close up shop. It took an hour to clear the parking lot, store the tables, and load the remaining items into his car.

"I'll take these donations to the shelter," he said, "and count the money this weekend. See how close we've come to our goal."

"We've surpassed it!" Jo said, grinning. "I can feel it."

Pastor Hamilton chuckled. "I love your optimism, Jo."

"Are you sure you don't need any help with that?"

He shook his head. "No, no. I'm fine."

"Well, okay then. I'll see you tomorrow morning for Sunday service. Bye, Olive."

The last sentence was quieter, off to the side, almost timid.

I returned her smile shyly. "Bye, Jo."

"Enjoy the rest of your Saturday!" And off she bounced, as awake and full of energy as if we hadn't just worked a six-hour shift.

I, on the other hand, was exhausted. The allure of an afternoon nap was growing stronger by the minute. It was second only to the growling of my stomach. "Bye, Pastor Hamilton."

"Oh, Olive! Wait a second!" Pastor Hamilton called.

I turned grudgingly.

"One more thing, if you don't mind. The poster. Out front. Can you get it for me?"

I sighed but did as I was told, grabbing the cardboard Open sign from the light pole. As I made my way back toward Pastor Hamilton's car, something pink caught my attention. Jo's sweater. In a pile on the ground.

"Jo's sweater," Pastor Hamilton said, pointing as if I weren't already looking in that direction. "She must have forgotten it." He took the poster from my hands. "Could you take it to her? I'd do it, but I have to get this stuff to the shelter and then I have a lunch engagement before prepping for tomorrow's sermon. Could you help me out?"

My stomach growled. Jo would be fine without her sweater for a night. More than that, he could very easily give it to her himself tomorrow morning because we all knew she wouldn't miss service. But saying no to Pastor Hamilton never really felt like an option— it might have had something to do with unsettled guilt over breaking the church window—and anyway, for all Jo had done for me today, the least I could do was return her sweater.

I accepted Pastor Hamilton's grateful pat on the back and vague directions ("On Michigan. About halfway down. The yellow house.") before he drove away, leaving me to collect the pink pile from its heap on the parking lot. Warm from the sun and even softer than it looked, the sweater smelled like Jo—all soap and flowers and piety.

Michigan Avenue was the "good" part of town. These houses were nicer, more elegant and stately. Two stories, wooden, with picket fences and large trees. They'd been here since the town was founded, not like the adobes south of Tenth, which sprang up as an afterthought. These weren't just houses. They were *homes*.

It wasn't difficult to find "the yellow house." It was the sunniest one on the street, bright and cheery and easy to spot amid its white and gray neighbors. It had twin brick columns on either side of the steps and two large bay windows on the upper story that looked like eyes. The front yard was covered with early sprouts of green grass. Pots of petunias—the first of spring—lined the porch, and a row of evergreens stood against the side drive, offering shade and privacy. Colors, colors everywhere, even in the desert.

A pang of jealous curiosity flared as I knocked on the bright-red door.

"Olive?" Jo opened it almost immediately. Her hair, which had been so tightly bound earlier, now cascaded around her shoulders. She smiled as she spotted her sweater in my hands.

"Oh!" she said, lifting it from my grip. "I must have forgotten. Thank you for bringing it by."

I tried to peer behind her, but she took a step backward into the doorframe, very obviously blocking my view.

"I'll see you tomorrow?"

I lowered my brows. There was something inside that house she didn't want me to see. Maybe it was full of fancy furniture or black-market cheese and sugar. Silly, yes, but so was the fact that I was standing on Jo Hawthorne's front porch.

"Bye, Oli—"

"Can I use your bathroom?"

Jo raised the sweater to her chest, sucking in her breath sharply, which she then tried to pass off as a cough. "I, um . . ."

"Please? I'll be quick. I didn't have a chance to go all morning." I hunched down and pressed my knees together, hoping to pass off my lie as authentic. "It's an emergency."

Her chest rose and fell with a suppressed sigh. The pained smile on her face was almost enough to make me feel guilty. "Okay. Yeah. Sure."

Stepping into the front hall and blinking against the dim light, I needed a moment to realize what I was seeing. The house wasn't stockpiled with rich people furnishings or covert baking goods.

It wasn't full of anything at all. The house was empty.

Hardwood floors, light-green wallpaper, an ornately carved banister leading to the second floor—it was all there, like I imagined it would be, here on the street where the fanciest of Alamogordo lived. Except there was nothing else. No furniture. No wall hangings. No shoes on the floor or coatrack overloaded with cardigans. Despite the warm colors and rising temps, the place felt cold.

I took another step forward. The floor seemed fragile, like it had never been walked on before.

"The bathroom is right over there."

But my fake emergency had vanished with the blunt force of truth. There was no point in pretending anymore. My mouth gaped as I turned around.

Jo remained just inside the doorway. Her cheeks were red, hands clenched together in a white-knuckled grip.

I couldn't believe I hadn't connected the dots before. Her mother was dead. Her brother was fighting. And her father was sleeping in my old bedroom sixty miles away.

"Do you . . . do you live here alone?"

Jo's hands dropped. Her shoulders curled over her chest.

"Jo?"

"My dad bought the house after my grandmother died. It wasn't until after I arrived that he found out he'd be heading up north for a few months to do . . . well, whatever it is they're doing up there." She gave a half shrug. "So . . . I'm here."

"But how do you eat? Pay bills? Live?"

She laughed. It was the first time I'd ever heard a chuckle from her I didn't believe was genuine. "I'm sixteen. I know how to cook and shop. My dad makes sure I have money and the bills are paid. It's not like he deserted me completely."

Actually, that's exactly what he had done, I thought.

"And anyways, Pastor Hamilton knows the situation. He helps out and checks in on me. I'm really okay. I took care of my grandmother for so long that taking care of myself is a piece of cake."

Her tone was so flippant, so completely indifferent to the reality in which she lived, but there was pain just below the surface. Pain I understood yet still couldn't fully grasp. I often felt alone. Jo, it seemed, truly *was*.

A sudden wave of sympathy swelled inside me. I had an urge to comfort her like she had done for me earlier, though I wasn't quite sure how. But before I could move, she brushed past me.

"Besides, I still have this."

She pushed open a wide door behind me, from which burst forth a distinctly different atmosphere from the hallway before. A breeze ruffled the lace curtains, blowing in the smell of oleander and creosote. There was a four-poster bed against the side wall. On it, a thick pink blanket lay smooth and tight over the top of the mattress. Shelves full of books and records lined the far wall, and a prim white dresser sat in the corner, covered in jewelry boxes and perfume bottles.

Jo turned around, arms outstretched, a brave smile on her face. Her eyes were trained in my direction, but I could tell they were looking at a spot just past my head.

I gave her a weak smile. "It's . . . it's great."

"My dad sends me all the latest books and music from Albuquerque whenever he gets the chance. He just sent me this." She held up the paper sleeve of a record, the words *Candy: Johnny Mercer, Jo Stafford, and the Pied Pipers, along with Paul Weston and His Orchestra* emblazoned in bright-red lettering on the front. "Have you heard it?"

I shook my head.

"I can listen to these records any time I want. Sometimes I let them play all night." Her breath hitched as she finished her sentence, as if realizing she'd revealed too much.

And she had. Because I could hear it. The sound of crooning voices and wailing horns echoing throughout this big, empty house at all hours of the day and night. Anything to fill the silence.

That's when I truly understood. This was the saddest room in the house. The most lived in, yes, but the saddest. It contained everything a teenage girl could ever want. Everything, that was, except the one thing I knew she so desperately wanted. Because it was the same thing I wanted too.

I rubbed at my throat, trying to swallow both the awkwardness and heaviness of that realization. "I should go."

"Don't you have to go to the bathroom?"

"Not anymore."

Her expression went as slack as her shoulders. "Okay. I'll show you out."

The journey to the front door took only seconds, but it seemed an eternity. Discomfort choked out any other attempts at conversation. It wasn't until we reached the threshold that Jo straightened suddenly, the snapping of her fingers so loud in the cavernous quiet that I jumped.

"Can you wait here just a second? There's something I've been meaning to give you."

"I really need to—"

"It will only take a second!" She disappeared back inside her room. When she returned a moment later, she held a leather book in her hand. "Here. I want you to have this."

It was a Bible. A *used* Bible.

I shook my head with more force than necessary.

"Please?"

"My grandma has Bibles at her house."

"I'm sure she does. But this one is special. It was my first one, given to me by *my* grandmother when I came to faith. It got me through some hard times. There's notes in it. And I thought, since you—"

"Jo."

She held it up. As she did, the soft leather cover flopped open to reveal the thin pages inside. "I know. I know. You're not a believer. And that's okay. I'm not trying to make you one." Seeing my face, she giggled. "I'm not! You just . . . you've been through a lot. And you asked about the things that have happened to me. How I'm not angry about it all." She patted the book's cover. "This is how."

Her pale-blue eyes were wide with sincerity, one side of her mouth curved upward in a half smile.

This girl had both everything and nothing at the same time. Her house was empty, but her heart was full. And somehow she was more concerned about *my* hurt than the depressing, overwhelming realness of her own.

She was a friend. I could admit that now. A real friend. Perhaps the first one I'd ever truly had.

Surprising both her and myself, I wrapped my arms around her in a tight, urgent embrace. She tensed momentarily and then returned my hug with full force. I thought I even felt her body tremble with quiet, relieved cries, though she wouldn't have admitted it, and I never would have asked.

No, I didn't want Jo's Bible. But I sure was glad to have Jo.

When we broke apart, however, I took the Bible anyway. The grin on her face made the absurdity of me holding Scripture in my hands worth it. I was only a few steps down her front walk before I turned.

"Hey, Jo?"

She stood in the doorway, silhouetted by the darkness filling the house behind her. "Yes?"

"Would you like to have dinner at my house tonight?"

CHAPTER SIXTEEN

JO

MARCH 1952

Jo was surprised at how fast the sun set out here. Ever since they'd left the ranch, time had quickened, like it was in a hurry to get away from this cursed ground. But even as night swept in, Charlie continued his westward journey, refusing to tell Jo their destination.

"Just wait," he'd promised through a wide smile each time she had asked. Her head cleared the farther they got from the ranch, and uncertainly replaced her initial excitement. She didn't know Charlie. Not really. She was heading out into a rapidly darkening desert wasteland with a man who was practically a stranger. He, on the other hand, only seemed to grow more relaxed with each passing mile, loosening his tie and unbuttoning the collar of his shirt. "It will be worth it."

The land outside the Alexander ranch was even more nondescript than the countryside before it. The mesa faded behind them, giving way to valley floors covered with clumps of spiky brown grass. Obscured by distance and the glare of the setting sun, the next row of mountain peaks was barely visible from their spot on the highway.

And then suddenly they were headed south on a dirt road, another path created in the rocky soil seemingly at random, with no signs or markers heeding any significance.

"What are we—?"

"Almost there."

Jo leaned back against the seat and tried to ignore the now-dry snake splatters on her pants. She had a headache again—stress, probably, or lack of water and the remnants of a hangover. Maybe both. Fishing two aspirin from her bag, she swallowed them dry. Her empty stomach revolted at the bitter pills, and she found herself wishing again she hadn't given Charlie her lunch. "Does this mysterious place have anywhere to eat?"

Charlie gave a sympathetic shake of the head but did not take his hands off the steering wheel. "Sorry. No."

"Well, is there somewhere we can stop along the way? A restaurant? Gas station?"

"Here." Charlie handed her a wad of yellow paper from the dash. "This is better than nothing."

Inside were a handful of limp fries, lukewarm and soggy from their time in the sun. Her already-tender stomach rolled.

"I'll treat you to some dinner after this," Charlie promised. "Real proper and everything. But for now, this is all I've got."

"I don't want you to take me to dinner."

"Okay. But maybe you do." He winked.

Jo looked out the window and shoved the squishy fries in her mouth, avoiding a response. She could *feel* the smirk on his face.

At that moment, the journey was mercifully interrupted by the appearance of a small white building, rising out of the desert like a mirage. Charlie pulled the car to a stop in front of it and allowed the dust from their tires to float onward before opening the door. "I'll be right back."

A man had emerged from inside, dressed in civilian clothes but his hair shorn in a military cut. The scowl on his face intensified when he saw Charlie.

Charlie, however, simply reached for his hand and shook it with vigor. The man's lips remained twisted in a frown. From her spot in the car, their voices were muffled, though it seemed Charlie was doing most of the talking. He pulled something from his coat pocket, small enough to be hidden in the palm of his hand, which caused the man to begin shaking his head aggressively. The muffled voices—Charlie's in particular—grew louder, then retreated back to a murmur. The man's eyes flickered in Jo's direction briefly before he allowed himself to be led back to the building, one of Charlie's hands firmly on his shoulder. Charlie shot Jo a smile and held up one finger before disappearing inside behind him.

She shifted in her seat, finishing the last of the fries and wiping her greasy fingers on a crumpled napkin. The silence seemed bigger out here, now void of the humming engine and crunching tires. Aside from this little white building, visibly bleached from the sun even in the dim light, there was nothing around them for miles. Alone in the car, the isolation pushed against her. She stared at the doorway, willing Charlie to hurry.

After what seemed like hours but could only have been minutes, Charlie finally returned. In his arms he carried a small white bundle, which he gestured with as he approached the car.

Jo stepped out, relief and apprehension simultaneously flooding into her extremities.

"You'll have to put these on." He pushed a ball of white, scratchy fabric into her hands.

"What?"

He nodded in the direction of the building. The other man stood just inside the window, face obscured by shadow but arms folded in a not-so-subtle disapproving way. "His rules, not mine." He slipped his set of covers over his shoes, the fabric puffing out like a cloud around the polished leather. With his crisp, professional suit and marshmallow-shaped shoes, he looked so much like a mismatched clown that Jo couldn't help but laugh. He pouted but his eyes remained light. "Alright, alright. Let's see just how fashionable they look on *you*, then."

Bracing herself against the car, she pulled the fabric over her own shoes.

Charlie whistled. "Doggone it. You can even make these stupid things look good, snake guts and all!"

Jo felt heat rise in her cheeks. She fussed with the shoe covers, thankful for a distraction.

"Well, we best get going. We've only got thirty minutes. And trust me, he's timing." He gestured again to the window. The man inside remained unmoving, watching them.

"Thirty minutes for what?"

"You'll see."

They returned to the car and continued down the road deeper

into the desert. Miles upon miles of dirt and scrub brush stretched out on either side of them. But there was something different about this area; it seemed bare, even for the desert. Bleak. There was an eerie emptiness to the land. Out here, it was easy to imagine they were the only two people on earth.

As they passed another half-dead yucca, Jo's skin began to crawl. She no longer cared about Charlie's surprise. She wanted out of here. Now.

But just as she opened her mouth to say so, he startled her by turning off the road and into a small dirt lot she hadn't even realized was there. Killing the engine, he waggled his eyebrows and grinned. "Ready?"

Jo followed him past a rusted barbed wire fence, from which a No Trespassing sign drooped limply. She expected something big on the other side, something secretive and exciting, something to warrant protective clothing and signs and fences and guards (for that was what that man had been, civilian clothes or not). But it was still just desert, flat and featureless.

"Charlie, where are we—?"

Even before the words came out of her mouth, she knew. It hit her before the ground began to slope gently downward, before the shimmering oasis at the bottom made itself known.

Trinity. This was Trinity.

This was where the world had changed, where the future of millions had been etched into sand. Hundreds of thousands in Japan, evaporated or—worse—left to die in a slow burn. Memories of Hiroshima floated before her. The core of that beautiful city had been reduced to vapors, with so many of its unlucky inhabitants now dust. She then thought of Pastor

Hamilton's words, of the people here, the unwitting test subjects in a game of war.

But it wasn't just here or in Japan. And it wasn't just the physical effects. Even now, years after the fallout had settled, millions more lived at the mercy of Soviet and American hands as they hovered over the nuclear trigger, waiting for one or the other to flinch. The blanket of fear now suffocating the entire world had been woven here, in this spot of dry, barren land.

Trinity loomed large in her mind. It was this *thing* from which everything else in her memory revolved, and yet it had remained a mystery, the dark place in her dreams from which all pain flowed. And now here it was. Out of her nightmares and spread out before her. A sea of green glass in the middle of the desert, frozen against the shallow depression of its earthly container.

She had never seen anything so beautiful—or so terrible—in her life.

"How did you . . . ?" She stopped, then started again. "I didn't think anyone was allowed in."

Charlie gave a mischievous grin. "They aren't anymore. But I have my ways." His eyes drifted over the glass crater. "Do you want to touch it?"

Jo started. "Is it safe?"

"Sure. In small doses. That's why we've only got thirty minutes." He glanced at his watch. "Fifteen now."

She took a step forward. Her white booties left no impression in the stiff earth as she bent down. Although hard like glass, the surface was anything but smooth. Swirls and bubbles lay trapped within, waves and ripples frozen in a moment of time.

"They call it trinitite. Formed when the bomb blast fused with the sand. You know, right after it first happened, people used to come out here for picnics. They'd take pieces of this stuff home with them as souvenirs. No one had any idea it was dangerous. Not the locals, not even the scientists who created it." He bent down beside her. "It *is* stunning, though. Shame they're getting ready to bulldoze it."

Jo stood and stepped back, surprised. "Who? Why?"

"The Army and the Atomic Energy Commission. Finally realized—or admitted—it's a hazard. The wind keeps blowing particles around, spreading the radiation. Easier to just break it up and bury it."

Easier. Nothing about this was easy. Not for the people in Hiroshima, in Nagasaki. The people *here*, the ones in the hospital. Dying from the air they breathed, the water they drank, the land they worked upon. Or for her, whose brokenness was tied irrevocably to that day, to this place, no matter how far away she ran.

A breeze whistled across the frozen sand, pushing pieces of dust across the glass toward her. By the time it reached her ears, it sounded like a scream. Desperate and forlorn, a plea from the very earth itself.

Goose bumps sprouted along Jo's arm. No, you couldn't bury Trinity under the ground any more than you could put the bomb back inside its shell. It was here now and would be—visible or not—for thousands of years. Yet it wasn't what was *here* that made this place so frightful; it was what was missing.

Never had Jo felt God's absence more powerfully than she did right here, right now.

As the last rays of the setting sun kissed the shimmering-green glass, Jo turned and strode from the crater, eyes focused only on the dirt beneath her fabric-covered shoes.

"Jo! Jo, wait up!"

The crunch of gravel signaled Charlie's advance, but she did not slow down. The walk seemed longer than before, the car miles rather than feet ahead.

"Jo, wait. Please—" His fingers dug into her arm with surprising force, causing her to jerk to a stop. But she could not bring herself to look at him.

"I want to leave. Now."

Charlie released her. "Jo, I'm sorry. I didn't mean to upset you."

"You didn't."

"I thought you'd like to see it . . . before it's gone, I mean."

Her shoulders sagged slightly as she exhaled. "Charlie, it's not your fault. It's . . . complicated, okay? I know to you it's names and dates and soil samples and experiments. But for me, it's more. It's my dad. It's . . ."

"Olive?"

Their eyes met. Lingered. "Yes," she said softly. "And Olive."

He took her hand. She let him. "What happened, Jo? You can tell me."

"We were friends. At least I thought we were."

"And now you're not?"

"Maybe we never were."

He rubbed his thumb over her wrist. "So you haven't spoken to her? Since when?"

"Since that day. She was supposed to . . ." Her voice trailed off. She couldn't talk about it. Couldn't think about it. Couldn't *breathe*.

And then Charlie, very unexpectedly, pushed his lips against hers. They were dry and tasted of tobacco. Anger welled up in Jo. Her body tensed as she prepared to shove him away, smack him across the face, storm off to the car, and demand he take her back to the motel. But then his warm hand was on the small of her back, and inexplicably, she began to breathe again. She pressed into his touch, his smell, his taste. Anything to make her feel something besides this pain.

"This place is about more for me too," he murmured against her neck. "I lost someone. Not here exactly. But in the war. My brother. He was murdered—killed, I mean, during a . . ." She felt his breath catch, his body stiffen under her arms. "I swore I wouldn't let it mean nothing. I wouldn't let it just slide. That's why I'm here. On the surface, his death had nothing to do with Trinity. But it all comes back to this place. Everything does."

She leaned into him, letting his heartache wash over them both. He was broken too. This seemingly smooth, confident, handsome man. He hid it better, but he was broken too.

However, rather than a sense of comradery, this realization made her feel even more alone. No one had survived Trinity, it seemed—not in any real sense, anyway. From Hiroshima to the Jornada, there was nothing—and no one—it hadn't damaged in one way or another.

There was no escape. There was no *hope*.

The guard had been glaring out the window when they returned with their booties, two minutes late according to his watch. Charlie waved off the man's irritation with a roll of his eyes. Afterward, they drove back to Alamogordo in silence, Jo curled against the passenger door. She watched the countryside pass in a blur as they moved away from Trinity, the green glass sea, the Alexander ranch. And yet, no matter how far they drove, she never felt quite removed from the emptiness that had nothing—and everything—to do with the desert around her.

CHAPTER SEVENTEEN

OLIVE

APRIL 1945

The window was ordered.

I'd had my doubts, but the rummage sale had been a success. We hadn't just met our fundraising goal; we'd surpassed it. Pastor Hamilton was able to put a down payment on a new window, which would be ready for installation and unveiling before the start of the summer monsoon.

It was a relief to be done. Things could go back to normal.

Well, "Alamogordo normal," that was. Because nothing had ever really been normal since I'd moved here.

Tim occupied much of a mind that was filled with too much free time; I'd received a few letters from him during basic training in Texas, but now that it was finished, all I heard was silence. I had no idea where he was, what he was doing, if he was safe. I spent a lot of time writing to him all the same. The letters piled up on my desk, ready to be mailed the moment they had a destination. Those letters—and the hope he'd one day get to read them—kept me going.

Those letters . . . and Jo.

That first invitation to dinner had led to another . . . and then another . . . and then another, until Jo's presence on Delaware Avenue became as ubiquitous as the dust. We studied together (she liked math, while I was much better at English), listened to music together (I was a Bing girl, while she preferred the more soulful crooning of Billie Holiday or Ella Fitzgerald), and chatted about clothes and makeup (about which Jo knew everything and I knew nothing). We couldn't have been more different. And yet the mutual pain of our past bound us in a way our polar personalities could not overcome. Her surprising friendship eased the pit of loneliness in which I'd been trapped since I'd moved to Alamogordo. In which—if I were truly honest—I'd been living my whole life.

But you could not separate Jo from her faith. While she wasn't pushy about it, if you were with her, you couldn't help but notice it. She prayed before every meal. She thanked God for *everything*, even silly things like a stray cloud on a hot day or an unusual amount of red Dots in her gumdrop box. She never—and I mean, *never*—cursed. Even that time when I accidentally dropped my history textbook on her bare toe, causing it to instantly purple, *I* had let out a swear while she'd merely peeped, "Ouch! Goodness gracious!"

I thought I'd gotten the gist of Christians from watching

Grandma. But this was a whole new level. I tried to ignore it. I mean, we were different in almost every other way. What was one more thing? But this wasn't as innocuous as disliking green chiles or her belief that Joseph Cotten was better-looking than Cary Grant (both grievous errors in my opinion). Her insistent, immersive faith bumped up against everything I thought I'd known about religion.

And it irritated me. *A lot.*

Still, I kept my mouth shut, not wanting to upset the delicate balance of our new friendship. Of my *only* friendship. And I did well, I think. Until one melancholy day in April when I could stay silent no longer.

Mr. Williams came into our classroom just before dismissal, a somber pall across his already-colorless face. His mustache had quivered, his thick voice nearly unable to speak the words:

Roosevelt was dead.

The release bell sounded immediately after his statement, but the normally welcome signal now seemed shrill and offensive. It wasn't true. Surely it couldn't be true. The entire classroom remained glued to their seats; the muted, solemn sounds from the hallway let us know we weren't the first group of students to have learned the news. It was only the gentle, sob-choked shooing of our teacher that eventually convinced us to join our peers in a melancholy retreat from the building.

Jo and I walked to Delaware Avenue in silence. The shock of losing the president who had led us out of the Depression and through these awful years of war wasn't confined to Alamo High; it covered the entire town like a black shawl, muting the blooming oleander and cottonwoods into sober shades of gray.

Grandma was gone when we returned home, probably on her daily run to the Piggly Wiggly. But it was for the best. I needed a chance to process the news before being able to help her, especially if one of her episodes decided to flare. I collapsed on the couch and buried my head in my hands. The blood in my temples pounded beneath the tips of my fingers. I thought about turning on the radio but decided against it. What good would it do? It would only fill the house with more grief. Never again would we hear Roosevelt's strong, confident reassurances or the news reports of his steadfast commitment to Hitler's defeat.

He was gone. And so too, it seemed, was America's hope.

Tears were just beginning to form in the corners of my eyes when I heard it. The familiar crinkle of thin pages.

I looked up. Jo was reading her Bible. Again.

No, not just again. *Now.*

Now, when yet another senseless act of misfortune had come down upon on our country. Now, when the evidence against a loving, generous god had once again been notched in my favor. Now, when faith in *anything* seemed most lost.

Weeks of pent-up aggravation fused with my sorrow. "What are you doing?"

Jo's head jerked up, her eyebrows furrowed in surprise. "I'm reading my Bible?"

"Why?"

"It helps me."

I clenched my jaw. "Our president just *died*, Jo! He died! In the middle of a war—a war in which your brother and my brother and my . . ." My voice fizzled, unable to categorize Tim. "They're all still fighting, and now we're vulnerable. A body without a head. How in the world can that . . . that stupid *book* do anything?"

Jo's lips turned downward.

"We're in trouble here. *Real* trouble. And we need *real* help, not the kind you can get from some imaginary—or at least apathetic—god and his silly fairy tales. Put the book away, Jo. For pete's sake. This is real life. Stop acting like a child."

Cheeks red, she closed the black leather cover and folded her hands on top of it. She did not look at me, but I felt her injury all the same.

Doggone it.

The tightness in my chest returned. But this time it wasn't from grief. It was from guilt. I'd thought I'd just needed to get those words out. Finally. Prove her wrong. But it hadn't made me feel any better. In my impotent ire, I'd wanted to hurt her God; instead I'd hurt her.

I let out a long sigh. "I'm sorry, Jo. I didn't mean it. I'm just scared and sad and . . . what do I know about anything anyway, right? Just read it, okay? If it helps you, read it."

But she didn't. She didn't move. Instead, her eyes remained focused in her lap, one hand pulling on the fingers of the other.

I removed my sweater, suddenly much too warm. I wanted her to look at me. I wanted her to speak. But more than anything else, I wanted her to open her book back up, if only to prove my big fat mouth and Russian temper hadn't ruined everything once again.

"Jo . . ." I moved from my seat at one end of the couch to the other, closer to her. "Please, I'm sorry. Books help me, too. I escape into Robert Louis Stevenson and L. Frank Baum. I—"

"Have you ever read the Bible, Olive?"

I leaned against the cushion, crossing my arms over my chest. I'd taken her Bible, yes, but had shoved it under my bed the moment I'd returned home. Unless Grandma had moved it, that's where it remained. Keeping my eyes on my knees, I gave a slight shake of my head.

Beside me, Jo let out a small burst of air through her nose; I wasn't sure if it was irritation or amusement. When she spoke, however, her tone was kind. "It's okay, Olive. I'm not mad. You can be honest with me."

The taste of blood assaulted my tongue. I'd bitten the inside of my cheek too hard.

"I know where you are," she continued. "Faith-wise, I mean. I understand your doubts and I can even understand your anger. But how can you attack me for something you haven't even read? You say books help you, too, but how can you say this particular one doesn't if you've never bothered to crack the cover? You don't have to believe a single word of it, but if you're going to make fun of me, can you at least try to understand what you're making fun of me for?"

I picked at some lint on my skirt, wrestling with a desire to defend myself while grudgingly admitting the truth in her words. I knew nothing about God or the Bible save Hershel's rants and the things Grandma had been trying to not so subtly shove down my throat. Did I really want to risk Jo's friendship because of my own close-minded stubbornness?

"Or if you don't want to read the Bible, can you stick to arguing other things instead? Like, for example, your clearly inferior taste in music?"

I looked up to find her grinning, her petite nose wrinkled with the strain of a stifled snigger. She looked so ridiculous I had no hope at self-control; I let out a loud, high-pitched giggle. Soon Jo joined me.

It didn't fix anything. Roosevelt was still dead. World War II raged on. The tension between Jo's religion and myself remained. But that was Jo. She didn't need everything to be perfect to find joy. She could love her God and her pigheaded, short-tempered, nonbelieving friend at the same time; she saw no contradiction between the two.

Because love wasn't just a word to her. It was her life.

That night, I opened Jo's Bible for the very first time. Not because of any desire to know God. But out of a desire to love my friend in the same way that she loved me.

—◆◈◆—

By the beginning of May, I understood Scripture even less than I believed it, but at least the weather had finally cleared, skipping straight over spring and heading directly into summer. The temperatures had already broken ninety, buoyed by incessant winds. The Sacramentos lay in a perpetual fog of dust. Even with the windows shut, Grandma still swept gypsum from the floor every morning, muttering under her breath. Because of this, reading outside was no longer an option, and I resigned myself to my bed, the softness of my pillow and the Bible's dry and minuscule print often lulling me into unintentional sleep.

"Olive, Olive, wake *up*."

My eyelids peeled open, heavy and confused. Pink sunlight streamed through my window. I must have fallen asleep last night while trying to read the book of Joshua and slept through to morning. Dread crept into my stomach as I realized I was probably late for school. "Humph. Wha—what?"

"He'd dead, Olive. He's *dead*!"

Even inside the warm cocoon of blankets, my blood froze. Not again. Who was it this time? *Tim? Avery? Please, no.* "Dead?"

"Yes! Finally!"

Finally? What a horrible thing to say! Is she having one of her spells again? I sat up groggily, my tired mind struggling to process a flood of emotions. "What?"

Grandma gripped my hands. "Hitler's dead! They just announced it on the radio!"

I blinked once, the words entering my mind one by one. *Hitler. Dead. Radio.*

"Two days ago," Grandma was saying. "Suicide in Berlin. The coward's way out for sure, but what did we expect? The devil himself probably greeted that man on the other side."

He was dead. Hitler was dead. Avery could return. Tim could come home. The Army could leave. I could go back to the ranch. It was over. It was finally over.

I wrapped Grandma in a hug, fighting the urge to cry. She smelled of coffee and sleep as she patted the back of my head. Relief rendered me limp inside her arms. It was as if I'd been holding my breath for years and had finally been allowed to exhale.

"Do you want some breakfast?"

As if on cue, my stomach growled. We both laughed.

"Wash up and get dressed. I'll try to scrounge up something special. No school today! Today is a day to celebrate!"

And celebrate we did. Grandma whistled while she made pancakes and eggs, even eventually allowing me to switch from the news (which had begun to repeat itself) to some music. Doris Day echoed through our kitchen, her angelic voice over the top of Les Brown's orchestra:

"My dreams are getting better all the time . . ."

The trumpets wailed as Grandma spun in her apron, her thick hips clumsy and slow but joyful. She held out her hands, inviting me to twirl. I giggled and joined her. Because when your seventy-two-year-old grandmother asks you to dance with her, you dance. Especially now when there was something to dance about.

"Let's take a walk," she said when breakfast was done and the dishes were soaking. "It's a beautiful day."

Our neighbors had the same idea. Everywhere we turned, people were emerging from their houses, like animals from a long winter, smiles on their faces and whistles upon their lips. We walked down Ninth Street and headed for downtown.

"Won't be long now!" an older gentleman said as he passed, tipping his hat. "We've got 'em on the run."

"Good riddance!" said another woman, sweeping her front walk.

"Last nail in the coffin."

"Tails between their legs, tails between their *legs*!"

Smiles spread across faces that had nearly forgotten how. Even the haze covering the Sacramentos abated, at least for the morning. The sun blazed and the wind whispered songs of hope. Music seemed to flow from every open window. In our long stroll down the sidewalks of Alamogordo, I noticed things I hadn't seen in the entire time I'd lived here. Like how the cottonwoods along Tenth Street all swayed in rhythm with one another. How the water tower on Pennsylvania Avenue wasn't just black—it shimmered with the purple hue of the mountains. And how the ducks in the pond at Alameda Park didn't just quack—they sang.

We returned to the house around eleven, just in time to see a car pull up in front.

Grandma spoke my thoughts. "Now who in the world . . . ?"

Before she could finish, a pair of long legs emerged from the driver's side, clothed in familiar drab khaki. "Well, hello there! Just the two ladies we were hoping to see!"

Sergeant Hawthorne smiled as he placed a hat on his head.

His appearance was shocking. What was more surprising was his use of the word *we*. Because that could only mean—

"Olive!"

My mother stepped out from the passenger side. Dark sunglasses covered her face, and her hair was pulled back on one side. She wore a brown-and-white polka-dot dress with brown heels on her feet that clicked as she rushed toward me.

I'd never seen that outfit before in my life.

I stiffened under her hug. Gone was the smell of lye. Of grease. Of housework. Instead, she smelled faintly of vanilla and something else I couldn't quite place.

"I've missed you so much."

"Why are you here?" It came out meaner than I intended, but I felt only slightly guilty as I watched her face fall.

"I missed you, Olive. I was planning a surprise trip, and then Richard—Sergeant Hawthorne—stopped by for breakfast and told me the news. About Hitler, that is. And he decided he wanted to tag along too. To see Jo." Her mouth twisted in an unnatural smile. "So I said of course. It's a day to celebrate, after all."

Suddenly I didn't know which of them I hated more. The two of them, showing up like this, together, smiling and laughing, knowing nothing of the struggles we'd been facing in their absence. The sheer enormity of their ignorance—about Tim, about me, about Jo, about the very weight of our hearts and our lives in this town. My mother should have been here. Sergeant Hawthorne should have been here.

But instead they'd been someplace else. Together.

The May sun no longer felt pleasant. It felt hot. Sweat dripped down my back, wetting my undergarments.

"I should go," Sergeant Hawthorne said, taking a step back. "Evelyn, I'll be back in a few hours. We'll need to return by nightfall."

It was only after he'd left that my mother finally removed her sunglasses. Her makeup was thick and dramatic. I noticed a faint smudge of eyeliner on her lid as she looked down at her watch. "So, Olive," she said, "tell me what you've been up to. I want to hear everything."

I pulled my arms to my sides, crossing them over my stomach. I suddenly coveted my secrets; just knowing she wanted to hear them was enough to make them weapons.

"Nothing. School."

She giggled. "I know school. But *what* at school?"

"Stuff."

"She's doing real good," Grandma said quickly, trying to cover for my attitude. "Passing all her classes. Top marks in literature, even. But we expected that, what with all the reading she does."

"And what about friends? Have you made any friends?"

"No." A lie. But she didn't deserve to know about Jo. She didn't deserve to know about any of it.

233

"Now, that's not true." Grandma's voice again, higher, faster. "She even had a date."

My mother, who had been checking her watch again, jerked her head. "A date?"

"Yes." Grandma winked. "With a very handsome boy."

"Olive! You had your first date? Why didn't you tell me?"

The box in my mind in which I tried to lock Tim flew open. Pictures from that night flooded forth. I closed my eyes, trying to force them back in. That night was mine and mine alone.

"Olive?"

"It doesn't matter," I said. "He enlisted. So he's gone now."

Ma tried to meet my eye. I stared at her shoes. Brown leather, a small silver buckle on the top. No scratches. New.

"Evelyn, dear, you should have seen her. She looked beautiful. This may have been her first date, but it most definitely won't be her last."

Grandma winked at me. My mother beamed. Their faces told me I was supposed to say something. But my mind was empty. Or rather, too full.

"Let's go out to lunch," my mother said suddenly. "To celebrate, I mean." She glanced down at her watch again. "Olive's date, Hitler's death, all of it. I'm starving, and I don't want to waste a single minute of this visit in the kitchen. Let's go out. My treat."

"That's a splendid idea. Let me get my shawl." Grandma took a step back toward the house, calling over her shoulder as she went, "How about the Plaza Café—?"

"No." Ma's voice was surprisingly forceful. "No," she repeated, gentler, seeing the bewilderment on Grandma's face. "I was thinking something nicer. Somewhere we don't usually go. Someplace . . . special."

"What did you have in mind?"

"Memories."

"Now, Evelyn, don't be silly. That place is way too expensive, and you shouldn't be spending money all willy-nilly. I know—"

"It's fine," my mother broke in. "Really, it's fine."

"Yes, but the ranch—"

"Mother." Her tone was sharper now, her word directed at Grandma but her eyes focused on me. "It's fine. Please."

My gaze flickered between the two of them, trying to read the conversation playing beneath their closed lips. I was obviously in the way of a discussion they'd had before. About the ranch. And money. I knew funds had been tight, but this felt bigger. More urgent. And more secretive.

My mother gave me a smile—strained, manufactured—and glanced at her watch. "It's a special occasion. Let's open the purse strings. Just a little. Please?"

Grandma stared at her for a few more moments before sighing and retreating inside for her covering.

Memories was a fancy little restaurant on the northern end of New York Avenue, away from the noise of Tenth Street and the bustle of downtown. There were no neon lights up this way. No window-shopping gawkers. It was a serious restaurant for serious people—dim lights and cloth napkins and dinnerware that probably cost more than Grandma's house. Even the lunch crowd was fancy—no ham sandwiches for these people. No, there was steak and roast lamb and something called eggplant, which sounded terrible.

Grandma and I looked completely out of place in our simple cotton dresses, both with wide collars and small pockets, hers a pale pink, mine a dark shade of green. My mother, somehow, fit in.

We were tucked into a table in a corner of the restaurant—my mother's request—next to a window that allowed a nice view of the mountains. We ordered salads with roast chicken—the cheapest thing on the menu—and iced tea with lemon from a waiter with silver hair and a thin mustache. While we waited for our food, Grandma excused herself to the bathroom, leaving me alone for the first time with the woman who'd birthed me, nurtured me, raised me.

A woman who was now a stranger.

"So . . . ," she said, twirling her glass and making the ice clink. "How's she doing? Grandma, I mean," she added as if I didn't know. "Any more . . . issues?"

I smoothed the corner of my napkin with exaggerated precision. "Fit as a fiddle." She wasn't, of course. Just two days ago she'd tried to force her way into the neighbors' house thinking it was her own. Luckily, I'd been home; even more fortunate, the neighbors hadn't.

"She seems well today," my mother continued. "But I wanted to make sure it wasn't getting worse. I know you can handle anything, but it can be frightening, I'm sure. She hasn't done . . ."

My jaw tightened. I stopped listening. I didn't care about anything she had to say. Her words were hollow and self-serving, thrown out under a guise of concern that couldn't quite mask her desperation. After months of silence and indifference, nothing she said could convince me that anything more than our proximity was responsible for her interest.

"Have you heard from Avery lately?"

It was a dare, the edge in my voice surprising even me. But more than that, it was a plea. For a moment of honesty, a glimpse into truth—that the letter was real, my suspicions were childish fancy, that whatever else I felt about my mother, at least she wasn't a liar.

There was a hitch in her breath, nothing more than a hiccup really, before a soft "No" escaped her lips. She twisted her napkin. "Not since his last letter."

And there it was. Truth without truth. It wasn't my imagination. Something *was* off about Avery's letter. My mother knew it too . . . but she wasn't going to tell me.

As if reading my mind, she reached out and clasped my hand in her own. Her skin was ice-cold. "Olive, please look at me."

I couldn't. I simply couldn't.

"I'm sorry, sweetie. I wish I had better news. And I should have been here for your date. I will regret that every day for the rest of my life. I will regret . . ." She coughed, violent and deep, before starting again. "I need you to know that, Olive. I wish things were different. I wish everything was different. The war, the ranch, the world . . . me."

The last word was a whisper. I finally looked at her . . . only to find she was no longer looking at me. She was staring out the window, misty-eyed. I opened my mouth to speak.

"Your food, ladies."

Our plates landed in front of us with a dull thud, breaking my mother's gaze and the moment. Heaps of colors abounded—green leafy spinach, bright-orange carrots, vivid-red tomatoes and radishes surrounded by strips of brown roasted chicken. It was like a painting, the most beautiful array of food I'd ever seen in my life.

And I was nowhere near hungry.

Grandma returned from the bathroom, wringing her hands. "What a fancy restroom!" she exclaimed as she sat down. "Three different kinds of soap! As if that's what the world needed now was three different kinds of soap."

My mother glanced yet again at her watch. She stood suddenly. "Well, this I just have to see. You all go ahead and eat—really, it's okay. I'll be right back." Grabbing her purse, she waved down Grandma's protests. "It's fine! Just eat. You've waited long enough!"

I watched her dark hair bob away from the table toward the back of the dining area, where she accidentally jostled a waiter on his way out of the kitchen. Thankfully, he was able to save his tray of bread before it hit the floor. Her body twitched as she apologized, her reaction seeming way too dramatic for a simple, inconsequential mishap. I saw her check her watch for the hundredth time.

Something was wrong here. And very, very off.

"This looks delicious!" Beside me, Grandma draped her napkin over her lap. "Wonder where they get all these fancy vegetables. Can't grow stuff like this in New Mexico soil. Trust me, I've been trying for years! Wonder if they haul it in from—"

"I have to go to the bathroom."

"You too?"

"Yes."

"You're just going to leave an old woman sitting here by herself?"

I gripped the side of the table, my face falling. "No. No, of course not, Grandma. I'll wait."

Grandma laughed. "Gracious, child, ain't you lived with me long enough yet to tell when I'm teasing? For goodness' sake, go to the bathroom. I'm not five years old, if you haven't noticed. I can sit here by myself for a minute. Ain't no one gonna snatch me away, and God help them if they try."

I tried to laugh. "I'll be right back."

I maneuvered around the other patrons, narrowly avoiding a server's tray loaded with wineglasses before ducking into the dark hallway down which I'd seen my mother disappear. The ladies' door squeaked as I opened it. The smell of lilac soap rushed forward to meet me. There were three stalls, each of them empty.

I checked again. I'd seen her go back here. I'd seen it. Where could she be?

I pushed out of the restroom, looking down the darkened hallway. From here, I could see Grandma at her corner table. She was chewing contentedly, gazing out the window to the mountains beyond. She was alone.

I glanced the other way. An unmarked black door lay at the end of the hallway.

I was being stupid. She'd probably just stepped outside for a smoke. I should go back to the table and wait.

And yet I found myself nudging the door open anyway. Just a crack, I told myself. Just to see.

An alley barely wide enough for the dumpster it contained and the stacks of crates lining the other side. One end open to the street, the other a solid brick wall. At neither end was my mother.

I sighed, irritated with my own foolishness. But as I released the door to let it close, I heard murmuring. I eased the door back open and strained my ear against the silence. I was imagining it. It was probably just the noise from the dining room making its way outside. But there it was again. The low hum of voices, muted but nearby—much closer than the dining room.

I pressed my face into the crack, too scared to open it further. My eyes scanned the alley. It was empty. Completely empty. But then, there, in the narrow gap between the wall and dumpster, I saw it. A flash of fabric. Brown fabric. With white dots.

But my mother wasn't alone. A pair of black shoes, shiny, and the tiniest sliver of khaki pants. Sergeant Hawthorne?

The murmuring increased in intensity, but the words were still indistinguishable. I heard my mother cough; it echoed through the narrow corridor.

The black shoes tapped against the pavement. A man's voice. Muffled. Too high-pitched to be Sergeant Hawthorne. And yet . . . I pressed my cheek against the door, straining to see, but there was nothing but shadows and whispers.

And then, very distinctly, footsteps. They were done talking. I closed the door and rushed down the hallway, sliding into my seat beside Grandma while blood pounded in my ears.

Grandma chewed, eyebrows raised. "Problems in the bathroom?"

"Sorry that took so long." My mother appeared suddenly, completely unruffled, her purse tucked under her arm. "I got distracted by all those soaps." Her voice never faltered; her eye never twitched. She smoothed her dress as she sat down next to me. "Well now, let's eat, shall we?" She stuck a fork in her spinach and raised it her mouth. Smiled at me. Like we were just a mother and daughter, having lunch together. Like she hadn't just been in the alleyway with a mysterious man. Like she wasn't lying through her teeth.

The salad should have been the best thing I'd ever eaten. Grandma said it was. But I don't even remember eating it. It was simply mush in my mouth, soured by suspicion and doubt.

———— ◆ ❈ ◆ ————

"I think I'll take a nap," Grandma said when we returned to the house a little while later. "All the excitement of the day has worn me out. I hate to waste away your visit sleeping, though, Evelyn. Would you come lay down with me?"

"I would love to," Ma replied. "I could use a quick rest myself. Just a short one, though. We could wake up in time to listen to a program? Abbott and Costello still your favorite, Olive?"

I hadn't listened to the silly comedians in months. "Sure."

"Come lay next to me, Evie," Grandma said, heading toward the bedroom. "Give this old lady the gift of your company as I fall asleep."

My mother winked at me as she followed. "Thirty minutes. And not a minute more. Do you hear me, Olive?"

I nodded. "I'll wake you up."

Grandma's door closed with a soft click. I collapsed onto her scratchy sofa with a deep sigh, as if I'd been holding my breath. My head hurt. The muscles in my neck ached. I pinched at them, trying to will my body to relax. I felt tired but the events at lunch would not let me rest. My mother in the alley, only not in the alley. Insisting we eat at Memories and then barely eating at all. Sergeant Hawthorne or not Sergeant Hawthorne with her.

Secrets. Lies. Mysteries.

I rubbed at my eyes. I was being immature again, overreacting. There had to be a logical explanation for all of this.

I shot up. Jo's. I could go to Jo's. She would know if her dad had gone missing an hour ago; if he had, it would give me at least one answer, maybe more. I grabbed a piece of paper from the counter.

Gone to Jo's, I scribbled. *Be home soon.*

I put the paper on the table, placing a book on the corner to keep it from blowing in the breeze of the open window. Taking a step back, I noticed Ma's purse on the table. The same purse she'd taken with her to meet the man in the alley.

"Don't do it, Olive," I whispered.

But even as I said it, I knew I would. I crept to the bedroom door and put my ear to the crack. Silence. They must both be asleep. Returning to the table, I pulled the purse toward me, making careful note of its exact position before moving it. The handle was there. The zipper in that direction. The brown leather smelled of the ranch, hay and dirt and home. Probing my hand into the soft lining, I found her wallet. Keys. Lipstick. Nothing out of the ordinary, although the lipstick I was sure was a new addition.

But then, strangely, a Jell-O box. Lime. Empty and in two pieces. I turned the two halves over in my hand. They were neat and precise. No jagged edges. The box had been cut deliberately. I placed both sections on the table, staring at them as I reached into the purse again. I knew what the last item was before I even pulled it out. A shiver ran through me as my fingers brushed against the smooth surface.

It was the notebook. The one I'd found in the shed at the ranch. Same brown cover, same yellow paper. I opened it.

The pages of scribbles were gone.

Numbers and letters swam up from my hazy memories. *STRAWBERRY* crossed out and replaced with the word *LIME.*

My pulse pounded behind my eyes as they drifted over to the Jell-O box. The *lime-flavored* Jell-O box.

From inside my grandma's bedroom came a cough and the squeak of the bed. Heart racing, I stuffed the items back into the purse, placing the strap just so before fleeing from the house.

Outside, the wind had picked up, sending tufts of seeds from the cottonwood trees swirling into the air. I kept my head down as I crossed Tenth and headed north on Michigan. I needed to see Jo. Because she would be able to tell me what was going on. She would have an answer. Somehow she always had an answer. Or at least a way to make me feel better.

Sergeant Hawthorne's sleek, Army-issued car sat in the gravel drive. Curiously, another Army vehicle was parked behind it, this one green, rugged, and not at all suited to an officer.

The trees shielded the porch from the incessant wind, making me feel as if I'd walked into another world. I pushed my hair away from my face, fingers snagging on more than a few new tangles, before raising my hand to knock.

The front door flew open, causing me to jump back. Two Army men emerged. Their faces were grim as they placed caps on their heads. Sergeant Hawthorne walked behind them, putting a hand on the shoulder of the first man.

"Chaplain Porter, thank you for—Olive?"

I hunched my shoulders, dipping my head into my chest. "Hi."

Sergeant Hawthorne leaned toward the two men and whispered something into their ears. They nodded. As they walked away, they kept their eyes very intentionally on the ground. It was only after their truck had rumbled down the road, heading north, that Sergeant Hawthorne turned to me.

"What are you doing here, Olive?"

"I came to see Jo."

He closed his eyes and I noticed for the first time just how long his eyelashes were. They fluttered over the tops of his cheeks. "Now might not be the best time."

"Oh. Right. Okay. I'll just come back—"

"Olive?"

Jo's face appeared in the doorway. She looked older somehow, her cheeks drawn, her lids heavier. That hint of a smile—the one that was always there, no matter what she was doing, no matter what she was feeling—was gone.

And in that moment, everything else disappeared. Because I knew. Grief welled up inside me at the sight of her—deep, penetrating, desperate grief, our country's collective sorrow come to make it personal. She didn't need to say it. But she did anyway.

"My brother."

I nodded.

"Perhaps you should go," Sergeant Hawthorne said gently, startling me. I'd forgotten he was there.

"I want her to stay."

Sergeant Hawthorne looked at his daughter. She looked right back. There was something being said between them, silently. A challenge. A plea. And it was the elder who broke first.

"Just for a few minutes."

Jo stared at him until he disappeared inside, closing the door behind him. I stood on the step, unsure what to say, unable to move, until Jo's eyes finally met mine. Heart breaking, I pulled her into a strong embrace, feeling her thin shoulders sag. She didn't cry. Instead, her grief seemed to ooze from every pore.

After a moment, she pulled back. "I have to go to California. They're saying the body should arrive next week. We'll have the funeral after that."

I nodded. *The body.* Like it was a package now. Because it was.

She tucked a long strand of hair behind her ear. It immediately blew back again.

I needed to say something. Tell her I was sorry for her loss, that it would be okay, spout off some kind of Bible verse like I knew she'd do if the situation were reversed. But there was nothing to say. It could have been me. It could have been any number of people in this town, breath caught in throats as the Army chaplains' vehicle rolled through the streets. But instead it was her. And no words would make that go away.

I hugged her again. When we finally broke apart, she threw one last glance over her shoulder before disappearing back inside. Staring at that closed door, I did something I'd never done before in my entire life.

For Jo and her brother, for Avery and Tim, for every hurting soldier and family in this cursed, never-ending war . . . and for myself and a world that seemed determined to break us all, I prayed to a God who seemed the only and last way to save us from ourselves.

CHAPTER EIGHTEEN

JO

MARCH 1952

The sun had barely crested the Sacramentos when Jo slipped from her bed. She pulled on her old black pants. They were crumpled and dusty but still an improvement over the blood-splattered khakis from the day before. She'd need to find a Laundromat. Or a dumpster. Did snake guts stain?

It didn't matter. She was too tired to think about it. She hadn't slept. Not even exhaustion could push the image of yesterday's events from her mind. The abandoned ranch. Pieces of serpent flesh in the dust. Charlie.

And the green glass sea. Every time she closed her eyes, she was there again, surrounded. Suffocated.

Separated.

She hadn't spoken to God in years, hadn't felt Him, seen Him, experienced Him in any way. And yet the distance she'd encountered yesterday felt bigger. All these years, she'd felt God was hiding; yesterday she wondered if He had disappeared altogether. And for the first time in a long time, she felt something other than numbness or anger.

What she felt was fear.

She walked to the Plaza Café, keeping her head down and slipping into a back booth. The smell of fresh bacon and old coffee filled the small space. Despite the early hour, the counter was full, crowded with men in dusty cowboy hats, most of them long past the age of ranching but holding on to their memories and opinions nonetheless.

"What can I get you, hon?"

The waitress had weary eyes and hair the color of night, streaked with gray. Pale-pink lipstick smudged her teeth, but her smile was friendly.

"Coffee," Jo said. "Black."

"Anything else?"

She wasn't hungry but knew she should eat something. The soggy french fries from yesterday hadn't exactly satisfied. "Eggs, please. Scrambled."

"Chile." It wasn't a question. Chile never was in New Mexico. "Green."

The waitress scribbled a note on her pad and disappeared, returning a few minutes later with a pot of coffee. Jo's eggs arrived shortly thereafter. The green chile caused her eyes to water. She'd never adjusted to the spiciness of the local cuisine, and she wasn't sure why she was trying now.

As she chewed, she glanced absentmindedly at a newspaper left on the table. Most of it was about the war in Korea, reminding people of the importance of a United States victory—even though it had been locked in a stalemate for months—in order to stem the threat of Communist spread. A smaller blurb underneath told of a protest in New York City, demanding clemency for the convicted Soviet spies, the Rosenbergs. It was inconsequential, the article said; their execution would likely proceed next June. Americans had little sympathy for "Reds."

Red. Everything was "red" now. How eager the Soviets had been to fill the void left by the Nazis. From ally to enemy in mere months, if they'd ever really been allies to begin with. But she was too tired to deal with the world's hate, even less inclined to deal with its fear. She had quite enough of her own.

She pushed the paper away and listened instead to the idle chatter of the other diners, the clatter of silverware, the rumble of cars as Alamogordo slowly awoke to the start of a new day. From her spot, she could see the bus station, the trickle of passengers arriving with their suitcases, buying tickets, and hugging goodbyes as they traveled to El Paso, Albuquerque, Amarillo. How strange to think that twenty-four hours ago, she'd been so sure she'd be among them, running away, free from all of this at last.

But now . . .

Running wasn't the answer. She knew that now. Leaving this place wouldn't fix things any more than coming here had. For there was nowhere left to run, nowhere else she could go in her search for the truth.

For Him.

Because that was what it came down to. Yes, she had come here because of her father. She could even admit now she had come for Olive. But she had really come because of Him. Because she'd searched everywhere for Him, around the world, in slums and cities, farms and schools, even inside the throbbing of her own exhausted body after a day of mission work. Everywhere, that is, except the place where she'd last seen Him.

Yes, she'd come back to find God.

But He wasn't here.

She pushed chile seeds in circles on her plate. All around her the diner bustled, plates clinked, bacon sizzled, neighbors discussed the ongoing battle of Hill Eerie and the unusually dry spring. Everything was so normal. Mundane. She was the only one aware the world had changed.

"Jo?"

She was so far inside herself she barely registered when a man sat down in the booth opposite her.

"What a nice surprise!" Pastor Hamilton clutched a newspaper to his chest, his smile excruciatingly warm against her drear. He put a hand on the table between them. "I thought you'd left town already."

She tried to smile back but wasn't sure she succeeded.

"How are you? How's your father?"

Green chile burned the back of Jo's throat. Surely it was just the chile. She gave a slight shrug.

"I see. I'm sorry to hear that. Were you able to get in touch with Olive at least?"

This time, all she could manage was a defeated shake of her head.

"Golly. That stinks. I felt bad I couldn't help you more. You know, I asked around after you left, seeing if anyone had heard anything. There was gossip aplenty but nothing concrete."

"Gossip?"

He rolled his eyes. "Yeah, you know how it is. This and that. The family moved back out to the ranch after the war. Edna passed, which you already knew, but from what I understand, Evelyn died too—"

Jo's breath caught in her throat. "Evelyn? You mean Olive's mother? She . . . died?"

Pastor Hamilton frowned. "Yes. Lung cancer, I'm told. Not long after Edna. Though there was never any funeral here in town for her. I heard she was buried out at the ranch."

Jo pulled at her knuckles. Olive did not deserve her pity. And yet it didn't stop her from feeling the first twinges of it anyway. "Anything else?"

"Well, there was a brother and an uncle, I believe, who disappeared during the war. But Olive stayed at the ranch for a few years, even after her grandmother's and mother's deaths. She sold the house on Delaware Avenue and retreated to the desert. Supposedly she used to come into town every so often, but no one has seen her for years. Rumor has it even the ranch is abandoned now. No one knows what happened to her. It's like she just disappeared. Poof!" he added for emphasis.

Jo shook her head. She'd seen the house, walked through the emptiness of the ranch. She knew they were gone. And yet she also knew Olive—at least she thought she knew Olive. It would take something big to make her give up the Jornada. Something that couldn't be summed up in the word *poof*.

"But that doesn't make any sense."

"I agree. That's why I don't believe it. A few of Edna's old neighbors over on Delaware said there were some detectives poking around her house for a little while after she'd moved out to the ranch. Asking funny questions."

"Detectives?"

Pastor Hamilton snorted. "That's what they say. It was probably just military folks, checking in after the test. They did that, you know? After they finally admitted there *was* a test, that is."

"What else did you hear?"

There was a long pause as he adjusted in his seat. He averted his eyes, folding and unfolding the corner of his newspaper.

"Pastor Hamilton?"

"Jo, this isn't really my place. I shouldn't—"

"Tell me."

He grimaced. "Some said the Alexanders weren't alone out there after the war. Some said the reason they got most of their ranch back when so many others didn't . . . was because Mrs. Alexander found an Army man and was out there playing house with him."

Even though she was still sitting, Jo suddenly felt dizzy. Like the diner had tilted underneath her. An Army man. Her father. He could only be talking about her father. She pictured them all together, reading by the fire, carving Sunday chicken. He hadn't just been there for Olive in a moment of grief. He had been there for her, *period*. Olive had found the dad she'd lacked while he'd discovered the daughter he'd never had. The one he'd always wanted Jo to be.

They'd sent her away so they could start over fresh. New. Better.

"I don't know if there's any truth to it," he said hurriedly. "No one had any proof. About the Army man or the detectives or any of it. So I wouldn't take stock in the rumors. All we know for sure is they're gone." He sighed deeply, running one hand through his hair. "I should have kept better tabs on them, especially after Edna left the church and moved out there. Once a part of the flock, always a part of the flock. But after the war ended, there was so much need here in town—grieving families and soldiers with wounded souls." He pressed his lips together. "Not that that's any excuse. I should have tried harder."

The burning in Jo's throat had returned. Her father had never really been a part of her life, even before Trinity. She thought it had been because of the Army, because of his work . . . but maybe it was because of her. His final words to her on that morning rang through her head, as sharp and agonizing as the day he'd spoken them:

"Get on that bus and don't ever come back."

It wasn't because he was too busy. Olive hadn't wanted her. And neither had he.

Maybe that's why she couldn't find God. He didn't want her either. He wasn't hiding; He'd fled from her like the rest of them to be with someone better.

"Jo?" Pastor Hamilton's eyebrows were raised. "Are you okay?"

The realization pulled at her insides, making her feel as if she would vomit.

"Jo?" He reached across the table and laid a hand on her own.

The warmth of his touch surprised her; she flinched. But rather than pull back, she left it there, trying to steady herself against the rising tide.

"Do you think . . . ?" she heard herself whisper, voice quivering at the edges. "Do you think God is still here?"

He leaned forward, mouth pulling down at the corners. "What?"

"Do you think it's possible for God to leave? That He gets fed up with us and He . . . He just leaves? To find someone better?"

Pastor Hamilton set down his newspaper and reached his other hand toward her. She released her mug, allowing both her hands to be wrapped in his. "No, child. No. To God, there is no 'better thing' than His children. No matter what we do, God doesn't leave. He doesn't give up on us. He loves us too much—Jesus is all the proof of that we need. Abandoning us is simply not in His nature; it's not who He is."

Jo dropped her head to her chest. His words, though kind, failed to comfort.

"But I think that's who *we* can be."

She raised her head to find his face drawn.

"God never leaves us. But I think we often try to leave Him. I think we can get so consumed by our misery, our bitterness, even our own selfishness or pride that, like Paul, it can grow scales over our eyes or build a wall around our heart, rendering us unable to discern God's presence or even hear His voice. And it's not because He's not there. He's always there, just on the other side of the hurt and the grief, everything we refuse to surrender at the cross."

Jo's mind flashed back to Trinity. To the sand hemmed in beneath the green glass sea. Contaminated, yes, but not destroyed. Isolated from the world by the residue of that day. Trapped. Separated.

Like Jo's heart had been since that very same day. Withdrawn and closed off from the world. Because of Olive's betrayal, her father's words . . . and her own determination never to be that naive again. Never to feel that way again.

Never to feel anything.

Pastor Hamilton squeezed her hand. His skin was dry, his touch gentle, a subtle gesture sweeping like a flame over the iciness within. As his words soaked into her soul, she searched the face of the man who had been her teacher all those years ago, a father all those times when her own couldn't or wouldn't be one, the person who had shown her what it meant to know Jesus, deeply and personally.

This man who had welcomed her with love and open arms after all these years apart, despite the damage she knew he could sense just beneath her surface.

A signal fire of God's presence that she'd missed for the world's smoke.

And she felt something inside herself crack. Sorrow and regret rushed forth, filling her body with weight as heavy as lead. She struggled to breathe. Everything was a mess. All of the feelings she'd tried to bury—the pain and the betrayal, loneliness and doubt—all of it was there, raw and bare, anguished and severe.

And yet somehow, therein lay the hope. After all these years of determined numbness, He was using this man to tell her to *feel* once again . . . because just beyond those feelings lay freedom.

Lay Him.

She'd been feeding herself poison for years, trying to kill her heart; after all, what good was a heart when it could only feel the sting of rejection? Yet it was in this toxic soil that a lie had taken root, without her even realizing it: the deficiency of her earthly father was not a signifier of the absence of her heavenly One. He had not run; she had. In trying to flee from the ruination of her past, she'd gotten confused between her father and her *Father*, closing herself off to the only One who could heal the ache in her soul she'd tried to deny even existed.

Yes, her father had rejected her. Olive too. But God had chosen her. And He was still choosing her. The evidence was in the pain that had devastated but not destroyed her, in the heart that continued to beat despite her attempts at silencing it. In the man in front of her who saw her, even now, and spoke truth to her grief. She'd put up a barrier and focused her eyes inward rather than up. But God had always been there, just on the other side of herself. Waiting for her to let Him in again.

She only had to tear down the wall, brick by painful brick, starting with her own bitterness. To break through the green glass sea . . . to find Him on the other side.

If there was still time.

She squeezed Pastor Hamilton's hand and gave him a real smile for the first time. Pained, but real. "Thank you. Thank you so much."

The side of his mouth curled in confusion. "You're welcome? But are you—?"

"I have to go," she interrupted, scooting from the booth. "I'm so sorry, but I have to go."

"Jo—"

"I'll come see you again before I leave. I promise!"

The bell over the café door jingled as she pushed her way outside into the dry, dusty morning air. As she glanced at her watch, she was surprised to find it still shy of nine. She broke into a run, headed east toward Tenth Street . . . and straight into a suited back.

"Jo!" the man exclaimed, turning around. His hair was greased and perfect, his eyes hidden beneath a pair of dark sunglasses.

Charlie. It was Charlie Wilson. Again.

"Fancy running into you here," he said, smoothing the front of his jacket.

"Charlie! What are you doing here?"

"Getting a bite to eat, of course." He gave her a grin.

Jo tried to return it, shaking off an unexpected niggling inside her. This wellspring of emotions bubbling up inside her was stale and out of practice; surely she was just *over-feeling* this coincidence. Because it *was* a coincidence. He was getting a bite to eat. Alamogordo was a small town, and this was one of the few diners open for breakfast.

All the same, though, somehow he was always just . . . *there*.

"What are you up to today?"

"I'm going to see my father."

"Want me to come with you?"

He was being sweet again. Concerned. He liked her; yesterday had made that much obvious. And yet she still stepped back. "No thank you. I really have to go."

"Jo, wait—come have breakfast with me. Let's talk. You seem upset."

She took another step back. "I already ate. I'm sorry, Charlie. I have to go. We'll talk later, okay?"

And as she took off down Tenth Street toward the hospital, she knew they would. Somehow she knew he'd make it a point to see that they would.

But for right now, she had more pressing issues at hand.

CHAPTER NINETEEN

OLIVE

JULY 1945

May brought the elation of V-E Day and, shortly thereafter, the despair of continued fighting in the Pacific. June ushered in the last day of school and triple-digit temperatures. Behind it rolled July and the hope of rain. Each afternoon, mounds of fluffy white clouds grew over the mountains, drifting into the valley like tourists, sometimes lingering, other times wandering onward, releasing their much-needed moisture elsewhere.

But the summer did not bring back Jo Hawthorne. Her usual spot in the front pew remained vacant, the house on Michigan Avenue empty. Pastor Hamilton said he'd been in touch with her. According to him, she was grieving but doing okay. However, as she was busy "tying up loose ends" back in California, he did not know when she'd return.

My heart cleaved in a way I didn't expect. I missed our chats and our sing-alongs, her easy laugh and peaceful silence. I missed *her*. More than that, I worried about her in her mourning. But if I was being honest, I was also worried for myself. Selfishly, I worried that she would be one more person to abandon me. I needed her to come back and prove me wrong. But I also needed her to be strong, to be able to get through this. Because if she couldn't, no one could. Because then all that stuff she tried to tell me about Jesus was worthless.

And Jesus, it seemed, was the only thing I had left. Grandma continued to slip in and out of episodes, my mother remained steadfastly silent away at the ranch, and both Avery and Tim lingered around the edges of my mind, their absences pronounced and tangible, but in very different ways. With no letters from either of them—real or fake—no friends to confide in, and no school to distract me, I had only Jo's Bible. The words on the pages were foreign and perplexing but somehow the only real thing in this hazy, never-ending nightmare.

And then suddenly, as if in a dream, Jo was there. One sticky July afternoon, she appeared on my doorstep, separated from me only by the thin mesh of Grandma's screen door.

"Hi."

I stared at her, too stunned to speak. Everything I'd felt, everything I'd wanted to say over the last few weeks, evaporated at the sight of her. All that remained was the faint smell of frying Spam wafting from the kitchen behind me. "You're here," I said finally.

"I am."

"When did you get back?"

"Last night."

I realized I'd expected her to look different. How could she not after all she'd been through? But she still looked the same. Her white-blonde hair was pulled back in a simple ponytail, and she was dressed in a light-green button-down blouse paired with a navy-blue skirt and brown loafers. Practical. Unassuming. A picture of sense in a nonsensical world.

"Jo!" Grandma appeared behind me, wiping her hand on her apron. "How lovely to see you, dear!" She opened the screen door and wrapped her in a hug, and for the first time, I saw Jo's face crack. A slight twitch in her eye, a tremble in her lip. For a fraction of a second, truth broke through: she was not the same. Nothing was the same.

"Do you want to go for a drive?"

Grandma released Jo, turning to me with raised eyebrows. "Olive?"

"I promised I'd take her out to White Sands when she got back. She's never been." Inspiration came on me at once, and the words fell from my lips as if I'd been planning them all along.

"You want to drive all the way out to White Sands? In this heat?"

"Please, Mrs. Burke," Jo piped up, catching on. "It's . . . it's been a stressful few weeks."

That's all it took. Any suspicion drained from Grandma's face. "Oh, Jo. Of course. Of course." She squeezed her hand again. "Just be careful. Don't you go driving like you're on the ranch, Olive. You may know how but you're not technically legal, and even though the cops look the other way, they won't turn a blind eye to your lead foot. The last thing I need is the police showing up with a ticket I can't pay."

I snatched the keys from the entryway table and pushed out the front door, nudging Jo forward. "I won't!" I called.

"And be back before it gets dark!"

Jo slid in beside me. She waved at my grandmother on the front porch as we pulled out of the drive. "So where are we really going?" she asked under her breath.

"Oh, we're going to White Sands."

She turned her head sharply. "Really? Why?"

"Because we wouldn't have gotten any privacy in that house. And because it might actually be the place you need right now."

Twenty miles outside of town, past the Army air base with its barbed wire and security posts, on the other side of the low, scraggly shrubs and windswept dirt of the basin desert, crisp white dunes rose out of the desert floor like a mirage. One minute we were in a wasteland; the next, we were surrounded by hills of gleaming white sand, stark and bright against the blue sky and black, jagged peaks of the Organ Mountains.

The heat pushed on us as we exited the car. "Up here." I squinted my eyes against the glare and gestured forward. "There's a spot where my dad and I would always picnic. This way."

We trudged up the hill, giggling as our shoes sank into the soft, white earth. We stumbled and crawled and laughed, then stumbled and crawled and laughed again. Soon we were out of breath and covered in a layer of thick sand, which clung to our sweat. I led her to my favorite spot: a towering, gnarled tree, completely out of place among the yucca and sagebrush, its wide green leaves like paint splattered on a white canvas.

"I can't imagine trying to carry a picnic basket up that hill."

I gave a winded snort. "Well, that part's not fun, no. But it's worth it."

Following my gaze, Jo looked out at the scene before us. Her eyes rolled over each crested hill, the swirls in the sand painted with perfect synchronicity by an unseen hand. The breeze was light, dry, the smell of desert vegetation stripped during its journey across the expanse of white nothingness.

Jo's breath caught in her throat. "This is incredible."

A pregnant pause filled the air between us as we stared out at the dunes. The landscape was bright and exotic in the otherwise-monotonous Tularosa Basin—as out of place in the desert as I felt beside Jo. I had nothing to say to her and, also, too much.

But to my surprise, she spoke first. "I wasn't going to come back. When they brought his body off that plane . . ." She shook her head, unwilling—or unable—to say more. "My father stayed for a few days after the funeral but then he had to go back to work. The war doesn't stop for one dead soldier."

My stomach tightened. "He left you? Alone? In all of that?"

She shrugged. "I get it. I understand. Thousands of men die every day. And Dad says he's trying to end it. So . . ." She chewed at a spot of dried skin on her lips.

"But, Jo, still. He shouldn't have left. You shouldn't have been alone."

The wind whistled between us in lieu of her response, grains of white sand tumbling down the dune. We watched it, silent, for a moment before she finally spoke again. "It was like living in slow motion. Do you know what I mean?" She didn't wait for me to answer. "The world is moving. Going on. Doing all the things the world does. And it feels like I can't quite catch up. One day Josh was alive and now he's dead, and we're supposed to just keep moving, like nothing's changed . . ."

She slipped off her shoes and ran her toes over the white sand, letting her words fall off. "It's cold," she said suddenly.

"What?"

"The sand. It's cold. How is it cold? At the beach, the sand burns your feet."

"Because it's gypsum. It reflects the sun."

"Oh." Picking up a handful, she let it trickle through her fingers, tilting her palm to watch it collect near her feet. "I'm not staying, Olive."

My own fingers, which I'd been using to mindlessly doodle in the sand, went numb. "What?"

"Being back in California, seeing my brother's casket . . . it made everything so clear. The world is moving on . . . and I should too." She wiped some sand from her nose with the back of her hand. "I tried to talk to my dad about it. He was very upset. Forbid me to go, actually. And I guess I understand. He's lost a lot, and he feels like he needs me here even if he's not actually here. But I can't . . . I can't just sit here. Not anymore. Not while so many people out there are suffering. I mean, I've always known I wanted to go into mission work but now . . . I feel like He's calling me, Olive. And now is the time to answer. I'm leaving tomorrow."

I looked at my lap, willing tears to stay in my eyes. I wanted to be angry with her. Or be happy for her. Or even indifferent. Anything at all but *this*. This overwhelming sense of hurt and abandonment. Again. Always again.

Everyone around me was always wanting something more. Avery, Tim, even Hershel and my mother. They all wanted something more than this. Than me.

And now Jo did too.

She dug her toes into the sand, trying to bury herself to the ankles, oblivious to my discomfort. "And . . . I think you should come too."

The ground roared forward as if to swallow me. It felt as if my body were shrinking. "What?"

Jo turned. Her smile was hesitant and shy. "That's why I came back. For you, Olive. I want you to come with me."

"But . . ."

"Look, I understand—you're still not sure about all this Jesus stuff, and that's okay." She put a hand on my shoulder. "I know this doesn't make any sense . . . and yet it makes all the sense in the world. Because I know it's what He's telling me to do. And I think maybe it's what He's telling you too."

"Jo, I . . ." My lips were numb and useless. "I'm not a preacher."

Her laugh echoed across the dunes. "No one's asking you to get in the pulpit! Mission work is about *people*, not preaching. Helping them see themselves as God sees them. Showing them they're loved. Showing them—" she squeezed my upper arm—"that they matter."

I trembled as tears streamed down my cheeks, my lungs burning with the force it took to simply keep breathing. It was absurd. It was stupid. It was unbelievable, irrational, and foolish. The thought of me going on a mission trip with Jo, doing work for a God I still wasn't sure about.

And yet here Jo sat. Offering me a purpose and a place. A *friend*. Could this God of Jo's really be answering prayers I'd never been brave enough to voice?

Could He somehow know? Could He somehow care?

Could He somehow . . . truly exist?

"What if I can't do it? I . . . I don't even know what I believe anymore."

Jo's face was serious, the pain in those pale-blue spheres as real as my own. "That's okay. For now, I believe enough for the both of us. I know one day you'll find Him. And even if you don't . . . at least we won't be alone anymore."

I wrapped my arms around her, surprising even myself with the force of my affection. She clutched me back. We sat there, holding on to each other as if letting go would allow the reality of the world to erase the future we'd begun painting in our minds.

The two of us, finding our place and doing good in a world determined to be bad. Together.

The sun was just beginning to kiss the tops of the Organ Mountains, the afternoon slipping away like the white grains beneath us, when Jo finally spoke again. "What is that you were doodling?"

I glanced down. Without realizing it, I'd drawn the same symbol in the sand over and over again. A line, up and then down again. The upside-down *V*.

I wiped them away, pushing against the ache rising in my throat. "It's nothing."

Jo raised her eyebrows. It was a mark of just how kind she was that she didn't press.

"It's something my brother and I used to draw," I said anyway. "After my dad died. The three points represent me, Avery, and the mesa. Home." I took a deep breath. "We had this secret place. It was on this one particular bluff behind our house. We called it the burrow. There was this boulder with a lightning-shaped crack that we could squeeze through and . . . it was nothing, really. But it was ours. Our special place. And when things were bad, we'd write this symbol in the dirt or slip notes with it under each other's door. Just to remind each other we always had the mesa. We always had each other. We always had home." A fresh wave of sorrow swelled within. "Not that it meant anything. Obviously."

Jo took her finger and drew the symbol in the white sand in front of her. She tilted her head, studying it for a moment. "I don't know," she said eventually. "I think it might mean something."

"What?"

She gestured at the three points. "Me, you, and God." The smile on her lips was serene. Hopeful. "Home."

— ✦ ◈ ✦ —

We drove back to Alamogordo in silence. The sun behind us dipped below the western mountains, drenching the desert in orange and red. There was too much to say, too many questions to ask, too many what-ifs to be considered. They rolled around in my head, the incredulity of what I was contemplating pushing against the echoes of my past, my present, my future. Was I really considering leaving New Mexico? My family? My home?

When I pulled up in front of Jo's house, she hesitated as she grabbed the door handle. "I know it's a lot to consider in a short time. But think about it, okay? Pray. Ask Him. He'll answer. He—"

"I'll go."

Jo's eyes widened. "Really?"

I nodded, still not fully believing I'd spoken the words out loud. "Yes. I'll go."

It was impulsive and illogical. Insane, even. And yet in this moment, my fear of losing out—of losing Jo—outweighed all those other things. Nothing made sense—not my mother, not Avery, not even this entire war. Why should my decision to go on a mission trip be any different? At least I'd be with my friend. No, she was more than my friend. My sister, in every sense of the word but blood.

The one person who cared enough to come back for me.

Jo hugged me so hard I felt as if my ribs would crack. When she finally pulled away, her eyes were glittering with tears. "The bus leaves tomorrow at eleven. I'll meet you there?"

I nodded. But before she could slide out of the car, I grabbed her arm. As soon as the decision to leave had crossed my lips, a cloud of doubts and fears had begun pushing into my heart; I knew once she left, it would swallow me. I didn't want to allow it the chance to change my mind. "Jo—"

"I'm scared too," she said, giving my hand a quick squeeze. "But just because it's scary doesn't mean it's wrong."

I nodded weakly, biting my lip. I was going to cry again.

"I wrestled at first as well. That's what took me so long to come back. My dad tried to tell me this whole 'calling' thing was baloney. On my weakest nights, I almost believed him. But now I know it's only his bitterness talking. Just because his plans didn't line up with God's doesn't mean mine can't."

"What do you mean?"

She shrugged one shoulder. "My dad's a professional Army man, but he's been stuck at a desk his entire career. When two of his friends were killed at Pearl Harbor, he begged his supervisor to send him to Japan. He felt like it was his duty—his calling—to avenge them, but he couldn't pass the physical. He swore the color blindness didn't affect his ability to fight, but the Army didn't see it that way. So he's stuck here, stateside. I guess it's a blessing, though . . ."

Jo kept talking, unaware the air in the car had soured. "What?"

"I said it was a blessing, really. Especially since my brother ended up there. I can't imagine both of them—"

"No, about the color blindness."

"My dad's color-blind. Has been his whole life. That's why they won't send him overseas."

Her mouth continued to move, but once again, the words evaporated into nothing, blocked by the thudding of my own heart.

Her dad was color-blind. So the Army kept him stateside.

Avery was color-blind . . . and yet he was overseas. Supposedly.

His weird letter, the only one I'd ever received. The mysterious notebook. The man in the alley. The Jell-O box. Lie after lie after lie. Pieces of a puzzle that didn't fit, and yet I knew they must. Somehow they were all connected.

I waited, waving and smiling, pretending everything was fine, until Jo disappeared inside. Then I slammed the car into reverse. I did not go back to Grandma's. Instead I turned the steering wheel north, heading out of town on Highway 54.

Sixty miles lay between me and the truth. And I would not stop until I reached it.

CHAPTER TWENTY

JO

MARCH 1952

Out of breath and dripping with sweat, Jo slipped into the hospital, clutching an ache in her side. She had walked as fast as she could from the diner and, when that was too slow, had broken into a painful run, her sensible heels no longer feeling sensible. But it had still taken her an eternity to arrive.

Miss Betty Thomas stared at her from the reception desk, bright-red lips parted in shock.

Jo wiped at her forehead, the grit of ever-present dust rolling beneath her fingertips. Her hair stuck to the back of her neck. "I'd like to see Richard Hawthorne, please."

"Visiting hours start at ten."

Jo glanced at her watch: 9:17. "But I'm his daughter. Surely you can—"

"Family or not, visiting hours start at ten."

"This can't wait. I . . . I've waited too long already." The emotion in her voice surprised her.

Betty's eyes narrowed behind her black-rimmed glasses. Her lipstick disappeared beneath the force of her grimace as her gaze flitted between Jo and the patient-wing door.

Jo let out a weary sigh. Logic told her she could wait; it was only forty-five minutes. But it wasn't logic pushing her forward. "Please."

After several excruciating seconds, Betty's shoulders sank. "Alright. But you best be quiet, you hear? I'll get it from the on-call doctor if you go waking up the other patients before it's time for their next round of meds."

"I promise. Oh, thank you. Thank you so much."

She gestured Jo inside with a wave of her hand. Stillness marked the air as the door swung closed behind her. Most of the patients were dozing. Jo winced as her footsteps echoed down the aisle of curtains, but no one inside stirred.

In sleep, the ravages of her father's disease were less apparent. His breathing was deep and steady, giving no clue to the battle waging within. He looked peaceful, serene even. Jo hated to wake him, knowing the physical anguish that awaited when he arose. But she *had* to wake him. And she had to do it now.

"Dad."

He did not stir.

"Dad." Jo took a step forward and grabbed his hand, forcing herself not to recoil at the cold skin. "Da—" She stopped. Her father's eyes had opened, glassy but intent, feeling her presence rather than seeing her. Weakly his fingers squeezed back.

Every muscle in her body tensed, every instinct telling her to flee. Looking at his decimated face, her anger swelled. She was allowing herself to feel again . . . and what she felt was hurt. A physical ache spread across her chest. The sting of his words on that long-ago morning pierced her heart again just like it was yesterday. Pain years in the making would not disappear in a day. She wanted to run away. Or perhaps to scream. But more than anything, she wanted to retreat into her shell, numbing herself once again from the intensity of this agony.

And yet something else pushed against those emotions. For years, she had permitted this man and his choices to hold power over her. But it was power only One was worthy to hold. It was time to let it go. She both craved and feared this surrender, every natural instinct rebelling against it but knowing true release was only possible if she ceded his power—and her own feelings—over to Someone bigger.

"Dad . . . I forgive you."

His eyes bulged. Shaking his head, he opened his mouth and released a quavering rasp, clutching at her with a desperation she understood without words.

"I forgive you," she repeated. The second time was easier; the words drifted from her lips, carried not by her own volition but by the force of something long dead finally awakening inside her.

A lone tear dropped onto his sunken cheek. And there, for the first time in almost seven years, was one of her own.

She reached up with her free hand, wiping at the wetness on her face with a bittersweet laugh. Because the ache inside her chest was no longer just for herself. She had loosed those feelings of resentment and rage . . . only to have something sharper and more intense take their place.

Genuine, heartbreaking grief.

Jo pressed her face into his side as sobs welled up in her throat. "I love you, Dad. Despite everything. And I'm sorry this has happened to you. I'm so sorry . . ."

Her words were swallowed up by the ferocity of her cries. Years of emotions she'd tried to deny now rushed forth in a flood of tears, dampening the sheets that lay over his broken body. She'd been too angry, too full of her own hatred to allow space for the truth.

Her father was dying. He was *dying*.

His breathing came forth in uneven gasps, whispered moans escaping his lips as she clung to him. The venom she'd stored inside for so many years drained from her limbs as she wept for the things that were, the things that should have been, and the things that never could be. For so much wasted *time*. She cried until there was nothing left and her sobs were reduced to whimpers. In the exhausted misery that followed, the sound of her heartbeat reverberated in the silence, steady with the rhythm of her father's chest, rising and falling beside her.

And the flicker of his fingers inside her palm.

She turned her head slightly to allow a view of his face. Absorbed in his task, his eyes were narrowed. His mouth twitched in concentration. The touch of his fingertips was like a feather, light and barely discernible. Clumsy. Determined.

Hair prickled on the back of Jo's neck. Writing. He was trying to write something.

"Dad, what . . . ?"

She swallowed the question as she focused her attention on the nerves in her palm. His fingers fumbled, heavy and unwieldy with the weight of a thought he was unable to communicate.

Using her free hand, she reached for his chart, which was tucked into a folder at the foot of the bed. She shoved a pen and piece of paper in his direction. "Write it down," she pleaded. "Write what you can."

The pen fell from his grip and onto the sheet beneath.

She scooped it up, curling his fingers around it. They instantly unfurled; the pen rolled onto the floor with a loud clatter.

Tears leaked from the corners of her father's eyes.

"It's okay," she said. She laid his fingers inside her palm once again. "It's okay. You can do this."

But it was no use. The weak fluttering was only an excruciating, indecipherable tickle.

Staring into her eyes, Jo's father released a pained breath, and then his fingers went limp. His eyes rolled into the back of his head. His rigid body relaxed, sinking into the starched sheets.

Jo grasped at him, pulling on his hand and shaking his shoulders. "Dad!"

But for the first time ever, he failed to respond to her touch.

A guttural howl released from her throat. "Help!" Jo screamed. "Someone help him! Please!"

Behind her, a sudden flurry of movement erupted. "What are you doing in here?" a nurse snapped. "Visiting hours aren't until ten!"

A doctor pushed past them both, unwrapping his stethoscope from his neck and digging his fingers into her father's wrist. "His pulse is weak," he said to no one in particular. "Nurse, I need you to grab—"

Their words jumbled. Her father's body was obscured by the frantic movements of the physician and several nurses who'd appeared out of nowhere. Jo watched, paralyzed, as the hospital staff worked hard to negate the truth, to turn back time, pumping and shouting, sticking his arm with needles and blowing air into lungs that refused to inflate. It took them so long to realize what Jo already knew. Not from the sound of their shouts or even the stillness of the body in front of her. She knew it from somewhere inside, from that place she'd unlocked after all this time.

Her father was dead.

CHAPTER TWENTY-ONE

OLIVE

JULY 1945

Just past Carrizozo, it started to rain. Highway 380 was deserted under a hazy moon. It had been forever since I'd seen darkness like this. No lights, no cars, no noise—just earth and sky. I crossed the lava fields and then felt rather than saw the gentle swell of the Chupadera Mesa rising up beneath me. And there, finally, barely visible in the night, the yucca plant that signaled the end of our lane.

Dust glittered in the headlights as the car bumped over the gravel drive. A sudden realization caused a dull ache in my chest: this would be the last time I'd see the ranch. For a long time, at least. No matter what happened, I was getting on that bus tomorrow morning. As I let my eyes wash over my childhood home, I couldn't help but wish this last visit were under different circumstances.

But then again, I wished a lot of things were different.

The main house was dark, the only light streaming through the thin curtains of the casita. I parked the car beneath the sycamore and kept to the shadows as I approached. There were no Army trucks now. No bodies. Just the gentle tapping of raindrops on the tin roof, the rustle of creosote leaves in the breeze, the hum of a generator. And from inside the casita, voices.

I grabbed the door handle with sweaty hands and hesitated. *Don't do it, Olive. You have a chance to be free. Take it. It doesn't matter what's behind this door.*

And yet it did matter. The truth mattered.

As expected, the door was unlocked. The lights in the living room were off, only a single kerosene lantern turned down low in the kitchen. I stepped over my mother's shoes. Dirty plates on the table, a couple half-empty wineglasses. The smell of rice and peppers in the air mingling with the faint scent of floral perfume.

Light shone beneath the crack of the closed bedroom door. The voices were coming from inside along with the purr of low music. Electricity coursed through my palm as I put one hand on the door.

I pushed it open.

The music grew louder, gentle horns and a tinkling piano from a large wireless that hadn't been there before. In front of the bed— my mother's bed, the one she had moved from the main house, the one she had shared with my father—stood two bodies, wrapped around each other, swaying to the beat. Their faces were turned toward one another. Eyes closed in a picture of serenity as Perry Como sang about the end of time.

Which was what it was. Because as I stood there, unable to move, unable to breathe, my mother stretched upward, ran a hand through his dark hair, and kissed Sergeant Hawthorne on the lips. The gesture was tender. Loving. Familiar.

Every other thought in my mind fled at the sight before me. This. *This* was what had been so important. For months, I'd been hurting, confused, alone, and scared. She'd pushed me away . . . for this. For *him*.

A sound escaped my throat, high-pitched and strangled, a cry competing with a scream.

My mother's head twisted. Her eyes widened. "Olive!"

Sergeant Hawthorne's hands dropped from my mother's waist. A trace of her lipstick still stained his mouth.

I wanted to run. But something held me to the ground, pinning my shoes to the shaggy rug. They stood there in front of me, no longer touching but still close, their intimate proximity screaming in the panicked silence. And Perry Como continued to sing.

After minutes or hours, my mother finally moved, stepping toward me with outstretched arms. "Olive," she said again.

Her movement gave me permission to move too. My feet free, I backed from the door, stumbling over the end table in the living room. The one my *father* had made. Bile rose in my throat as I staggered toward the exit.

"Olive!"

But I was already outside. The rain was harder now. Stinging my eyes and causing me to slip in the mud. I started toward the car, then hesitated. I could drive, but where? I couldn't face Grandma.

I couldn't tell Jo; she was just as much a victim of this as I was, and I couldn't bear to think of her carrying the weight of this betrayal so soon after her brother's death.

"Olive!"

My mother's voice rang out through the night. I ran. Away from the car, splashing through puddles, sending water flying all the way up to my knees. It was surprisingly cold, even in the warm July air.

"Olive!" My name again dissolving into a fit of coughs.

But the voice was distant now, drowned out by the rain and my own breathing. Darkness folded in on me the farther I got from the casita. Past the shed, the corral, the barn. Out into the open desert, where the cattle once roamed. When the world made sense. Before the Army came.

Beneath my feet, the ground began to rise, the foothills of the Chupadera Mesa meeting me in my pain. Still I ran. Tripping over rocks, slamming into a prickly pear, scraping knees and elbows as loose gravel gave way beneath my shoes. The darkness was intense, blinding. It had been a long time since I'd been out this far. And yet I still knew the way, as if the very dirt spoke to my soul.

Onward and upward until, at last, the ground leveled. My lungs struggled to take a breath. I moved on rubbery legs through the split in the rock shaped like lightning and into the burrow. Swatting the cobwebs with an old comic book, I pulled out a flashlight, thumping it several times before it finally turned on.

It was still the same. Stacks of books, a dusty quilt, even a tin full of crackers. It was all still there. The world hadn't touched this place. Everyone out there was killing each other, betraying one another, lying, hating, hurting . . . but the Chupadera Mesa had been forgotten.

Shaking out the blanket for scorpions, I pulled it over my pounding head and lay down, feeling as if I were eight years old again. Deep sobs rattled my chest. My mother, Sergeant Hawthorne. All the pain and rejection I'd felt just so she could canoodle in privacy.

And Jo, alone in her house on Michigan Avenue. Grieving in solitude in California. While her father was here. With my mother. All under the guise of duty.

I wrapped my arms around my body, chilled from the inside rather than out. Jo and I had been pushed to the edges, thrust into a world that had no room for us. Not children but not yet women. We were unsteady, inexperienced, scared.

All while the two people who should have cared had instead been wrapped up in each other.

The rain had lessened, falling now in a gentle mist. From somewhere in the night came the sound of a mourning dove, its doleful cooing acknowledged and returned by a companion nearby. My throat grew thick as I pulled my knees to my chest. The two birds called for one another again. Crying out in the night . . . and answering.

Like Jo and me. And—the thought struck me suddenly—like my mother and Sergeant Hawthorne?

The idea came from nowhere and yet, once planted, wouldn't let go. Was I being juvenile? Could they merely have found one another in the darkness? Amid the pain and grief, Jo and I were proof that fellowship could be found in loss, even when it was unexpected. Even when it was unwanted. When life gouges a hole in your heart, sometimes an unexpected someone can rush forth to fill it. And as easy as it would be to discount their pain in favor of my own, my mother and Sergeant Hawthorne had suffered their share of loss. The late Mrs. Hawthorne, my father, Jo's brother, Avery . . .

I sat up suddenly, banging my head on the ceiling of the burrow. In my shock, I'd forgotten the real reason I'd come out here. Avery.

The truth.

The thaw hardened as quickly as it had begun. I could understand a relationship with Sergeant Hawthorne. It would explain Ma's new dresses, girlish behavior, and sustained silences. But it didn't explain everything. The numbers in the shed. The alleyway meeting. The empty half box of Jell-O. Avery's letter.

I traced the mesa symbol carved into the side of the rock, fingers drifting over the smooth edges. Maybe it truly was time to grow up. To move past the time of secret symbols and childhood hideouts, of cursing the world for not making a place for me in the present when I wasn't willing to let go of the past. Everyone around me had moved on; it was time I did too.

There was a life for me out there, if only I was willing to go live it.

It was time to leave New Mexico, make a fresh start. And I would let my mother do the same.

She only had to give me one thing: the truth.

——— ✦❖✦ ———

I sat up with a start. My body had drifted into a restless sleep as adrenaline gave way to exhaustion. I wasn't sure how long I had slept, but something had woken me. A booming noise. I was sure of it. And yet as I crawled out of the burrow, a calm spread out across the Jornada. I glanced at my watch: 5:28 a.m. The sun would be rising soon. The ranch was below me, quiet and dark. I wondered if Sergeant Hawthorne was still there.

And then, out of nowhere, an explosion. I jumped, causing a few rocks to tumble. A rocket of some kind in the distance. In the early morning darkness, I could see dozens of lights. The new Army post. The one they were working on. At just minutes before 5:30 in the morning, the Army was throwing up rockets.

Fantastic.

I'd moved to take a step when a flash of light burst into the sky, brighter than White Sands at midday, brighter even than the sun itself. I gave a shout of pain as my eyes slammed shut. The flash burned into my pupils, still visible even beneath closed lids. A blast of air, hot and sour, barreled in behind it, knocking me onto my back. I tried to let out a shriek, but all the oxygen was pushed from my lungs. Beneath me, the ground vibrated and shook, pebbles rolling along as if fleeing, bumping into my arms and scratching at my back. The mesa was collapsing. It was *collapsing*. The noise came last, a roar that wasn't a roar, a boom that was so much more than a boom, like the moon itself had lost all hope and crashed into the earth.

And then, as suddenly as it started, it stopped.

The ground stilled. Even with eyes closed, I could tell the white light was gone. Orange, red, and yellow swirls danced over my pupils. My ears still rang with the sound that had long since faded, pounding against my temples like phantom waves.

I eased open my eyes, surprised by the darkness. Spots hovered around the corners of my vision. I ran a hand over my elbows, fingers coming away with fresh blood. A hot stickiness at my back told me I could expect more there. Rubbing my head, I felt a hard knot forming under my hair. Every single thing on my body hurt.

I sat up slowly, feeling dizzy, and struggled to stand. The desert beneath me was quiet, holding its breath. The first rays of pink light were just beginning to season the eastern sky. Like it was a normal day. But it wasn't normal. The flash, the earthquake, and now, billowing out before me, a cloud like no other. Coming not from the sky, but from the ground. Mushroom-shaped and multi-colored in the early morning dawn, it grew larger by the second, until it obscured the view of anything except itself. At its base, smoke rushed out like tentacles, crawling over the Jornada as if to devour it.

I tried to look away. But I couldn't. The cloud held me, binding me to the mesa as it spread. Soon I could see nothing but haze in every direction, my beautiful New Mexico buried under a tapestry of smoke.

CHAPTER TWENTY-TWO

JO

MARCH 1952

One day. She was supposed to have spent one day in Alamogordo. In and out, business done, gone before nightfall. She should never even have seen the sun set on the dusty ground.

And yet here she was, watching it dip once again over the distant mountains. Its orange glow stretched across the crumbled dirt at her feet, casting a shadow on the earth that now covered her father's body.

The other mourners were long since gone, a couple of neighbors and a few Army friends the only remaining strands of her father's life. A part of her had thought—hoped—Olive would show, but of course she hadn't. Olive was gone. *Poof.*

She'd been surprised at the *busyness* surrounding death. From the moment the last breath had passed her father's lips, people hadn't stopped asking her questions, seeking answers she hadn't the slightest notion how to give. Mr. Purcell had stepped in, miraculously producing papers that would take care of the whole thing. All she had to do was sign. How absurd it all felt. *Just sign here and your father will be gone.*

The very thing she'd come here to do in the first place.

Condolences dwindled as the crowd dispersed. They could retreat to their lives, breathing a sigh of relief that duty had been done and they could be home in time for supper. Jo even outlasted Pastor Hamilton, who stuck around for nearly an hour after the memorial, hugging her, praying for her, his sermon having been for her father but his presence truly meant for her. And she was grateful for that, even if she couldn't quite express it. To see and be seen, to *feel* . . . even if those feelings were grief.

Charlie had come, though he kept a respectful distance. He had given her a soft kiss on the cheek before withdrawing to the outskirts of the service. Jo was vaguely aware of his lingering presence during her time with Pastor Hamilton, as if he were waiting for the man to leave before approaching again; she was surprised to find afterward that he had left.

No, not surprised, she realized. *Relieved.* She needed to be alone with her thoughts. And with her God.

When the mourners had gone and the glare of the sun became too much, burning her skin through the black fabric of the cheap dress she'd bought without trying on at a run-down shop on Maryland Avenue, Jo retreated to a nearby tree, far enough away the gravediggers felt it appropriate to finish their work but close enough she could see every grain of dirt they tossed into the grave.

She sat watching as the hole became level ground, as the workers patted it flat with their shovels and hoes, wiping their brows and walking away, satisfied with a day's work well done. She watched as the sky faded from blue to orange to red, until the shadow reached the spot on the ground where her father now lay forever entombed in New Mexico earth.

So many things she wished she had told him. Asked him. That cross he'd drawn on her hand. Or what she'd thought was a cross. The last words he'd tried to write on her palm. Had her father finally come to know God?

All those years doing mission work, and her greatest mission had gone unfinished. All because of her own stubborn heart.

She prayed for forgiveness. She prayed for peace. She prayed for the grace God had shown to her, undeserved and unnoticed, a grace her father had never understood and she'd never known how to share with him.

It wasn't until the deep purple of twilight that she finally returned to her motel. The stars were beginning to appear, somehow obscene on this night. A note was slipped under her door.

If you want to talk, I'm here. All you have to do is call.

A scribbled number, a barely legible *C.*

In the morning, she thought with a sigh. Maybe. She didn't have the heart or mind to deal with Charlie right now. Instead, she slid between the sheets, not even bothering to change out of her dress. Her exhaustion was sudden and powerful. She drifted into a deep and thankfully dreamless sleep.

◆ ✦ ◆

"Jo!"

She was awoken early—too early—by a banging on the door and the sound of her name. Out of blissful nothingness and into the memory of the past few days. The heaviness of her heart felt like a weight pinning her to the mattress. Sleep. She just wanted to sleep.

But the pounding persisted.

Sighing, she wrapped the sheet around her to cover her rumpled dress and shuffled to the door, squinting against the sun as she opened it. "What? Who—?"

"You didn't call me last night."

"Charlie?"

"You didn't call me." His tone was sharp. Accusatory.

"I didn't . . ." Jo rubbed her eyes, her tired brain struggling to reconcile the scene before her. Charlie. It was Charlie. And he was . . . mad?

"You didn't call me. I . . ." He sighed. Pinched the bridge of his nose. When he continued, his tone was lighter. "I was worried you'd skipped town without saying goodbye."

"No, I didn't . . ." Her voice trailed off as her vision finally cleared. Charlie was dressed impeccably again, navy-blue suit, polished black shoes. His familiar hair and smile, even the now-recognizable smell of his cologne. The unexpected coldness was gone, his face as warm and flawless as always, save for the tiniest remainder of a scratch upon his cheek.

The scratch.

The ghost of her father swelled before her, causing her skin to prickle. In all of Charlie's charm and her own self-absorption, she'd nearly forgotten. But now the faint mark—practically healed and barely larger than a paper cut—was all she could see on his otherwise-perfect face. She tried to tell herself it was just her grief, seeking out any remnant of her father to which she could cling, but it was more. The memory of that morning knotted her stomach. The words her father had tried to speak. The ideas he'd tried to communicate. And his face when he'd seen Charlie . . .

The way he'd lunged at him, determined and almost instinctual, even in his dilapidated state. The anger she'd seen in his eyes. The *fear*. Because that's what it had been. Fear. In her hardened heart, she'd assumed it was the cancer, but now . . . He'd spent his last few days trying desperately to communicate with her, and something about this man was included in that. But what?

In front her of, Charlie smiled, waiting.

Jo scratched at her throat. Her mind was racing.

"Water under the bridge. Let's get breakfast." He took a step toward her, hand outstretched.

She stepped back, avoiding his touch. "I have to meet Mr. Purcell at nine."

"Do you want me to come with you?"

"No." The word rushed from her lips with startling intensity. "Thank you, though," she added gently.

"I don't mind. I'd like to come. I don't think you should be alone."

"I'm fine."

He gave a pointed glace at her wrinkled clothes, visible now that the sheet had dropped from her shoulders.

She was still in her funeral dress. She pulled the bedsheet up around her again. "Really, I am. I'm just tired. I'll be fine. I *am* fine, I mean."

"Fine people don't need to tell people they're fine." It was a joke, but his words held an unexpected edge.

"I really need to get ready," Jo said pointedly.

He stared at her for a moment before breaking into another smile. "Alright." His stiff suit barely moved beneath his shrug. "I'll catch up with you later? Lunch?"

"Yeah, maybe."

"Well, call me. You have my number."

Jo did not wait for him to walk away before shutting the door. After a quick shower and a stale breakfast of yesterday's uneaten toast from the café across the street, she threw on a pair of navy-blue trousers and a light cotton button-down—another cheap boutique find because apparently snake guts *did* stain—before slipping from her room. She half expected to find Charlie waiting for her, but the stoop was blissfully empty. The sky was white and cloudless, the sun already intense enough to send shimmering waves up from the sidewalk. Mr. Purcell's office, however, was as dark and cool as ever, the clicking of the oscillating fan greeting her as she entered.

He hugged her awkwardly. His squat body reeked of sweat and yesterday's cigarettes, but for once, Jo didn't mind. His kindness covered all manner of imperfections. He said little as he placed paper after paper in front of her, a courtesy for which she was thankful. He simply pointed out where to sign, pausing only long enough to explain the purpose of each document in foreign legalese, most of which she didn't understand but signed anyway.

"I'm sorry there's so many. We're almost done, I promise." Mr. Purcell wiped his brow with the back of his pudgy fist as he laid another sheet in front of her. "Right here. For the insurance policy."

Jo signed without reading. Her hand was starting to cramp from the repeated swoops and swirls of her signature. Three more papers and then two needing her initials passed in front of her before Mr. Purcell finally sighed.

"There. That does it, I believe."

Jo dropped the pen and stretched her fingers, rubbing at the joints. "Thank you for your help, Mr. Purcell. All of it, I mean. Everything."

He gave her a sad smile. "It's the least I could do, Miss Hawthorne."

She smiled back, realizing guiltily it might have been the first time he'd ever seen hers. "Well, anyways, I guess I'll be—"

"There's just, uh, one more thing." Mr. Purcell waddled to the other side of his desk, pushing aside folders and notebooks. "It's rather short, I'm afraid. But still . . ." He ran his fingers over the mess. "Ah, yes. Here we are." He pulled a yellow folder from beneath a stack of papers. "Your father's will."

An unexplained feeling of dread washed over her. She'd come so far on this road to healing; somehow she knew the contents of that folder would be like a freight train pushing her back. "Mr. Purcell, I'm really not interested—"

"He's left you the house on Michigan Avenue and everything in it." He stretched out his arm. A small metal object rested in the palm of his hand.

A key.

Jo gripped the armrest and closed her eyes. She'd faced a lot of things over the past few days. But she still wasn't ready to face *that*. "You knew that first day he'd left it to me," she said. "When I came in for the power of attorney. Why wouldn't you just let me sell it then?"

His hooded eyes refused to meet hers. "Because ownership of the property would only pass to you after your father's death. At our first meeting, you were still technically—legally—unable to sell it. And if I'm being honest, I was hoping that maybe you'd change your mind, considering—"

"Nothing's changed. I still don't want that house. Sell it."

"Are you—?"

"Please." Weariness mixed with anxiety, causing her voice to come out as a squeak. "Just sell it."

His gaze softened. "Very well then. I'll have the papers drawn up."

She bit the inside of her cheek, feeling as if she should say more. She wanted to defend herself, to explain, and yet she had the sense that Mr. Purcell already knew too much. About her, about her father. And that exposure made her feel too vulnerable to speak. So instead she merely nodded, hoping to betray both her apologies and her gratitude in a single gesture.

As she made to move toward the exit, a gentle touch on her wrist stopped her. Mr. Purcell's eyes were moist as he pressed something into her hand. "Just in case."

The key shone up at her. "Mr. Purcell, really, I don't—"

He wrapped her fingers around it tightly, causing the metal to bite into her skin. "Just in case," he repeated, "there's something in the house you've been looking for."

Her mouth suddenly went dry. In her palm, the skin around the key seemed to tingle.

Mr. Purcell gave a slight nod, his lips disappearing beneath his forced silence.

He couldn't say. And Jo would never ask. Because instead she was gone, her blonde hair flying behind her as she raced from the office, ignoring the heat and blinding glare, dodging traffic and pedestrians, her mind too fearful to hope and yet already irrevocably certain of what she would find.

The house on Michigan Avenue looked the same. The yellow paint hadn't even faded in the harsh sun. How was that possible? Her father's truck still sat in the driveway, like a dog waiting for its master. The lawn was well maintained, the front stoop swept, and the porch tidy. No doubt some neighbor or Good Samaritan. Perhaps even a cleaning lady her father had hired.

Or someone else.

She shuffled up the sidewalk, careful to avoid the left side of the third stone, uneven because of a tree root hidden under its base. An obscure memory to resurface now, of all times. The porch steps creaked beneath her weight, the only sign of age, and she grabbed the bronze door handle with icy hands. For some reason, she was surprised it didn't give way beneath her grip. Locked.

She pulled the key from her pocket, hesitating just for a moment before inserting it in the lock. Entering this door would change everything, and she wasn't sure if that was good or bad. She only knew it was necessary.

"Hello?"

Silence swallowed her as she entered. The air was stuffy and thick. When she had lived here, the hallway had been empty; now it had a coatrack. Her father's brown Army jacket hung limply from one of the pegs, a few pairs of shoes lined up under it. On the staircase sat a small stack of books, waiting to be carried to what Jo could only assume were shelves above. The wallpaper had faded to a sickly green, and the hardwood floors were dull and scuffed.

"Hello?" she called again. She pushed open the door at the end of the hall. The kitchen was just as she remembered it too. Except it wasn't. It was tidy, no dishes in the sink or crumbs on the counter as one might expect from a bachelor's residence. But there *were* dishes. Stacks of them inside the cabinets. Pots and pans in the cupboards. In the pantry, boxes of oats and rice, cans of vegetables, a bottle of oil.

Signs of the life her father had lived here. Without her.

She blinked back tears as a familiar ache spread. It should have looked like this seven years ago. A father and a daughter. Not just a house. A home.

Closing the pantry door, she took a deep breath, allowing herself to feel for a moment, to accept the truth that would probably be with her for the rest of her life: she might have forgiven her father for what he had done. But it still hurt.

She moved back through the hallway, climbing gingerly up the stairs to the second floor. She tried to look without seeing. A bedroom. A bathroom. An unmade bed and forgotten toothbrush. Relics of a past she wasn't here to relive. No, she was here for something else.

But as empty room gave way to empty room, it soon became obvious that nothing lay within these walls but ghosts.

She went downstairs and sat on the bottom step, sighing. It had been foolish to think Olive was here. No one had seen her for years, and Jo expected her to be sitting in her father's house in downtown Alamogordo? She shook her head, letting out a laugh she did not feel. The nerve of Mr. Purcell to get her hopes up like that.

She sat there and listened to the stillness of the house. It was only now, nerves deflated, that she noticed a slight smell in the air. Old tobacco, yellowed newspapers, and something else—muted but there just the same.

Her father's cologne.

Tears rolled down her cheeks, disappointment and mourning combining in this house that had once been her own. A place full of hope and heartache filled now with the last remnants of a man she had always loved but would never truly understand.

Eventually she stood and wiped her face with her palms. There was no reason to linger. Not anymore. As she took a step toward the door, she breathed out a last goodbye and let her eyes swing over the stairs, the hallway, the—

She stopped, stomach twisting. A familiar white door lay in front of her. She'd tried so hard not to look at it when she'd come in, pretending it didn't exist. Now, in her sorrowful state, she'd allowed her eyes a glance—just one glance—and she knew. The one room she hadn't checked. The one room she didn't want to check. The one room she *had* to check.

It was supposed to have been a sitting room, and he could have easily reverted it to one after she'd left. But he hadn't. Instead it remained a bedroom. *Her* bedroom. Her books and her records, jewelry boxes and perfume bottles—all still there. Lace curtains and movie posters (though Joseph Cotten's tie had faded from blue to gray in the years since *I'll Be Seeing You* had been released), even a few rumpled dresses hanging off the back of her chair. Her four-poster bed was still pushed against the far wall, thick pink comforter tucked tightly over the end of the mattress, one corner turned back in invitation. Just waiting for her to come home.

And on her pillow, a Bible.

Jo's hand trembled as she raised her fingers to her lips. Not just *a* Bible. It was the one she'd given Olive all those years ago.

The leather cover was cracked, the spine broken from use. Flipping through the pages, she noticed the thin paper was rumpled and ripped in several locations. When she reached the book of Acts, something small and white fell onto the bed.

She stared at it, mouth dry. The rolling sensation in her stomach verged on nausea as she slowly picked it up by its edge.

There were no words. Just a small black mark, uneven, unimportant. Unmistakable.

The paper slipped from Jo's hand as her fingers went numb. They fumbled clumsily as she snatched it back. No. It was impossible. It couldn't be. And yet there it was.

A line. Up to a point, then down. The upside-down *V*.

Jo sprang to her feet as if released from a snare. Finally, at last, she knew where she had to go. But she'd only taken one step before realizing she had no way to get there. No, she thought, shaking her head. She would figure that part out. This would not be the thing that stopped her.

She ran into the hallway, pausing just long enough to grab her father's old Army jacket. It was too big, but she put it on anyway, breathing in deeply. It wouldn't always smell like him, but at least it was something—a small part of him she could see and touch and remember.

The good and the bad.

She put one hand in the pocket as the other reached for the doorknob. Something metallic lay within its depths. A silver key. She turned it over in her palm and laughed—a real one this time, rich and incredulous and relieved.

Her father hadn't been able to speak. But that didn't mean he'd been silent.

She burst out the door and ran for the truck, soaring once again over the cracked third stone, every step forward fueled by hope, a frantic thawing of the past seven years, until it felt as if it was her sixteen-year-old self sliding behind the wheel.

CHAPTER TWENTY-THREE

OLIVE

JULY 1945

The cloud drifted in all directions, shrouding the mesa and obscuring the desert beneath. I knew the way down but struggled, disoriented by smog and dizzy from the blow to the back of my head. The sun had risen by the time I reached the bottom. Particles in the air glittered like a dream.

The ranch was quiet. No sign of anything out of the ordinary. The sycamore was still standing, although several leaves dotted the top of Grandma's car, along with a fine layer of dust. If it hadn't been for the smoke, thinner down here but still hanging over the ground like a canopy, I would have thought I'd imagined the whole thing.

"Olive?" From just behind me, my mother's voice. She'd been waiting for me. "We need to talk."

"What was that flash?" It wasn't what she meant, but it was the first thing out of my mouth. How could it not be?

Silence. Thick and unnatural. And not just coming from my mother. For the first time, I noticed there was no breeze. No birds. No insects. The air was full of absolute nothingness. The hair on the back of my neck stood on end as I finally turned.

My mother stood before me in her pale-blue housecoat, hands clasped to her chest. Dark hair was piled loosely atop her head. Her face was tight, eyes ringed in red, with dark circles beneath them. Sergeant Hawthorne stood beside her, gaze downcast.

"What was that flash?" I repeated, swallowing a lump in my throat.

"Please come inside, Olive."

"No."

"Your mother's right," Sergeant Hawthorne said. "We should go inside and talk."

I threw my hands in the air. Any sympathy or understanding I'd garnered the night before had vanished; my fear and confusion were too big to let anything else in. "You want to talk? Fine. We can talk right here. Where's Avery?"

My mother recoiled as if struck.

"And don't you dare try to tell me he's in the Pacific. Because I know they don't let color-blind men serve on the front lines." I gave a pointed stare in Sergeant Hawthorne's direction. "So where is my brother? *Where is he?*"

Jo's father twisted his hands in front of him, looking back and forth between my mother and me. He was frowning. Gone was the strong, confident, self-assured sergeant. In his place stood a deflated, uncomfortable wisp of a man, Army jacket lopsided on his shoulders. "Evelyn?"

She ignored him. "Olive." A whisper, echoing through the stillness.

I backed away, holding my arms behind me to find the car, never taking my eyes off her face. Waiting, wishing, begging her to say it. Tell me he had run off. Tell me he was dead. Tell me something, anything, so long as it was the truth. Just love me enough to tell me the truth.

Tears streamed down her cheeks, leaving trails of old mascara in their wake. But still she said nothing.

And that silence told me everything I needed to know to finally be able to leave.

My breathing was shaky and painful as I started up the car. Through the side window, I could see my mother crying, her lips forming the same words over and over again: "Olive, please. Olive, please."

I did not stop. I did not look back. Bumping over the gravel drive one last time, I kept my eyes forward. It was done. Over. I'd given her a chance, and she had chosen not to take it. Now it was time to move on. I pressed harder on the accelerator to further the distance between us; I would not allow my mother—or myself—the opportunity to change my mind.

The cloud above me continued to descend. As I pulled onto the 380, three black cars came screaming out of the smoke, headed east. The haze swallowed them before I could get a good look at the drivers. Police, maybe. More likely Army. It didn't really matter. Neither one would be much help if the sky was falling. In every sense of the word.

I drove slowly, squinting against blindness. The road remained the same, exactly as it had been last night. I kept waiting for the end, for the drop-off, for the place the flash had destroyed. But the blacktop pressed on through the Jornada, past the blackened hills of the lava fields. I slowed as a brown blur materialized on the roadside up ahead. An animal, I realized. Someone's mule, escaped from a pasture somewhere nearby.

I rolled down my window, prepared to shoo it away from the highway, lest a stray car lose control in the smoke and strike it. "Hey!" I shouted, waving my arm. "Get! Go on, get outta . . ."

A wave of terror eroded my words. It was a mule, alright. But it was frozen. Jaw slack, tongue hanging over its great gray teeth like a pink slug. Its rib cage rose and fell with deep, heavy breaths, but the rest of its body remained rigid as its vacant gaze stared west without blinking.

Repulsed, I shrank back into my seat and rolled up the window. The car sputtered and groaned as I pushed on the gas, but the mule did not react to the sound. When I crested the next hill, I allowed myself a glance in the rearview mirror; the animal remained where I'd left him.

I arrived in Carrizozo, heart pounding, surprised to see all the buildings still standing. Cars drove up and down the quaint streets, even at the early hour. Pulling to a stop at the corner gas station, I rubbed my eyes until they stung, but the image of that mule was burned inside my brain.

Two men with dirty cowboy hats atop their heads passed by my car. "I don't rightly know," one of them was saying. "Ain't never seen nothing like it in all my days."

The other one spat, sending a wad of tobacco flying. "The

sun done rose in the west and then went on down again before coming up in the east. If that ain't a sign of the end times, I don't know what is."

His companion murmured in agreement as they walked away.

So something *had* happened. I hadn't been the only one to see the flash. And the smoke. It was less here but still hazy; even if you'd slept through the flash and the noise, you couldn't miss the smoke. What could cause such a thing—seen, heard, felt with such intensity even here, miles away from the ranch?

Taking a deep breath, I pulled the car back onto the road, heading south on Carrizozo's main drag. A man ran past me in the opposite direction, arms in the air, eyes wild. "They're here! They're here!" he shouted. "It's the Japs!"

I watched him run in my rearview mirror, stomach knotting. Could it be true? There had been rumors for months but still . . .

And then, just as suddenly, a new terror formed in my mind. Grandma. She was all alone. Sick in her mind. If the Japanese really were attacking . . .

Never had the drive to my grandmother's seemed so long. The smoke faded the farther south I went, but my panic did not. In the sleepy town of Tularosa, all was quiet. The houses were dark, the sun just now high enough over the Sacramentos to glare off the eastern windows. I blew through two stop signs as I raced toward Alamogordo, not slowing until I reached the city limit sign.

But there were no Japanese. No planes. No bombs. Barely even any cars. Most of the parking spaces on New York were empty. The shopkeepers hadn't yet opened for the day. A few pedestrians meandered along Tenth, walking dogs now to avoid the heat that would be blazing by midday. A few flags, left over from the Fourth of July parade not quite two weeks ago, fluttered in a slight breeze at the base of the cottonwoods.

It was an average Monday.

I pulled to a stop in front of Grandma's house, bursting in the front door with muscles so tense they ached. Quiet in here too. I pushed toward the back bedroom. Grandma was snuggled under a quilt, releasing quiet snores.

Too spun up to stop myself, I jumped into bed beside her, patting her plump middle and jiggling her arm. "Grandma! Grandma, wake up!"

"Wha-what? Evelyn? Evelyn, is that you?"

"Did you see it, Grandma? Did you see the flash?"

She blinked a couple of times, rubbing her eyes with the back of her hand before grabbing my arms and pushing me away as if to get a better look. "What? What flash? What are you talking about, Evelyn?"

I didn't bother to correct her. Not now. "The flash. It was . . . it was like the sun had fallen. You didn't see it?"

"The sun? Heavens to Betsy, child, no. I didn't see anything like that. I did rouse up around five thirty, though. Felt like the house was shaking . . ."

"An earthquake?"

She nodded. "It didn't last long. Thought I must have been dreaming."

"And there's been nothing else since? No alarms, no sirens, nothing?"

She sat up straight, fully awake now. "Evelyn, what in the world are you talking about? Where have you been? What did you see?"

I pressed two fingers against my temples, sighing with equal parts relief and dread. "Nothing. It was . . . well, it wasn't nothing. Some kind of explosion. A bomb, maybe. But not like anything I've ever seen or heard before. I thought the world was ending . . . or the Japs were coming."

"The Japs! Here? In Alamogordo?"

I shook my head firmly. "No. No, I don't think—"

She pushed me aside. Springing from her bed, she rushed to her closet. "We need to leave, Evelyn. We need to leave right now." She threw a blue suitcase to the floor and began filling it with dresses, some still on their hangers. "I knew this would happen. I just knew it. Lord, help us." She lifted her head briefly toward the ceiling, eyes closed, lips murmuring a silent prayer. "But I won't sit by and just let 'em come. I—"

"Grandma." My shoulders sank even as my voice rose.

She paused to look at me, but I knew she wasn't truly seeing me. Because she wasn't Grandma. Her eyes were clouded, the alarm on her face muddled by confusion. Her past was battling with the present, the terrors of the current world forming connections with memories she didn't know were memories.

"Evelyn, why are you still sitting there? I told you to pack!"

I pulled at the sleeves of my shirt, trying to curb my tears. In this moment, when I felt the most like a frightened child, I had to somehow be the adult. "I know. I . . . Shouldn't we turn on the radio first? Find out what's going on?" The notion sprang up suddenly, desperate and asinine. But at this point, I was willing to do anything to buy us time—time for Grandma to emerge from her spell. "We don't know where they are, which way we should go."

The corner of her mouth twitched. It was the only outward sign of internal struggle. "Fine," she said at last. "But quickly."

Her bare feet slapped against the tile as she shuffled from the bedroom and switched on the wireless. The gentle crooning of the Pied Pipers drifted into the kitchen. Their serene chorus was at odds with the tense air.

"Bah!" She waved one hand. "Garbage. They've probably already taken over the radio towers." She moved to turn it off.

"Wait! Let's . . . let's at least wait for the song to end."

I was stalling. She knew it just as well as I did. But she lowered her hand anyway.

The music finally faded. Several pops hung in the air before a nasally voice cut through the static. "This just in from the commanding officer of Alamogordo Air Base, Colonel William Eareckson: 'Several inquiries have been received concerning a heavy explosion which occurred on the Alamogordo Air Base reservation this morning.'" The announcer paused, audibly licking his lips. "'A remotely located ammunition magazine containing a considerable amount of high explosive and pyrotechnics exploded. There was no loss of life or injury to anyone, and the property damage outside of the explosives magazine itself was negligible. Weather conditions affecting the content of gas shells exploded by the blast may make it desirable for the Army to evacuate temporarily a few civilians from their homes.'" A deep breath before continuing. "Again, this is coming from the commanding officer of Alamogordo Air Base, Colonel William—"

I turned the knob with a sharp click, willing myself to exhale. It wasn't true. I was no expert, of course. But I'd been there. I'd seen the glare of that light, the cloud it left behind. That flash was no ammunition magazine exploding. No amount of explosives in the world could make a flash like that.

First my mother. Now the Army. Everyone around me was lying.

Swallowing my angst, I gave my grandmother a weak smile. "See? Nothing to worry about."

"Don't you feed me that baloney, Evelyn. You didn't believe a word of that any more than I did." She let out a short huff. "I'll pack. You run over to the mill and grab your father."

A rock dropped into my stomach. "What?"

"Your father! Your father! Go get your father! He probably has no idea what's going on, it being so loud in there and all. No radios, no nothing. Take the car if you have to, but just go get him. And quick!"

My grandfather had died before I was born. Before Avery, before my mother even met my father. I didn't know for sure in what year my grandmother's mind was lingering but I did know that in all the episodes she'd had since I'd been here, she'd never gone this far back before.

"Grandma . . ."

"Go, Evelyn! Why do I keep having to ask? Go! *Go!*" Her voice was shrill and unnerved.

My lip trembled as I shifted my weight from one foot to the other, unsure what to do. I wanted to cry. I wanted to *leave*. All of this, the weight, the responsibility, the anxiety—it was too much for me. I wanted to pack my bags—for real—and run to the bus stop without looking back. To find Jo, climb aboard, and put all the lies, secrets, and heartache behind me.

"Evelyn! Why are you being like this? Don't you know we're in danger?" I winced as her nails dug into my flesh. "We need to get your father. We need to get out of here!"

Instantly shame flushed into my cheeks, the truth more painful than her grip. I couldn't leave her. Not like this. I could not start my future while my grandmother was still stuck in the past. The world was splintering; if I left her alone, she would most assuredly fall into the cracks.

The only solution, I realized with a sinking feeling, was to not leave her alone.

"Come on," I said, heart wrenching within my chest. "We'll grab our bags and get Father. He's not at the mill. He's . . . he's at a special site out in the country. We'll meet him there."

She narrowed her eyes at me. I put on my bravest smile. The stare down was short-lived, however; she eventually retreated to the bedroom to finish packing. I swallowed hard, trying to ignore the guilt over the very same kind of falsehoods for which I'd denounced my mother earlier.

I glanced at the clock on the wall, rubbing at the space between my brows. It was only 8 a.m. If I hurried, I could be there and back before eleven, easily. No, that wasn't what was worrying me. What was worrying me was the uncertainty of the decision that had just hours ago seemed so concrete. What was worrying me was if I had the strength—or the heart—to say goodbye to my grandmother, especially in her current state.

What was worrying me was having to face my own mother one last time.

CHAPTER TWENTY-FOUR

JO

MARCH 1952

The drive seemed longer this time, long enough that Jo started to doubt herself. Her foot's pressure on the gas fluctuated with every demand of logic to turn back. That symbol on the paper . . . she'd misinterpreted, misunderstood.

Only she hadn't. Somehow she knew she hadn't.

She didn't have to guess where to turn this time. The yucca stood out like a beacon beside the hidden drive, even though it differed little from the other plants dotting the landscape. She pulled to a stop under the Arizona sycamore, a dust cloud engulfing the car before continuing its journey westward without her. She didn't allow herself to hesitate. Instead, she exited the car and headed not for the casita, looming in front of her like a tombstone, or even the main house, but beyond it. Past the decaying barn and crumbling shed, the empty corral and barren pastureland, out into the open where the gently sloping hills of the ranch met the sharp, rocky incline of the mesa. She didn't know where she was going; all she had were Olive's words, all those years ago. Those words she should have forgotten but had instead kept locked away, bursting forth now with clarity as if they'd been spoken only yesterday. Those words, and this feeling, as if the ground were whispering in her ear, pulling her upward with a force she couldn't have fought if she wanted to.

She chose the hill with the path snaking up its side, barely visible through a tangle of overgrown brown grass. It had to be the right one. But maybe it wasn't. She only knew, if it came to it, she'd check every last knoll on this mesa.

Breathing hard, she pulled herself to the top, ignoring the stitch in her side and the sweat dripping down her spine. For all the clothes she'd bought, she still only had her low black heels; her ankles ached from their multiple twists and slips. Thankfully, the ground at her feet had now leveled. Even up here, the rocks were the same reddish brown as the New Mexico soil hundreds of feet below. She could see for miles, the faintest speck of houses suggesting the nearest village, the black of the lava fields behind her, and—if she squinted hard enough—the gleam of gypsum dunes far in the distance.

But up here . . . up here was nothing. Boulders and gravel, a maze of rocks with no prize to be found upon completion. No sign of life or habitation. No sound. Not even a breeze. Nothing to see except mounds and mounds of worthless rock, all the same, dull and nondescript.

Except one. A lone boulder with a cleft in its side shaped like a lightning bolt.

Even before Jo squeezed through the crack, she felt her. Before she saw the makeshift door, the box garden, the smoldering ashes, she felt her. But it was still a surprise to finally see a woman with long dark hair leaning against the rock, cracked blue mug in her hands, peering at Jo with those eyes that had haunted her dreams for the past seven years.

Olive didn't move from her seat. She didn't smile or frown, laugh or cry. She simply stared. "I knew you'd come." Her voice was gravelly but still tinged with the girlishness Jo remembered. "The Bible on the bed. The note. I knew you'd find it. I knew you'd remember."

Gone was the roundness in her cheeks, the playfulness in her deep-set eyes. She was thin, and her skin was now as dark and leathery as the shoes on her feet. It was hard to believe she was younger than Jo; life and sun had aged her well past her years. She coughed wetly, wiping her mouth with the back of her bony hand, but her eyes never strayed.

Jo tried to speak. She really did. But her words evaporated before they could form. She'd dreamed of this moment and dreaded it all the same. So much love, so much hurt, so much rage and affection. A bond once severed that refused to die now lay bare between them.

"You're angry and confused," Olive said as if reading her thoughts. She finished the contents of her mug and dropped the dregs into the glowing coals.

"No," Jo said, finally finding her voice. "You don't get to tell me how I feel."

There was a flicker of discomfort in the corners of Olive's eyes. "Okay."

Jo's gaze rolled around the mesa. So many emotions and yet it was the questions that burst forth first. "What is this? Do you live here?"

Olive shrugged. "No. And yes." She stepped aside and gestured toward the rotted door behind her. An invitation.

Jo hesitated briefly before stepping past her and into the burrow. Inside, it was dark and smelled faintly of kerosene. In the dim light, she could make out a cot and blankets, stacks upon stacks of paperbacks, and a pile of pots and canned goods. Other shadows lurked toward the back. Clothes, Jo guessed, or other household items.

"I've been on the move for a few weeks," Olive said, appearing behind her and making her jump. "Grandma's old car is locked up in the barn. I use it when I have to but try to stick to buses as much as I can. Carrizozo, Corona, San Antonio. Yet I always end up back here."

"Why?"

"It's . . . it's a long story."

Jo turned sharply, heat rising in her cheeks. Her fury was sudden and powerful. She stuck an accusatory finger in Olive's face, causing the two of them to back out into the blinding sun. "Don't you dare. You don't get to do that."

"Do what?"

"Leave me in the dark. Not anymore."

"Jo . . ." The stoniness in Olive's face faltered. Her dark eyes watered.

Jo didn't know what she'd expected to feel, but it definitely wasn't this. She'd forgiven her father, thought she'd released all her anger and resentment. And for the most part, she had.

For him.

But not for Olive.

It was still there. Festering, just waiting to be released. And yet behind all that anger lay something else, something only recognizable now because of the vulnerability she'd allowed herself to feel with her father.

Pain. So fierce and so deep, it felt as if she had been stabbed. Jo took a step backward, struggling to swallow the lump in her throat. She would not cry. Not for the pitiful state she found Olive in, a shell of the girl she'd known, the truth of whose condition was worse than she'd ever imagined. A nomad, a wanderer, practically homeless.

No, she would not cry for that, no matter how much it hurt her to see. The tears that fell from her eyes came from somewhere much deeper. They came from the shadow of herself she saw in Olive's eyes. From the hint of youthful promises she'd once imagined, eroded by the harsh reality of life. Seeing Olive not only brought her face-to-face with the past but also reminded her of the future that should have been . . . and wasn't.

Blinded by tears, she started at the feel of a hand on her arm, soft and tentative, yet more powerful than her anguish. She turned and grabbed Olive, breathing in the smell of dirt and sweat as she wrapped her in a tight embrace. Olive's frail body heaved, crying tears as silent as Jo's were loud.

"Why didn't you come?" The words fell from Jo's mouth in between sobs. "Why did you leave me?"

Olive pulled back. Tears left trails of mud down her dusty face.

"Why did you leave me?" Jo said again. Releasing her grief had allowed strength to return to her resolve. Urgency. "Where were you?"

"Jo—"

"You said you'd come. It was supposed to be you and me. Together. And then you . . . you never showed. My dad came, and he said . . ." She shook her head, trying to force her father's words from her mind. She'd forgiven him. Repeating the words would only restore the power she'd vowed never to allow them again.

"I never meant to hurt you."

Jo turned her body away from Olive's. "I went alone. I did the work. The work I always knew I was supposed to do. God's plan, right? My calling." Fresh tears welled inside her, but they were different from before. "So I went and I . . . I lost God. Do you know that? I lost Him. At least I thought I did. I thought, if I was so wrong about you and His plan for us, then maybe I was wrong about everything else too. And I lost Him."

Olive's chin dropped to her chest.

But Jo didn't stop. "I worked myself ragged, hoping with each new project, each new location, that the doubt would subside and He would show up again. But He never did. The only one who ever showed up . . . was you. A ghost I could never escape."

Olive clutched at her pant legs, avoiding Jo's eyes. Fresh drops stained the tops of her dusty shoes.

"So I built up this wall, trying to keep you out, trying to keep my dad out, trying to keep myself out. Yet all it really did was keep Him out. All it did was break me." Jo's voice was thick, coated with the memories of that painful, lonely time. "It was supposed to be different. Supposed to mean something. It was supposed to be *us.*

But you never showed." She crossed her arms over her chest, trying to stop the trembling. "The least you can do is tell me why."

Several moments of silence passed. And then:

"Jo." Just her name. Quiet. Painful. Spoken in supplication.

Her old friend's watery gaze pierced her, pleading, but Jo would not be shaken. Not when she was this close. "Olive, what happened that day?"

CHAPTER TWENTY-FIVE

JO

JULY 16, 1945

The sky was cloudless when Jo left the house on Michigan Avenue for the last time, all traces of yesterday's rain evaporated by the summer sun. Her nostalgia surprised her; it had never been a home. Not really. More like a waiting room. Someplace she could bide her time until real life started. Until what came next.

Until now.

She had packed light, leaving behind most of her things. Toys, clothes, books. Her childhood. And a note, written to her father with as much poise as she could muster. She knew he didn't want her to go. It would break his heart when he found out she had gone anyway. But this wasn't about him, and she hoped someday, maybe, he would understand that. This was about God. About her.

And about Olive.

She hurried her pace, wondering if Olive would already be at the bus stop. What a thrill it had been to see God working, that moment of breakthrough, His Spirit triumphant through her willing obedience. She had witnessed the moment Olive had witnessed Him.

There was still trepidation, of course. And not just for Olive. Jo could admit now that she'd begun to doubt, worried she'd misheard His calling, afraid He'd forgotten her in the chaos of the world around her. But faith had sustained her through the uncertainty and months of isolation, both here and in California, this hope and belief in God's faithfulness, His goodness, His plan. And now she was seeing it. She could see it all over Olive's face. Not only was He opening the door to the future, He had brought her the family she'd always craved. And not just in the sense of God's family, which she'd always known she was a part of. With Olive, she had a friend. With Olive, she had a sister.

For the first time in a very long time, she would no longer be alone.

Traffic on Pennsylvania Avenue was light, the curious scent of distant smoke mixing with the ever-present dust in the morning air. She crossed the street at a run and scanned the handful of people milling outside the bus station. Men in uniform, women in dark dresses with small, cranky children, a few older couples with tattered suitcases and frumpy sun hats. But no dark-haired girl to be seen.

Apprehension tried to push its way back into Jo's heart. *What if . . . ?*

But Jo wouldn't allow herself to finish. Perhaps Olive was inside, waiting. After all, Jo hadn't told her which ticket to buy.

Tucking her bag against her side, she pushed into the lobby, smile wide.

It was empty.

Well, not empty. A very bored, very tired-looking ticket agent sat in her booth, clicking her nails against her coffee cup. The sound echoed through the small room. She stopped as Jo approached.

"Where you—?" Her question was interrupted by a deep yawn. She covered her mouth with one hand sheepishly. "Sorry about that! Where you headed?"

"San Diego?" She wasn't sure why it came out like a question.

The woman nodded and shuffled through some papers on her desk. "Got one leaving in fifteen, with stopovers in Lordsburg, Tucson, and Yuma."

"That's fine."

"Just the one ticket, then?"

"Yes." Jo reached for her bag, hesitating before pulling out an extra bill. "On second thought, make it two."

"You bet."

It was an act of faith. No, of confidence. Because Olive would need a ticket. And since this was Jo's idea, the least she could do was buy her ticket. For when she got here. *When.*

Inside her booth, the ticket agent yawned again. "I am so sorry! I'm usually a morning person. You have to be with this shift. But that doggone quake woke me up before I was able to get my eight hours—"

"Quake?"

The woman's green eyes bulged at Jo. "You didn't hear it? Feel it?"

Jo shook her head.

She let out a short burst of air through her nose and returned to her shuffling. "Some people can sleep through anything. It's a gift, I tell you. A real gift. I wake up when a mouse sneezes." She chuckled at her own joke. "Ah, well. It didn't last long. Got me out of bed quick, though. I'll tell you that. Heard a rumble like the earth itself was breaking apart. And—my husband says I'm crazy—but I swore there was a bright light that went along with it."

"A light?"

The woman waved her hands in front of her. "I know. I know. My husband thinks I must have been dreaming. He didn't see or feel a thing. But the radio's saying it was a munitions explosion over at the base, so I know I'm not crazy."

A chill prickled the hair on the back of Jo's neck. "Munitions explosion?"

"That's what they're saying. But I don't know." The woman tilted her head side to side as she scratched some numbers on a notepad in front of her. "I swear, something just feels . . . off. It's been that way all morning."

Jo struggled to release a breath. A munitions explosion. An accident. It had nothing to do with her. Or with Olive. Or her dad.

So why was she suddenly feeling as if she was going to be sick?

"Well, anyway—" the woman extended her hand, oblivious to Jo's discomfort—"here you go. Two tickets to San Diego. Your bus will be leaving from stand number three. Out the front door and to your left."

Jo took the tickets with numb hands, trying to force a smile onto her lips. "Thank you." She tucked the tickets in her bag as she stepped back outside. The air was no better out here; though a slight breeze rustled some nearby cottonwoods, the atmosphere remained stagnant. Heavy. Unsettled. Had it been like this before she'd gone inside?

And still Olive was nowhere to be seen.

Her bus was already parked in its spot at platform three. Its chrome sides gleamed in the sun. A small crowd huddled near its rear, loading suitcases and bags into the storage compartment while a man in a Greyhound uniform smoked a cigarette nearby.

Jo walked over to the waiting area. Shielding her eyes from the glare, she strained for any sign of her friend.

"You on this bus?"

A deep voice caused her to jump. She spun around, clutching her bag to her chest.

It was the man in the Greyhound hat. The driver. He gave a small laugh. "Sorry, ma'am. Didn't mean to frighten you. I was just wondering if you needed help storing your bag."

Jo exhaled, feeling foolish. "No. I mean, yes. Yes, I am on this bus, but no, I don't need help with my bag, thank you. I'm waiting for my friend."

The driver tipped his hat. "Sure thing."

Jo stepped back out of the crowd and craned her neck. Where was Olive? There was now only ten minutes until departure. Her stomach knotted as more passengers joined the queue, none of them familiar, none of them Olive, all of them talking about the mysterious early morning quake few had experienced but about which all had theories.

"It's the Japanese, for sure. First step in an invasion. That's why we're getting out of here. Now."

"Nah, it was just some kind of test over at the air base. They're always up to something."

"Baloney. I saw it. I felt it. Ain't nothing man-made can make a glow like that. Like the sun done come up twice. Like the very finger of God."

Jo took yet another step back. She didn't want to hear any more. Something wasn't right. Only minutes ago she'd been so confident, so hopeful about the day ahead. But now these whispers. This feeling. As if the very air around her had soured.

She hadn't seen a thing. Heard a thing. Whatever it had been—earthquake, explosion, or something else entirely—had nothing to do with her. And yet a niggling in her core said otherwise. Something—everything—had somehow changed without her knowing it.

"Jo."

Her own name pierced her like a needle, both searing hot and bitterly cold. She knew the voice well, and yet it was not the one she was so desperate to hear. Steeling herself for what was to come, she turned.

Her father stood before her. His brown Army uniform, usually so crisp, was wrinkled and skewed. His tie was loose around his neck, and one tail on his shirt was untucked. Dark stubble covered his normally smooth cheeks. And while the space around his eyes was hollow and gray, it was the eyes themselves that were the most striking: no longer vibrant but dead. Clouded. Empty.

A sudden pang of guilt gripped her heart. Another crack in the plan that was already beginning to splinter under the weight of self-doubt. "Dad . . ."

"Jo." He wrapped her in a hug. He smelled of tobacco, days-old cologne, and unwashed clothes. But his embrace was strong and his arms stilled her trembling body. "I'm so glad I caught you in time."

"Dad, I'm so sorry. I didn't mean—"

He cut off her sentence with another hug. "Shh. Shh. There's no need to apologize. I found your note, and I rushed over here as fast as I could. I'm just glad I caught you before you left."

She clutched his jacket, the coarse fabric beneath her fingers the first real thing she'd felt all day. "I was so sure," she whispered. "I was so sure I was doing the right thing. And now I . . . Everyone's talking about an explosion and an earthquake and a bright light, and I'm scared. Something feels wrong. I want to go back home." She leaned into him, needing another embrace, and was surprised to find him tense.

"Jo, don't be silly. You have to get on that bus."

His tone was kind and even, no hint of malice, yet her stomach clenched as if punched. "What?"

He put his hands on her arms, staring deeply into her eyes. "I came to say goodbye. I wanted to see you one last time. But you have to get on that bus."

"I don't—"

"I was wrong to discourage you from your dream. Your 'calling,' I think is what you said. It was selfish of me." He rubbed her shoulder. "You know I've never understood this religion stuff. Not that you haven't tried." He gave a small smile she did not return. "But I can't deny the impact it's made on you. And if you say this is what you need to be doing, I can't hold you back, even as much as I'd like to. I can't keep you all to myself anymore."

His words were touching. Jo had always known her father cared about her, but it was in a distant, disconnected way. The Army came first; it had to. It was a painful truth, but a truth nonetheless. She'd had her brother, though, and her grandma, to fill the void. And most importantly, she'd had God. Still, she'd longed to hear tenderness in her earthly father's voice. To be understood by him and to know, without a doubt, that the Army was his duty but she was his heart. Now finally those words were here, hanging in the air between them.

And they were completely hollow. Because in his eyes, it wasn't love that she saw. It was fear.

"You have to get on the bus, Jo. You have to go."

She took a step away from him. Out of his touch, the memory of his hand on her shoulder tingled. She looked down at her feet, trying not to show the disappointment and unease curling around her heart. "I'm waiting for Olive."

"What?"

"I'm not leaving without Olive," she repeated, louder this time, despondency strengthening her nerves. "We're . . . we're going together."

"You're leaving together? When did you decide this?"

"Yesterday."

A slight twitch beneath his eye. "When was the last time you saw her?"

"Yesterday after . . ." A sudden chill sprouted goose bumps along Jo's arms. "Wait—why do you . . . ?"

Her father glanced at his watch. "Jo, please . . ."

The vehicle behind them gave out several annoyed sputters before settling into a constant hum. "Five minutes!" the driver called, one hand cupped around his mouth. "Bus number seventeen leaves in five minutes! Lordsburg, Tucson, Yuma, San Diego from platform three leaving in five minutes!"

Panic clutched at her, but she tried not to let it show. She craned her neck past her father. *Olive, Olive—where* are *you?*

"Jo, don't be silly. You need to get on the bus." His voice was cheery. Forced.

"No." She stamped her foot like a child. "Not without Olive. She's coming. She said she was coming. I've got her ticket."

Her father glanced over his shoulder, his eyes scanning the parking lot impatiently. "Don't be ridiculous, Jo. You're wasting time." He made as if to touch her again but she ducked from his grasp.

"The explosion. This has something to do with the explosion, doesn't it?"

He met her eyes briefly before looking away again.

"The one everyone's talking about. It was you, your work near the ranch." Anxiety wrestled with her rising anger. "Do you know something? What happened? Is Olive okay? Where is she? What did you do?"

"Jo!" His outrage was sudden, loud, and chilling. Several people turned to stare. Her father gave a weak smile, rubbing his temples with cracked knuckles, and waved dismissively. When he spoke again, his voice was quieter but no less fierce. "Stop this."

"Not until you tell me what happened to Olive. What *was* that explosion?"

"The explosion had nothing to do with her!" His rage was barely contained. He struggled to keep his tone at a whisper. "Or with you. Just get on the bus."

"Not without Olive."

"Olive isn't coming."

"What?"

"I saw her. Olive, I mean. I saw her this morning." His eyes roamed through the crowd, looking at everyone but her. "She told me she wasn't coming."

Jo's throat felt as if it were being squeezed from within. "No, that can't be right. She said—"

"She isn't coming." His words were tinged with exasperation. "She told me to tell you."

"But she said she would."

"Then she must have changed her mind."

"But . . . this is God's plan. I know it is. Her and I, we—"

"Enough!"

Jo stepped back. Her cheeks felt as hot as if he had physically slapped her.

"Enough with all this ridiculous God stuff, Jo! I am so sick of hearing about it! I can't bear one more word about such irritating, irrational hope!" His skin grew splotchy as he spat his words. "People like you—you walk around telling everybody about this wonderful God of yours, while the world burns and evil grows like weeds! For pete's sake, open your ever-loving eyes already!"

Jo's shoulders hunched. She tucked her head, trying to shield herself from the blows.

"There is no good, no hope, no grander plan. There's only corrupt people and the hurtful things they do to one another." He shook his head. "I'm sorry, Jo. But there's no God. And if by some miracle there is, then He doesn't belong here . . . and neither do you."

Tears streamed down Jo's cheeks as the breath in her lungs

dissolved. Every fear, every doubt, every whispered insecurity that once haunted her in the night now lay bare in the desert sun, stacked in the space between her and her father. It was a wall she knew would never again be breached.

The crowd around them stared without staring. Many had begun to push onto the bus, presumably to get away from the uncomfortable tension filling the platform.

Her father sighed. His strength seemed to wilt now that the truth had been spilled. "For pete's sake, Jo," he muttered. "Just go. Take your hope and your Jesus someplace else." His green eyes were rimmed with red and brimming with tears she would never understand. "You're a silly little fool. Stay a silly little fool. Get on the bus and don't ever come back."

When bus seventeen pulled away from the station only minutes later, Jo was on it, alone, curled into the last seat with a suitcase in her lap and her head in her hands. She wept for hours; it wasn't until she crossed the California state line that she finally, stoically, dried her face and cemented her soul. Eyes focused ahead, she vowed to never look back, not yet knowing that the darkness she believed she had fled was already spreading inside her heart.

CHAPTER TWENTY-SIX

OLIVE

JULY 16, 1945

The smoke had finally lifted. Yet again, I could see for miles across the Jornada. The creosote and yucca, the sporadic cottonwoods—they were all still standing. The land rose and fell gently, still the same red-and-brown earth as always. It was as if this morning—whatever it was—had never happened. Like New Mexico had already forgotten. But I knew I never would.

The mule was gone. Thank goodness for that. Even in my rush, I didn't think I'd be able to stomach seeing it again. But the spot on the other side of the lava fields was bare, no sign of a carcass. Perhaps he'd wandered away, having been only momentarily stunned by what he'd seen. Hadn't we all been?

There were no more cars in Carrizozo or racing down the 380.

The earlier excitement had faded. The Japanese weren't coming. It was just an ammunition explosion. How readily we accepted the lie. Anything to let us keep on living our lives.

When I reached the ranch, all was quiet. No Army men milling about. No cars out front. But I knew she was in there somewhere. Maybe he was too.

I eased open the casita door. Inside was dark, the red curtains still drawn against the sun, casting the room in an eerie, blood-like glow. The dishes were gone from the table, but the smell still remained. Peppers and men's cologne. I moved through the room silently, careful not to touch anything. Grandma followed me, her earlier apprehension fading the farther we got from Alamogordo, even as my own rose. She seemed smaller now, like a child.

"Olive."

It was the last voice I expected to hear. And yet somehow it did not surprise me.

Avery appeared out of the shadows, standing near the back door. Dressed in a white T-shirt and jeans, he looked just like he had the last time I'd seen him . . . but also completely different. Older, his already-thin face now gaunt and bony. His hair was long, most definitely not in Army regulation, and darkness circled his eyes. As he stepped into the light, the shadow around him did not dissipate.

"What are you doing here?"

The query came from his lips but it was the same one upon my own. I, however, lacked the courage to speak.

"Avery?" Behind me, Grandma tilted her head. The fog had lifted enough to enable recognition of her grandson, though her tone spoke a confusion larger than her episodes.

His eyes flitted toward her, then away just as quickly. He took another step forward, smaller this time, as if afraid to get too close. "You shouldn't be here."

"Where's Ma?" It wasn't the most important question but it was the only one I could muster. I stared at my brother with a mix of elation and dread. He was here. He was alive. And yet it was these very truths that seized at my heart, fanning my earlier suspicions and flooding my body with fear. *He* shouldn't have been here.

"You need to get out of here. Both of you."

"Where's Ma?"

"Olive, honey, I'm here." My mother rushed in behind Avery, wrapping me in her arms before I could push her away. "I'm here. I'm here. I was so worried about you."

I breathed her in, wanting to stay in her embrace, fighting the urge to surrender to youth. But even as I allowed her to hold me a little longer, my eyes were forced to Grandma, to Avery, to Hershel, who'd quietly stepped inside behind her. Reality slammed down on us, prying us apart as if by physical force.

"Grandma," I stammered. "She . . . she's having an episode. A bad one. The flash . . ."

The look of hurt on my mother's face quickly changed to concern. "Mother," she said softly, touching her on the arm. "Mother, are you okay?"

"Your father. We have to get your father. The Japanese . . ." But there was no conviction in her voice anymore. Only weary uncertainty.

"The Japanese aren't here, Mother. I promise." She looked toward the ceiling, blinking rapidly. Her eyes, already red and sleepless, glistened in the low light. "Why don't you lay down and rest?"

"Evelyn." The name came out as a warning on Hershel's lips.

But she ignored him. Pulling gently on Grandma's elbow, she tried to lead her away.

"No," Grandma said. "I don't need to rest." Yet even as the words fell from her lips, she slumped, allowing herself to be guided to the back bedroom. Ma glanced over her shoulder at me, trying to plead with me through her silence. *Stay,* she seemed to say. *Please stay.* The door clicked behind them, muting their murmurs and filling the space left in their wake with a rigid unease.

Avery looked at the floor and toed the ground with scuffed boots. Hershel, however, stared right at me.

"Your mother done told me what happened. What you think you saw. Her and Sergeant Hawthorne. The flash."

Heat flushed under my collar. "I know what I saw."

"You don't know a doggone thing, girl. And it was supposed to stay that way." He ran a tongue over his yellow teeth, lifting his hat to scratch at the bald patch beneath. "Now you best be getting on out of here. Your mama will bring your grandma back once she's caught the bus out of Crazy Town."

Bus. Jo. I glanced at my watch. If I left now, I could still make it. But the glint in Uncle Hershel's eye as he curled his fingers around Avery's shoulder gave me pause.

I stuck out my chin, hoping he didn't see it wobble. "I'll go," I said. "I'll go and I won't ever come back. I can promise you that. But first you're going to tell me what's going on."

Hershel let out a snort.

"Just tell her," Avery said softly, still looking at the ground. "She's a part of this family too. She deserves to know. To understand why." He glanced up at me finally. There was a hunger in his eyes. Exhaustion and pain, yes. But beneath it all, a cold, merciless hunger.

It was enough to make me want to flee. And yet I could not force myself to walk out that door.

"The flash you saw this morning. It was a test of a new kind of bomb. Atomic, they're calling it." Uncle Hershel took a step forward.

Instinctively, I took a step back. "What does that mean?"

He waved a hand. "I don't really understand the science. Something about plutonium and uranium and some other *-ium*. Dangerous stuff. All I know is that it's big. And powerful. More powerful than any bomb ever made before. It can wipe out a city the size of Albuquerque in seconds."

"That's not possible."

"It didn't used to be." He raised his eyebrows as if daring me to contradict him.

"How do you know this?"

The smile on his lips was wicked as he gestured toward the bedroom. "Ask your mother."

I closed my eyes, feeling very much like the night I'd had too much wine. Only this time, there was no wine.

"Olive, will you please sit down?"

I hadn't seen my mother emerge from the bedroom. But there she was, looking pale, her long dark hair falling messily from its bun. A cigarette hung loosely from her fingers.

I backed away with lead feet and grabbed the doorknob. I'd

come all this way for the truth . . . and suddenly there was nothing in the world I wanted less. I would leave. I had to leave.

"Olive, please."

"Bah," Hershel growled. "If she wants to go, let her go."

"No." There was a firmness beneath the quiver in my mother's voice. "No. Olive . . ." A pause. "For the past several months, I . . . we . . . have been working for the Union of Soviet Socialist Republics. For Moscow. For the Communists."

My hand slipped from the knob. "What?"

"Gathering information about this bomb. This test. Their construction methods, their testing facilities, their site. That's the real reason I stayed behind . . . and the reason why you couldn't."

It seemed to take hours for her words to reach my brain, and even then, they failed to connect. "But the Soviets are our allies."

Avery gave a short, bitter laugh. "We're on the same side against the Nazis, yes. But don't mistake that for friendship. The Americans have been secretive about this weapon, denyin' it, refusing to share anything, even the science. *Allies* don't do that, Olive."

My head spun. I placed one hand on the couch to steady myself. As I struggled to make sense of Avery's words, a bigger, more urgent thought pressed forward instead. "But this is our home. *We're* Americans! We're—"

"We are Russians first." Uncle Hershel's lip curled into a sneer. "My parents may have chosen to leave, but your pa, me, even you and Avery—Russian blood still flows through our veins no matter what land lays below our feet."

I shook my head, trying to clear it, trying to make something— anything—make sense. "No. No. Pa was . . . well, he kept to himself, self-sufficiency and minding your own business and all . . .

but he was an American through and through. He would never have betrayed this country."

"America betrayed us first!" Avery's voice was nearly a shout. "A pledge of alliance, all while keeping their fingers crossed behind their backs. They want Russian men to die for their cause, to weaken the strength of the Soviet Republic, so after the Nazi defeat, they can rule the world unchecked. They even deny their own citizens the right to fight, while the Soviet people—men and women—are dying all across Europe." The last sentence dripped with disdain, spoken more to himself than to me. "Look around you, Olive! They've been doing it for years. First the Native Americans, now us. They've taken our home and destroyed it, all for their own selfish gain. This isn't for peace. It's for power!"

Hershel squeezed Avery's shoulder roughly. Shadows fell over my brother's face, darkening his eyes. I'd always thought Avery to be the spitting image of my father. But here, in this light, in this moment, he was Hershel. In looks, in bitterness, and in hostility.

It was as if Pa had died all over again. My lip trembled. "Please tell me you don't really believe that."

He crossed his arms over his chest, grinding his teeth.

It felt as if my very soul was shrinking inside me. "Avery . . . what did you do?"

His eyes gave me only a moment's glance before turning downward. "I've been in Los Alamos. Outside a research facility, working in secret with others who share our view. Doing my own duty for Moscow, who gladly accepted my willingness to serve. Unlike others." The last words were spoken with a snarl.

I sank onto the couch. The room seemed to sway. All this time, all those people praying for my brother half a world away—and he'd been less than three hundred miles north, slinking in the shadows, undermining the very war effort they all worked so hard to support. None of this made any sense. And yet, inside this version of the truth, all the pieces fit. Avery, denied overseas service due to his color-blindness, had been sucked into Hershel's vitriol. And my mother . . .

The mysterious writings in the notebook. The secret meeting in the alley outside the restaurant. Sergeant Hawthorne.

She had used him.

I retched twice, my entire body convulsing, though there was nothing to lose. I dropped my head between my knees, trying to stem the waves.

My family wasn't just broken. They were spies.

I felt the couch depress as my mother sat down beside me. Her spindly hand reached for mine. "It's okay, Olive. It's okay—"

I jumped up, repulsed by her touch. "It's not okay! It's *not okay*. This is . . . this is treason!"

"It's not treason. It's—"

"That's exactly what it is!" I backed away from her, stumbling over the corner of the couch. "You're a traitor! And you and you." I gestured at Hershel, at Avery. "And Sergeant Hawthorne too." The nausea swelled again with the realization. Jo. Oh no. *Jo.* Her father had been brought into this; *she* had been brought into this.

"Olive—"

"Enough, Evelyn. Just enough." Hershel threw his hands up. "This is exactly why I told you she had to go. Why she couldn't be a part of this. She's too young and weak, too brainwashed by this country and now that doggone church I told you to put a stop to!"

He raised an accusatory finger at her. "But I will not waste another second on this nonsense. Avery, let's go."

He grabbed my brother by the shoulders and started to push him toward the back door.

"Hershel!" For the first time, the calm, matter-of-fact tone left my mother's voice. "What are you—?"

"The boy comes with me."

My mother's already-pale face drained of any remaining color. "That was never part of our agreement. You said—"

"You got your money, didn't you? The CPUSA came through and gave you what you wanted."

"Yes, I got the money. But you promised you would leave, that you'd take your Communist friends and—"

"That's what I'm doing!" he snapped. "But the boy comes with me."

"No!" A soft wail from my mother's lips. "This was not part of it. You promised . . ." Her words died, then re-formed harder, more desperate. "You cannot take him."

Hershel's eyes narrowed. His hand dropped from my brother's arm. "Go on. Tell her. Tell her I ain't *taking* you. Tell her you want to leave."

Avery's shoulders hunched. He looked at nothing but the floor.

"Avery," my mother murmured.

"I want to leave," he said quietly.

Even in my devastation, his words still rattled my heart. But it was nothing compared to the torment I saw on my mother's face.

"Avery," she said again, her voice cracking.

"There ain't nothing for me here, Mama. The ranch ain't

making no money, and pretty soon there won't be no ranch left. I want to go with Hershel."

"But—"

He talked over her objections. "The CPUSA's goal was always to change America, to make them see Communism's light. But the time for that has passed. This is just the beginning, Ma. One war is ending; the other is just getting started. The real war. And it's time I face the truth: there ain't nothing for me here. No plan, no purpose. The ranch don't need me. This country don't need me. But CPUSA needs me. Moscow needs me. They have a place for me." Hershel's words but my brother's mouth. "You ain't—"

"*I* need you, Avery. We need you." She gestured limply in my direction. Her eyes brimmed with tears. "Your place is here. We only have a little time left."

Avery met my mother's gaze for the first time. His face remained stoic, but his mouth gave a small quiver, the only sign of a crack in his hard expression.

"Enough of this," Hershel barked. "Clock's a-ticking. Let's go."

Avery gave a grunt as Hershel's hand landed with a thud between his shoulder blades. The moment had passed; his lips solidified back into an unreadable line. Whatever he had meant to say would remain with him, and my mother's heart would go with it.

"Avery," my mother whimpered. "Please."

But he didn't look at her. Instead he glanced over his shoulder at me.

I'd thought I was the only one with a void in my life, the only one searching for meaning, purpose, and belonging. Turns out Avery had been too, but that pain had pushed us in very different directions.

Holding his gaze, I lifted my hand. With trembling fingers, I made one small motion in the air between us. Up to a point and then down again. The upside-down *V*.

I wish I could say there was regret in his eyes, sadness, or maybe even a little bit of love. But they were blank and expressionless, his face a mask of nothingness. And it was for this reason that a lone tear finally broke from my eye. Not because I knew without words that I'd never see him again. But because he was already gone.

Their absence left a palpable presence in the home, bigger than their physical bodies ever had. My mother stared at the door without blinking, so long I almost believed she'd forgotten I was there. Until finally she spoke.

"He—they're going to Canada, I think. For a few months, until they know for sure they haven't been found out." She took a long, shaky breath. "And then likely . . . maybe . . . Russia. I don't know. That was Hershel's original plan, anyway. But now . . ."

I stared at the door, no words sufficient to express my disbelief and sorrow. In the last twenty-four hours, my world had been flipped upside down; this revelation had set it on fire. There was nothing else to do . . . except leave. I stood and walked out of the casita on wobbly legs. Outside, the air was warm, thick with the hint of a monsoon storm yet to come. There was no more smoke. No more Army trucks. Somehow ridiculously, perfectly ordinary.

"Olive! Olive, wait!"

I did not. I walked toward the car, grabbing the handle and yanking open the door with numb fingers.

"Olive, please. I . . . I'm sick."

I closed my eyes, willing myself to get into the car. It was another lie, I told myself. Another lie from the liar that was my mother.

"It's . . . cancer. Or so the doctor says. In my lungs." As if on cue, she let out a deep, scraping croak. It was a cough just like a million others I'd heard my mother make. She was always coughing, had been for years; it was the ever-present dust and the cheap cigarettes. Not cancer. Just a cough.

Except it wasn't. Because the time for lying had passed. There was nothing left between us but the truth. The hard, agonizing, unbelievable truth.

"I . . . I should have stood up to Hershel. Should have told him no when he asked me to fish for information, to pass it on to Gus, his contact, though I don't know if that was his real name. Code, more likely. But Hershel did it all—the ciphering, the correspondence. Even came up with the place to meet—Memories—and the way I'd find the agent in Alamogordo: a Jell-O box split in two. I should have told him no. But he . . . he told me they'd give me all this money. More money than I could ever want or need. Enough money to keep the ranch going, for you, for Avery." Her breath choked on my brother's name. "Long after I was gone."

I spun around, stuffing my sorrow beneath anger. "And you honestly thought I'd want the ranch at the cost of my own mother? That treason was worth the price of a few acres of land?"

"It was worth our freedom!" Sobs erupted from her throat. Strands of windblown hair stuck to her cheeks. "I've made so many mistakes in my life, been so lost, so weak, so *pushed around* since your father died. Like I had no foundation anymore. I wasn't a mother. I was a ghost. I let Hershel come in and walk all over me, all over us; I let this world decide who we were and what we should be. And then I got the diagnosis . . ." She pressed a weary hand to her forehead. "I should have been better, done better. Given you kids more than just memories. You deserved a future. A *real* future. I went about it all wrong, but you have to believe, deep down, I was trying to finally do something right."

I pressed my fingertips to my eyes. I wanted her to stop talking. I wanted to stay angry.

"The money would secure a place. Hershel's absence would supply peace. And maybe, just maybe, you'd learn enough from your time with Grandma to bring us all a little hope. In the last days."

My breath caught in a painful, burning hitch. Church. My mother had wanted me to go to church. The faith she'd given up, abandoned for my father, still flickered in her breast. Weak and dim, fractured and nearly forgotten, but when everything else had been taken from her, she still remembered enough—believed enough—to want that faith for me.

Because she was broken. And alone. A traitor and a liar.

And still my mother.

The misery in that truth pierced me. I crumpled against the side of the car.

"I told him, you know. Richard. I told him the truth this morning. I never meant to hurt him . . . I genuinely care about him. But I had to tell him. He didn't yell. He didn't scream. He didn't do anything. He just . . . left, Olive. Everybody just left." She pressed her palm to her chest. "I've made such a mess of things. Such a mess. I deserve whatever happens to me. But he doesn't. And you don't. And neither does she." She gestured toward the casita with a limp wave of her hand.

Grandma. In my selfishness, I'd left her inside. In all of *this*. My heart seized as I imagined her back in her house on Delaware Avenue, longing for the daughter she could never find. Confused, fearful, unsure of the day, the year, of this world and her place in it.

And then there was Ma. The Feds would get her if the sickness didn't take her first. I pictured her, toiling on the ranch alone, drowning in remorse and rejection, wasting away and waiting for the day of her reckoning.

And me. A thousand miles away with Jo. Doing good works, pressing onward into something honorable and true. A plan and purpose.

Racked by guilt and haunted by a past I could never truly outrun.

I didn't want this to be my "something bigger." This mess, not of my own volition, but rather created by those around me and dumped at my feet, was surely not the future God had in store for me. He hadn't been nudging on my heart, opening doors of opportunities and freedom . . . only to force me back into darkness and grief.

But still I let go of the door handle. Something other than myself turned my body from that car and moved my legs toward the casita. I knew less than a hundred miles away, Jo was getting on a bus, moving on from this place with all of its wretchedness and despair. Maybe she was wondering where I was. Or maybe not. I would never know. Because instead of driving away, I swallowed my tears and gripped my mother's bony shoulders. Her body collapsed against mine as I led her back toward the house.

Jo had found her purpose in life, and I had wanted it to be mine too. But as the dust swirled at my feet and the weight of my mother's grief pulled at my soul, I could only pray that God wasn't just for those out there; I hoped He was still here, too, in this forsaken piece of New Mexico wasteland. And with the broken, flawed people in it.

CHAPTER TWENTY-SEVEN

JO

MARCH 1952

For a long while, there were no words. Olive's story hovered over them like an unexpected cloudburst in a clear sky, raining truth over a past Jo had written inside her head a million times. But never, ever like this.

They had remained standing for the duration of the story, and it was only after its conclusion that Jo realized she had taken several steps back. Or had it been Olive? They were no longer within arm's reach of one another. The spell of their nearness evaporated as verity grew between them.

"I haven't seen or heard from Avery or Uncle Hershel since. The plan was Canada, but who knows where they ended up. Somewhere the Feds couldn't reach, I'm sure."

The Feds. She said it casually, like a line from some cheap spy novel. Her face, however, was anything but fiction.

"I stayed at the ranch with Ma and Grandma. Every day we went through the motions, just waiting for the police to show up, sure today would be the day. But somehow . . ." She ran one shoe over the gravel, scraping it. "After a few weeks, your father moved in too, finally being done with the Army and all. Well, I say 'moved in,' but it never really felt like he was all there. His mind was always . . . He wanted to come after you, you know? Almost did, several times."

"Then why didn't he?" Jo's voice was flat; unable to choose an emotion, she chose none at all.

"I want to say it's because he loved my mother. Because he wanted to take care of her, make what they had together mean something real. Maybe if true love came from what they had done, he could forgive himself. And I think maybe he did. Not necessarily forgive himself, but I think he did love her, in his own way." She gave a sad smile. "Or maybe that's just wishful thinking. But I know it's not really why he stayed."

Jo poked her tongue into her cheek, throat tight.

"The real reason he never went after you wasn't because he loved my mother. It was because he loved you."

Jo shook her head violently, her blonde hair whipping across her face. The past several minutes had been filled with the most outrageous, implausible information, things she would never have believed if she weren't standing in this place, here and now. But this—*this*—was the most unbelievable thing of all.

"You weren't there. At the bus station. You weren't there. You didn't hear the things he said."

"I didn't have to," Olive said quietly. "Because I saw him every day afterward."

The air was laden with the words she didn't say, lending authenticity to a sentiment Jo didn't want to be true. She had forgiven him. She had given him that much. But the pain . . . the pain was hers and hers alone; allowing for the possibility of his own was more than she could bear.

"The shame of what he had done and the inevitable consequences to follow—he couldn't have you be a part of that. The web in which he'd become tangled, the one he'd helped spin—he knew it would catch up in the end. If not the Feds, then his own guilt. He had to push you away from here, even if it meant hurting you. Away from this. Away from *him*. All the light he knew you were going to bring into the world . . . he couldn't be the one who smothered it."

Black spots swam at the corners of Jo's vision. It was all wrong. How could the truth be more excruciating than the lies? All the wasted years and poisonous hate, the faith she'd almost abandoned, the ruined man she'd very nearly condemned.

And the shell of a woman standing in front of her, carrying the weight of it all.

"I wanted to be a part of what you were doing," Olive continued. "I hope you know that. I really did. To go out into the world and do those amazing things you talked about. But that day I finally figured out *my* calling, my purpose. It was to stay. I couldn't fix things . . . but I could stay and deal with the mess. I could stay . . . so you could go."

Jo's knees started to quiver. Olive's confession felt too heavy to withstand. "Olive . . ."

"It was the right choice," she said, speaking over her. "I know it hurt you, and I'm sorry, but it was the right choice. Ma had horrible dreams in those final days, and I'm glad I was here for her. Grandma was gone by then and Ma . . . her guilt and shame were so big, I'd swear that was what killed her, not the cigarettes. She begged me for forgiveness, begged Avery and my father too. I wonder if she saw them in her nightmares." She paused for a moment. When she resumed, her voice was husky. "She cried out to God. Searching for His love, His forgiveness. I don't know for sure, but I hope she found it. In the end."

Jo opened and closed her mouth several times, unsure what to say. Turned out she didn't need to say anything. Olive wasn't finished.

"After she died, your father moved back into town. He didn't want to leave me out here alone, practically begged me to come with him. Said he had enough money saved for retirement for the both of us. But I promised I'd be okay, that I'd come and visit, though I never really intended to. Truth was, it was a relief when he left. Like that chapter of our lives was finally over. But once he was actually gone, I found I couldn't bear it. It was almost like losing you all over again. And judging by the way he welcomed me into his home every time I visited, I think he felt the same. We were each other's last remaining connection to you."

Jo rubbed the insides of her palms with her fingers. She felt Olive's eyes but was unable to meet them.

"When the Feds came, your father wanted to confess. But he didn't. Not because of any sense of self-preservation, but because of me. He knew without any other Alexander scapegoats available, I would have been an easy target. So he kept his mouth shut. Even when the Feds were tearing up his home, my home, threatening his arrest, he stayed quiet. They had their suspicions, but they could never find any proof. It was pretty intense there for a while, but then they got their Rosenbergs and their Greenglasses and Fuchs, and it seemed to appease them. They finally left us alone, and I was able to be there for him when he got his own diagnosis. When the cancer got worse, when it stole his strength and his voice and it finally became apparent that . . ." She swallowed loudly.

"But in these last few weeks, once he moved into the hospital, the Feds came back. Well, one of them did. It's like he knew time was running out; your dad was the last chance at learning the truth. And this one—this one was crazy. Aggressive. Not in line with the bureau at all. That's why I've spent so much time up here. I've had to be careful, stay out of his way. Your father wanted me to run . . . but I couldn't leave. Not yet. Because I still had one more thing I needed to do."

Jo's eyelids felt gummy. The raw ache in her chest had spread into every part of her body.

"I knew you'd come back. And I had to make sure you knew the truth. He never meant to hurt you. He went about it all wrong—everything about this was wrong—and he hated himself for it. But he loved you. He pushed you away because he loved you; I stayed because I loved you. We loved you and we hurt you—and ourselves—because of it. And that kind of love—that painful, reckless, self-sacrificing love that didn't make any sense at all—that was where it finally clicked: the God who shouldn't love us but does, who sacrificed everything just to make that love known. In our damage, we see His perfection. In our sin, we see His grace. And in this mess, we saw the God who loved you . . . and us, too." She pressed her lips into a tragic smile. "We found Him, Jo. *He* found Him. *I* found Him. And I couldn't leave until I was sure you knew that . . . that something good came out of all of this."

Jo lowered herself to the ground, suddenly feeling light-headed. The air was too thin, the sun too hot, the light around her bright and piercing. She felt weak, exhausted, as if she were being pulled underground, seeing and hearing things through layers of dirt and rock.

"Jo?"

Olive's voice was far away. God's hand . . . God's hand in all of this. The sin and the hurt, the mess and the misery. His hand was somehow, miraculously, in it all. He had never left. Years of grief and isolation, yet He was always there, working in the background, answering prayers she'd long since abandoned. The cross in her palm, the Bible on her bed. Her father had found God. Olive had found God.

And she had found Him. Again.

Head in her hands, she pressed her eyes closed, trying to stop the ground from swaying.

"Jo." Deeper now, no longer a question.

No longer Olive.

Swallowing her dizziness, she blinked against the sun. Olive still stood where she'd been, though her once-melancholy face was now twisted in panic. "Olive, what—?"

"Jo."

The voice came from behind her. She spun around on her bottom, ignoring the sharp tear of gravel against her legs.

Charlie was standing on the edge of the mesa, both hands wrapped around a silver pistol.

Jo sprang to her feet. She rushed toward him, arms outstretched. "Charlie! Charlie, it's fine. I know her! She's a friend. She's—"

"Step back, Jo." His tone was foreign, deep and cold.

"Charlie, what—?"

"I said step back."

"You're not going to shoot me," Olive said calmly. "We've already played this game."

"The rules have changed," he replied, corners of his mouth upturning. "Thanks to her."

Jo stepped back as if the gun had discharged. Her head swiveled wildly between them. "Me? Charlie, I—"

"I'm not a scientist, Jo. I'm with the FBI."

"The FB—"

"You're not!" Olive yelled. "You're not in the FBI, not anymore. He's the one, Jo. The rogue one I was telling you about. He's—"

"I used to be," he continued as if she hadn't spoken at all. "They suspended me for refusing to let this lie. But this—this is what I need to get reinstated. The truth. I've been trying to catch up with Miss Alexander here for a long time now." His eyes narrowed. "They can call you innocent all they want, but I know Commie blood runs deep, doesn't it, Olive?"

"I ain't no Commie," she spat.

Charlie waved the pistol in a way that made Jo wince. "So says you. You may have everyone else in the FBI fooled, but not me. I knew you knew more than you were saying. You knew not only what your mother was doing, but where she was getting her information."

For the first time, his eyes flickered to Jo. The kindness and compassion in them were long gone; those beautiful blue orbs were now full of rage.

"I knew you were in on it, and I knew it was Hawthorne."

"They said you had to leave me alone now. The case died long before he did." Olive's voice struggled to mask its tremble. "Everyone else let it go. Why can't you?"

"Because those dirty Commies killed my brother!" Silence rushed in behind Charlie's scream.

"He . . . he died in battle," Jo said hesitantly. "You told me."

He shook his head. "I never said battle. I said war. The war the Russians started with us the minute the one with Germany was over. Killed in Berlin the night before he was supposed to come home. By one of our 'allies.'" He scowled at Olive. "They were celebrating together. Friends, victors. Until one of them decided he wanted something my brother had. His watch. A watch his wife had given him as a wedding present. Gold, but simple. Nothing worth dying for. And yet he did. A bullet right in the stomach and left to die in a Berlin alley, while the Russian returned to the bar and raised a toast with the rest of the members of my brother's platoon."

Jo closed her eyes, picturing her own brother's body. Bloody and dying, lying on a German street thousands of miles from home. She knew Charlie's pain. No matter who was accused of pulling the trigger. "Charlie—"

"That has nothing to do with me," Olive interrupted. Her face had softened but her voice was still angry. "I'm sorry about your brother; I am. But I had nothing to do with his death."

"Maybe not you specifically. But your people. That's how they fight, Jo." Although speaking to her now, he sneered at Olive. "That's how they all do it. They're sneaky. They'll pat you on the back with one hand and then stab you with the other." He pushed hair off his forehead with his free hand. "They said to leave it alone. They said the investigation was dead. But no. No, I will bring down every single traitorous Commie I can, with or without the FBI's help."

"I'm not a Commie!"

Charlie laughed. A real laugh this time, a joke only he found funny.

"You used me." The words tasted vile in Jo's mouth. "You used me to get to Olive."

Charlie's eyes flickered in her direction. The bitter smile on his face wavered slightly. "I'm sorry, Jo. I really did like you. *Do* like you. But *this* . . . I've spent years waiting for this moment. Nothing—not even a pretty little thing like you—was going to stand in my way."

Chills crept down Jo's spine, like a dark cloud covering the sun. Despite her fear and confusion—or perhaps because of it—she no longer saw Charlie. She saw herself. In his callousness and venom, she recognized the bitterness and hate that had nearly consumed her too. Her soul would still be lost if not for the grace of God as well as the unrealized yet overwhelming love of her father.

And the woman on the other end of the gun.

"It won't bring him back, Charlie," she said softly.

He blinked twice, his eyes darting from her to Olive and back again. "What?"

"Killing Olive won't bring your brother back. Your grief—it's lying to you. This won't solve anything. We can't undo the past."

"You don't know what you're talking about."

She nodded in the direction of Trinity, the green glass sea hidden from their view but conspicuous all the same, as she took a tentative step forward. "It's like that. Thousands are dead, countries are at war . . . all for something men created, thinking they were doing the right thing—ending a war and avenging our fallen. Instead it's poisoning us in ways we're just now beginning to understand. But we can't undo it. We can't stuff the bomb back into its casing, wash the nuclear particles from the ground. That contamination will never truly go away. But we can press it into the hands of the One who can redeem us from the poison."

Behind her, Olive was crying quietly. Charlie's entire body trembled, the silver tip of the gun bobbing in his hand.

Jo took another step, slow and steady. She was close now. So very close. "I almost let that chance slip away from me. And the same thing is happening to you too. But killing her is not going to bring back your brother. It's not going to take away that evil. It's only going to spread it. Not just in the world, but in you."

"Shut up, Jo!"

His scream caused her to jump. She stumbled backward over a large rock, a crimson gash slicing across her arm.

"Just shut up! I've worked too hard, waited too long!" His body continued to shake but the gun in his hand suddenly steadied. "This is for my brother. For every American we've lost to the betrayal of so-called friends and comrades."

Jo lunged before she could think, driven by feeling rather than thought, before the shot rang out, before the smell of smoke ever reached her nostrils. It wasn't until her body hit the ground, where gravel tore at her back and dust billowed out beneath her, that she even became aware of the pain. Warmth and coldness spreading simultaneously across her chest near her shoulder and then a throbbing that erupted into agony.

"Jo!" Olive was by her side, blocking the light. "Jo, are you okay? Jo!"

Her vision swam. She couldn't speak. Her body understood but her mind struggled to catch up. Shot. She'd been shot. By Charlie.

"You shot her!" Olive gave voice to the impossible. "You shot her!"

Charlie stood frozen in place. The gun was still raised. "I didn't . . . I mean, she . . ."

Olive pulled Jo's head into her lap, causing a fresh swell of pain. "Do something! Please! Go get help!"

But Charlie didn't move. His eyes were glued to the bright-red spot on Jo's chest.

"Go!" Olive screamed again.

Blinking rapidly, Charlie took one step back and then another before he finally lowered his gun. He turned to make his way down the mesa, but his eyes remained fixed on the deep stain on Jo's shoulder. He never saw the rock, the one that caused his feet to trip and his body to lurch awkwardly and uncontrollably toward the edge. It sounded as if he said her name as he began to plummet, but Jo couldn't be sure. She was fading, a blanket of coldness creeping over her body even as the sun bore down on her. Through her haze, all she knew was that his face never registered his fall; it was still a mask of disbelief as he slid backward, hands grasping at the air. She saw without seeing him tumble down the side of the mesa, his body flipping end over end until it came to rest on a ledge, just feet above the desert floor, and was still.

A ripping of fabric, intense pressure on her wound.

"Stay with me, Jo. Stay with me. Come on."

She was vaguely aware of being weightless, of the strength of Olive's arms and the smell of New Mexico air on her skin before the coldness overtook her, and she was aware no more.

CHAPTER TWENTY-EIGHT

OLIVE

NOVEMBER 1952

"You know you don't have to do this. In fact, I recommend against it."

Pastor Hamilton frowned in that way Olive still remembered too well all these years later. It had been ages since she'd set foot inside this church; yet for the past few months, she'd been drawn here almost daily. And Pastor Hamilton, for all the grief she'd given him when she was younger, had simply welcomed her back with a silent nod and a warm smile. No questions. No comments. No condemnation. And while her faith had grown exponentially outside these walls over the years, there was something about being inside them that made her feel like she could breathe again.

Especially now.

Olive smiled. "I know you do. You've told me several times. But it's what she wanted."

He tapped the back of the pew and sighed as he glanced up at the ceiling. Probably asking God to give him patience with her. Again.

"You never stopped trying to take care of her." Olive patted his shoulder gently. "You're a good man. I hope you know that." Then she wrapped a scarf around her neck and made her way up the aisle before the tear she saw in the corner of his eye could fall. She could handle a lot of things, but she couldn't handle *that*.

Sunlight filtered through the stained-glass windows on either side of her, basking the threadbare carpet in hues of reds, blues, and greens. The ever-present dust shimmered in the air like glitter. But as she passed, one particular window shone brighter. You could say it was because it was newer—and it was—but Olive liked to think it was because of a different reason. Because it was the window she and Jo had destroyed and mended, the literal and figurative pieces of Jesus coming together as the world around them crumbled.

Abide In Me, the lettering around the Messiah's head read. Green glass vines curling around Jesus's outstretched hands. *Abide In Me.*

And they had. Thousands of physical miles, even more emotional, and yet it was the Vine that bound them to hope.

And to each other.

Olive made her way to the front of the sanctuary, staring up at the wooden cross behind the pulpit and praying for the strength she knew she wouldn't get through this day without. She said a small prayer for Tim Bucknam, as she always did; he'd never made it home from the Pacific, but his memory lingered, and she found she still couldn't say a prayer without whispering his name before she was done. She prayed for Avery and Hershel, wherever they were, needing daily to release the heaviness their ghosts still held. She wasn't angry anymore; instead she felt only sadness for their diverging paths and the uncertainty of their fates. But there was still hope—there was always hope.

She breathed out her *amen* before turning from the podium. "It's time."

In the front pew, a head of white-blonde hair rose, startled from deep prayers. Pale-blue eyes met Olive's dark ones—and the two girls smiled.

Jo

"Are you ready?"

Jo put a hand over her chest. It was aching today. There were days it was numb, when the wound seemed to shrink into nothingness. Today was not one of those days. Today her scar was making sure it was remembered. "As ready as I'll ever be."

Entwining arms, the two girls walked up the aisle, nodding a brief goodbye to Pastor Hamilton on their way out before stepping into the sunshine. The brisk November air stole their breath but did not slow their stride.

Jo's very survival was a miracle, or so the doctors had said. She'd been brought to the hospital with barely a breath left to give, the bullet found a mere hair's width from her artery. It had fractured bones, severed nerves, shredded muscle . . . but it had left the gateway to her heart unscathed. It had taken three surgeries to remove all the bullet fragments, each one more painful than the last. Even now, a few small pieces remained lodged below her shoulder, too near her heart for the doctors to risk extracting. Advancements could be made in the future that might enable them to fix it, they said. But for now, she would have to live with pieces of bullet inside her chest.

Pieces of violence and hate. Pieces of Charlie.

He'd had his own miracle. He'd survived his fall, though his injuries left doubt about his ability to ever walk again unassisted. After a few months in the hospital—a different one from Jo's, a small blessing the police had granted her—he'd been transferred to a jail cell to await trial. Only there had been no trial. Still groggy from the anesthesia from her third surgery, Jo hadn't believed it when she heard he'd pleaded guilty.

Today the frigid temperature had kept most of the curious at bay, but several people still milled in front of the courthouse doors, waiting for the judge's sentence, curious about the renegade FBI agent who'd attempted to murder his lover in a fit of passion. That was one of the rumors. The other—about the Communist spy he'd risked his life trying to uncover—was worse. Jo pulled her hat down lower. Today wasn't about rumors. Today was about truth.

They'd been standing only a minute or two when a white van pulled up to the curb, and two police officers emerged from its depths. The meager crowd of onlookers pushed forward as Jo stepped back.

"Are you okay?" Olive gripped her arm. "Do you want to leave?"

Jo shook her head, throat already too tight to speak.

The crowd blocked her view, but she didn't have to see it to know what was happening. The opening of doors, the clang of metal as a wheelchair was hefted to the ground. The polite but firm commands to step back, move aside, make room.

And then he was there. His once-tall frame was lessened, his broad shoulders now shrunken and withdrawn. Gone was the crisp, fitted suit, replaced with a drab, baggy prison uniform. Dark stubble covered his chin. His hands were folded in his lap, his feet tucked into the platforms of the chair that carried him toward the courthouse door.

A throbbing spread through Jo's chest that had nothing to do with her wound. Her mind floated back to the man she'd known before—the man she thought she'd known. To the day he had rescued her at the ranch from the poisonous serpent ready to strike. She remembered the feel of his strength, the firmness of his grip, the certainty in his eyes. He had saved her that day, for sure, but real salvation had come on the mesa when he had nearly taken her life . . . and somehow, simultaneously, given it back. Learning the truth about him—about herself—had broken her heart; discovering the depth of God's love had slowly begun to mend it again.

But healing had come at a cost, both to her and to Charlie. And that was why she needed to see him today. She needed to find out if maybe, just maybe, the price had been enough. Not only to free her, but Charlie as well, if not from his shackles, then at least from the prison within.

A hush fell over the crowd as the police officers wheeled him toward the glass doors. Jo stood back, clutching Olive's hand for support, trying to see but remain unseen as the audience parted.

Charlie's head stayed bowed as he passed. His shaggy hair drooped in front of his face, obscuring it. And then suddenly, as if sensing her, he looked up.

Jo held her breath. She took a step forward out of the crowd. Away from Olive, away from the chance to turn back, until she stood on her own, alone with Charlie in a sea of onlookers.

His eyes widened when they met hers. Though his gaze caused a stinging in her scar, she did not look away. She saw it all again in his stare, felt the piercing of the bullet, the coldness of her own breath that day on the mesa. The moment was frozen in the space between them. Impenetrable. Irrevocable.

He continued to gape at her as his body moved past, revealing the pain that lay beneath his shock, the regret and sorrow, the defeat and remorse.

Or maybe that's just what she wanted to see. Because all she could really see on his face was emptiness.

The glass doors opened. She was running out of time. She opened her mouth to say something . . . and found that she couldn't.

Then the doors closed, finally breaking his stare, swallowing Charlie within.

Her body deflated. The moment had passed, and she'd missed it. There was so much she should have said, felt, done . . . and in her weakness, she'd done nothing at all.

She felt a sturdy arm around her shoulders. "Are you okay? Do you want to go home?"

Blinking, Jo pulled herself from the shadow and looked at the girl beside her. Olive. Her friend. Her sister.

Slowly, painfully, she began to breathe again.

Her healing had begun up there on that mountain, but it wasn't complete yet. Like the fragments of bullet that lay buried within, the memory of that hurt still lingered, at times a blazing inferno, at others a residual smolder. She wasn't strong enough to put it out. Maybe she never would be. But this time it would not consume her. This time she was placing those coals at the feet of the One who heals, trusting that someday, someway, a time would come when He would extinguish those flames once and for all.

And He would bring beauty from the ashes.

Yes, her heart still had a long way to go to be whole. But she wasn't alone on the journey anymore. And really, she never had been.

JO

JULY 16, 1955

Even after all these years, this day was still different.

Out here on the ranch, there wasn't much need for calendar keeping, but this day . . . somehow she always knew when this day arrived. Perhaps it was the increase in traffic, audible even a mile back from the main road. A morbid tourist destination now. Or perhaps it was something in the air, a shift in the wind, the scent of memory on the breeze.

But all the locals knew it was more than that. This was a day they all could *feel*. Jo could feel it now too.

Trinity. Ten years ago today was Trinity.

Jo rose, wincing at the stiffness in her shoulder as she stretched. She pulled on a pair of jeans and one of her father's old shirts, feeling the familiar warmth she always did when she was close to him again like this. It no longer smelled of him, of course, his musk or aftershave. Now it only smelled like hay and dust, the spice of the chiles that never really left the New Mexico air. The sun had not yet crested the mountains, and the back of the house was quiet and dark. Jo moved toward the washroom but stopped at the nearest door instead, placing a hand on the wood as she heard movement from within. "Olive?"

The window was open, allowing the orange predawn glow to wash over the room and cover Olive's bed in serene radiance. The light made her dark hair glow like fire as it spread across her pillow. It brought color and life to her pale face. Her eyes were tired but sparkling, drawn cheeks appearing full for the first time in weeks.

It was a trick of the light. Jo knew that. But it made her smile just the same. "Good morning."

Her friend grinned. It was one of the few aspects of her appearance not yet ravaged by disease. "Morning, Jo."

She crossed the room and settled herself on the edge of the bed. "It's gonna be a hot one today."

"Bah. Not for long. It'll storm this afternoon."

"You're crazy. It's been dry for weeks."

Olive tilted her chin to the ceiling. "Why do you still doubt me? Am I ever wrong?"

Jo let out a small chuckle. "We best get to work then. The adobe needs a fresh coat of paint. The barn too. I was hoping to get that done today, but I'm guessing it will have to wait. We'll be lucky to get the morning chores done before the rain. If you're right, that is."

Olive made a move to rise, releasing a grunting noise that disintegrated into a cough. She lifted a hand to her mouth to stifle it, very purposefully looking away.

The illness had progressed at an alarming rate, though the doctor said the cancer had probably been growing undetected for a long time. Years even. But it had seemed only to gain strength at the doctor's prognosis, as if the words had released the monster that was now eating Olive from the inside. It was absurd, but Jo couldn't help but wonder what could have been if she hadn't spotted the blood on Olive's hankie. Hadn't forced her to go in for that checkup. If they'd just stayed at the ranch like Olive had wanted and had never heard the word they both knew but prayed not to hear.

But that was stupid. The cancer was there, whether they admitted it or not, and had been for a while, perhaps even before Jo's father had passed. It was Trinity, of course. Everything came back to Trinity. Even if the government wouldn't admit it. Those boys hadn't really known what they were doing when they exploded that bomb; the true fallout was just starting to emerge, and the battle over consequences loomed on the horizon. But the only battle Jo cared about right now was Olive's. The one she was waging inside her own body.

The one she was losing.

"You want breakfast?"

Olive shook her head, hand at her lips. Jo knew she was holding in another cough, afraid of upsetting her.

Jo suppressed a rebuke. It wouldn't do any good to scold Olive for not eating. She'd tried that before. It only made her sullen and withdrawn. The cancer might have been destroying her body, but her will was still as stubborn as a mule's. "Coffee then," she said instead.

Olive gave her a half smile and nodded.

"I'll get it started."

The water from the well stank like sulfur and was often tinged gray with sand. It was one of the harder things to get used to, living out here. But after a long, hot, dusty day, the water was wet and cool; it cleaned the grime from your face and relieved the ache in your throat. And it still made for a decent cup of coffee every morning. So that was something.

The house on Michigan Avenue had sold quickly. She'd been surprised about the lack of grief she'd felt watching her father's things being packed up and sold at the estate sale, but she shouldn't have been. The house had never really been a home, the things inside remnants of a life she'd never really been a part of. She'd kept a few books and pictures, a couple boxes of clothes, and her father's Army memorabilia. Everything else was snatched by bargain hunters or lookie-loos, those who'd perhaps heard whispers and hoped to be the one to finally bear proof.

Whatever secrets they had betrayed, both her father and Mrs. Alexander took to their graves. But even though they were gone, the battle between the US and the Soviet Union showed no signs of abating. "The Cold War," they were calling it. According to McCarthy, "Reds" were everywhere. His paranoia certainly didn't help the rumor mill surrounding the Alexanders. But eventually, without any concrete evidence, even the most stalwart of local Communist hunters grew tired of stale crumbs. Hearsay and gossip could only get you so far. Jo and Olive were left alone. Forgotten.

For the most part.

The government men came around once more, but it wasn't to badger Olive or interrogate her yet again about Trinity. It was to ask about Charlie and find out exactly what had transpired up on that mesa. A formality, really. Their questions had been stiff, their true words lying just under their scripted questions: *We won't bother you if you don't bother us. Okay?*

Fine.

Jo pulled her hair into a ponytail and poured coffee into two mugs. Turning, she was surprised to find Olive standing in the doorframe, staring out into the desert beyond. She hadn't even heard her come out of the bathroom. She held her Bible under her arm.

"I'd like to do our reading outside this morning." The threat of a wheeze was just audible under her words. "So we can see the sunrise."

Jo gripped the mugs tighter. The days were getting harder, no matter how much they tried to pretend otherwise. Like a breath she could never quite catch. They could leave. *Should* leave. Spend what time Olive had left in comfort and ease, away from the strain and hardship of the ranch. Not that Olive ever would. Much like the plants just beginning to sprout up through what remained of the green glass sea, staying was a way to both honor the past and defy it, clinging to what remained of the good and refusing to be defined by the bad.

The people of the Jornada were moving forward, bravely facing a future they hadn't chosen. And now Jo was too. She didn't know what would happen tomorrow. Or the day after. Or the day after that. When the cancer won and Olive was gone and the ranch was hers . . . what would happen then? She didn't know for sure. All she knew was that Olive had found her purpose—practically given her life—protecting her, and Jo was determined to live a life worthy of that sacrifice. One way or another, she would redeem the trauma from which they'd all suffered. Maybe she'd stay on the ranch, working the land her friend had loved. Maybe she would move to town and help Pastor Hamilton with his Trinity outreach. Or maybe she'd get political and start campaigning for atomic survivors, giving a voice to the voiceless.

The possibilities were endless. After all her years doing mission work abroad, she'd found her greatest mission here, in the sands of New Mexico from which she'd spent so many years running. Though she didn't know what lay ahead, she knew she was being called to love those here in her adopted home. Perhaps even to fight for them. For her friend. For her father. For the people of the Jornada who continued to suffer all these years after Trinity. For the travesty of the past . . . and the possibility of a future.

But all that could wait. Because for now . . . for now there was Olive.

"Okay. Okay, sure."

Olive stepped outside and slipped into a metal chair, Bible in her lap, cupping the mug as she stared out toward the brightening sky. Jo, noticing goose bumps sprouting on Olive's arms despite temperatures hovering near ninety, retreated inside to grab a blanket. She tried not to feel the sharpness of Olive's bones beneath her skin as she placed the red wool around her shoulders. "Better?"

Olive smiled and nodded. Her breathing was ragged but steady.

Trinity had gotten her friend. It had gotten her father. And it had gotten countless others in this "uninhabited" stretch of desert. The men had sent the cloud up, forgetting that it had to come down somewhere. It seeped into every grain of sand, every molecule of air, every nerve of their bodies and beat of their hearts. It was in the food they ate, the water they drank, the words they spoke, in the lives that should have been and the lives that were. The green glass sea had been buried; the scientists had long since moved on. But there was no escaping Trinity.

In the same way, her father and Mrs. Alexander had created a storm of secrets, perhaps not realizing it too would eventually burst, raining toxins on those they loved, those whose only crime was living in the fallout zone. The ensuing deluge of lies and betrayal should have destroyed Olive and Jo in ways much deeper and more permanent than the nuclear history that had occurred this very morning, ten years ago, in a spot where, even now, hordes were gathering to celebrate the science, relive the history, and ponder the future of a world capable of such destruction.

But Jo's and Olive's eyes were focused eastward, away from Trinity, where the sun was just peeking over the mountains. The rays reflected off the gathering clouds—Olive had yet again been right—turning them from stormy gray to magnificent red and washing the basin below in shades of gold.

Olive's hand found its way into Jo's. It was cold and small, thin white fingers pressed beside Jo's now-calloused ones. She smiled, the rising sun reflecting the fight still left in her tired eyes.

Jo squeezed and smiled back. Yes, Trinity might have stained this land. Grief might have defiled their past, and heartache would most certainly come again in the future. But there was still beauty in the here and now. It came from a Trinity bigger than the one behind them, whose bright light brought life and not death, joy and not despair, healing and not hurt.

The One who had brought them home, in every way.

With their entwined fingers resting upon Olive's Bible, the two friends watched the rising sun overpower the storm clouds, painting the sky with the richness of hope and the promise of the day ahead.

Discover a story of resilience and redemption set against one of America's defining moments—the Dust Bowl

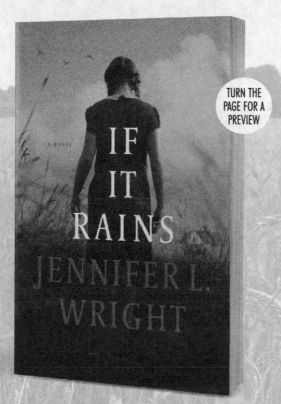

TURN THE
PAGE FOR A
PREVIEW

"[A] lovely debut. . . . Wright's adept depiction of the times capture the grit of the Dust Bowl."
—Publishers Weekly on *If It Rains*

IN STORES AND ONLINE NOW

CHAPTER ONE

KATHRYN

Helen lost her third baby on the day of my sister's wedding.

I'd tried to tell Melissa. Told her Helen was too pregnant, the late-April sky was too ripe, and—most of all—that getting married was a stupid idea anyway. She told me to stop being hateful and help her with her dress. Her *dress*. All this dirt and dead crops, and what she cared about was looking pretty for Henry.

Sure enough, the sky turned black by midafternoon. But not from rain. It was never from rain anymore. The wedding party scattered before they so much as cut that ridiculous white cake. A few escaped to their cars; the luckiest were able to start them before static cut the ignition. Even then, not many would make it home. Most would pass the storm stuck in a sand drift. At least the wedding would give them something to talk about while they waited. Rubberneckers, all of 'em.

We didn't even have it that good. We would have to walk. Pa's truck hadn't started for weeks. Too much dust or not enough gas. Or both. Sure, we could have stayed at the Mayfields'. Waited it out like the other sheep. But I would rather chance a duster than spend another second with the new Mr. and Mrs. Mayfield. So I left. Pa and Helen followed.

A cloud of earth swallowed me when I stepped out the front door. Melissa had tried to make her old pink dress look new for me, but the fabric was still thin. Nothing she could do about that. I pulled it up over my mouth and nose, gagging on the cheap perfume Helen had doused me in that morning. "I won't have you smelling like a pig even if you insist on looking like one," she'd said. "Not today." Like it even mattered.

Helen slowed us. Her stomach threw off her balance in the wind, making the two-mile walk home seem longer. If not for Pa, I would have trudged ahead. Forget her. But I couldn't leave Pa. He was all I had left now. And since he insisted on helping his wife, I knew I had to be the one to count fence posts or we'd miss the house completely.

House. We hadn't had a house since Ma died. Sometimes the blood won't come out, Pa said, even when you can't see it no more. But the dugout was good enough. Cool in the summer, warm in the winter. And at least it kept the wind out.

"Get that sheet under the door."

I did as I was told, eyes stinging, trying not to listen to Helen's moans and wheezes. Did she have to make all that *noise*? The whistling, the scratching, the rattling—I could take the storm. But *this*? It was her own fault for making us go to that circus wedding. A woman in her condition weren't in no fit state to be walking.

Come to think of it, it was Melissa's fault, too, for having a wedding in the first place.

Helen's voice, desperate in the darkness. "James."

I felt around until I found the cabinet door, pulling a rumpled sheet from within. Two steps over was the water bucket; then it was eleven steps back to the door. Listening to Pa fumble for the lantern, I punched at the wet sheet, willing it into the cracks. The sooner it was in there, the sooner I could plug my ears. The door popped and creaked like a monster was seeping into the very boards. I missed Melissa already.

The stench of kerosene and a sudden flare of light. Helen stood at the table, clutching her swollen belly. Her eyes were shut, hair matted to her forehead. "James—" she started again but broke off as if strangled. At her feet, water began to pool, thick and shiny in the flickering light. The soft dripping was louder than the storm raging just outside our walls.

I squeezed the sheet in my hand, feeling my fingernails penetrate the thin fabric. It wasn't the baby. It couldn't be the baby. It was too early.

But it was always too early.

Dirt lay in the creases of Pa's face and coated his thinning hair. His eyes were red with grit. Yes, grit. There was no way he was crying. Helen just had an accident, that's all. She couldn't make it to the outhouse in all this dust.

We stood silent, staring, unable or unwilling to accept the injustice of truth, as if remaining where we were would change it somehow. For minutes or for hours. It was impossible to tell. And then, with the faintest of sobs, Helen made it real.

Pa pushed past me, grabbing her arm to steady her as another pain twisted her face. "I have to go get Emmalou." His voice betrayed none of the panic twitching his eye. "Kath, you'll need to stay—"

"No!" The word slipped from my lips before I could stop it. Loudly. Urgently. "I'll get Mrs. Patton. You stay."

Outside, the wind roared, but my plea hung heavy and immovable in the airless dugout. Pa cleared his throat. Helen shifted where she stood, one hand gripping the table, the other rubbing the sweat-caked dust on her brow. She very purposefully didn't look at me. She didn't need to. I already knew.

The only thing stronger than her aversion to my help was her memory.

"She won't make it," she said finally, defeat souring the edge of her words. "Please . . . not again, James." The last part softer. But not soft enough.

The midwife lived in a small house about three-quarters of a mile south of here, across a stunted wheat field plagued with plow ruts and rabbit holes. Last time it had been clear, not a cloud in the sky, and I'd still failed. And although it wasn't my fault the barbed wire had been covered in dirt, it *was* my fault my brace had gotten tangled and the midwife didn't make it in time. Helen made that perfectly clear. I had killed her baby. She told me so right after we buried her. In a voice low enough Pa couldn't hear but loud enough I would never forget.

"James . . . ," Helen whimpered.

There wasn't time to argue about what I could or couldn't do. Not now. I stuffed my pride into the window with another wet blanket and nodded without looking at him. The dust was making my eyes water, too. A scream of wind, a blast of dirt, and he was gone into the storm.

Helen wailed and coughed. Like she was the only one scared.

I rewet the sheet and shoved it beneath the crack of the door again. *This* I could do. Maybe if I kept wetting sheets, she wouldn't ask me to do anything else.

"I need to lay down."

Helen's dress was saturated with sweat, leaving muddy stains under her arms and across her chest. I could see her belly button through the fabric. It was hard and knotted, heaving with each shallow breath.

A sudden gust of wind knocked a spray of dirt against the window, startling us both.

I could make it to the barn. I knew the way, even in a duster. Helen didn't want me here, and Pa would be back soon with the midwife. It was better for everyone if I stayed out of the way. And still I found myself saying, "What . . . what do you want me to do?"

"Water. I need water."

I hobbled to the kitchen area, gasping as a sharp pain shot through my leg. I'd pushed too hard today. The traveling, the wedding . . . I needed to sit down. But I couldn't. Not when Helen was staring at me like that.

Our water bucket was only half-full. Pa would be mad. The last duster had clogged the well, and I was supposed to pump through it this morning. All this wedding stuff had me distracted. I pulled up a cupful, watching particles float to the bottom. How much water did one need to have a baby?

I returned just as Helen let out another scream. Startled, I dropped the cup. The water bounced against the dirt floor, too hard and dry to soak it in.

"Kathryn."

The water puddled at my feet, nudging against my shoes.

"Something's wrong."

"What—?"

"Come over here. You need to check."

Check? No. No, no, no. She didn't mean . . . ? "Water. I was gonna get you more."

Tears rolled down Helen's gray cheeks. "Kathryn, please. I need you to check. Which way is the baby facing?"

"Facing?"

The water was mud now, holding my feet in place. I wasn't a midwife or a doctor. And she wasn't even really family. Just a step-mother. Not that either one of us would ever call her that.

"Please." She moaned as another pain erupted. It was an eternity before she could speak again. "Something's wrong."

Of course something was wrong. Everything about this was wrong. I needed Melissa. She'd helped with the others. I wasn't supposed to be doing this. I was only fourteen. I knew where babies came from. I'd helped with the cows and pigs before most of them had starved. But this . . .

Was this what it had been like for my mother? Had I made her scream like this before I killed her?

"Please . . ." Helen's voice was barely above a whisper.

The window rattled. I couldn't look at her; instead I counted my fingers. Right now she needed me. My new brother or sister . . . he or she needed me, too. Needed me to help. Needed me to look. And I just couldn't.

"Kathryn, what do you see? Can you see the head?"

I backed away. I shouldn't be here. I'd only make it worse. Where was Pa? Where was Melissa?

"Kath—" Helen's words choked as another pain gripped her.

I closed my eyes and stumbled backward, smashing into something that hadn't been there just minutes before.

Pa. Pa was back. He grabbed my arms and shook me. "Kathryn, what's happening? What's wrong?"

I couldn't speak. My foot throbbed. Bile pooled in my mouth.

The midwife rushed past us, bag in hand.

Helen shrieked again.

My father dropped my arms, forgetting about me. He ran toward the bed.

Ignoring the protests from my foot, I pushed out the front door, coughing as dirt filled my lungs. But I could breathe out here. Somehow, in the dirt, I could breathe. I felt around blindly until I found the rope leading from our house to the barn. Pulling my dress over my nose and mouth once again, I stumbled through sand drifts until I felt the worn wood of the barn door beneath my fingers and pushed.

The chickens scattered. Our one remaining cow glared.

The lantern gave a comforting glow as I pulled my book from its hiding spot in the rafters. My mother's book, my real mother, the only thing I had to remember a woman I'd never met. *The Wonderful Wizard of Oz.* The book from before Helen. Before the babies. Before the drought.

Melissa's face floated before me in the dark.

"Now, Kath, listen. You can't talk and listen at the same time."

"But I know it already," I said. "I don't even need the book anymore."

She sighed and closed the cover, like we hadn't done this a million times before. "Well, if you already know the story, I guess we don't need to read it no more. I'll be going."

I'd known she wouldn't really leave. She never left. But still I would cry out, beg her to stay, read a few more pages. I'd be quiet and listen, I'd promise. If only she'd stay and read just a little more.

But this time she hadn't stayed. She'd really left. And all I had was my mother's book and this barn, where I could get away from the nightmare she'd left me in.

Dorothy lived in the midst of the great Kansas prairies
with Uncle Henry, who was a farmer, and Aunt Em,
who was the farmer's wife. Their house was small, for
the lumber to build it had to be carried by wagon many
miles. . . .

Helen's screams outlasted the wind. By sunrise, the storm had finally passed, leaving dust and death hanging in the air. The house quiet, I retreated from Oz to dig yet another hole in the parched earth near the fence line.

A NOTE FROM
THE AUTHOR

Come Down Somewhere is a work of fiction. That much must be made perfectly clear. Olive, Jo, and the others in this book were created in my mind. The Alexander ranch never existed, nor were contractors assisting with the Trinity site housed in the outlying rural community. But as in every work of historical fiction, many aspects within these pages are based in truth.

Despite being an ally to the United States in its fight against the Nazis, the American government was already growing wary of the USSR in the early 1940s. Their bridge of friendship was built on the desire to defeat a common enemy, but that allegiance went no further than the battlefield. So when the US government began work on a secret military weapon in the mountains of northern New Mexico, they kept it a secret from everyone.

Including their Soviet allies.

Because not only did the US recognize the inherent danger Communism posed to a free republic, it also understood the brutality and ambition of Stalin's regime. It was obvious that Russia was a possible future enemy and one from which they needed to closely guard their secrets.

What they failed to identify, however, was that—at least to the Communists—the future was already here.

Although there is no concrete evidence that any sort of Soviet espionage occurred in the area bordering Trinity, nor within any of the ranches requisitioned for the test site, Moscow operatives did infiltrate the Manhattan Project in various ways. The leaks came all the way from scientists such as Klaus Fuchs to Army men like David Greenglass. It wasn't until the Soviets tested their own atomic weapon in 1949—over a decade before US Army officials believed they would, based on the Communists' lagging science— that the US government truly became aware of the treachery from their so-called ally.

What's surprising is that a large number of these operatives were not Russian nationals; they were, in fact, American citizens with Communist sympathies. Outwardly, the Communist Party USA proclaimed itself loyal to the United States and sought to bring reform to the American system, allowing it to fly under the US government's radar and avoid any real suspicion. In reality, how- ever, its inner workings were full of people faithful to the USSR and more than willing to do its bidding. For example, both Julius and Ethel Rosenberg were American citizens who provided top secret information to the Soviet Union regarding radar, sonar, and jet propulsion engines. They were executed in 1953 for their crimes.

The United States declassified the Venona project, its Soviet counterintelligence program, in the early 1990s. Over the course of almost forty years, agents decrypted nearly three thousand mes- sages between KGB agents and the USSR. The sheer depth of undercover Soviet permeation within the United States' borders was astounding.

If you're interested in reading further about atomic espionage during the 1940s and 1950s, I highly recommend *The Atomic Spies* by Oliver Pilat and *The Venona Secrets: Exposing Soviet Espionage and America's Traitors* by Herbert Romerstein and Eric Breindel. Both of these works were monumental in helping me understand the mentality and atmosphere surrounding spy work during World War II and the time immediately following.

While the occurrence of spies within the confines of the testing site is fiction, sadly the effects from the Trinity test on the people of southern New Mexico are all too real.

The Jornada del Muerto, or "Route of the Dead Man," is a ninety-mile stretch of desert lying between Socorro, New Mexico, and El Paso, Texas. It's hot, it's dry, and it's barren. But the very characteristics that made it so appealing to ranchers also made it attractive to scientists from Los Alamos searching for a place to test their secret bomb. Although chosen for its isolation and accessibility (most of the land was already owned by the government and in use as the Alamogordo Bombing and Gunnery Range), the land was *not* completely empty. Several towns lay scattered throughout the desert nearby. In fact, nearly forty thousand people lived in a fifty-mile radius around the test site. Nearly one hundred families had their ranches "leased" for testing purposes, with the understanding that their land would eventually be returned. The fallout from Trinity, as well as the creation of White Sands Missile Range, however, meant this was not the case. The government simply continued to "rent" the land year after year, despite the protests from owners. Although outrage led to some ranchers eventually receiving payment, most of them, to this day, have never gotten their property back.

Bigger than the land grab, however, were the consequences of the test itself. Scientists were concerned about the effects of the initial blast, even hiring a seismologist to assure any quaking from the explosion would not cause damage to nearby homes and villages and also assessing vegetation location to rule out any possible wildfires that could result. The issue of fallout, however—what would happen hours, days, weeks, and months after the test—was barely considered. Although consulting physicians raised several red flags, their concerns were, for the most part, pushed aside. To appease these issues, the Army outlined an emergency evacuation plan for the surrounding area, though they didn't really expect to use it. When it came down to it, the priority for scientists was the test; anything that happened afterward wasn't their problem.

On Monday, July 16, 1945, at 5:29:45 a.m. Mountain Standard Time, the bomb ignited. The flash was so brilliant, it was seen in three states, and the resulting mushroom cloud surged thirty-eight thousand feet into the atmosphere in only seven minutes. The heat created by the ensuing fireball was so intense, it fused together sand particles and created a greenish-gray glass within a half-mile crater, a substance scientists would later call trinitite. Every living thing—plant and animal—within a mile radius of the blast was killed instantly.

The radioactive cloud split into three parts. The lower section drifted north, the center went west, and the upper—the brunt of the cloud—moved toward the northeast at around forty-five thousand to fifty-five thousand feet. Teams of scientists followed the clouds with devices to measure radiation. Very little fallout occurred for about two hours, giving the men a false sense of security. Instead, the fallout began to intensify in the days following the blast, due to the nature of the particles as well as wind patterns. Although an evacuation plan had been developed, there was no agreement on how high radiation levels needed to be in order to enact it; because of this, a full-scale evacuation of fallout areas was never put into place.

But even as scientists began to collect high readings, they did not really understand the danger. At the time, scientists believed the fallout to be a "onetime" exposure that would eventually dissipate and pose no long-term danger to residents. The test site became a tourist destination (although time inside the blast area was limited) and trinitite was sold as souvenirs, the only caveat being not to hold it close to the body for an extended period of time. Because no effects were immediately apparent, many scientists and military personnel soon became lackadaisical in their protection efforts around the test site.

Areas of contamination stretched to a hundred-mile radius, from Las Vegas over to Roswell and all the way down to El Paso. The heaviest area of contamination, outside the restricted area, was the Chupadera Mesa, nearly thirty miles away from ground zero (and the site of Olive and Avery's fictional ranch in the story). During that time, these areas were predominantly rural. The people lived off the land, both in terms of livestock and agriculture, and much water was collected in outdoor cisterns or ditches. When the fallout began to come down, it settled on the very things these people needed to survive. Cows began losing their hair and showing abnormal blotches on their skin. But because the cattle appeared otherwise healthy, researchers decided they were safe and they were allowed to continue to reproduce and be used for food. Rodents and birds in the area were also discovered with unusual mutations and discolorations. Plutonium was discovered in the soil as well as nearby plants, with the desert wind pushing particles even further outside the original contamination zone. Although scientists from the Atomic Energy Commission made yearly trips from 1947 to 1955, funding soon dried up and the monitoring ceased. The world's attention moved on.

For the people of the Jornada and the Tularosa Basin, however, the effects of Trinity are still being felt. A 2019 article in the *Bulletin of the Atomic Scientists* showed that, following a decline in infant mortality in the years leading up to 1945, there was a spike in infant death in the area with no known cause other than it began after the Trinity test. In 2020, the National Cancer Institute released a study on the high cancer rate in southern New Mexico, finding that many "probably" got sick due to radioactive fallout from the atomic bomb blast of 1945. A consortium of survivors and their children, known as the Downwinders, continue to fight for recognition and compensation for the land—and lives—lost to this atomic test in an "uninhabited area."

If you're interested in learning more about the Trinity test, as well as the fallout that occurred afterward, I recommend Ferenc Morton Szasz's book *The Day the Sun Rose Twice*, as well as *Trinity: The History of an Atomic Bomb National Historic Landmark* by Jim Eckles. I also highly encourage you to visit trinitydownwinders .com to hear from their own mouths the stories of those affected by the test, as well as to understand and support their legislative efforts.

The title of this book comes from a quote attributed to Dr. Louis Hempelmann, a physician who worked on the Manhattan Project. Upon witnessing the Trinity test, he remarked, "All I could think of was, my God, all that radioactivity up there has got to come down somewhere." And come down it did—on the homes, farms, and lives of the people of southern New Mexico. I wrote this book in an attempt to honor their stories and aid in their pursuit of validation. I hear you. I see you. And now I hope others do too.

DISCUSSION QUESTIONS

1. While most people know that atomic bombs were dropped on Hiroshima and Nagasaki to end World War II, fewer are aware that the bomb was tested on US soil or that it caused lasting consequences to people who lived in the area. How much did you know about the Trinity test? What is the fallout—both literal and emotional—for the characters in this story?

2. Olive and Jo initially seem like polar opposites in personality and in the way they view life. Where do they find common ground? What makes Olive so determined to push Jo away? Why do you think Jo continues to pursue a friendship with her anyway?

3. Jo leaves Alamogordo as a hurt and bewildered girl and returns a hardened and angry young woman, after years of believing she was betrayed and abandoned by those she loved most. What did she not know or misinterpret about the events of the day she left? How does she misinterpret God as a result? Were her hurt and bitterness justified?

4. At times both Olive and Jo take refuge in anger, calling it an anchor, a buoy, a source of strength. What lies behind the anger for each of them? Have there been times when you found anger a comfort or a "safer" emotion than what you might otherwise feel?

5. Each thread of this story—in 1944 and in 1952—contains elements of mystery. When did you begin to suspect Charlie's motives might be different from what he claimed? What did you think was behind the strange goings-on at the Alexander ranch—the notes Olive finds, the odd letter from Avery, the confusing behavior from Evelyn? Were your conclusions correct, or were you surprised?

6. Olive starts out believing that religion is absurd and belief in God is a sign of delusion or weakness. But as she watches Jo live out her faith, she sees that Jo "didn't need everything to be perfect to find joy. She could love her God and her pigheaded, short-tempered, nonbelieving friend at the same time; she saw no contradiction between the two." How does this begin to change what Olive thinks about God? Is there someone in your own life whose faith you find especially winsome or compelling?

7. Standing at the Trinity site, Jo realizes, "Never had [she] felt God's absence more powerfully than she did right here, right now." Have you ever believed God was absent from a place? Or from your life? How would you describe what that felt like? What does Jo come to believe about God's absence?

8. As a teenager, Jo is certain of God's path for her—His calling on her life and His plan for how she and Olive will work together—only to find herself cruelly disappointed and left doubting. Do you think she was wrong about what God wanted for her life? How do you discern or define God's plan or purpose?

9. Though Olive wants to follow Jo into mission work, she concludes that is not God's path for her. How does Olive find her own purpose? What do you imagine would've been different if she'd gone with Jo?

10. Sergeant Hawthorne and Evelyn Alexander love their daughters but are caught up in "a storm of secrets." What actions do they take to try to protect Jo and Olive? In what ways do they fail them?

ACKNOWLEDGMENTS

I began work on *Come Down Somewhere* just as the COVID-19 pandemic started shuttering schools, closing businesses, and wreaking havoc on life as we knew it. I'm a person who needs solitude and quiet in order to write—two things that were in short supply in March 2020. In addition to trying to re-create the world of World War II–era Alamogordo, I was suddenly homeschooling two kids, fighting for office space with a husband now working from home, and planning a military-mandated move—because the Air Force mission doesn't stop just because of a pandemic.

Although I know my struggles pale in comparison to the heartache faced by so many others during that same time, I will not sugarcoat the experience. It was *hard*. It was *scary*. And there were many times I didn't know if this book would ever reach my editor's desk (or your hands).

The fact that it did can only be attributed to God. To His goodness, His mercy, and above all, His patience with me. Even in my times of deepest doubt, He never left my side. His grace alone allowed me and my family to withstand the absolute mess that was 2020 (and 2021) and somehow turn this manuscript in on time. To Him forever and always be the glory and the praise. Thank You, Jesus, for never giving up on me.

To my husband and two amazing kids: Thank you for dealing with a stressed-out-quarantined-writer-on-a-deadline-wife/mom for months on end. I know at times I wasn't the most pleasant person to be around. To my kids, thank you for being incredibly flexible, astonishingly resilient, and the biggest cheerleaders I have ever had. I'm sorry I didn't write *The Mouse and the Motorcycle* or *Superfudge*, but your enthusiasm nevertheless for my writing means the world to me. You two are the reason I do what I do. To my husband, thank you for giving me the opportunity to chase my dreams. None of this would work without you. Thank you for being the calm in my chaos, the voice of reason in my madness. Most of all, thank you for loving me for me . . . and for giving me a house with a wall full of books.

To my agent, Adria Goetz: You always make me feel like I'm your most important client, not simply one among dozens—no small feat in this business. Thank you for your warmth, your energy, and your positivity, even in the most negative of times. Thank you for believing in me.

To Jan, Sarah, Elizabeth, Isabella, both Andreas, and the entire team at Tyndale: Thank you for making my debut experience even more amazing than I could have possibly imagined. Your support and enthusiasm calmed my nerves, and I never doubted for a second that Melissa and Kathryn were in anything less than the best possible and most capable hands in the publishing business. To be able to do it all over again with Olive and Jo is a gift. Thank you for everything. And I do mean *everything*. Because you all are superwomen.

To Susie Finkbeiner, Naomi Stephens, Elizabeth Laing Thompson, and the many other Christian writers who have served as my applause sign over the past few months: Thank you for welcoming me into the Christian fiction community with open arms. It's always a weird feeling being the new kid (especially among authors whose books you've read and admired), but you all never skipped a beat and invited me to sit at your table on the very first day. Thank you for simply being so *kind*.

To my parents, my extended family, and my Melissa: Thank you for supporting me. Having someone you know read your book is way scarier than having a stranger read it. You always wonder what weird, subconscious notions you've unknowingly written into it (and which those who know you best will pick up on!). Thank you for not recognizing them (or at the very least, not calling me out on them). But in all seriousness, thank you for your unwavering excitement and for getting the word out about my book to everyone you meet—even the checkout lady at Walmart.

Last of all, to my readers: Thank you for taking a chance on a new author. Whether you gave my story a little bit of your time or money (or both), you made a sacrifice in allowing my words into your life, and it is one I do not take lightly. Thank you for allowing me to share my passion. Connecting with you all has been one of the biggest joys of this entire experience. Thank you for blessing me; I pray this book blesses you in return.

ABOUT
THE AUTHOR

Jennifer L. Wright has been writing since middle school, eventually earning a master's degree in journalism at Indiana University. However, it took only a few short months of covering the local news for her to realize that writing fiction is much better for the soul and definitely way more fun. A born and bred Hoosier, she was plucked from the Heartland after being swept off her feet by an Air Force pilot and has spent the past decade traveling the world and, every few years, attempting to make old curtains fit in the windows of a new home.

She currently resides in New Mexico with her husband, two children, one grumpy old dachshund, and her newest obsession—a guinea pig named Peanut Butter Cup.

By purchasing this book from Tyndale, you have
helped us meet the spiritual and physical needs of
people all around the world.